1.

Figment of the Imagination

I was enjoying a cup of coffee at the café on Corn Market Street at the centre of the city. When the coffee was nearly half finished I lit a cigarette; a strategy I had adopted when I took up smoking during my college days back home in the then East Pakistan. Players no. 6, the brand of cigarette I began to smoke when I arrived in the UK was roughly half the size, both in length and in girth, of other makes, and consequently half the cost. By taking short puffs at long intervals I managed to make each cigarette last a reasonable length of time, at least until the last gulp of coffee. That brand, by today's grading standard, most probably would have hit the top of the nicotine content league table for cigarettes. I had another practical reason for sticking to this brand. I had hoped that one day, in the not too distant future, I would be the proud owner of a dressing gown (bar the undertaker getting to me first) if and when I had collected the required number of cigarette coupons.

My expectation was that the combined effect of the caffeine and the nicotine would help me to be a thinker and an intellectual, allowing me to hobnob with other intellectuals and giving others the impression that I was one of them. In those days, examples of intellectuals addicted to smoking abounded. Harold Wilson, the prime minister of the day, who I suppose could be said to set an example of conduct for the whole of commonwealth, was never seen in public without his pipe.

I frequented that café not particularly for the quality of its coffee, but for its lower cost in comparison with most other coffee houses within the city centre. That was probably the reason why this place was abuzz with students in the evenings, particularly at weekends. For most hard-up students, it was the perfect spot to meet up and hang about with friends and make new ones. Unless I had buddied up with someone new or met an old acquaintance, I usually tried to occupy a seat near the window to watch the world passing by.

While enjoying the last few puffs of the cigarette, sitting on a chair near the window, I was pondering my options for the evening. The Beatle-blessed Ravi Shankar was going to give a solo sitar recital at the Town Hall. As an aspiring connoisseur of 'high culture' this had to be an important event for me to go to. Surely, there I would meet other like-minded people and make new friends. However, there was a competing event to be considered. A debate at the Oxford Student Union on the motion, 'The British East of Suez policy in 1947 was immoral', which promised to be an equally interesting and intellectually stimulating event. Some heavyweight luminaries, including our own Pakistani-born hero, Tariq Ali, as well as a few other left-wing internationalists were expected to grace the occasion with their presence.

Once, not long after my arrival at Oxford, I met Mr. Ali at the Union hall after the end of a debating session. He did have an over-powering personality and was a passionate talker. He tried to persuade me to go back home, join the 'Naxalites'- a revolutionary Maoist communist cadre in West Bengal in India, which was to take on Government forces. The goal was to wage a guerrilla war to establish an enclave unifying India, Pakistan and Burma. This was to be the beginning of the creation of a new world order, a world without boundaries. It appeared to me that he was holding the sole agency of the so called, '4th International', one of the factions of Trotskyite ideology.

'Why aren't you in the field and spearheading the movement?' I quizzed him,

'If I were there doing that, who the hell will be here recruiting talented future revolutionary leaders like you?' He snapped.

He lectured me on the need for a new world order to alleviate the sufferings of the hapless people of Asia, Africa and Latin America. I suspected that he might have ambitions for me to become the next Che Guevara. I was not convinced and decided to ignore his advice with no hesitation. I thought it would be wiser to achieve excellence and fame, all risk-free, as an armchair revolutionary and as an intellectual like him.

Before finally deciding between my choices I took a casual and leisurely look at people walking along the street just beyond the glass window of the café. Through the large glass shop widow on the opposite side of the road I noticed a display of variety of ware galore, illuminated with bright neon lights. Fashionable clothes and bedlinens made of a unique new material called nylon dominated the display. In addition, a host of other gadgets, wrapped up in glittering packaging, with tags displaying not the price, but the percentage of discount being offered, were on show.

This was my first Christmas in an affluent society of a prosperous West European country. Back home I nurtured the idea that Christmas was a religious occasion to celebrate the birthday of Jesus Christ (also one of our Muslim Prophets); to be observed with great reverence. This was a time for purifying the mind, a time for achieving tranquillity of the soul, a time to establish universal brotherhood among humankind. But so far, to my dismay, I hadn't heard, either from people around me or from the media, anything about peace and tranquillity or about universal brotherhood. What I saw and heard was incessant advertisements for the sale of commodities on television, radio, newspapers, and invariably in display behind shop windows. I was, however, excited about the arrival of Christmas, expecting lots of festivities and fun, and a new experience of being party to a major Western cultural and religious event. But for now my immediate and pressing concern was to decide how I was going to make the best use of that Friday evening.

My idle thoughts on the erosion of spirituality of Christmas and the influence of materialism in Western society vanished at the sight of Rolf. He was window shopping at the Boswell superstore on the opposite side of the café. I had learned that this was a favourite pass-time for many people in this country. Although I couldn't see his face I recognized him instantly from his back profile. He had a balding head with a tidily manicured narrow rim of salt and pepper coloured hair around it. That was perhaps not such an unusual feature in middle-aged men, but the feature that was unique to him was his firm but stooped posture. I was relieved that the immediate problem of deciding my next move was now solved. I knew Rolf always had a fixed programme for his evenings and often, being like-minded, it coincided with that of mine.

I stood up abruptly, stubbed my cigarette butt in the ashtray and gulped down the remaining dregs of the coffee. Then, grabbing my overcoat and long Oriel college muffler, I ventured out of the café to meet and greet my friend. I stood behind him and gently tapped his shoulder. Rolf jumped, turned around and was speechless for a few moments. I was taken aback because normally he would greet me with a funny anecdote, laughing at his own humour, and then ask me about my plan for the evening. We would then find a quiet corner and discuss what we might do for the evening together if we were both free. In most cases in the past, on such unexpected encounters, we usually cancelled our individual pre-conceived plans and made new ones to suit our mutual interests and mood. But on that occasion it was surprisingly different.

Without responding to my greetings and with a very serious

face and tone, Rolf said,

'I am very upset. I have been looking for you, couldn't find you at your flat. Don't know who else to turn to at this time of dire need. I know for sure you are the only one who has the courage and integrity to help a friend in need.'

He paused for a moment and added,

'I desperately need that help now. I genuinely believe you are my true friend and well-wisher, you won't let me down.'

Knowing how over-expressive he could be at times I was not unduly concerned and said,

'I am really sorry to hear you're in trouble. Of course I'll do whatever I can to help. That's what friends are for, isn't it? Tell me frankly, exactly what the problem is?'

He raised his head and glanced sideways at me and replied in a doleful tone,

'It's quite a serious matter. I can't discuss it in a public place. I strongly believe you know or at least have some inkling about the matter which is troubling me. Anyway, we shall discuss this shortly; for now, would you just follow me please?'

He started to walk briskly and I followed him. I guessed from the direction he was taking our most likely destination was his flat in Banbury Road. It was located approximately halfway along the stretch from St. Giles to Summertown. I was not used to walking briskly, particularly while breathing cold air on a winter evening. I had to force myself to keep up with him, panting time to time. While walking I tried to make conversation, but his lack of enthusiasm to talk and his short and sharp answers to my queries made me give up.

During my frequent encounters with him over the last four months I had never found him in such a mood. I could sense that he was very concerned and deadly serious about something.

I just couldn't fathom out what that might be and what on earth I possibly could do to help him alleviate his anguish. I surmised, he may have unwittingly got the 'wrong end of a stick' and fallen out with some friends, or made an enemy of someone through a gross misunderstanding. Perhaps he had fallen foul of the law, or maybe he was over-reacting to an exchange or dramatizing an event that had a simple explanation, and his blinkered and obsessive mind was unable to come to terms with it. I started to get worried thinking, perhaps he really was in grave trouble. I resolved, as a good friend, albeit a recent one, it was my bounden duty to help him as much as I could.

Although I felt benevolent towards him I was, at the same time, aware that my involvement in his private affair ought not to be too deep to cause problem for myself. I pondered - I must not get too wrapped-up in something harmful from which I might find it difficult to extricate myself. Surely, such involvement would make demands on my time which I could ill afford.

While pontificating on these concerns I was conscious of the sole purpose of my being at Oxford. I had to avoid any time-wasting extra-curricular commitments at all costs. My priority had to be my studies and research in order to obtain my qualification. My spare time was already committed to a few social activities. However, I would be prepared to help a friend in need. But what was the need? It seemed to me that the journey from the city centre to his flat was never ending.

After about twenty minutes brisk walk we arrived at the ground floor entrance of his flat, which was on the third floor of a large Victorian detached house. He had to wrestle with three locks to enter his fortress flat. One was for the ground floor entrance to the communal area for all the flats in the house. The other two keys were for opening two doors, one leading to the porch and the other to the reception room of the flat. Previously he told me he had been renting the flat for an indefinite time, and contractually he had the right to live there for as long as he wanted, so long he paid his rent regularly, and this was duly reviewed every couple of years.

Rolf effortlessly climbed the steep stairs to the third floor whereas surprisingly, being the younger man, it was more of a struggle for me. Once inside the house I had ample time to catch up my breath because there I had a good few minutes' wait before he was able to let me in, unlocking and bolting down another two doors with two different keys.

His obsession with security, I thought, was way over-the-top. It made me wonder if he had some very valuable items in his flat, perhaps he was hoarding gold bullions or precious diamonds. Once inside, the first thing he did was to switch on the electric heater in his library and then he took my overcoat and muffler, carefully put them on a hanger and stored them in a cupboard. He sat me down on a sofa near the electric heater and asked me to make myself comfortable and offered to make me something to eat or drink. I declined with thanks.

The situation was very tense, and I was tired after the long walk and a steep climb. I was not in the mood for any food or drink. I simply wanted to know at once what all that fuss was about – the suspense was killing me. Rolf sat on another sofa, positioned himself opposite me and looked me in the eye. He usually avoided eye contact by not looking at me directly. For the first time, I noticed that his left eye was different from the right one, it had a starry reflection. I wondered if his left eye was made of glass. Perhaps he didn't want anyone to know that he was a one-eyed man.

With a pathetic expression and in an earnest but hushed voice he pleaded,

'I beg you please do me the favour. It will allow me to expose the heinous activities of the agents who are chasing me all the time – making my life a hell. They want to destroy me both mentally and physically. I want you to help me get rid of them. Once the culprits are behind bars I shall be able to live like any other normal human being without facing constant harassment, persecution and intimidation. Please, please tell me you will do me this favour. I swear that no harm will come to you. I shall make sure of it.'

I couldn't believe my ears. I had never expected such a dramatic outburst from a wise, intellectual and mature person like him. I was sure that he was not play-acting or having me on with a prank. His plea was in earnest. But I couldn't fathom out what this was all about. I found the situation very uncomfortable, but kept calm, thinking that he must really be in some sort of trouble. I leaned forward and in a composed and serious tone said,

'I promise I will help you in any way I can. But first you have to trust me and explain everything without getting so uptight about it. I assure you I am one of your most sincere well-wishers. Believe me; I do not have the faintest idea what you are talking about. I can't make any heads or tails of your request. I promise, I shall listen to your story sympathetically, but you must explain everything to me in detail without being so emotional and dramatic.'

Rolf replied in a mocking tone,

'Without being emotional! Ha! Did you say dramatic?' He paused and continued,

'Yeah! But tell me one thing my friend, are you not talking to a professor now? That is, Professor Kosterlitz!'

He paused again, I was bemused; it was as if he was rehearsing for a part in a play. He then continued,

'Surely, by now you must have guessed what I am talking about!'

I shook my head a few times from side to side in despair and disbelieve. His words sounded surreal. I was at a loss to find a response to his weird comment.

'I don't understand why I am suddenly talking to a Professor

Kosterlitz, instead of my good friend Rolf?' I enquired and continued, 'I am now even more puzzled about the cause of your distress my dear friend. Unless you tell me in plain English and without being cryptic about the matter that is tormenting you, I can't see how I can help. I promise I shall do my utmost to help you. But to be honest, what you're telling me appears to be nonsense.'

Rolf looked visibly unhappy about my accusation of dramatization and said,

'I'm sad but not surprised that you, a close friend and a genuine well-wisher, feel that I'm being dramatic and fictionalising an actual event. Perhaps you think I'm deranged or imagining things. Probably you didn't realize it at that time or, maybe now you cannot recollect the circumstances and the time when you became involved in this murky business. But you cannot deny the fact that you often address me in front of others as 'professor'.'

I retorted in an agitated and offended tone,

'I am quite upset that you can even think of me getting involved in anything that could harm you.'

Rolf shot back,

'I don't mean you did so intentionally or even knowing that it might be a part of a conspiracy against me. Someone at some point in time must have intentionally told you that I am a professor of the University.'

Still a little angry with him, I countered,

'Admittedly I do address you as 'professor' from time to time. But I do it as a jest, and not because I have been prompted by someone to do so to demean you. I find it quite ridiculous that I have to justify why I occasionally introduce you to others as 'professor'. I continued,

'Let me tell you something Mr. It's not uncommon amongst my friends and co-students to sarcastically address some one as 'professor' if he presents himself, unmindfully or deliberately, with the characteristics of a forgetful academic. Why does it matter so much now? Anyway, you never objected to such humour and often smiled and always nodded your head in approval – so I thought.'

By this time Rolf had calmed down a bit and said,

'You have known all along that I am not a professor and have no connection with the University. Still you keep on addressing me as 'professor' in the presence of others. You could have addressed me as 'sir', or 'king' or 'boss' or even, 'doctor', which I am. But why call me 'professor'?'

I was dumbfounded; anger nearly got the better of me. The idea that I was a party to a dirty conspiracy to harm him was just ludicrous, unthinkable.

As I opened my mouth to object, he interrupted,

'Please don't waste your breath trying to explain this to me. You don't need to tell me anything now. Just do me a favour and come to the police station with me and tell them the name of the person who tempted, cajoled or perhaps even blackmailed you into addressing me as 'professor' in front of others. If for any reason you can't disclose the agent's name or don't know it, at least admit that you have been approached by a stranger to do this. Surely, you can now see that this is a conspiracy by an organization. Its plan is to make me appear to be a fraud. Your admission that someone prompted you to address me as a professor in the presence of others will give credibility to my many complaints to the police. They refuse to take them seriously. Once, one of the police officers said quite categorically that this business of 'agent of an organization' was simply a figment of my imagination. Can you believe it? He even dared suggest that I consult a psychiatrist! They whisper and laugh at me behind my back. I feel helpless. They are not prepared to listen to my story. How can I convince them of the threat facing me? They will take my complaint more seriously if I have a witness. That is why I need your help, Rafi, please, please!'

By this time I had had enough; my heart was thumping and hands shaking. I needed a cigarette to calm my nerves, but smoking was not allowed in his flat. I got up from the sofa and paced to and fro across the room. I was thinking of leaving him unceremoniously to avoid an outburst which would otherwise damage our friendship for good. I even peeked through the window asking myself – did Rolf's unusual behaviour have anything to do with a full moon; a lunar effect? But there was no full moon; in fact there was no moon at all, despite the clear sky. Rolf was gazing at the wall waiting for an answer. I pulled myself together, sat down and said in a firm but calm tone,

'Listen, my friend, I don't know what your game is. Are you seriously suggesting that I could unwittingly be a party to a conspiracy against you? Whatever your motive, let me tell you sir, don't like playing games with people's emotions and I don't like this conversation. If I had been approached by anyone to address you as 'professor', I would come to the police station with you to confirm this without any hesitations and fear whatsoever. But I am completely at a loss to make any sense of this at all. I am not even sure if you are serious or playing a prank on me. I swear on my mother's life, no one has approached me to do anything of the sort.'

As far as I am aware, that was the first time, and certainly it would be the last, I had sworn on my mother's life, that's how desperate I was. I could see Rolf starting to shake his head in disbelief even before I'd finished my passionate response to his wild allegations.

'I'm not surprised', he said, 'I was afraid that your mouth, like that of Mack and Hanna, would also be shut by the cunning designs of the agent.'

Something must have happened that day about which he hadn't yet told me. That could have triggered his anxiety about the so called 'secret agents'. I found myself in a dilemma - my friend was in trouble and I was unable to help him. Worse still, I was unable to bear his company any longer. It seemed we had nothing else to say to each other, but at the same time I was uncomfortable at the thought of rushing off unceremoniously and leaving my close friend alone in such a distressed state.

I was worried – feeling unloved, isolated and tormented Rolf might become suicidal. I couldn't make up my mind what to do next. He stood up and asked me again if I would like a cup of coffee or something to eat. I politely declined and took the opportunity to stand up and make a move towards the door. I assumed that this offer was the age old English custom, indicating it was time to 'call it a night'. I mentioned, I had to catch up with some work the next morning and I had an appointment with my academic supervisor, I needed an early night. I thought he was expecting me to leave him alone by then. But when I saw his sullen expression I realised that this wasn't the case and that he didn't really want to be left alone. In a low, distant voice he wished me good night and watched me leave through the door.

I left with a heavy heart and a guilty conscience. I lit a cigarette as soon as I hit the road and started walking slowly towards my flat, feeling very low. I hadn't gone very far before I stopped, about turned, walked back to Rolf's and rang the bell. He came down and opened the door without a word.

In a matter of fact tone I said,

'I have decided to accept your offer of a cup of coffee and a bite to eat.'

He ushered me in as if he had been expecting me. I sat down in the same place as I had before and made myself comfortable.

He went to the kitchen shouting,

'Let me fix you something to eat and then I shall tell you what you came back to hear. Yes, my friend, I can read your mind; reading people's minds is, and has always been my passion and was one of my professions, you know.'

The situation was a bit surreal but somewhat less tense. He came back with a tray containing some slices of Emmental cheese and a couple of pieces of buttered pumpernickel bread on two plates and two cups of coffee. Again I protested my innocence against any charges of being a party to any conspiracy to harm him.

He sat down with his head in the cusps of his palms and elbows resting on his legs and eyes focussed on the floor, and said,

'I had a premonition you'd be back, so I didn't even lock the doors. Anyway, now that we are both relaxed and you are vehemently denying any knowledge about this vexing issue I have to give you the benefit of the doubt. I have to trust in your innocence in this matter. To be honest with you I can't afford to lose a friend like you, particularly during this period of turmoil in my life. You will surely understand and appreciate the seriousness of the matter when I tell you what brought this matter to a head this evening. That's what you have come back to hear,' he paused then leaned close towards me. 'Haven't you?'

I looked at him sympathetically and promised him my undivided attention to his story. He brightened up during our late-night light supper of bread, cheese and coffee. He even quipped with an impish expression,

'You eat the holes and leave the cheese for me.'

Rolf didn't beat about the bushes and straightaway got on with his story,

'This afternoon I experienced something quite uncanny. This convinced me beyond any shred of doubt that an agent of the organization is here. He is working incessantly to undermine my integrity, expecting that eventually I will breakdown mentally and harm myself physically. You see, the people who run the organization are like Mafiosi bosses. Their policy is to eliminate anybody who poses a threat to their interest. They sometime recruit local agents to do their unsavoury work. They can intervene anywhere in the world. They have targeted me because of the fear that I am a threat to their reputation and most probably to their survival. Now you know why the agents are so desperate to shut me up.'

I encouraged him to tell me what had happened earlier in the day and said, 'Please don't keep going on about those so called secret agents, and just tell me what happened this afternoon?'

Rolf snapped, 'But what I am about to tell you has everything to do with the activities of those agents. You will have an idea as to how they are trying to destroy me when I tell you what happened today. Just wait and be patient. I can't give you the whole history of my involvement with the organization now; it's too long a story.'

I apologised for my impatience and he resumed his account of the day's events: 'Nowadays I spend a good deal of time at the Bodleian library. I am writing an academic paper which I want to publish in the British Journal of Applied Psychiatry. As you know, I am not associated with Oxford University now, or for that matter, any University. The paper is based on my private research through literature search and on private communication with people who have proven expertise in subjects relevant to the topic of my research. For that I need to collect lots of data. I find the Bodleian is a treasure trove for information on the very esoteric topic of my interest.

'Lately, I struck up a friendship with Mack Bergmann. He is a mature student at the University of Utrecht in Netherlands, reading for a doctorate. He is preparing a thesis on symbolism and its origin in ancient cults and occults. He has come here under an Inter-University exchange programme only for six months, and is attached to Balliol College. He got a bursary from the Dutch Government under an Anglo-Dutch educational collaboration scheme. Although he lives and studies in the Netherlands his parents are of Austrian origin. He spends most of his time at the library, studying old books and documents on cults, the occult and ancient religions, incessantly taking notes. We became good friends and started to meet regularly to discuss philosophy and psychology. Another thing we shared which made our discourse more interesting, you have probably guessed it, is our mother tongue.

'This afternoon I met Mack at the entrance hall of the library. He was accompanied by a friend and introduced me to him as 'Professor Kosterlitz'. I was a bit surprised but not unduly alarmed straightaway, as I have noticed that you and one or two others have also done the same. His friend, Wolfgang Dewitt, shook my hand and expressed his pleasure and honour to have met a genuine Oxford University professor. Before I could try to explain that I was not a professor of the University and that I had no connection with it, he asked me about my field of research. I politely stated that I preferred not to discuss my research topic then and there, as it was rather complex and needed a lot of explanations. I showed eagerness to discuss this with him at a mutually convenient time and at a suitable venue in the near future. From his accent I realized he was a German speaking Swiss. It was then I smelt a rat. I took leave of them abruptly by saying *Auf Wiedersehen*.

'I walked a small distance along the Parks Road and stopped. Out of curiosity I looked back to the entrance to the library and saw Mack and his friend shaking hands and parting company. I hurried back to the foyer in front of the entrance to the library and caught up with Mack on his way back home. I apologised for being nosy and asked him in a low voice to tell me a little bit more about Herr Dewitt. He informed me that Wolfgang was an employee of the Jung Institute of Psychiatry in Zurich. He was going to be here for three months for literature search and to attend the winter school on the scientific basis of interpretation of dreams and its use in psychoanalysis.

'It was very strange, I thought, Mack had introduced me as a 'professor' to an employee of the very institute which is behind all my problems with the secret agents. Instantly I was convinced beyond any doubt that this 'Dewitt' chap was one of the agents who are trying to implicate me in falsehoods; most probably with the connivance of Mack. I've had disagreements with the bosses of the Jung Institute in the past but never thought they would go so far as to seek me out here to make me out as a fraudster, selling myself as a professor. It seems they are prepared to go to any length to protect the interest of the Institute, even if it means eliminating people they view as a threat to their existence.'

Before he could go any further I interrupted,

'I haven't got a faintest idea about your so called 'organization'. Unless you tell me all about it how can I give any credence to what you're telling me?'

'You are very impatient,' he snapped, 'The episode of my life connected to this organization is a long and complex story. You don't need to know about it now; just have patience. Please just listen to the story in hand.'

He shot me with his customary sideways look to make sure that I was in agreement and resumed:

'It sent a chill down my spine to think that my friend Mack was somehow involved with an agent of that dubious organization. My heart started to pound heavily. I thanked him for the information and left.

'I moved around the shopping centre and spent some time in the park. It was nearly 5 pm and already dark. I had to strike while the iron was hot in order to get to the bottom of the conspiracy they were hatching. The urge was uncontrollable, I had to go back and confront Mack without delay. I made my way to his flat and knocked at the door, I was excited and apprehensive. His wife, Hanna was surprised and perhaps not pleased to see me at her door unexpectedly, particularly at that hour of the day. Nevertheless, she politely greeted and ushered me into the flat. Mack was busy reading something and came out to the door, welcomed me cordially, and asked if there was a particularly urgent reason for my unexpected visit.

'He had every reason to be surprised, as we had met and talked only a couple of hours earlier. I said I wanted to speak to him alone. Hanna went back to the kitchen where she had been preparing their evening meal. Mack asked me to sit down and offered me a drink. I refused and apologised again for the intrusion. Then I asked him directly, why did he introduced me to a stranger as 'professor'?

'He paused for a while and with a show of surprise enquired, "What's wrong with that?"

'I felt he was pretending to be surprised and started getting a bit irritated. I told him that there was a lot wrong with that. I was not a professor and I had never ever told him I was one, and he must certainly know that.

'He didn't look straight at me. With his face bend towards the table he said, "I have only done so because I have heard someone addressed you as a professor, therefore I assumed you are one."

'Of course, I did not believe him. I begged him to tell me the truth and to admit that his friend, Wolfgang, was an agent of the Jung Institute and somehow he had cajoled him to address me as 'professor' in his presence.

'Mack looked confused and pretended to be dumbfounded. He asked me, "What purpose would that have served even if it was true?"

'I told him that the institute then would have evidence that I was a fraudster, promoting myself as one of the professors amongst the academia at Oxford, enabling me to continue practicing as an accredited analyst.

'Mack continued to pretend to be very surprised to learn that

I was not a real professor and began praising my knowledge on symbolism in ancient cults. According to him, my knowledge far surpassed that of many other professors, including his own supervisor. I sensed some insincerity and flattery in his assertions and I didn't believe it when he said he had no knowledge of any conspiracy in this matter. When I insisted on knowing the truth about his relationship with Wolfgang, he became very angry and accused me of talking nonsense. When I asked him if he was, for any reason, unable to talk about it, he became furious and said in a raised voice that I was crazy and talking nonsense. I then realized that the agent had secured his silence on this matter. At that point I stood up and left his flat unceremoniously with a bitter taste in my mouth. I then made my way straight to your flat. You were not there so I came to the town centre to pass time. That's when you caught sight of me loitering in front of the shop.'

Rolf's sudden unusual agitated mental condition surprised me beyond measure but did not unduly unsettled me, as I'd had lots of experience in dealing with such people in my younger days back home. However, the situation there was quite different. People with disturbed mental conditions were never left alone and were always surrounded by family and friends. Besides, the many day-to-day problems of living and keeping alive in third world countries generally kept mental breakdowns at bay.

Rolf was all alone with no family ties or close friends. Cultural constraints of the society here made it restricted, even for a close friend like me, to tell him that this talk of the so called "secret agents" of an organization was simply a figment of his imagination. I knew if I had told him that, it would have only strengthened his conviction that I was a party to the conspiracy and a client of an agent of that 'organization'. I was increasingly concerned for his well-being, and at a loss to figure out how to help him. I knew, "Time is the great healer", and these strange ideas he held would soon be gone out of his head and peace and normalcy will prevail in his mind.

For a thinking man, beliefs get established in the mind through reasoning and proofs. But when obsession sets in, logic goes out of the head. I felt Rolf had lost his way. I was hoping that this attack on his psyche was just a one-off incident, and this bizarre episode would soon be forgotten and my friendship with him would continue as usual. On the way back to my flat along the dimly lit footpath by the side of the Banbury Road, I tried to put Rolf's sudden madness out of my mind. I remembered the old saying my grandmother used to tell us: "the water in the river doesn't move without the wind." I was convinced that the 'effect', that is, his fear, must have a cause. An obsessive need came over me to find out the cause. Rolf was a wise and learned man with vast knowledge of human psychology. He had dealt with people's mental problems professionally. It was my turn to help him in his journey to recovery, simply by being a friend and well-wisher and listening to his stories.

2.

Days of Wonder

The word 'Oxford' was familiar to me from the tender age of six, although I did not fully understand what it meant. I only knew that it was associated with a special pair of shoes. During the annual Muslim festival of Eidul Fitre, my parents always took me and my sister, Zarina on a trip to the nearby town of Kishoreganj. On one occasion they bought me a pair of real leather 'Oxford' brogues. Up until then I'd only ever worn sandals, or gone barefoot like the other children. Wearing shoes made me feel like a grown-up. The only problem was I had to learn how to tie the laces. My mother sat me down and knelt in front of me, murmuring:

'You hold the first part of the knot in place while you make the first part of the bow,' she said, 'then wrap the loose end around that, thread it back through, make another bow and then, and only then, pull everything tight.'

Tongue out with concentration; I tried it a few times. The laces remained untied. My mother showed me again, and I had another go. I looked across at my sandals, waiting patiently on the other side of the room. Finally, after ending up with great big knots in both my shoes that I couldn't undo, I wrenched them off, threw them into the corner and slipped on my sandals. English shoes might look very good but you had to learn how to wear them.

That year the trip before Eid was particularly exciting because, in addition to becoming the proud owner of a new pair of proper shoes with real laces, I had the joy of watching the afternoon steam train pulling its carriages over the bridge across the Narashundha

River. My sister and I spent hours sitting on the side of the bridge in the hot afternoon, watching the turbulent flow of the water roiling beneath our feet, lingering long after the train had passed by, and the white smoke puffing from its chimney had mingled with the snowy clouds of the summer sky. Another attraction of these trips was the 'cinema or film show', early moving and talking pictures made into what was then called 'bioscope' which we were excited to see at the local cinema hall.

Back home, with the laces finally mastered, I showed off my brand-new shoes to my playmates. Later, I came to understand that Oxford was not just the brand name of a shoe, but also the name of a city in England, where exists a centre of excellence for acquiring knowledge. That country, we were told, was 'seven seas and thirteen rivers' away from where we lived, and populated by a very intelligent, white-skinned people who had colonized and ruled half the world, including, until very recently, our own country.

I arrived in England to study at Oriel College, Oxford in 1967 with a Commonwealth scholarship. I was enrolled to read for the degree of Doctor of Philosophy in Engineering Science. My parents were not that well-off, so I had to travel light, wearing my only dark suit, made to measure, and my only one dark pair of shoes which were handed down from my friend and companion, Mushfiq, coming from a rather wealthy family. The shoes were not 'Oxford brogues' to which I'd become accustomed, but they fitted me well and they were fairly new.

Quite a few Pakistani students landed at Heathrow Airport late that morning from Karachi, the then Capital city of Pakistan. We were all escorted by a representative from the local British Council office to a hotel in Strand. Our sojourn there was for briefing and training on British life-style and etiquette before sending us off to different Universities. My first bus ride experience in London, the awe-inspiring city that we talked about and, dreamt about to visit one day, in our younger days back home, is now a classic story.

I sat next to a middle-aged Englishman (then all white people were English to me). I looked through the bus window and tried to read the signs in shop windows, which was not easy from the moving bus. I was not surprised by the big spectacular buildings and parks, which I was expecting to see here. However I was not only surprised, but shocked by some things which I didn't expect to see the word, 'GIRLS' being displayed in big block letters in glass windows of some shops and, displays of models of naked girls behind the window of another. I also felt revulsed at the signs in window panes of some eating houses, advertising SNAKES, which were on offer. I thought – as far as I know only the Chinese eat such things.

I decided to strike up a conversation with my fellow passenger seated next to me. I extended my hand and said,

'Hello, my name is Rafi. It is my first day in London. You are the first Englishman with whom I have the privilege to introduce myself.'

Instead of shaking it and reciprocating my friendly gesture by telling me his name he stood up, muttering,

'Sorry I have to get down at the next stop.'

I let him pass and was surprised to notice, instead of alighting from the bus, he took another empty seat. I found his behaviour very odd and utterly rude. I looked around, and to my great amazement noticed that no one else was talking. This could never have happened on a public transport back home. I then realised perhaps the gentleman I had tried to engage in conversation might have found my behaviour odd. Perhaps it was some sort of English paranoia – a stranger is a potential enemy and cause for trouble.

Back home we believed that familiarity breeds friendship, but I learnt later that the English people believed it 'breeds contempt'. Perhaps it was just as well that I didn't quiz him about the signs in the shop windows and the naked dummy models.

The programme for my training and pep talk on English customs and etiquette at the British Council office was on the afternoon of the second day of my stay in London. The morning was free and I wanted to explore one of the seven wonders of the modern world – a train which not only travels under the ground but also under the river Thames. I was determined to travel on a train running under a river before this wonder was destroyed by some wacky disaster; something I felt sure to happen sooner or later. On my way to the underground railway station I was able to read shop signs more clearly and saw that the word was, GRILLS displayed on restaurant windows advertising fried food items, and not, 'girls' as I had thought advertised in brothel windows. I had also misread the sign for SNACKS. English people did not eat 'snakes', they took snacks. The plastic models of naked girls in the windows of clothe shops were just mannequins waiting to be dressed and not for attracting punters into places of ill repute.

At the nearby underground station I bought a ticket for Paddington main line station. I chose Paddington because the British Council had explained that I had to catch the railway train from there to get to Oxford. That day on the underground I had a similar experience as that I had had on the bus. People were not talking to each other, instead, to my utter surprise, I found almost everyone glued to the pages of their newspapers as if a terrible disaster had taken place and a cause for breaking news. After my previous day's experience, I knew better not to engage my fellow passengers in conversation. On disembarking at Paddington station I bought a newspaper to find out if something drastic was happening around the globe. There was no news of an imminent third world war, a catastrophic earthquake or any other major calamity. The brutality of the Vietnam War had been going on for some time and did not constitute 'breaking news'. I couldn't find any news which would make people 'en masse' be glued to their newspapers that they would miss the opportunity of getting to know a potentially interesting foreigner sitting next to them by initiating a conversation. I concluded that it was true English men do not speak to strangers unless introduced. Later, my Pakistani mentor, Shaukhat gave me the following definition of an Englishman – a white-skinned man who reads newspapers and fornicates.

I discovered later that he'd borrowed the description from Albert Camus, who used it to describe all Western males.

The British Council had arranged accommodation for me right in the centre of Oxford, in St John's Street. My 'digs' consisted of a small bedsit room with shared toilet and bathroom facilities. The rent included breakfast and one bath each week. There was no shower and I had to put a shilling in the gas meter for any additional baths, which had to be scheduled in advance par consultation with the landlady. The landlady, Mrs Capper was a small, wiry woman in her mid-forties. She had a head full of very pale, almost white hair.

I arrived from London late one Friday morning clutching my battered suitcase containing a change of underwear, a shirt and a pair of trousers and my black suit along with a matching black tie, some socks and a few books. Explaining that she was a widow, and only 'took in' to make ends meet, Mrs Capper showed me the room. It took me some time to realise that by the term, 'took in' she meant that she rented rooms to the likes of me and the other student lodger, Alfie.

I expressed suitable praise for the very sparse, not to say Spartan furnishings, which consisted of a single iron-framed bed, a rickety desk and a chair in front of the window, and a chest of drawers with one of its knobs missing. Mrs Capper appeared to be quite pleased and kindly invited me to tea on the following Sunday.

Inside my room I noticed a small hand-written note on the desk. It was from a chap named Shaukat. He was a senior research student under the same supervisor. He had asked him to help me settle-in. Shaukat's note said that he would visit me on Saturday morning.

My excitement at the prospect of new experiences was overwhelming. I woke up unusually early on the Saturday before the landlady's knock at the door. She entered my room, put the breakfast tray on the side table, bade me good morning and assured me that it would be a lovely day. I forced a smile on my face and echoed her greetings. I was hungry and excited, and got up straight away. The breakfast of fried egg and tomato, a piece of toasted bread and baked beans went down quite easily, thanks to the hot coffee. I got ready and while waiting for my visitor I read the folder of the house rules kept on the table – No baths without prior permission. No visitors in the room after 10 pm. No parties. No cooking in the room. The last one was odd, as there were no cooking facilities anywhere in the room. As expected, there was a knock at the door, when I opened it I saw my landlady again; this time accompanied by a tall, well built and reasonably handsome young man. She disappeared without a word.

Unlike the Englishman on the bus, the stranger extended his hand and introduced himself,

'I am Shaukat Khan,' and then asked me, 'What shall I call you; Sheikh or Rafi?'

'You can call me anything you like as long as it isn't a swear word. My friends call me Rafi,' I replied flippantly.

We became friends instantly. We set out for the Engineering department. On the way he pointed out some University colleges and departments. These didn't mean anything to me but I was impressed when he pointed to a tall multistory and most modern looking building and said,

'That's going to be your *Alma Mater* for the next few years, Rafi, hope you like it.' The main entrance remained locked during weekends, but Shaukat, being a post graduate research student, had the privilege of having his own personal key. Inside the building there were a few other research students moving about but no staff members. He showed me my corner in the laboratory room, which I was to share with three other post-graduate researchers each having their desks in the remaining three corners. My niche was equipped with a desk, a couple of chairs, a filing cabinet, a book case and some monitoring equipment and various laboratory tools spread out on a long side bench.

After having refreshed ourselves with a cup of coffee at the departmental senior students' common room Shaukat suggested that I wonder about and explore the city's 'Dreaming Spires'. Noticing my puzzled expression he said, with a wide flourishing gesture using his arms,

'Once you soak in the atmosphere enriched by the beautiful and harmonious architecture of the city you will understand why a Victorian poet coined this attribute – 'city of dreaming spires' to glorify this university town; surely the oldest in the English speaking world.'

The weather was fine and he assured me that I wouldn't get lost within the city even if I tried. We parted company, agreeing to meet again on Monday.

I wandered along some of the narrow cobbled streets in the city centre passing various colleges. The 'paramount' beauty of 'dreaming spires' was not in my thoughts at all. I knew I would have plenty of time for savouring that later. I was more interested in exploring the cloister-like colleges and experiencing the austere undergraduate life-style. After all, I thought, in this highest seat of learning the robed students and teachers surely lead a monastic life, dedicated solely in pursuit of knowledge. But again, there would be plenty of time for that too, I thought. One thing however was certain I was definitely not going to be able to concentrate on anything as I was so hungry. I was craving not just for any food, but for rice and curry. A Bengali without his fix of rice and curry for three consecutive days is indeed a desperate and dangerous man.

Like a sharp eyed hawk I caught site of a sign in capital letters, TAJ MAHAL RESTAURANT, with the following inscription in smaller letters below – 'Authentic Indian Cuisine'. The thought ran through my head; Indian Cuisine! We had fought three wars with India over Kashmir, and being a Pakistani I couldn't possibly patronize an Indian restaurant. It was a matter of principle and patriotism.

Alas, my need was so desperate that when the aroma of freshly cooked curry wafted through the open kitchen window and entered my nostril, principle just flew out of my mind. I entered the restaurant climbing up the steep stairs. It was a bit early for lunch, and I couldn't see any other customer or even a waiter. I hesitated at the entrance door if I ought to go in, wondering if I had come too early and should leave to come back later. Then an Asian waiter appeared, asking me if I was looking for something or somebody. I said,

'I'm looking for a meal of rice and curry.' He ushered me to a seat and said,

'You have come to the right place for that, young man' and enquired, 'are you a Bengali by any chance?'

I was surprised, 'How did you guess that?'

'I'm Bengali too, I can recognize a hungry Bengali anytime, brother', he said patronizingly.

I felt real good and completely satisfied after a meal of boiled rice with spicy chicken curry and *Dal* (Lentil curry) with a hot green chilli and some mango chutney, and had a heartfelt chat in our mother tongue with the waiter, Abdul. I forgot to ask why the owner, a Bengali speaking East Pakistani, had called it an Indian restaurant. As I was leaving, Abdul tapped me on the shoulder and said with a carefree expression and in a loud voice,

'If you are going to live in this country, you will need the heart of a lion and not to be frightened of anything or anybody.'

I knew it was not in my nature to be frightened of anything or anybody, but he must have got that impression when he saw me hovering outside the restaurant.

The next day was Sunday and as arranged, I went downstairs and knocked on the landlady's sitting-room door. This, as Mrs Capper had made very clear in the course of her introductory tour, was strictly off-limits to lodgers, as in fact was most of the house. The invitation to join her for tea was plainly an honour and a privilege.

Instead of Mrs Capper, an attractive young woman opened the door,

'Hello,' she said, shaking me by the hand,

'You must be Sheikh. I'm Jennifer, Mrs Capper's daughter. She'll be with us in a moment; she's just making the tea. Why don't you sit down, while we wait?'

I asked her to address me as 'Rafi' while sitting down, and we chatted about the weather for a while. I'd been told during my initiation events in London that, when all other conversation fails, or instead of actually having a meaningful conversation, British people like to talk about the weather, which changed very frequently and abruptly, and thus rarely led to awkward silences.

Jennifer was taller than her mother, and prettier. Her hair was less pale, more of a straw colour, but still very bright. She wore a green mini-skirt that showed off her legs to good advantage, a floral-patterned blouse, a large number of bangles and big looped earrings. Eventually, having exhausted the subject of the weather she looked up and said,

'I shouldn't really tell you this, Rafi, but my mother's taken a bit of a shine to you. If you play your cards right, you'll be quid's in.'

I stared at her in astonishment. What did she mean exactly? Almost nothing of what she'd just said made any sense to me, "a shine"? "Play my cards right"?' What could she possibly mean?

Just then the door opened and Mrs Capper came in bearing a tray laden with tea and cake. I couldn't see a pack of cards, but no doubt they would produce one when the time came.

'I'll be mother,' the landlady said mystifyingly, and set about pouring the tea. We drank for a while in polite silence, except for my slurping noise.

To break the silence, I said,

'What game are we going to play? I only know, snap!' I'm afraid, 'Where I come from students don't play cards all that much.'

They both stared at me as if I'd gone mad.

'Pardon me?' Mrs Capper said.

Jennifer started to laugh, then checked herself, and without her mother noticing, shook her head and compressed her lips with her index finger pressing against them, as if warning me to shut up.

Anxious to change the subject, since I'd clearly made a mistake, I blurted out the first thing that came into my head,

'You remind me so much of my grandmother, Mrs Capper.'

There was a short silence. Mrs Capper stared at me, her eyes narrowing. There was something about her gaze I didn't like. It was steady, and seemed full of disapproval.

'Did you say your grandmother?' Why?' She said in a flat tone.

Dimly, I sensed that I might once again have said the wrong thing. Trying to make amends, I cast about for a suitable reply,

'Well, only because she has the same colour hair as you.'

There was another pregnant silence. Then my landlady asked, 'And what colour would that be?'

'White,' I offered tentatively.

Mrs Capper set her tea cup down in the saucer, a little too firmly for my absolute comfort. She was incensed,

'Are you saying I look old, Mr Ach-mad?'

With a rush of embarrassment and shame, I realised I'd made the most terrible mistake. I felt the blood blaze in my cheeks. My shirt collar suddenly felt a size too small, and despite the tea, my mouth had gone dry. I tried to make amends,

'No, not at all – it's just that your hair's the same colour…'

There is an old English saying I learnt later, sadly too late to help me on that particular occasion – when you're in a hole, stop digging. Mrs Capper stood and raised herself to her full height, which was not very great, perhaps only up to my chest,

'My hair, Mister Ach-mad', she said slowly, separating each word and some of the syllables for greater emphasis, 'Is NOT white – it is BLONDE, which is its NATURAL COLOUR.'

Hastily setting down my own cup, I rose and backed towards the door and the landlady followed me,

'Do you,' she continued in the same tone, 'understand what blonde means?'

I bumped into the door and grabbed the handle, much in the same way a drowning man will grab at a lifebuoy.

'Thank you very much for the tea, Mrs Capper,' I gabbled, 'I am very sorry if I offended you. I only meant –.'

Glancing at Jennifer, who was standing behind her mother, I saw that she had her fingers stuffed in her mouth, and was making strange squawking noises. She was trying not to laugh! But what was there to laugh about? Truly, the British are extraordinary!

'I think you've said enough, young man,' Mrs Capper concluded grandly. If I were you, I'd go and take some lessons in English language and manners – before it's too late.'

"It's too late for what?" I wondered, making my way disconsolately back up to my room. I'd only been in the country for a few days, and already I'd made my landlady, the very last person I should have upset – angry. And I'd have to live under the same roof as her for at least a year – what a blockhead I was! But the fact of the matter was I'd never, ever, been up close to a person with blonde hair before.

As if I was in any doubt at all as to what my landlady meant by, 'too late'; the next day I started getting the notes. The first one, which was pinned to my door so that I couldn't possibly miss it, read:

"NO SMOKING IN BED"

It was printed in large black capital letters on a sheet of white A4 paper. I stopped on the landing and stared at it. My bowels became a little watery. It was true that I had already smoked in bed a couple of times; make that all of the time, but how could Mrs Capper possibly knew that? Was she spying on me, through a tiny hole she'd bored in the wall? Then I realised, she was probably just guessing, or rather, deducing, in the manner of the great Sherlock Holmes, from the evidence of the butt-ends I'd left in the ashtray on the mottled and scarred bedside locker. 'Elementary, my dear Rafi!' – I said to myself.

Having no television or radio or any other facilities to entertain myself or my visitors I found my digs to be quite claustrophobic and used it only for sleeping at night. Life started to become more and more restrictive as Mrs Capper's house rules gradually became more and more stringent and life under her baleful eye made me feel like a caged bird.

She would knock at my door every morning precisely at 7:30 am, except on week-ends, when this was extended to 8:30 am. Without waiting for my answer, she would open the door and put the breakfast tray on the small side table, draw the curtains and leave the room after politely bidding me good morning and addressing me as 'Mr. Akh-mad'.

On weekdays, I usually got up at about 9 am and, on weekends even later. By that time the fried egg was like a piece of leather and the slices of toast were like pieces of tree bark. I would put a shilling in the electricity meter to use the heater for long enough to swallow the cold breakfast, wash and brush my teeth, get dressed and leave. I usually re-heated the cold pieces of toast on the protective grill of the electric heater and gobbled them with cold beans, piece of tomato and the rubbery egg, washing the tasteless food down the throat with cold coffee. I could only start functioning properly when I'd reached my desk in the department and lit my first cigarette of the day with a cup of hot coffee from the machine.

In addition to the tyranny of breakfast, I was ruffled by the barrage of hand-written notices, like the ones I received immediately after my acrimonious encounter with Mrs Capper over the tea party at her lounge. Those read, "NO BREAD CRUMBS ON THE FLOOR; NO VISITORS AFTER 10 PM; NO SMOKING IN THE TOILET". The 'shine' she was supposed to have taken on me had been very short-lived, I thought. She hadn't forgotten or forgiven my sin of likening her to my grandmother. To avoid any further confrontations with the Gorgon, on weekdays I made the corner of my lab space my home, slinking in late at night after watching television in the departmental common room.

The first year of University, for most students, was a time for familiarization, exploration, adventure and, most importantly, a time for personality building. There was much to do, learn and enjoy in the University, but for most of us, beyond the chores of the academic activities, there was precious little time to participate in most of these. We had to be quite selective in our choice of involvement in non-academic pursuits. There were also some activities - cultural, political, and recreational, in which ex-students or members of the public took part. My new friend, Rolf was one such member of the public.

My first encounter with him was at the weekly evening event at the British Council auditorium during my first week at Oxford. He was there busily chatting up a couple of beautiful Venezuelan girls. It was quite amusing to see a middle-aged man laughing and joking and flirting with young girls, trying to befriend them without a shred of inhibition. One of my acquaintances told me his name was Rolf and that he was often the heart and soul of these gatherings and the occasional parties which took place there. It seemed to me that a bit of flirting with young girls was a harmless enough way to have some fun. I approached him and extended my hand and used the old cliché with a cheeky smile,

'Professor Rolf, I presume!' I did not know his surname then.

'I didn't know he's a professor!' One of the girls expressed surprise with a giggle,

'But now you do,' I retorted, again with a mischievous smile.

Rolf stared at me at sideways for a while and then reluctantly shook my hand. He was more interested in one of the girls than in speaking to me. However, it was of some help to him when I kept the other girl engaged in small talks. After a very brief exchange of niceties Rolf went back to the business of flirting with a particular girl who had caught his fancy. I noted that he didn't object to me calling him 'professor', but it seemed he was not amused either.

On Monday morning, I made my way to the department to meet my academic supervisor, Professor Donald Walsh. I was proudly wearing my sombre dark suit with a matching dark tie and, of course, my well-polished black shoes. I knocked at his office door and heard a voice from behind the door, 'Enter.'

So I did. The room was packed with books, journals and papers. These were all scattered everywhere, on the chairs, desk, shelves, filing cabinet, even on the floor. But the chair on which I was expecting Professor Walsh to be sitting was empty. I got worried – was I hearing voices? Was I hallucinating?

Professor Walsh, a middle-aged man, wearing a pair of powerful glasses at the end of his nose and wearing a peeved look, appeared from underneath the table mumbling,

'Can't find the bloody paper, it was right here on my desk, a few minutes ago. Where the hell has it disappeared? It isn't under the desk either.'

I cleared my throat to draw his attention. He apologised for his bad language when he saw me stood in front of him. In response I said,

'It's quite OK professor, as long as it is not directed at me. (As a matter of fact, I was getting used to being abused often at night when the drunken occupants spill out of pubs onto the street. They shout "Paki" at me with a 7 letter adjective before it, gesticulate and tell me to go back home.)'

He didn't catch the innuendo in my tone and asked me to move the pile of papers from one of the chairs and to park my bottom there.

'Good morning Professor Walsh,' I said, as I had been trained to do so during my initiation sessions on local social manners and etiquette. Unfortunately, the trainer had omitted to inform me that comparing your landlady, or for that matter, any lady, to your grandmother, is a thoroughly bad idea. Anyway, Professor Walsh came up to me, shook my hand and said drily,

'I was expecting you Sheikh, welcome to the department. Now tell me, how do you do; young man?'

I wasn't sure what he meant, "How did I do, what?" To which

particular activity was he referring? This time, instead of blundering on, I decided to be cautious and replied nonchalantly,

'In the same Bengali way as I always do, sir.'

I could see he thought I was making a joke, because he smiled. Rephrasing his question, he said,

'I mean, is everything alright with you?'

Later, I found out that my supervisor's peculiar question was a common English way of asking how someone feels about life. It took me a long time to learn that this kind of peculiarity is the very meat and drink of the English language. After we'd exchanged a few more misunderstood pleasantries, Professor Walsh told me that the department had a tradition of informality between the students and the academic staff. I asked what that meant.

'Well,' he said, 'for a kick-off you can call me by my first name, instead of sir.'

I thought, 'Kick off? Were we now going to be playing football, as a means of cementing our relationship?'

In my strong Anglo-Bengali accent I said,

'No, no sir; I'm sorry. I absolutely cannot do that. According to my English primer back home, Donald is the name of a cartoon duck. You are my much-respected teacher and supervisor, how can I call you by your first name?'

From the expression of amusement in his face I could tell that once again he thought I was joking. Little did he know that people from the Indian subcontinent never make jokes at the expense of their elders and betters, let alone their teachers! For us, teachers are considered as the givers of knowledge. We regard them as gurus, i.e. virtual demigods, who command the highest respect. I couldn't commit a mortal sin by addressing a guru by his given name, least of all when it was the name of a Walt Disney cartoon duck.

After briefing me on various aspects of my research activities, Walsh raised an inquiring eyebrow,

'Are you on your way to a funeral, Sheikh?'

I failed to notice the ironic edge to his tone. Whereas to a certain class of educated British persons irony is more or less of a default setting; to foreigners it can very often seem as if, instead of joking, they are speaking the literal truth. Following my contretemps with Mrs Capper, I was beginning to realise what a minefield life in Britain could be. Despite my best efforts to be polite and learn the ropes, I kept treading on mines. Oxford life was much like Oxford shoes – you couldn't just slip into it, you had to learn its secrets first.

I was wondering why on earth he had asked me such an extraordinary question, and hoping to match him in levity, I shot back,

'Why? Does the department provide funeral services, as well as education?'

Walsh smiled and rose to his feet. By now, one thing was perfectly clear, his sense of humour, which consisted almost entirely of mild irony, designed to unseat his interlocutors was the polar opposite of my own. Shaking my hand at the door, he caught my gaze and said, 'I should dress casually from tomorrow.'

I looked at his jeans and his scruffy jumper and said,

'But you're already dressed casually, sir,' and, thought - why would he want to dress more casually, after all he is a professor!'

After a brief pause when he realized my predicament with the English idioms he said with a smirk before closing the door behind me,

'I meant, if I were you.'

Outside in the passageway I stood for a few moments pondering on our last exchange – he was never going to be me, so why didn't he just ask me directly to dress more casually!'

It dawned on me, I had to improve my command of English language in earnest to get on with life and enjoy it. In particular I needed to get cracking with learning to decipher it's weird and rather wonderful idioms. I had to consider Mrs Capper's advice quite seriously.

🌑

Over the following days, my mentor, Shaukhat, took on the challenge of training me to blend in:

'There are two sides to Oxford,' he began, 'discounting the tourists, that is; the 'Town', the sphere in which ordinary inhabitants who are not students of the university belongs; and the 'Gown', the academic sphere, the members of which are identified by the black gowns that they have to wear on some occasions.' He continued with his lesson:

'If you want to fit in with the 'Gownies' you will have to get rid of your black suit and stop wearing tie. It might be how students dress back home to impress others, but here it looks terribly square.'

I looked at him. Now he was speaking in riddles, I thought, 'how could a suit be 'square'?'

Seeing my confusion, he added,

'By 'square' I mean, it looks old-fashioned, Rafi.'

With Shaukhat's advice ringing in my ears, and with my first tranche of grant, I went straight out and bought some new clothes; a pair of flared jeans, which I roughed up and ripped a bit here and there to make them look scruffy as was the fashion; a couple of T-shirts, one bearing the handsome features of Che Guevara, since everyone in Oxford under the age of 30 appeared to be preparing for an imminent leftist socialist revolution; and a smart flowery shirt with a matching slim knitted tie for best. I took my dated black suit to a charity shop in Walton Street, hoping to get a few shillings for it, but the shop assistant looked at it and laughed. In a fit of pique, I grabbed the suit, left the shop and shoved it in the nearest litter bin. Ironically, it transpired later that this was a big mistake because shortly after this incident

I got an invitation to a banquet in honour of Queen Elizabeth II, in Oriel formal hall. The dress code specified – men: black tie or lounge suit and tie.

Oriel is a relatively small and apparently insignificant college, just behind the mighty and famous Christ Church. Some people, not least Christ Church students, jokingly referred to Oriel as "the stable attached to the castle"; but as far as I was concerned it was a very beautiful stable. The Chancellor of the University at that time was none other than the ex-prime minister, Sir Harold McMillan, a great admirer of the Queen and a close friend of the Provost of Oriel. That was probably why Her Majesty was gracing us, Orielenses, with her presence. I was told by Shaukhat that, as a token student representative from the Commonwealth countries, I was very lucky to have this rear opportunity to hobnob with royalty and other luminaries. My good fortune, I later found out, was the result of my name having been entered into a lottery and drawn from a hat. Nevertheless, I felt honoured.

Even with a relatively handsome Commonwealth scholarship grant from the British Council, I couldn't afford to hire a dinner jacket, let alone buy one. Besides, I have always been a bit of an anti-monarchist and, therefore, wasn't that excited about the prospect of dining with the Queen of England. I was however prepared, indeed even eager, to relax my strong anti-royalist principles in return for a free slap-up dinner. I convinced myself that the compromise was a 'one-time only' exception to prove the rule. Having thrown away my suit, my next problem was how I could attend the banquet without the obligatory attire. Shaukat had a quiet word with the banquet's organizers and it was agreed that I'd be permitted to attend the event in my national costume. By asking around, Shaukat, who had turned out to be an absolute brick, managed to scrape up the full Pakistani regalia from a variety of sources. This consisted of skin-tight white *pyjama*, a long Pakistani '*Sherwani*', or tunic; a *Jinnah* cap and decorated sandals known as '*Nagrai* sandals'. Cometh the hour, my allocated seat was so far away from the high table where the Queen and the other bigwigs were seated that I could barely make her out. The whole purpose of this tradition seemed to be to put the lowly chaps like me in their places, while making those in the offices of power feel even more important, which, to my way of thinking is a pitiful state of affair.

I shall never know if the Queen noticed me. But if she did, she must have gone away with the impression that I was the college's resident jester.

꽃

Within a few weeks of my arrival at Oxford, my pre-conceived vision of life at the University, the highest seat of learning in this country, probably in the world, evaporated. The students here did not lead a monastic existence in search of knowledge and wisdom, devoting all their time in pursuit of excellence for broadening the mind, like the scholars of an elite school in Herman Hess's famous book, "The Glass Bead Game". They worked hard to pass exams, get good grades and to meet deadlines for the submission of assignments. It became apparent to me that the student life here was not much different from that of ours back home; that is to say, mostly routine and hard grind.

All students got monthly remittances, being funded by their local authority, parents, or by the Government and other charitable sources. Making a monthly spending budget of the stipend to see through the month was not something in vogue amongst the student body then. At the end of each month a state of near-famine affected them; post-grads were particularly affected. As soon as the opportunity arose I moved out of my digs to share a flat with a friend in Norham Gardens, with my £56 monthly grant and my flat mate's similar income as an articled clerk at an accountancy firm, we were relatively better-off than most other students. We managed to keep our heads above water during the days leading up to the famine period by acquiring mastery in the art of cooking minced meat curry and rice, thus avoiding the expense of eating in restaurants and public houses.

Our relative prosperity and generosity were no secret, especially amongst the Pakistani student community. To maintain this status we were constrained to run a *Longar Khana*, a sort of Indian 'soup kitchen' at the end of the month. We provided rice and minced meat curry to a steady flow of unexpected famine-stricken visitors - some, who dropped-in near dinner time, became regulars. We were particularly popular amongst the postgrads from the Indian sub-continent. Akhtar Hamid, a Rhode's scholar from Pakistan, was a regular visitor in the lean time at the end of the month. He would knock at the door and say,

'I was just passing by and caught a rather disgusting pungent smell wafting out of your flat. I thought I'd better look in, to see what is going on and if everything is OK.'

On hearing his familiar voice my flat mate would shout from the open door of his room and say in Urdu, "*Saloon May Aur Thura Hari Marcha Dhal Dew.*" He was asking me to put few more green chillies in the cooking curry pot. He knew that a hot curry would go further when we had to share our dinner for two with an unexpected guest.

Despite financial hardship and the ever present stress of exam and deadlines, most students found some time for extra-curricular activities. Some were passionate with the naïve dream of changing society's attitudes to life-style or transforming the world to a better place for the so called, 'have not's. Others got involved simply to feel the joy and exhilaration of experiencing some new achievement or amusement. An unprecedented cultural revolution started in the late sixties throughout the 'developed world'. Students at Oxford University were amongst the forerunners of this radical change, which encompassed a plethora of movements and cults. Krishna consciousness led by the Maharishi Mahesh Yogi, the post-Vietnam peace movement, the nuclear disarmament movement, the Hippy flower power mob, the anti-globalization movement etc. are just a few to mention. Changes in musical taste and fashion were led by Beatle-mania, the Rolling Stones, and Mary Quant's daring miniskirts. Stadium sized events were organised for rock and pop festivals. The 'Swinging Sixties' was the name coined to immortalize this Cultural Revolution. There also emerged a liberal student drug culture influenced by Timothy Leary. It was an exciting time for student body as a whole and there were something for everyone to belong to or take part in.

While so much was going on around me and the temptation of making my own mark on this epoch making-cultural revolution was alluring, I found the pull of attraction towards my enigmatic and mysterious friend, Rolf to be overpowering. Our intimacy grew in leaps and bounds; life was exciting in his company.

3

Soldåt – A Unique Cigarette

Fresher's fair at the Town Hall, just before the first session of the University's Michaelmas term, was quite abuzz with starry-eyed freshmen as well as older students. I found out that there were quite a few invited guests, and some curious dons were also lurking about. The older students were mostly minding their stands, trying to promote their clubs and activities and trying to recruit new members. I guessed about 60 to 70 stands; most of them were only with a small table containing a few leaflets and a hand-written placard showing the name of the club or the organization. Some had elaborate posters and pictures, set on billboards behind the table. All had a record book on the table for the interested visitors to note down their names and addresses. Someone was always minding their respective stalls and explaining their aims and activities to any interested passer-by who cared to stop and listen.

I felt important and elated by the attention I received from many students vying for my involvement and patronage for their supposedly 'noble' causes. They were promoting a wide range of activities or ideologies from mundane, such as, 'Save the Tree', Animal Protection, Gay Right (the term 'Lesbian' was not in vogue then) etc., to some serious ones such as, Ban the Bomb, Human Right, Racial Equality etc. In addition to these, there were religious and political groups, individual national groups such as Pakistani Student Association, Afro-Caribbean Student Association etc. Then there were some topical ones which almost was 'cult like' such as, Therapeutic Drug Culture

Society (following the cult of Timothy Leary), Monty Python Appreciation Society (MPAS- a weird-comical television serial) etc.

Since I had already been head-hunted by my mentor Shaukhat to become the secretary of the Pakistani Student Association, I decided not to get wrapped up in too many extra-curriculum activities. However I couldn't resist the temptation of joining the MPAS. I thought it would be great fun without much involvement or waste of time. I attended the first of the MPAS's impromptu meeting and became one of the organizers of the first and last ever mass 'silly walk' along avenue of St Giles, a landmark of the city. It was a mimic of one of many weird and funny television sketches by the group by that name and was an emerging cult. It was advertised in the University's weekly Vade Mecum. On the sunny spring Sunday morning, scheduled for the 'silly walk', there were no shortages of either participants or on-lookers along the avenue. It was a public display of the most awkward and hilarious manners of walking by scores of students.

I asked some of my *deshi* (country men) fellow post-grads to participate in the fun. Their comments were all much in the same vein,

'This is too silly for us, or for any serious under grads for that matter; ok, for school kids.'

I thought a bit of silliness would be good clean fun, good for mind and body. Rolf joined me without a bit of hesitation. His enthusiasm was, to say the least, 'over the top'. He got rid of all inhibitions and immensely enjoyed himself. If there was a competition for the silliest walk, I am sure he would have received the first prize. It was hilarious for all of us, and Rolf and I had a really great time playing the silly fool.

At the end of the Fresher's fare week when Michaelmas term was going to start in earnest in couple of days' time, I bumped into my mentor, Shaukat on a Saturday morning. He asked me if I was going to the party that evening at the Students' Union.

I was not sure what 'going to a party' meant. Back home we normally go to a 'function' and attend a party meeting (usually political). On enquiry, he told me that this was a traditional annual event organized by the Union, to allow freshmen to make new friends and enjoy themselves drinking, dancing and getting to know each other. I didn't think that sort of thing was really 'my cup of tea', but surprisingly, come 8 pm, I found myself at the door of the Union Hall, forking out 5 shillings for the entrance fee.

I said to myself – "I don't drink alcohol and I don't know how to dance; so what the hell I am doing here? Then it dawned on me, I would surely enjoy meeting new people, particularly of the opposite sex, and as for dancing, there is always a first time for everything, who knows, I might even enjoy it."

The hall was getting quite crowded, particularly around the bar at the opposite side of the stage. There was a local band playing music very loudly to encourage people to dance. I bought myself a drink and found a corner some distance away from the stage to avoid the ear-piercing music. Only a handful of people were dancing. Most of the men were busy drinking beer and chatting up girls or talking amongst themselves about upcoming national league football or the county cricket matches.

I found an empty chair amongst many dotted around the hall. I was drinking my lime and lemonade leisurely so that I did not run out of an activity whilst waiting to meet someone. I was looking around, desperately trying to find a familiar face. I didn't immediately find one but I did spot an Asian looking guy whom I thought could be the person who was often being talked about, a target of sniping derogatory remarks, by my few friends and acquaintances. Last year, the person in question had been the occupier of that corner of the laboratory which was then in my possession.

I was told of his research supervisor's comment about him,

"I have often seen his corduroy jacket hanging on the back of his chair, but always failed to trace him anywhere within the vicinity of his jacket."

His fellow research students reportedly had spotted him from time to time roaming in the city centre, usually in the company of pretty girls. It so happened that he was one of my Bengali speaking fellow countrymen and had been admitted to read for a D. Phil degree under the same supervisor as mine and on a topic similar to that of mine.

Just like my friend Mushfiq, who was studying at the Sorbonne in Paris and abandoned his studies on a doctoral thesis for a better and higher cause, - a journey in the path of Allah, he also took a similar but more deviant path, deducing – there must be more to life than being confined in a laboratory corner for four years, that's nothing less than a prison sentence.

At the end of his first year he chose freedom and pleasure in lieu of hard and dry academic pursuit. I was warned by some to be careful and steer clear of 'that playboy'. I was also advised not to venture too far from my jacket while I was at the department. I mulled over in my mind – "Is he that ex-student of my department? He fits the bill."

He was sitting on an armless chair with a pretty young girl on his lap. Another blond girl was standing behind him with her bare arms round his neck, pressing her well-developed breasts against his shoulder. He had a pipe in his mouth and was wearing a pair of expensive looking spectacles and sporting a moustache, in a style similar to that of Clark Gable. Everything about him gave the aura of him being, the much talked-about playboy.

He noticed me, stood up brushing the girl off from his lap

and casually removing the arms of the other girl from his neck. He walked towards me leisurely and when right in front of me, moved his pipe from his mouth with his left hand and extended his right one towards me and with a broad smile he started a conversation with the well-known cliché,

'Rafi Ahmad, I presume!'

I stood up and while shaking his hand said,

'You have presumed correctly, Mr. And you must be Asad Choudhury, the previous occupier of my desk at the Engineering Department. I have heard quite a lot about you. I guess you are quite famous, particularly within the Asian student circle.'

He smirked, took his glasses off and with a twinkle in his amber coloured eyes said, 'You need to take some lesson in English my friend. You probably mean, infamous, don't you? He continued,

'Yes, you have guessed it right; I have become a playboy and have forsaken the prestige of academic life. It is my choice. I hope you don't follow suit. Mind you, I don't advise you to lead a hermit's life either. Best policy, my friend, is to work hard and play hard. I just happened to have devoted myself to the latter.'

I was not sure if he was joking or seriously trying to correct my English. It reminded me of Mrs Capper's advice. I simply didn't want to insult him by using the correct adjective. Anyway, I did take his advice and didn't become a total hermit in pursuit of academic excellence during my time at Oxford.

Without exception, all of us, Asian overseas students, to start with, nurtured the lofty ideal of acquiring knowledge and skill while at such an advanced seat of learning and use them for the benefit of our countrymen when we went back home. We were also aware of the fact that a good qualification would be a valuable asset for our own personal career development.

I often wondered how relatively small island country like

England (that's what we called the UK back home), acquired the ability to rule the waves and colonize so many far away countries. England, in our folklore, was a country beyond 'the seven seas and 13 rivers'. We were also told at school that 'the sun never sets on British empire'. I was sure that I had lot to learn from this highly advanced and civilized society. At the same time I had a desire to enjoy and experience life in an open and free society. Back home, such freedom was out of bounds. Our society was steeped in tradition and taboos which the youth found claustrophobic.

Speaking with a posh English accent was, in our circle of friends, a sign of aristocracy and good breeding. Consequently most of us were trying hard to learn to speak in proper English; the Queen's English', some to supress their humble breeding. At the beginning we, the Pakistani students, followed an unspoken practice of avoiding social interactions with our fellow countrymen as far as possible. We busied ourselves making friends with the English speaking students of the host community, particularly those having 'Public School' background Alas; it didn't work out quite as we hoped. Those students had their own circle of close friends, toffs with posh accents and were mainly interested in sport and beer and women.

Sooner or later, most of us found ourselves being drawn towards our fellow *deshi* men for company and formed a cluster. The need to exchange jokes in one's own mother tongue and to get involved in heated discussion about one's own country's politics and culture was unstoppable. Therefore, regular gatherings in a restaurant or in a café for the students from the Indo-Pak subcontinent became inexorable. As time went by, the 'meeting up' in this way, i.e. 'hang-out' as is known here, became a life line for our *deshi* student community members. This kind of antics back home, was popularly known as *adda*, and it is something we the Indo-Pakistani students, just couldn't do without.

The student liaison officer, Mrs Smith, was responsible for organizing weekly evening events at the British Council (BC) auditorium. The aim was to provide opportunities for overseas students to get together and to get to know each other and have fun. For the latter, she organized a variety of cultural and social events such as Scottish and Irish folk dancing, discos, musical recitals by local artists, magic shows, international cuisine evenings etc. Home students were encouraged to participate in such activities for the benefit of the overseas students. However, very few Asian students visited the British Council, even fewer participated actively in any of its organised events.

Members of one group, Voluntary Overseas Services Association (VOSA), consisting exclusively of white Brits however actively participated in these weekly events. They were mainly postgrads who had spent a year or two abroad after graduation or occasionally they were students who had taken a gap year during their undergraduate studies. They had volunteered to go to some developing countries, mainly, ex-British colonies to teach for a nominal subsistence.

Simon, a final year undergrad reading for a degree in Geography at Jesus College, was the group's leader. He organized some additional weekly activities, such as talks on various topics, particularly on their overseas experiences. He easily cajoled me into joining the group as the organizing secretary. A few overseas students, including myself, were regular visitors to such events at the BC's premises on Tuesday evening, hoping to have a good time, meet old friends and make new ones from other countries. There was no cultural or social bar or barrier of language, colour, religion, sex or age to take active part in those events. My good friend Rolf was a regular participant in those activities long before I came to Oxford.

Rolf hadn't attended the BC for the last two consecutive events since the acrimonious encounter more than a fortnight ago.

I hadn't met him at all since then and I badly felt his absence despite my busy and eventful life. He often came into my mind because of that rather disturbing encounter at his flat. I felt, for some reason not clear to me, he was emotionally in need of some help. Of late he had become my closest friend, and a companion with whom I hung out at many social, cultural and recreational activities. I didn't want to fall out with him over that episode, and at the same time, wanted to avoid becoming too involved in his personal affairs. I was hoping that my hankering for his company would disappear with the passage of time – "out of sight, out of mind". But it didn't. My yearning for his company grew stronger by the day.

My resolve not to get involved with Rolf weakened; but at the same time I was apprehensive that he may be quite cool or even unfriendly towards me after the last episode should we meet. I felt he had not taken it easily that I couldn't or, according to him, didn't, want to help him with a police investigation into the mysterious 'secret agent'. Despite my fear of being unceremoniously rejected as a friend and a companion, I wasn't able to stay away from him for long and ended up on his doorstep one evening.

There was no telephone at my flat to announce my intended visit. Although I could have used the phone at the department I deliberately didn't do so. I was afraid that over the phone he would be able to brush me off, something I believed was less likely to happen in a face-to-face encounter. From the opposite side of the Banbury Road I saw the light in the kitchen of his third floor flat which assured me that he was there alright. After I pressed the doorbell, I heard the familiar voice.

'Wait a minute, I'm coming down.' He opened the door and with a troubled look on his face said,

'If you have come to see Professor Kosterlitz I am sorry to say he does not live here anymore.'

'Professor Kosterlitz! Why mention this!' I thought perhaps

he was still in a pique with me regarding our last meeting. I couldn't work out if he was joking or seriously showing, in his own peculiar way, his annoyance at my unexpected and unannounced presence at his door-step. He immediately broke down and doubled up in laughter. He did not usually shake hands with friends; instead he held my shoulder and led me inside.

While I was making my way upstairs behind him he asked,

'How are you, my good friend? What have you been up to during my absence?'

Instead of answering his question following the English custom I replied formally enquiring about him,

'I was concerned about your well-being, you know. It is not like you to miss the evenings at the British Council for two weeks running. I was worried you might have been cross with me for not understanding your plight. I am extremely sorry that I could not help. I hope you are now able to take this, 'professor' thing lightly and with humour.'

I was relieved that he'd welcomed me warmly. This made me gabble incessantly during the arduous climb to the top floor flat. By the time we were inside his flat and in his library I was exhausted. Rolf attributed my breathlessness to excessive smoking. Such comments always annoyed me. I believed that the conjecture relating breathlessness to smoking had no scientific validity. His constant nagging to quit the habit fell on deaf ears. He took my coat and hung it in the cupboard, sat me down on a sofa and in a rather exultant tone said,

'Do you know that you talk too much? People who do that tend to talk a lot of rubbish. Let me tell you something, you're not the only one who was unable to help. Besides, as I told you before, I cannot afford to keep losing friends; especially one like you when I'm fighting a life-threatening battle with heinous agents of the organization. I have to face them and beat them and survive on my own. In time, I'm sure somebody will turn up and testify against those agents to help me expose the conspiracy. Anyway, now let me answer your query about my absence at the BC events. Well, there are many reasons why I did not go to the BC for the last couple of weeks. One of these is that I was away for a short visit to Venice.'

He looked at me with his familiar sardonic smile and continued,

'I believe you don't need to hear other reasons.' He continued, 'Of course I am not angry with you. I thought about you. Truth be told, I even sent you a card from Venice. There could be several reasons why you may not have received it. One of them, the main one I believe, is that I forgot to stick a postage stamp on it and I remembered it immediately after shoving it in the mail box. Don't worry; I have bought another one for you with the same motif – a picture of the painting of the crucifixion of Christ by Giovanni Bellini, to hand it over to you in person.'

He fetched a card from the drawer of one of his antique chest of drawers and handed it over to me. He immediately snatched it back saying with a smirk,

'Let me write something on it. At least it should have my name and signature. You never know, once I become famous, this may be a valuable collector's item.'

I thanked him for remembering me in Venice and said mockingly,

'It was very thoughtful of you. There is surely a world of difference between a postcard picture from Venice where the original painting is alive, and that available in books on classical paintings in book shops. Besides, personal hand delivery must be a lot superior and more desirable than the very impersonal delivery by the postman through the letter box.'

Completely missing my sarcasm, Rolf said,

'Anyway, it is good to see you. Now tell me what liquid refreshment can I offer you?'

'I would like to have the usual please, if I may.' I said.

He asked me to remain seated comfortably, turned the electric heater on and went to the kitchen. He knew that I always preferred a cup of hot Assam tea. He didn't offer me any alcoholic drink although he kept a few bottles of wine in his flat and would drink a glass on special occasions with friends. He wouldn't have any aversion to a glass of sherry or red wine in a party or function as long as he did not have to pay for it. While he was busy in the kitchen with his ritualistic tea-making procedure using a special tea pot, I stood up and casually browsed the books on shelves covering two walls of the room. On my last visit when I was brought to this room I noticed that the books were carefully arranged according to the size and colour of the spines. The situation then was tense because of his predicament with the 'secret agents', and I was not in the mood and the circumstances wasn't right for me to browse through his collection of books.

This time, the thing that struck me immediately was that unlike University professors' study rooms, which are normally cluttered with books, papers, journals and a host of other items all over the places, Rolf's study was fastidiously well-organized and the books on one side of the walls were carefully and meticulously arranged like a work of art. My first reaction to the books on this side of the wall was that these could be wooden objects designed to look like an array of books, showing their spines with some writing along them. I had seen such design fashion in some novo-rich people's lounges in Hollywood films. On close inspection, I found that they were real books alright but in the German language. The books on the shelves on the other side of the wall, however, contained books in English and were not arranged according to size, shape or the type of spines. Those shelves gave the impression that they held a collection of some old books, perhaps, rare ones. Later I found out, in the whole of his three bedroomed flat, there was nothing that could be remotely considered to be modern. Antique-looking objects included not only his books but also his furniture, household items, objects of fine art, paintings, musical instruments, wall-hangings etc. I couldn't see any television, radio or newspaper anywhere in the room.

I thought - only a hermit could live without a newspaper or television these days. It seemed Rolf was living in the dark ages, rather like a monk within the confine of his flat.

To contrast his domestic life style with that of a normal modern man a recent episode came to my mind. Once I was invited to the home of a married English colleague for dinner. When I arrived at his door at about 8 pm he did not look very happy, but welcomed me anyway. He pointed out that I was late and that they went to bed by 10 pm. I had to eat a re-heated English dinner on my own as they had theirs at 7 pm. After the meal, I was ushered into the television room, which used to be called the lounge or drawing room before.

My host sat on the sofa beside me and offered me the newspaper and switched on the television, apologising,

'Sorry I just couldn't miss this week's episode of the Coronation Street, hope you don't mind.'

I knew he was going to watch the programme anyway with hardly any consideration as to whether I did mind or not. I couldn't blame him; I had my own addiction to smoking. I was amazed by this style of hospitality and the addiction of average English people to television and to newspaper.

Rolf was different, he was not an 'average Englishman'; in fact, not an Englishman at all. He was a German, later became a naturalised Briton. He liked to talk to people and had an innate aversion to modern technologies and gadgets. He was interested in real people with real-life stories and not the phony people in television soaps with make-believe stories. While browsing through the writings along the spines of the books in English I noticed that these were on topics all to do with ancient religion, culture, subculture, symbolism, rituals, cults, occults etc.

I picked out a book entitled, 'The Cults and Occults of Primitive Man'. I sat down and start flicking through the pages, a couple of hundreds of them. I noticed a pencil-marking and some notes on the side of a page. I also noticed that it referred to the cult of *Naga Panchami*, the worship of the deity *Mansa*, the snake goddess in ancient Indian cults. I continued to flick casually through the pages of the book, and stopped at the topic entitled, 'Cave painting–who and for what?' While I was grazing through the pages of that very interesting topic, Rolf appeared with a tray laden with a china tea pot, matching milk and sugar pots and, two pairs of equally matching cups and saucers. There were some small iced fancies, carefully arranged on a beautifully embellished two-tier cake stand.

Sitting comfortably on a sofa in front of me, holding a hot cup of tea, he was in a radiant mood and said,

'Good to see you, my friend. You couldn't have dropped in at a better time. I was impatient to share the magical beauty of a masterpiece with someone like you. I am over the moon at being the owner of such a treasure with very little investment. It could be the jackpot I had been dreaming of.'

He asked me to close my eyes and then when I opened them on his command I found him standing before me with an old-looking, rather faded painting of Jesus Christ on the cross. He rested the painting on a small easel and sat beside me on the sofa. He appeared ecstatic. With an elated tone he said,

'I bought it at an auction in Venice. There is an old and insignificant synagogue in the Jewish quarter of the city. The ancient Rabbi there was the custodian of this for over three decades. I was informed that there was no signature or record of its origin. The local community needed to raise funds for some restoration work, so they had an auction of some selected items stored at the vault. I had a gut feeling that it could be a valuable piece since it had been kept hidden in the vault.' Rolf continued, 'Before the start of the auction I made my way to the room adjacent to the synagogue where the auction was going to take place. Glancing through the items to be auctioned I found this oil painting. From my familiarity and experience I realised that this could be an almost unknown early work of Giovanni Bellini, a very well-known Italian master of the renaissance period. I felt I had to take a gamble and thought – "since miracles had happened to me before, they could happen again." I bid in the auction and got it for a reasonably low price.'

Before he could go any further I interrupted,

'Please forgive me for not being able to share your joy and enthusiasm over your prized new acquisition. You can't expect someone with my background to have the ability to judge the quality of an old painting which you presume to be by a famous master of the Renaissance. I may be cajoled into saying that I am enjoying looking at the painting but I am definitely no judge of its quality. I have to apologize for not even trying to pretend to appreciate the beauty or the value of your new found treasure. On the other hand, I'm fascinated by your collection of books on ancient cults, particularly those associated with the Hindu religion. I'm also very interested in your opinion and knowledge of cave paintings. I have noticed you also have books on this topic on your shelf.' I continued with my blurb,

'Classical paintings per se and those depicting religious motifs in particular, do not evoke much feeling in me. I know these provide focus for religious people. But I am sorry to say that they are of little interest to me. If you don't mind me saying this, I am more interested in the 'pre-history', the crude drawings on the walls of caves by primitive people. I noticed you have jotted down some remarks on the margins of some pages on this topic in this book. Let me hear your analyses as to why they went deep inside the cave to draw such pictures on the walls of the caves. I have read some books and articles on this topic in the past, and often pondered – Why did they do it? There has been much speculation about the answers to the questions, "How? Where? And, When?" But so far there has not been any sensible hypothesis to answer the question "why". Perhaps, you might be able to shed some light on this.'

Rolf was not at all perturbed at being interrupted. My interest in this topic seemed to have inspired him to talk about his own recent study. The topic of his research, "The role of symbols in the evolution of the man," had a lot to do with the very question that I asked.

He began his monologue with renewed enthusiasm:

'I am glad you are interested in cave painting, particularly on the question of why did they do this? What motivated them? As a matter of fact, this very topic will be the major focus for my research. It will constitute an important part of my thesis on the "origin of the man".'

I shot back to interrupt his speech,

'Hang on please; as far as I know, Charles Darwin has exhaustedly researched this topic in his treatise on the 'origin of species'. Is there anything new that you are trying to add to his theory?'

Wearing a peeved expression and using a curt tone he answered,

'First of all you have to understand that Darwin and I are not talking about the same "man". His definition of "man" and my concept of "the man" are very different. For now, just listen, and listen very attentively and stop trying to be too wise; if you do that you will soon be the wiser.'

I apologised for my interruption and he resumed,

'Being able to read the mind of our cave dwelling ancestors we need to look deep into the history of the ancient religions. These, as you are aware, have evolved from a variety of cults and occults of the pre-historic men. The un-written history of this evolution is hidden in the symbols used in the practices of their cults and occult. Analyses of such symbols, used by the isolated tribes, not yet influenced by modern civilization, may provide some clues to the status of their mind-set. The symbolism is and, has always been an integral part of all religions and cults. But my quest is to find the symbols which represent the birth of 'the man' and not the one Darwin called, Homo sapiens.'

Rolf leaned forward and took the book from my hand which I took out from the shelf. He noticed that the chapter on the cave painting was opened. He closed the book and put it down on the table. He then resumed his lecture on the theory of the creation of "the man": 'According to the creationists, man was created by divine decree at a specific time and for a specific purpose. This concept, enshrined in the scriptures of major religions, as you know, contradicts the scientifically validated theory of 'evolution' by Charles Darwin. According to his theory, man evolved from apes over millions of years. This "man" has no specific purpose on earth other than to propagate and preserve his species at all cost. This sense of purpose is not adopted through any logical thought process. It is instinctive, somehow written into his genetic code. On the contrary, the belief in the divine cosmic creation of the universe exists from antiquity. In this belief "man" is the ultimate reason for this creation, and this faith is ingrained in the human mind and had been written into the psychic code of modern man. The question is how can these two diametrically opposite concepts be reconciled?'

Rolf paused, lifted his head and was waiting for my response to find out the extent of my interest in, and understanding of, the topic. I butted in to express my view,

'In my opinion, for what it's worth, there can't be any resolution of a conflict between a concept based on faith and the one on science.'

He realized that I was interested in the topic and retorted,

'Of course there is a resolution. Darwin describes the evolution starting from a creature moving on all fours to an ape, walking on two feet, the 'Homo Erectus'. This then evolved into Homo sapiens, the "wise man", fashioned by ever evolving intelligence. But he didn't give us any tangible definition of the essence we call "wisdom" or how it evolved.'

To emphasise the point he said, 'Read my lips, certainly not through the process of evolution. 'Wisdom', another essence, also known as 'consciousness', came to some Homo sapiens miraculously. These Homo sapiens were surely inspired by a natural force. They are the ancestors of the modern man. That's my hypothesis and that's what I am talking about'

Rolf paused briefly, and then while nodding his head in a gesture of agreement to his own assertion he spoke in a rather dramatic tone, 'Yes my friend, this transformation took place suddenly and, not through an evolutionary process. I tend to believe this transformation was triggered by a cosmic signal. The answer to the question, why our pre-historic ancestors left impressions of his palm or drawings of animals on cave walls may lie in that sudden event. This miraculously acquired attribute had triggered an urge in that "Homo sapiens" to leave signs or coded messages to posterity. In my analysis the decoded message reads, "The man is born". That also triggered a propensity in his conscious psyche to pass on his skill of survival to the next generation. Without this attribute, primitive man wouldn't have passed on the knowledge and the skills, such as making and using the wheel, to future generations. Now you see, the 'consciousness', or if you like, the "self-awareness" has prompted "the man" to arrive at the modern age rolling on that wheel. The ape, without this gift, remains an animal, and survives as such using only its instinct and to some extent to its intelligence. If the creationist wishes to call this 'cosmic signal' the decree from God, I wouldn't have any qualms with that.'

Rolf's hypothesis was interesting and provided a plausible answer to the question of reconciliation of the two concepts of the creation of "man". I couldn't take Rolf's deep-rooted conviction quite literally just as I had not done so for the concept of the creation of "man" in the scriptures. When I asked him if it was the basis of his present research, he replied,

'Attributing the concept of consciousness to define "the man" is merely the starting point of my ambitious thesis.' I was in a receptive mood and Rolf resumed his monologue on his thesis: 'The instinct of 'modern man' is very different from that of his primitive ancestors. In the subconscious state, primitive men lived by his instinct. I have to find the nature of this instinct which still lies hidden in the psyche of the modern man. Its expression must be hidden in symbols used in the practices of their cults and occults and also in some religious practices of modern men. Such symbols should bear the signatures of their inner thoughts and should bear clues to the expressions of their hopes and fears, and their concept of birth, death and survival. We, the modern men, will only be able to read their minds from such symbols if we look at these with the conviction that the creators of these symbols are consciously trying to tell us something. Symbolisms of the modern man clearly indicate that the future man will shed the religious shroud and turn back to life based on instinct, which governed the lives of their ancestors, the primitive men. All these point to the fact – "Return of primitive instinct to the 'future man' in a new psycho-physiological framework"; and this, my friend, is the working title of my thesis.'

Rolf paused briefly, as he usually does during his long monologues. This was, perhaps, to allow me, the sympathetic listener, to digest the content of his theory, and also to feel if I was still interested and not dozing off. I was listening but was not happy with his often woolly interpretation and use of 'self-made' terminologies. I wanted to show off my knowledge in classical philosophy and, at the same time to assure him of my undivided attention and interest in his preaching. I took the opportunity of his brief pause and commented,

'As far as I understand, you have categorized 'man' into different time frames as primitive man, modern man and future man. But this concept is not new. Jung's classification of 'state of mind' in terms of sub-conscious, conscious and super conscious is similar to that of yours. He has also categorized 'man' in terms of the level of consciousness as, ordinary man, higher man and ultimate man. I believe your concept is very similar to that. Anyway, this is not his original idea either. These ideas come from the ancient Hindu scriptures.'

I was very interested in the topic but I had to express my criticism of his hypothesis, so I continued, 'Your theory is simply, "old wine in a new bottle", and lacks originality.'

He raised his voice, not to express anger but to emphasize the point he was making and said,

'I am glad you are listening and trying to impress me with your knowledge on Jung's philosophy. I am also impressed that you have made a valid criticism. But, you have misunderstood me. Perhaps, this is due to your half-baked and superficial knowledge of Jung's philosophy. Please do not take offence. I am not hinting at the misquoted dictum that "a little learning is a dangerous thing". In my book, "a little learning" is better than "no learning" at all. But that is not the point. I am not claiming that these are my ideas. I am just re-defining the concept of Jung's or Nietzsche's concept of 'super man' or 'higher man' that possesses the attribute which has brought him to become the 'modern man'. Occasionally under some circumstances, and I emphasize, quite rarely, the modern man may possess super-consciousness, and, may be elevated to godhead. In my book, he is simply the future "man", what Nietzsche called, "ultimate man". He, unlike the godhead of primitive man, is vulnerable and will be concerned for his own survival. He will, therefore, create his own gods, as is stipulated by Jung, just as primitive man did. Let me explain.'

I stood up, fearful that he would continue long into the night, and said,

'Please forgive me my friend, it is quite late and I have to get back to my flat to catch up with some sleep. I will have a long and hard day tomorrow in the lab. I didn't intent to spend so much time with you this evening. I am also a bit tired. So, I am afraid, I have to go now. I am sorry about leaving you so abruptly and unceremoniously.'

Rolf was determined to hold on to me. He was not going to let our discussion end just then when it had come to a head and the topic had got more interesting for him. He also stood up and said,

'The night is still young my friend. It's only a few minutes past midnight. I think we are in tune, and it will be a criminal offence for you to leave now before even I conclude the introduction of my thesis. Sit down and I shall bring you another cup of coffee and some nourishment. That will rejuvenate you.'

I responded in an indignant tone,

'I understand how you feel, Rolf, but you should also consider my predicament. You know that I can't go on for a long time without a break for a smoke. I haven't had a cigarette for the last two and a half hours. I know smoking is strictly forbidden in your flat. I don't really intent to go out and loiter in the street at this time of night in cold weather for my fix. Surely you now understand why, even if for no other reason, I have to go now and hope you will understand my need and let me go!' He responded with a sly smile,

'Let me make a deal with you. I will make an exception for you, just for tonight. You may go to the bathroom and have your fix, if that helps you to get back to the mood for listening to the rest of my theory of the origin of "man".'

I was, of course, very surprised by his offer of breaking a

life-long rule just to entice me to listen to his lecture. It showed how desperate he was to strengthen the logic of his concept of "the origin of man and his primitive instinct" by bouncing it off me. Surely his unusual eagerness did not arise from a benevolent desire to educate me. Perhaps he was trying to learn something and was adopting the policy, "the best way to learn is to teach". He was certainly using me as a mirror, trying to reflect his ideas to consolidate them in his mind. It must have been quite a rare occasion for him to find a sympathetic and eager listener like me who would seriously listen to his theory and interact with him.

I took up his offer reluctantly and stood up to go to the bathroom. I put my right hand on my jacket pocket to take out the cigarette packet. I always carry the packet there and it always contains sufficient number of cigarettes for my own need and also allowing for any unexpected eventualities, like offering them to others in a gathering. But most unusually and quite disappointingly the packet was not in the pocket, although I found the lighter. I had inadvertently left it on the table in my flat while changing my clothes – a very rare occurrence. When I informed him he moved his head from side to side a few times, paused for a while and asked me to wait for a few minutes and went to the guest bedroom adjacent to his bedroom.

I wondered "What trick would he be playing on me now?" I was pacing up and down the empty space in the library where we were sitting. I didn't find any reason to hang about under these circumstances and was desperate to take leave. After about ten minutes Rolf came out with a packet of cigarettes in his hand and handed it over to me.

I found the event somewhat bizarre. I looked at him and then at the cigarette packet. On the front of the packet was a picture of a neatly uniformed soldier mounted on a beautiful horse, holding a lance in one hand and the rein in the other. There was something written at the bottom in German and in bold alphabets. I read the writing and it sounded like "Soldat". I presumed that it was a brand name meaning, 'Soldier'.

After I had overcome my amazement I said in a grave voice,

'Rolf, I know you hate the smell of cigarette smoke and detest the habit. The first time I came to your flat under some stressful circumstances I wanted to light a cigarette. You then promptly announced your house rule that smoking was strictly forbidden. And now, not only you allow me to smoke here, but also provide me with cigarettes, albeit German ones. I find it strange, I don't get it. Could you explain please?'

In a pensive voice Rolf spoke,

'Yes, my friend, you are absolutely correct. I hate the smell of cigarette smoke, it chokes me. I have successfully resisted succumbing to the habit, but my father, like you, was addicted to this. He managed to give up the habit after he immigrated to this country. Probably he couldn't afford it. That was a long time ago.' I asked,

'Did you ever enquire as to why and how he gave up smoking?'

'No, I didn't, and now it is too late.' He replied,

'My father passed away many moons ago, gone to meet his maker. He is 'no more' and, that's why you are in luck, my dear friend. You may ask why you are in luck. Let me explain,

'My family immigrated to the UK in haste. They didn't have the opportunity to bring much luggage with them. Amongst their scanty belongings, there was a small leather suitcase which belonged to my father. In this he kept some items of mementos of his time in his fatherland. For reason known only to him, he kept this case packed with things associated with his everyday life back home. This packet of cigarette was one of those items. I inherited his treasure trove and have kept it in the same box for over two decades now. Tonight is the second time I have opened the box. It took me a long time to find the key and unlock the box. The lock was a bit stiff as it had not been opened for a long time.'

I tried to engage him by asking,

'Why and when did your parents leave Germany?' The first question was quite loaded, which I probably shouldn't have asked, as I sensed that he may have been living under Hitler's rule. I should have thought about the fate awaited the Jews trapped in Germany at that time. Anyway, he only answered my second question very briefly,

'They left sometime before the Nazi bandwagon started to roll over Germany.' Curiosity got the better of me, I asked,

'Tell me, Rolf, are you a practicing Jew? Do you believe in your parents' religion or any religion at all?'

He paused for a while, turned his head away from me and said,

'Yes of course, by birth I do belong to the Jewish faith. But in practice and in truth I do not believe in any organized religion at all. I am basically a humanist. The people who you would like to brand as 'atheist'. But I like rituals, rituals of all kinds and of all religions. These fascinate me and inspire me to look for the origin of "the man" and his basic instincts. But, we shall talk about that another time.'

I looked again at the cigarette packet and went to his bathroom as instructed. I realized that these cigarettes must be at least two decades old. I sat down on an antique chair at the corner of the bathroom and lit one cigarette from the packet. It tasted like inhaling the smoke from a burning piece of wood. It reminded me of my childhood days in a remote village in present Bangladesh when I smoked the stalk of the jute stick with a few other children, in secret of course, to copy the grown-ups. The stick when broken into a small length did resemble a cigarette in a manner of fashion.

I thought about Rolf's father. He had to leave his fatherland and his ancestral home for survival. He kept some of the everyday items he used as mementos. Perhaps he had enjoyed the silent melody of the memories of his childhood days in a small town on the outskirts of Munich. This packet of cigarettes might have reminded him of his father and his own childhood. The box must have been a treasured memento for Rolf himself. I wondered why, then, he was getting rid of some of its contents now?

Perhaps time had done the trick of healing the deep wound created by the melancholy memories of the past and he did not need to cling on to any such memorabilia. I wondered if this healing was superficial, and the melancholy memory and the hurt were hidden deep in his subconscious state of mind. Under some circumstances painful memories do surface and enter into the conscious mind and haunt one in some way or other. I realized that it was unwise for me to bring in the subject of his parents' emigration which might have opened up a floodgate of emotions relating to his past life. I was afraid that the memories associated with his long-deceased father and mother could prick a raw nerve, even after two decades.

I came out of the bathroom pretending to be intoxicated and rejuvenated by the nicotine, sat down and asked him to resume his saga of the origin of man. He was, at that time, standing still, facing his newly acquired painting of the crucifixion of Jesus Christ resting on the easel in the dimly lit ambience of the room. He did not move, he did not turn his face, he just said,

'It is no good pretending that all is well, my friend. I felt the spirit of my dead father coming out of the suitcase. I am overwhelmed. I have lost the will to continue. It will be better for both of us if you were to leave me alone, if you don't mind.' I stood up and said in a sombre tone,

'I fully understand my dear friend. Please do not bother to show me the door. I know the way out.'

He bade me goodnight without turning to face me. I left his flat wishing him the same in response, knowing very well that the night wouldn't be good for him. I was rather relieved that I didn't have to see the despondent face of my usually radiant friend before I left. This would have played a melancholy tune in my heart in my solitary moments. At times, even long after that event, when in a pensive mood, lighting my cigarette stick, jogs my memory of a unique cigarette I smoked called 'Soldåt' which did not have any nicotine but was full of memories of Rolf's deceased father.

4

The Ecstasy of Agony

On my first meeting with Mr Jones, the warden at the local British Council office, he enquired while shaking my hand, with the phrase,

'How do you do, Mr Ahmad?'

By then I knew what he meant and answered saying that I was quite well, but finding the weather too cold to feel comfortable.

He cautioned me like a wise old man,

'It's only the beginning of September, young man. Life will be more uncomfortable when the real winter arrives at your door, slowly but surely. My advice is – "what can't be cured must be endured, so you have to put up with it and try to make it as comfortable as you can, without complaining."'

When I enquired if it was autumn or winter, he asked me to take my pick saying,

'If it's foggy and wet it could be the beginning of the winter. If it's sunny and mild and the leaves are changing from green to brown it's probably the beginning of autumn. However, if it's still warm and sunny and the leaves are turning red and the trees are shedding them, it has to be the beginning of the end of autumn.'

Finally just to confuse me further he added,

'If the weather continues to be warm and sunny for more than a couple of months from now we call it an Indian summer.'

He also gave me a tip, saying with a wink and a cheeky smile,

'Never trust English weather and English women, both of them are unpredictable.'

I said it to myself "I know about women, Mrs Capper gave me

the first lesson. As for the weather, I have to wait to find out I suppose."

From Mr Jones's description I sussed out that the weather might be cold, but for all intent and purposes it was still autumn, the season of "mellow fruitfulness", made famous by the poet Keats in his classic poem; "Ode to Autumn". This, we had to memorize as a part of our English lessons in secondary school back home.

Back home we were used to six seasons, each descending on us sharply, with its characteristic tell-tale sign. I knew in my college days that here in England, one season blends into the other with no sharp boundaries.

Keats' "Ode to Autumn" made me dream about nature's colourful canopies of leaves on trees that lined the streets and filled the woodlands of England. I was impatiently waiting for that dream to come true. How I longed to witness the changes in the colour of the leaves. However, following Mr Jones' caution I was all too aware to the fact that this festival of colour would not last long and that the nature would soon render the trees leafless and barren except for a few scatterings of coniferous foliage. This would be the beginning of the long harsh winter.

The impending arrival of winter was not a matter of my immediate concern at that moment. I had to adjust to the new social environment and face tuff academic challenges. The daily routine of my life started to take on a regular pattern. Outside academia, this comprised, among others, daily lunch and evening meals at the *Moti Mahal*, one of the two Indian restaurants in the city

🌰

The first year of University, for most students, was a time for familiarization, exploration, adventure and, most importantly, a time for personality building. There was much to do, learn and enjoy, but for most of us, beyond the chores of the academic works, there was precious little time for most of these. We had to be quite selective in our choice of involvement in non-academic avocations. There were also some activities – cultural, political, and recreational; in which ex-students or members of the public took part. My new friend, Rolf was one such member of the public.

He was different from all other students there. Firstly, he was not a student as far as I was aware. Secondly, he was lot older than the rest of us. The mark of old age, or 'maturity' to be politically correct, was impressed quite vividly on his face, but not at all in his mind-set or in his spirit. Not only did he have a near balding head but also there were couple of deep parallel corrugations across his forehead. His nose supported a pair of high-powered thin metal-rimmed spectacles which partially shielded his deep seated eyes. All told, he gave the appearance of a University professor in pursuit of excellence and knowledge.

꩜

Miss Simpson, the middle-aged spinster with unlimited energy, was the liaison officer for the overseas students. She organized and supervised the Tuesday-evening activities with great enthusiasm. The activities took place at the big hall of the ground floor of the two-story BC office, equipped with other facilities, such as furniture, kitchen, toilets etc. It was almost next door to my digs at St John Street. She maintained an open-door policy, allowing people who were not bona fide students to join in activities as long as they were, in some way or other, connected to the university. Rolf was entitled to use University's Bodleian library and was known widely as an academic. He was, therefore, quite welcomed at the weekly events on Tuesday evenings.

The gathering at the BC provided the opportunity, mainly to shy overseas students, to socialize and make friends. Students from different parts of the globe congregated there allowing them to learn the history, culture and tradition of people from many different countries, some of which we had not known existed.

Rolf would always be there unless he was out of the country or indisposed. Before long Rolf and I became close friends, meeting mostly at the BC. We often exchanged stories and jokes, and on occasions, got involved in serious discussions, sometimes in the company of others in a group. We both had a healthy interest in members of the opposite sex and tried to befriend them when we got the chance. Having noticed Rolf's mastery in flirting with young women at our first encounter at the BC function I realized I had a lot to learn from him. I was gradually picking up the tricks of the trade in his company; it was all fun and exciting.

I had no hesitation in talking to Rolf about my personal life, my experiences and my aspirations for the future. It was quite natural for me to be inquisitive about his life and his present personal circumstances, but for quite a while I didn't get the opportunity to enquire about these. Besides, I felt we needed time for friendship and trust to grow deep enough to explore delicate personal matters. On one occasion, I did ask him about his profession and his association with the University.

With a coy smile and a couple of soft taps on the right side of his nose with the index finger of his right hand, and moving his mouth close to my ear he muttered,

'Don't be nosy my friend; all will be revealed in good time.'

Being nosy, however, was one of my passions. I was interested in other peoples' business, particularly if I thought them to be unusual. I started to nurture an insatiable, rather unhealthy, curiosity about my recently acquired enigmatic friend. But as a freshman at the University, my life, like that of others, was getting too busy and exciting with many other events outside my academic commitments to find time to delve into Rolf's life history. While I managed to fill my time with activities during weekdays, I did find myself wanting for something to do over the weekends, when most students had pre-planned programmes.

☙

I woke up late on a cold Saturday morning in late November. I got out of bed and drank the cold coffee but didn't feel like eating the cold breakfast. Before going back to bed and inside the comfort of my quilt, I casually opened the curtains to look out what the weather was like. I remained bewildered for a while by what I saw. For a moment I thought I was dreaming. It was a sunny morning alright, but everything was shrouded in a gigantic white blanket. I was no longer sure where I was. Dazed, I met Mrs Capper on my way to the bathroom. She explained that there had been a very heavy snowfall the previous night and warned me of a repeat of the same, as par forecast, the next night. I sat on the chair and kept my gaze fixed along empty Pusey Street, musing on the exotic spectacle of snow-covered streets and houses. My first experience of seeing snow was absolutely mesmerising and thrilling.

My bewilderment was interrupted by the sight of two human beings, slowly approaching my digs like two cartoon pandas in a children's television show. The only difference was that the pandas on the show were white in a green environment and these two human beings appeared to be brown in a white environment. I watched as they checked the house numbers until they reached our door. I recognised one of the faces, Dilder Husain, a friend from my University days back home. I had known that he was scheduled to come here to study at the Nuclear Physics Department as a post-graduate student, but I didn't have a clue as to when he was due to arrive and where he would be staying.

I came out of my room, ran down the steps, opened the door and stepped into the street in my pyjamas and slippers. I was ecstatic to find an old *Deshi* friend in this foreign and frozen land. I hugged him and ushered him and his companion inside the digs. He introduced me to Masud Hasan, a mature Bengali speaking Pakistani civil servant, who had come to pursue a one-year Master's course in political science at Jesus College.

Masud immediately took a commanding role and advised me to wear some warm clothes and to put on a dressing gown when going outside in the perishing cold. I thanked him for his advice and said I would certainly put the item on the shopping list when I went out next time. I dressed myself in some warmer clothes and we went out to the 'Moti Mahal' restaurant. On my way out with companions I put the tray with untouched breakfast plate and the empty cup on the small table outside my room. We had a heart-felt *adda* over an extended rice and curry Brunch.

It was, by far, the most enjoyable morning since my arrival at Oxford nearly two months ago - my first sight of snow and the company of two other fellow Bengali-speaking *adda baz* (*adda*-addicted) students.

It transpired that on most evenings, Dilder and I ended up at the senior common room of Jesus College for the company of Masud, our self-appointed mentor, after our fix of rice and curry dinner at Moti Mahal. I never asked him about his age as I thought it would be discourteous, but I guessed he could have been 5 to 7 years older than me and, hence was entitled to the attribute *Bhai*, meaning 'big brother ' when addressing him by his name. There were two things common between us – our common root, i.e. we were both Bengali speaking East Pakistanis, and our inexorable dependence on cigarettes.

The *adda* in Masud's company was different from that of conventional ones in typical hangouts of Pakistani students. When he was speaking for the most part we were mere listeners, especially after he had downed a few cans of beer. The topic of his monologue changed gradually without any prompting from us, or without any relevance to what he was talking about previously. The topics varied from the intimate details of his misdemeanours and sexual antics in his early life to national and international politics and life and living in Oxford. He often put forward convincing solutions to international problems. Highly impressed and totally convinced we went back to our digs with a feeling of great relief that major international problems would soon be solved when the world's political leaders took heed of his advice and sprang into action.

Sometimes, high on alcohol and nicotine, Masud spoke passionately of his loving Pakistani wife, Banei, and the two little boys he had left behind. Sometimes when he was talking about his family, his eyes would grow moist and occasionally the tears run down his cheeks. We couldn't entirely relate to this melancholy since we were not married, but we did, from time to time, hold out a box of tissues for him. He told us in a desperate voice how much he missed his wife and how eagerly he was counting the days and the hours until dear Banie would join him, leaving the children with their maternal grandparents in Lahore. We felt lucky that we didn't have to face such a predicament.

To begin with, Masud captivated me with his eloquent monologues and I ended up spending most evenings in his company. I felt that he was in desperate need of someone to listen to his stories of intimate and, sometimes, embarrassing events from his past. His varied experiences made him something of a guinea pig for me. I took the opportunity to indulge in a bit of psychoanalysis, to add to the dossier of unusual people I had been studying for some time.

It was quite enjoyable for the first few weeks, but then his stories and confessions became repetitive and mostly emotional nonsense. But I kept meeting him and listening to his monologues mainly out of respect and kindness for an elder countryman in desperate need of a sympathetic ear. I felt that, Masud, like a Catholic sinner, needed a confessor and he made me that. He told me that his misery would soon be over when his wife joined him in a few weeks' time.

But a 'few weeks' was too long for me to have to endure his company since I was becoming bored, and so I tore myself away from his influence. I felt no regret for that, since I knew his darling wife would soon be with him and my company would then be the last thing he'd want. Eventually, I came to realize that he was quite normal and his tales were rather too commonplace to be included in my archive. The world beyond was alluring me. I had to explore that world. My friend Rolf lived there. He was much more fun to be with, and he, I am sure, had more interesting stories to tell. My desire for his company became stronger than ever.

The large age-gap between Rolf and me gradually disappeared and so did our cultural differences. We were buddies. Together we frequented theatres, concerts, public debates and seminars at the Students' Union Hall and attended many social and cultural functions. In particular, the thing that bonded us together was our common insatiable obsession for understanding the human psychology of unusual people.

Rolf appeared to be considerably well-off, because he often went on overseas holidays as well as attending expensive concerts and art-exhibitions in London and abroad. I also found that he procured expensive artefacts and would throw lavish parties, albeit for a handful of selected friends and well-wishers. On the other hand, he also behaved like a hard-up student, always trying to save a penny or two whenever he could. I did not know the source of his income. Out of curiosity once I asked him about that. As before, he tapped the side of his nose with his index finger and asked me not to be nosy.

On one occasion, we were returning home after a nocturnal party in a friend's flat somewhere on the Iffley Road. It was just before midnight and we were almost a mile away from my digs, and still lot further away from his. It was a rather cold night and I suggested that we take the bus back home.

He insisted that we walk and commented,

'For young and able-bodied people like us, particularly for a pauper student like you, it would be an unnecessary expense and an unforgivable luxury.'

'Don't be a Jew, my friend. You can't take it to your grave.' I retorted with a mocking tone.

'But I am a Jew. That doesn't mean I have to misuse my money.' He shot back angrily.

'Then don't be a double Jew,' I retaliated, 'Let's catch the bus; I shall pay for your fare.'

Such propositions always fell on deaf ears and, in his company I was often constrained to move about on foot.

Rolf usually found his way into informal parties, where students could get to know each other and spent enjoyable evenings; dancing, chatting and joking and sometimes making acquaintances leading to lasting friendships or even become lovers. I was most often his companion, both before, during and after these. As a long-term resident of Oxford he was well-known in many circles. Some of my friends and colleagues couldn't accept my close friendship with an old man like him, behaving as he did, like a young student. His fascination for, and flirtation with young females was unacceptable to some. Many thought he was a dirty old man. Some of my friends and well-wishers, Masud being one of them, advised me to avoid all contact with him as, according to him, he was a mentally derailed sex maniac. In some parties I saw students teasing him openly and even making derogatory remarks. He mostly ignored them and occasionally responded with such good humour and grace that most young people got to like him and accepted his behaviour with a pinch of salt.

I remember the occasion when I was invited to a private party for the first time by one of my female acquaintances. I took Rolf with me. He was not invited but that didn't stop him accompanying me to the party. I apologised to my friend for bringing an uninvited guest. But I didn't need to; she knew him and was cordially welcomed anyway. The gathering was known as a 'bottle party', where everybody is expected to take bottles of drink to share. Rolf took a bottle of wine and I took a big bottle of Coca Cola. The host provided snacks, generally known as finger-food, consisting of sausages, small pieces of cheese and pineapple on wooden sticks, pieces of bread, baked potatoes wrapped in tin foils, etc.

The background music came from a record player. I could hear the newly released popular song 'A whiter shade of pale' by Procol Harum being played. This was followed by songs from the recently released Beatles' album 'Yellow Submarine'. At first we engaged in small talks with people we already knew. Most of the guests were sipping beer or cider and hardly anyone was listening to the music. When conversation started to get dull and strenuous I excused myself and sat down on a chair at a corner of the room. I noticed that Rolf was already dancing with a girl and was trying to impress her with his moves. The music was fast and his dance sequences were hilarious to say the least. I explored the room with my eyes for any unattached girl and approached one standing alone and decided to try my luck. When I asked her for a dance, she rejected my invitation with thanks and was rather cool towards me. She re-joined her friends who looked my way and giggled. I felt very dejected. I wondered why it was that Rolf could get girls to dance with him so easily whereas I could not. Later I realized, 'it was the personality and confidence, stupid'.

Within the academic community students were so pre-occupied

with their studies and extra-curricular activities that hardly anybody would have time or interest to indulge in idle gossip about my unusual intimacy with an older man. However, once I did encounter an exception to this.

A newly acquainted fellow post-grad from Sri Lanka was unable to hide his curiosity and said,

'The other day I saw you with an elderly gentleman at the University Park. You two seemed to be absorbed in discussion, sitting on a bench close to each other. You seem to be rather too close to your academic supervisor for comfort, it's a bit unusual. Isn't it?'

'My supervisor is a much younger man.' I replied, 'The gentleman who you are referring to is my buddy, Rolf, the philosopher. He is a researcher like you and me, but his research isn't for a degree but for the fulfilment of his quest for understanding and to quench his thirst for knowledge.'

He thought I was joking and, from the expression on his face, I gathered that he probably didn't like what he felt was my weird humour.

'I am not sure about the 'understanding' and 'knowledge' bits,' he said, 'As far as I am concerned, my research is for acquiring a qualification. However, sometimes I have seen you hanging around with him like a pal. It is rather unsavoury. You must avoid such company, my friend; else, soon people will start to talk, you know.'

I parted company with him soon after, hoping not to see him again. I said to myself – "let the people talk, dogs bark but the caravans pass by regardless."

Rolf was not unique in doing research without any patronage or supervision or even recognition by the University authorities. My friend, Jamil, told me stories of weird looking people at the Bodleian Library, day in and day out, sifting through rare old documents trying to acquire information and gather knowledge.

He himself also spent nearly 3 years searching, reading, assimilating and cataloguing information to write his doctoral thesis on the history of municipal services in the city of Dacca (renamed later as Dhaka) during the first half of the 18th century.

'What benefit will posterity gain from the knowledge of the public service system in a faraway British colonial city in the distant past?' I once asked him.

In answer to my query, my friend gave me a mouthful,

'You must understand Rafi that there are certain things which cannot be judged in terms of materialistic cost-benefit criteria. You don't read history for any material benefit. You read it for pleasure and to broaden the mind. History often guides the future. Besides, there is a thing called, "knowledge for knowledge's sake", just like "art for art's sake". The same is true for history, whatever that may mean.'

I still wondered who on earth would take pleasure in reading about the history of municipal activities in the city of Dhaka in the early 18th century! The examiners of his thesis and, of course his academic supervisor had to read it, because they were paid to do so. Perhaps this is a bit of history of interest to a few people. But that cannot be knowledge for knowledge's sake. I started to doubt the authenticity of my own display of interest in fine art to my friend Rolf. Perhaps, in my heart of hearts, I was a philistine.

I was given to understand that Rolf's visits to the library were for the purpose of acquiring knowledge and understanding from the wisdom of great minds, hidden in the pages of rare old books and journals. The Bodleian has the most extensive and invaluable documents in its archives on the cultural history of the world, particularly of British colonies. I didn't have any need or particular interest in visiting that library. But I had to venture into the Radcliffe science library from time to time. There, I had encountered people like Rolf, and some much older than him, researchers or academics, trying to gather scientific knowledge for their theses or scientific papers. Some looked and behaved like retired professors. For them, there was no world outside academia.

But it was different for Rolf. He might have given the impression of being a professor to me and few others, but unlike many of the real, all-absorbed forgetful professors of the University, he was very much an active participant of the vibrant world beyond academia and, a mysterious one at that.

✿

I was by that time settling into a life at Oxford and ready for another change – freedom from my claustrophobic accommodation and the strict regime of Mrs Clapper. I moved from my digs to share a flat in Norham Gardens with my new acquaintance, Aziz Qureshi.

Moving from my digs to the flat was an experience I shall never forget. I gave notice and was asked to move out by 1 pm. I didn't have a car-owning friend to help me move and, hiring a taxi for the removal of my few belongings was out of the question. So I enrolled my trusted friend Dilder to help me carry my meagre possessions to my new flat, quarter of a mile away. We have had a long leisurely lunch at the Moti Mahal and at about 2 pm sauntered back to the digs to collect my belongings. We both were gobsmacked to find them in a pile on the pavement outside the house. I was furious and my poor friend seemed bewildered, being unable to comprehend what had happened.

I rang the bell. Mrs Capper came out in a rage. I could see her true nature, anger was written all over her face. She started to swear at us pointing to her watch. My friend, a sensitive man with a nervous disposition, became very upset. He later told me he thought that her behaviour was motivated by racism and was a direct proof of the prejudices of working class white people against Africans and Asians.

When she had asked me to vacate the digs by 1 pm I didn't take it to mean exactly at that time and thought plus or minus an hour or two wouldn't make much difference. I was at a loss to try to convince my friend that it was a one-off event and the vast majority of the people here were not racist. We couldn't understand why English people were so preoccupied with time keeping. I took it philosophically and consoled my friend to take heart with the thought – "they have the watch, but we are lucky, we have the time".

My friend was upset and shaken. I, on the contrary, being made of a sterner stuff, was not at all upset or even surprised by the incident. I put two and two together and realized that Mrs Capper hadn't forgiven my sin of comparing her with my grandmother.

I was quite comfortable sharing the two-bedroom flat with Aziz. We were free to do whatever we wanted, even having small house parties on weekends, as long as guests were out by 11 pm. Our ground floor flat was a part of a large 3-story detached Victorian house, owned by a fastidious middle-aged English widow, Mrs Malik. Her late husband, Mr Malik, was a clergyman of Indian origin. Here I didn't feel anywhere near the draconian restrictions I had under Mrs Capper's regime.

Occasionally, she would call me from her window while I was on my way to the laboratory late in the morning and ask me to go back to the flat and comb my hair, in a very affectionate tone. She didn't have any children of her own, but her motherly instinct was obviously there. Sometime, if she could get hold of me, she would invite me for tea and give me a sermon on the importance of cultivating good morality, particularly sexual morality and the evils of the erosion of this attribute in modern youths.

Talking to the spirits of long deceased people to answer questions using an Ouija board was one of my pranks at the University back home. My flatmate Aziz believed in my ability and wanted to experience such an event. I thought why not! He was of a gullible disposition and it would work on him. I had a session with him on an ordinary board with alphabets written on it. We put our index fingers gently on top of a small disk to slide it over the letters to construct the answer under the influence of the spirit as and when it had answered my call to arrive within the confinement of the board. I made sure that the disc slid freely with very little effort from me. Aziz genuinely believed in my power over the spirits.

Rolf wanted to see me in action, although he thought it was a fluke and a confidence trick. He thought he would catch me out and disclose my trickery to Aziz. Besides, he might have thought that this, like his other tricks, could be another tool in his psychoanalytical practice. One night I was persuaded to go into a trance to call on any spirit present in my room to come into the confine of the Ouija board, in the presence of two other guests. It was past 11 pm. These spirits were supposed to be more active at night when human activities were at a minimum. I asked both of them to call out, in an audible voice and with deep feeling, to any spirit in the vicinity to come within the confine of the board. Suddenly there was a thumping noise from above the ceiling.

'It is here, it is here.' Aziz cried out.

I was familiar with this noise. Mrs Malik was reluctant to come down to knock at the door when visitors overstayed their time in our rooms. I said in a hush voice,

'Calm down, calm down. Don't talk so loudly, you have, probably scared off the spirit.'

Aziz wanted to know if he was going to pass his exam. He was desperately waiting for the results. The spirit, according to him, rightly predicted that he was going to fail. I knew very few candidates passed the Chartered accountancy exams on the first attempt. He was also very pleased to know from the spirit that the souls of his parents were in peace in heaven. I tried the trick with Rolf's finger, along with mine, to bring the spirit on to the board. The disk didn't move. A non-believer's finger was too tightly fixed for mine to make it wander around to spell 'Y-E-S' when I asked to tell us if the spirit was present there. The exercise failed, which I attributed to human interference from above.

We released the spirits lurking about the room and agreed to have another go at a later time, and parted company.

Rolf made the parting comment with a smirk,

'I think the noise was God's warning not to mess with spirits. The world of spirits is out of bound for humans and is a 'no-go' area for the living. In any case, when all fails, we may be able to seek help with a glass of Scotch, a good spirit, you are welcome to join me sometime?'

According to Rolf, anyone he knew well enough to be considered as a friend was, in one way or other, connected to the "grand conspiracy" against him. He divided the people with whom he associated, into two broad categories - friendly foes and deadly sub-agents, all working for the organization that was hell bent to destroy him.

Being a wise and intelligent man, his mind rationalized that to survive in this harsh world as a normal human being he had to make peace with friendly foes like me, but at the same time he had to face and fight off the deadly sub-agents. The organization was trying every possible means to destroy him, to break him down and to take away his sanity. He was determined to fight against the heinous conspirators and survive. Not only that, he was also battling against time, time which was slowly but surely, according to him, eroding his youth and depriving him of the sweet taste of the nectar of life.

But who were these agents? What was the issue? What was the organization to which they belonged? Why were they dead-set on destroying such a timid unassuming gentle academic? I pondered – "the answers must lie in some events in his past life". I was sceptical about his conspiracy theory, to say the least. Nevertheless, the desire to know his story got the better of me and I expressed my eagerness to hear it.

He was most certainly waiting for such an offer. He desperately wanted to tell someone special what had happened to him. It would be like removing the cork from a champagne bottle to release the pressure. He told me there had been a chain of events that had culminated in a deadly enmity with a powerful organization, causing a most devastating change and debilitating effect on his life. It occurred to me that he could not sit down with just any Tom, Dick or Harry in a café or a public house to tell such a story. The listener had to have the right mental frame and adequate intellectual capacity to grasp the importance and intricacies of the events leading to his present mental condition. His listener had to have adequate time and patience to sit through the saga without getting fidgety. And the last, but by no means the least important requirement was the suitability of the ambience for such an important story-telling session.

The time came sooner than I expected when I was invited to dinner at Rolf's. I thought he was finally ready to open his heart and unload his anguish – must be a gripping real-life saga. I was mentally prepared to pay the price – my dedicated attention to his tale. I had to abandon all my other thoughts and be mentally prepared to listen to his story with all explanations, interpretations and deviations and, without any limit to the time.

It was a pleasant Saturday evening, what appeared to be of the so called Indian summer. Having had my weekly shave and bath, and wearing a clean shirt and trousers with a scarf round my neck I arrived at Rolf's flat and pressed the doorbell. Surprisingly there was no sound from above announcing his descent to open the door and asking me to wait a minute. But I could hear the sound of his footsteps, getting louder. The man who opened the door was Rolf alright, but barely recognizable, not because he was wearing a dark suit, but because of the expression on his face. I bade him good evening and from his facial expression I apprehended what the matter was and apologised profusely,

'Sorry I must have come to visit you on the wrong date. I must say you look dashing, might I say, quite elegant. I did not know you were going out, perhaps taking a young lady out to dinner. I am not appropriately attired or else I could have joined you. Anyway, we will meet another day, enjoy the evening.'

I felt embarrassed thinking that I came to him on a wrong date and at an awkward time. The reason of my long speech was to make him feel at ease. I was about to take leave of him when he stared at me sideways for a while without a word. I saw a hint of a smirk on his face; anger and dismay had disappeared. I realized that he had judged the situation and accepted the inevitable consequences of inviting a Bengali student to dinner. He, by then, had come to terms with the fact that for students from the Indo-Pak subcontinent like me, there was no such thing as dinner time. They ate food when they feel hungry and when it is available.

Calmly, he gave me a short lecture on etiquette,

'No my friend, you haven't come on the wrong day. I did not expect you to wear a suit for the dinner party on my birthday either, as I know you don't have one. I didn't tell you about the occasion for the party tonight for the simple reason; by the end of every month you are usually pretty skint and would feel bad coming here without a birthday present.'

'I would have certainly brought a present for you, if I had known it was your birthday today. I would probably have had to borrow the money from you in the first place,' I joked.

Rolf didn't react to this and made his sermon,

'By family tradition we like to present ourselves in our best attire to receive guests on special occasions. The least I was expecting from you was not a present but your arrival for dinner on time. When I invited you I did emphasize that dinner would be served at 7:30 pm.'

He pointed to his antique but still working grandfather clock and continued,

'Look at the time now. It is nearly 10 minutes past 8. That means you are 40 minutes late. That's unacceptable. Anyway, I have no other choice except to forgive you this time. I cannot over-emphasize the importance of timeliness in the presentation and consumption of food at dinner time. I hope you will respect my wishes and be on time on future occasions, particularly at dinner parties in my flat.'

I thought of an effective explanation and words to apologise for being late and said, 'You see, I am not used to such accurate time keeping. I don't even wear a wrist watch. Of course I have learnt the lesson. The lesson is clear and simple – I have to abide by German Jewish's tradition when invited to Rolf's dinner party.

'To emphasize about the precise time for the dinner I asked you to read my lips, if you remember,' he quipped.

'How could I read your lips over the telephone, mister?' I snapped.

This changed the smirk on his face into laughter.

To make the atmosphere still lighter I said,

'Look at the bright side of this situation my friend. Don't you think it is better late than never? In any case, by being late and skipping lunch I have cultivated a very healthy appetite. I am sure I shall do justice to every scrap of food that you may care to place on my plate.'

Rolf did not react to my banter. On the way to the lounge he pointed to the bathroom, 'You may use this for washing your hands.'

I was not expecting to eat dinner at his house with my fingers. Although when I consumed a meal of rice and minced meat curry, cooked by my flatmate, we usually put the food on the plate directly from the cooking pot and used our fingers. This practice saved eating and washing-up time to allow more time for our evening entertainments.

'I am quite happy to eat using knife and fork. I do not need to wash my hands.' I quipped.

He looked at me with amazement, shook his head from left to right a few times and paused. After a long breath he said,

'I know you will not eat my food with your fingers. Let me tell you something. Washing hands and mouth before dinner is considered to be hygienic and is considered to be good dinner etiquette. Never mind, you relax on the sofa and I shall fetch some food shortly. It will have to be re-heated, you see. I don't like doing this. It takes away the flavour from the food. But, I suppose it is better to eat re-heated food than to have no food at all.'

He went away to the kitchen refusing my offer of help. He considered this to be an unacceptable interference in a very serious matter. Since my first visit to his flat nearly six months ago when he commanded me to do so for a specific purpose, I had visited him a few times for informal chats and for tea parties. We always had such get-togethers in his library-cum-study, but this time he brought me to a new room. He said it was primarily used as the music room and a formal dining room. I noticed a piano in one corner.

Being a Victorian house the flat had large rooms with small windows compared to modern houses. Apart from two quite large antique cupboards on two walls, all the other spaces on the walls in the room were covered with old paintings. The suite, tables, chairs, carpets, curtains, everything in the room gave the feel of a Victorian household, such was often portrayed in classic films or dramas depicting that era.

I felt a bit uncomfortable being the only guest at a formal dinner with a close friend in a suit as the host in such an antiquated and formal environment in his own flat. There was not a single item in the room which could be considered remotely modern. I moved around inspecting the paintings and other antique objects which were displayed quite neatly on small tables or on the mantelpiece or on the walls. I noticed that the paintings were mostly classical types, depicting religious themes. There were a few bearing African, Indian, Chinese and Japanese motifs. It was like being in an antique shop or a classical art museum.

After a while I sat down and started to scan the paintings hanging on the walls with my eyes. My gaze stopped and got focussed on to a particular one. It looked familiar. I stood up and took a closer look. There was no title to read. I stepped back a bit to get a better view. The picture was of a nude woman riding on a seashell. She was flanked by winged angels and ushered by a maiden on the sea shore with gold-embroidered clothes to adorn her exquisitely beautiful body. My attention was broken by Rolf's appearance in the room. Gloatingly he said,

'Beautiful isn't it? Breathtaking, I am sure. You like it then!'

Suddenly I remembered that this painting was one of the items discussed by chance on a recent television programme on paintings of the Renaissance period. Opportunity knocks only once and I wouldn't miss it to impress my friend with my knowledge on, and interest in classical fine art.

With all the seriousness that I could muster I said,

'It is indeed a wonderful work of art, a thing of beauty no doubt and certainly a joy for ever and for anybody who would care to savour such gifts from paradise. I can't remember the name of the painter but I know it is by a Renaissance Italian master. But as far as I know it should be at the Uffizi museum in Florence. But --'

Before I could complete my sentence he interrupted,

'Don't be alarmed my friend, it is not a stolen merchandise. The original one – Botticelli's 'The Birth of Venus' is still there in the Uffizi. The more I meditate on this one, the more I find it to be as pleasant as the original. The fact is that I have had the pleasure of seeing the original one only twice in my life, whereas this one is with me and I look at her every day and, I enjoy and wonder in amazement, it is my intoxicant.'

'It's uncanny that the Hindu goddess, Parvati, like Venus, is also depicted with both physically and spiritually desirable attributes,' I said, 'such a concept of goddesses, morphed into human form represents the inseparable existence of sexual desire and spiritual devotion in human psyche. I believe the Western thinkers and artists have borrowed this idea in their writings and paintings from ancient Hindu scriptures.'

'You're quite right, Rolf said, 'Spirituality and sexuality are integrated in most ancient religions and cults. You will find it in the Hindu Tantric Yoga philosophy. It is like the two sides of the coin. But modern man, for better or worse, has changed that and has removed spirituality from sex. Anyway, I am pleasantly surprised by your interest in fine art. I believe we have something in common.'

When I enquired what that was he answered,

'A cultured mind I suppose.' He continued,

'I believe you must have done some homework on this. We must go to Florence together some time. The city has many shrines for art lovers. I am not particularly interested in sculptures; these abound all over Italian cities. Once, when I was in Fluorescence, just out of curiosity I ventured into the David Museum and stood in front of Michelangelo's "David". It was mesmerizing, something out of this world. I thought god's hand must have been at work in its creation. It's awe-inspiring and exhilarating experience, something you must have at least once in your life time.'

'Yes, my friend,' I replied, 'we must. But before that we should set up a "Fine Art Appreciation Society (FAAS)", just like the MPAS. I wonder if we would be able to recruit a viable number of memberships.'

'It's a good idea, Rolf commented, but I doubt if the membership for such a society will exceed that of a football team. Mind you, we would be able to fill a football stadium for a silly walk competition under MPAS, anytime. The fact of the matter is paintings by old masters are like manna from heaven for mankind. It is disappointing that I can't find many to share and savour the pleasure of such a gift.'

My stare at the iconic picture of Venus was diverted when Rolf drew my attention to a fairly large Chinese vase on an antique table at the far corner of the room. I remembered him once talking to me about the arts and crafts of the Ming dynasty. It was, therefore, not difficult for me to guess that it might belong to that era. That amazed Rolf beyond measure. He thought, at last he had found a soulmate in me. He got carried away. Pointing to a medium size oil painting on the wall, he said,

'I see that you have a good knowledge of Chinese and Italian paintings. I wonder if your knowledge extends to paintings of other masters of that period. Can you guess whose masterpiece it is?'

I was not going to push my luck any further by wild guessing, so I shook my head. Rolf was very surprised that I did not recognise such a famous painting. With renewed enthusiasm he said,

'This is it, my friend; Michelangelo's all-time great masterpiece, "The Creation of Adam". This painting epitomises the pinnacle of the high renaissance in early sixteenth century. I spent a couple of days looking up at the ceiling of the Sistine Chapel in Rome. I was in a trance when I entered the inner world inhabited by this master, a saint indeed. It was an enthralling experience, something out of this world. No wonder in his time he was known as the *"Il Divino"*, the divine one.'

I commented, 'But, as far as I'm aware, Jesus Christ is the anthropomorphic form of God in Christian belief, one of the three forms. The bearded man in the picture hardly resembles the conventional forms of young Jesus depicted over the centuries, with a crown of thorns on his head or as a dying man dangling on a cross with a bleeding wound in his chest.' Rolf interrupted, 'You are being a bit flippant, my friend. You know jolly well that Jesus was not represented as an anthropomorphic form of God. He is considered simply as the son of God by the Roman Catholics of the ancient world. Manifestations that you see in many paintings and sculptures are that of the son of God. I did not know 'God the father' had a form as a strong-muscled white bearded man until I saw the painting in the Sistine chapel. I do not believe in any organized religion, but I do believe in God, and from that painting I got to know what he looks like and how he created man.' He paused to draw breath, and continued, 'Some master-painters are truly divine. They are born with the gift of passion to express their divine creativity which results in works of breath-taking beauty. Behind the anthropomorphic forms there lies the truth as a quality, like the Hindu gods and goddesses.'

I listened to his half-baked philosophical "sermon" on art and culture and tried to feel the immense power and unfathomable beauty of paintings by masters. I looked at Michelangelo's painting again with utmost concentration. Somehow it did not evoke the emotion that I thought it would. It could have been because of the familiar signal that had reached my head from my stomach, generally known as hunger pain. I am not able to concentrate on anything serious like fine art by masters until I have taken measures to get rid of that signal. On the other hand, the lack of my interest could have been due to the fact that the painting that I was looking at was only a reproduction, not the original one.

Rolf was too absorbed in the appreciation of his treasured

possessions to notice my predicament and appeared to have forgotten about dinner altogether. Since it was meant to be consumed at the right moment and that moment had elapsed some 40 minutes before my arrival, perhaps further delay did not matter to him.

He looked at me and sensed that I was not as impressed as he would have liked me to be and said,

'I know what you are thinking. But I must tell you, my friend, this is no ordinary reproduction. I do not go for such things. When I look and concentrate on this one, I lose the sense of time and place and I feel I am back inside the Sistine chapel, gone back in time and, floating at the microcosmic space of the inner world in Michelangelo's mind. It is like heavenly music, coming out from the master's brush strokes. The energy emanating from my inner world makes that picture come to life for me. I feel that man is not merely a product of the evolutionary process as proclaimed by Darwin. He did not tell us about man's divine instinct of creating heavenly things on earth. Prophets of all major religions have propounded in the scriptures that God has created man in His own image, like the way it has been shown, metamorphosed in Michelangelo's masterpiece.'

I interrupted, 'It appears to me that this particular reproduction painting is very dear to you.'

'Yes, indeed.' He said, 'It is my most prized possession and I have a special attachment to this. You will find the story behind it most touching.'

Before he could proceed I said, 'Have you forgotten that we were supposed to have dinner together? I was eagerly waiting to listen to your story of the organization. That's why you invited me tonight, haven't you?' Rolf stood up and rushed to the kitchen, muttering,

'Good heavens! Our dinner must be grossly over-cooked by now. I am sorry I got carried away and forgot all about this evening's main purpose. You must be very hungry.'

'Well, unlike you, I am a mortal man and my belly does not get filled purely with the beauty of a reproduction painting and the philosophy behind it. Now you see why I was not able to give due attention to your words of wisdom and concentrate on the underlying heavenly beauty of the painting.'

Rolf apologised profusely and brought through whatever edible food he could salvage from the oven, saying,

'I shall tell you the interesting story about how I acquired this painting after we finish dinner or whatever is left of it. Don't worry; there is no shortage of pumpernickel bread and holey cheese.' I stared at him.

He added, 'This is authentic German bread, specially made for me by the local bakery. You will like it.'

Over dinner our exchanges were initially limited to small talk about our mutual friends and acquaintances, or girls we had met and tried to befriend. I was rather enjoying the dinner with light hearted tittle tattle and without having to participate in serious analysis of the microcosmic mind-set of the painter and the spiritual ethos of his creation.

But Rolf had invited me to listen to his story. I was in his grip and felt doubly obliged to do so as penance for being late. After the main course, he brought two bowls of pudding and after we finished we moved back to the sofa with two steaming cups of coffee.

Once settled and comfortable I said,

'Would you like to start your story about the mysterious organization?'

He paused for a moment and said,

'It is too late to start that saga. Besides, the debacle with the dinner has changed my mood. I nearly forgot I promised to tell you the story about how I acquired the painting. I bet you will find it quite gripping.'

I did not believe he had forgotten about it for a moment, but I was not there to express doubt as to his motive, but only to listen. The story was mercifully short, albeit an interesting one. He just wanted a special company to share his birthday. It appeared I have to wait for another suitable occasion for his "painful" story of the organization, and for the time being, content with a supposedly equally heart-rending story of the painter. He began:

'I met the painter of this reproduction masterpiece for the first time on Charles Bridge in Prague. Cities like Prague, Venice and Florence have long histories of culture in fine art and classical music. These cities have souls, because the attributes of their cultural heritage are still very much alive and vibrant even now. Whenever I feel tormented I just leave everything and go to one of these places and wander the streets and alleys, visit the fine art galleries and frequent the cafes and bars which were the meeting places of the great masters of art and literature in the golden days of the Renaissance.

'It was a sunny spring morning and I was taking a stroll along the bridge, casually observing vendors trying to sell their wares to the tourists looking for bargain souvenirs. My attention was drawn to a man with deep-seated piercing eyes, standing in front of an easel with a paint brush in his hand. With deep bold lines on his forehead, unruly mixed black and white long hair and nearly salt and pepper stubble on his face, he looked different from the other vendors. He was painting something from memory without the benefit of a scene or model in front of him. Some of his completed canvases were propped up along the side wall of the bridge.

'I noticed that he was painting da Vinci's masterpiece, 'The Last Supper'. I was aware that in tourist areas most vendors and shopkeepers learn just about enough English vocabulary to be able to haggle. The best customers for commodities like paintings and other esoteric artefacts are mainly the nouveau riche from the English speaking world with dollars in their wallets. I stopped and out of curiosity enquired,

'How can you reproduce a masterpiece like this just from memory?' He probably felt that I was not a prospective customer and it wouldn't be worth his salt to waste his time talking to me. Shrugging his shoulders, he said,

'Me no English'.

'I was about to continue my stroll when I heard him say, 'Guten Morgen', to a passing acquaintance. I immediately realized that he was either a local German speaking Czech or an expatriate from Germany or Austria. I repeated my question in German.

Pointing to the propped up canvasses and with an alluring dry smile and in a rueful tone he said in colloquial German, "I shall tell you the secret of my craftsmanship if you would like to buy one of my paintings. I can assure you these are almost as good as the original ones".

'I began to walk away as I had no intention of buying a reproduction painting, or, for that matter, any painting from a street vendor.

'Beckoning with his palm, he shouted, "Hello, Mister. Please come back. You don't have to buy anything. I just want someone to appreciate my work".

'I didn't go very far. The sound of his call in my mother tongue was haunting. I couldn't help but drift back to him. He took out a canvas from the propped up piles and showed it to me. It was an oil painting of 'The Madonna and Child'.

'He said with a relish, "I have copied this mostly from memory. There are many masterpieces on this theme alone. I have seen quite a few originals of Virgin and Child Jesus. But the one which impressed me most was Raphael's piece. I saw the original one in Pasadena when I was in the USA quite a while ago. I painted it from the vivid impression I carried of that captivating painting after my return home. I have to confess I do make sketches and sometime use pictures from books or cards for reproducing such well-known masterpieces."

'He showed me another canvas showing Jesus Christ on a cross which he had reproduced from one by the Spanish Master, Velázquez and said,

"I spent two weeks in Seville and visited the Velasquez museum every day to make this." He asked my opinion about his works.

'I thanked him and told him apologetically, "Your paintings are of an excellent quality but I am not currently buying any. As a matter of fact I don't have any place in my flat to display or even store anymore paintings. Besides, the British market is now quite down for reproductions."

'He wouldn't let me out of his sight and said,

"I understand sir. But before you go I must tell you something. I have one special painting and I call it my 'masterpiece'. If you see this, I am sanguine that you will change your mind. You will most certainly fall in love with it. I know it; I can read one's mind when I see the face."

'Curiosity got the better of me and I agreed to see his so-called 'masterpiece'. He then said, "It's not here with me. It has been hanging on the wall of my flat for the last one and a half years. I never thought of selling it. However, my circumstances have changed now. I have fallen on hard times and I am constrained to sell almost anything of value. But that painting I cannot sell as cheap street merchandise. Very few people will appreciate the beauty and the value of this piece. You have to visit me at my flat to see that. I have a feeling that you are a connoisseur of fine art and have the gift of recognizing and appreciating an evocative painting of inner beauty."

'I took his name and address and despite the risk of being persuaded to buy his painting, I made my way to Josef Kaufmann's flat one evening, a couple of days before my scheduled flight back to England.'

Rolf paused and made me a mug of coffee and asked if I was comfortable. He didn't ask if I was still interested in the story. I shook my head to indicate, "Yes", and he continued,

'It was a small flat with only a few possessions. We sat down on an old sofa on one side of the lounge. This was also his dining room with a small table and a couple of chairs. His reproduction masterpiece of Michelangelo's original painting, 'The Creation of Adam' was staring at us from the wall.'

Rolf continued with the story as was narrated by Josef:

'His ancestors had immigrated to Bohemia on the outskirts of Prague from Germany during the last quarter of the 16th century. Even after several centuries he, like other Jewish diaspora in Bohemia, maintained his Jewish traditions and kept German as his mother tongue. He became an orphan and was brought up in a Jewish foster home. He went to an art college but didn't get any qualifications. He and his small family, a wife and daughter, moved into the Jewish quarter of Prague where he earned a living as an art teacher at a nearby school.

'Alas, misfortune did not come alone. His wife eloped with another man and took their 3-year-old daughter, Natasha with her. He was feeling the curse of loneliness and was pining for his family; most of all he missed his daughter beyond measure. He got depressed and took to alcohol and was unable to keep his job. Not a single day went by when he did not think of his darling daughter and cried. He couldn't bear it any longer. He disposed of most of his belongings and went travelling across Europe with his paint brushes, hoping to be away from painful reminders of his dear Natasha and to devote himself to creating something remarkable for her, and in her memory.

'He went to the Vatican City to experience the beauty of the frescoes created by the great masters. He knew of Michelangelo's most famous masterpiece stretching across the ceiling of the Sistine chapel, and was longing to experience its aura and savour its beauty. He told me that when he looked at it for the first time his heart was pounding and he got so emotional that tears rolled down his cheeks. He gazed at it until his neck was hurting badly. He went to the chapel every day for a week and gazed at the painting as long as he could. At times he would enter into a state of trance. Perhaps he was trying to know God or to venture into the painter's mind to look for 'the man' that God had created. It was all to do with enjoying the ecstasy of agony.

'His urge to reproduce the painting was inexorable. He had to capture the image on a canvas for someone very special to him, who was, according to him, the reason for his existence. He was worried that time could soon wipe out the image, not only from the fresco on the ceiling, but also from the screen of his mind. He approached the Vatican authority and begged permission to be allowed to work on reproducing the painting inside the chapel. The permission was not granted. He set up his canvas on an easel in the room of the guest house where he was staying. It was not very far and he visited the chapel every day, sometimes several times a day. He made profiles of various subjects and objects in the painting in his sketch book. The sketches helped him to produce the framework for the painting. His frequent and extended visits to the chapel were necessary to give flesh and depth and eventually, to give life to the skeletal profiles by giving right colours and shades. He finished the painting in eight weeks. He returned to Prague with only one painting in his possession, that was the one hanging on that wall.

'He took the painting down from the wall, rubbed it very gently with a clean linen cloth and held it in front of me. It was in a frame with decorative gilded edges. I looked at it – the aura emanating from it was overpowering. I felt not only the body but also the soul in it. I asked him to put it back on the wall. The picture captivated me and I gazed at it silently for a while. I had been to the Sistine chapel many times and had often been mesmerized by the awesome beauty and the deep meaning of this heavenly artwork. I felt I was, once again, sitting inside the chapel and watching the same painting, but this time without having to suffer the discomfort of proverbial "pain in the neck". I fell in love and decided to have this painting at any cost.

'I asked him how much he wanted for it. He, in turn, asked me what I thought it was worth. I wondered how one could put a price on a masterpiece like that, albeit a reproduction! I felt guilty, as if I was trying to buy someone's baby because he had fallen on hard times. But if I didn't buy it someone else with spare cash, like a hawkish art dealer, would surely consider it to be a good investment. I persuaded him to name his price. After some hesitation, he did. I paid him a lot more than he asked for, and still felt guilty that I did not or could not pay him enough.'

Rolf paused and asked if I wanted a refill. He came back with two mugs of freshly made coffee. I helped him clear the dining table. He then took out an easel and a spotlight from the guest room and rested the painting on the easel and illuminated it by focusing light from a small lamp. He then switched off the room lights and sat down on the same sofa by my side with the painting in front of us.

Like a schoolteacher bestowing words of wisdom Rolf said,

'There is a reason for this elaborate arrangement. If you want to really appreciate and enjoy a good quality painting you need the right ambience and company; of course you also need to be in the right frame of mind.'

'I am not in the right frame of mind for this', I protested, 'I cannot so easily change my mood. You wanted to share your fears concerning the organization that is allegedly hell-bent on destroying you. I came mentally prepared to hear that story. Isn't that why you invited me for dinner this evening?'

'As a matter of fact I wanted to enjoy my birthday in your company. I could have told you the story anyway, but circumstances have changed. I am in a different mood now and have no intention of spoiling the evening by bringing in the filth and garbage of the real world, in which I have to live. Let us enjoy the beauty of this masterpiece. You just relax, gaze at the painting and try to forget that you exist. I shall tell you about the saga of the organization and its agents another time.'

I had no alternative, so I did what he asked me to do. I stretched my legs, lay back and fixed my gaze on the painting, remaining as relaxed as possible. I scanned the painting bit by bit, very slowly, reconstructing it in my brain. There, in a microcosm of my own creation, I became the subject of the picture – both the creator and the creation, but not at the same time. I was bewildered – "was I Adam, the first man, the most exquisite creation of God or, was I the creator, the ultimate man – the godhead?" I felt light headed as if I was intoxicated and confused. I thought I heard a voice asking me to justify why I created something in my own image. "It was the pleasure of creation, stupid", I retorted in my thoughts. I heard a voice again, asking me to look at my perfect creation – "Adam", the most exquisite of all living beings. I did that and found myself to be one with him. I felt that through his existence I could understand the mind of God. I felt fashioned by both God and Adam. My ecstasy was ended by Rolf's gentle tap on my shoulder. I realized that the voice was his. He was grinning and nodding with pleasure at my entrancement. Composing myself, I said,

'Now I also know what God looks like. As a matter of fact, I have encountered similar gods in flesh and blood many a time back home. They are in our language called *Bhagwans*, translated literally it means, 'gods'. Often such *Bhagwans* would go into a trance, while high on 'ganja', a type of marijuana, uttering *Mantras* or singing devotional songs accompanied by the rhythm of a single-stringed musical instrument. They all seem to have long hair and long, 'salt and pepper' coloured bushy beards. I wonder if Michelangelo ever visited India!'

'No my friend, he did not visit India.' Rolf said, 'He didn't need to copy the form of God. God was in his heart. As a matter of fact, God exists in the hearts of all of us. Only, Michelangelo was able to elevate himself to the status of an 'ultimate man' and be one with Him and was able to depict His face on a canvas for the mortals like us to see. This is the God who personifies the qualities of kindness, love and strength, all intertwined in one Supreme Being, pervading the Universe. If you look at this personification and are able to lose yourself, you may have the pleasure of ecstasy, the feeling of being the ultimate man and, for a moment, may gain the status of the godhead.'

I thought the old wizard had tried to hypnotize me. I felt very satisfied that he had not succeeded, but again, I wondered – "Was I stupid to see a living God, the so called, 'ultimate man' in a reproduction painting of the creation of Adam?" Whatever the truth, it had been a really ecstatic experience. It was quite late by then and I was dying for my fix of nicotine. I stood up to call it a night and wished him good night. Rolf made no reply.

He stood up, looked at me and said, 'You can't leave without listening to the last and most touching episode of the story of the painter of this masterpiece. I know what is bothering you, my friend. My bathroom is no longer out of bounds for you; you may use it as a den as and when you wish; you are free to have your fix there.'

I was rejuvenated after my fix and Rolf continued with the story of the painter:

'I returned home with my prized possession a couple of days after my last encounter with Josef. I couldn't wait to put it into a new frame, befitting its quality. After tearing off the packaging paper I turned the frame over to take off the hard paper board holding the canvas inside the frame. I noticed something written there in German. It read, 'Dedicated to darling Natasha, my legacy.' Beneath this, there was no signature or date, only the word, Papa.'

Rolf continued, 'I felt a sharp prick in my conscience. This treasure belonged to someone else. It was bequeathed to his daughter. I didn't have the moral right to own it even though I'd paid for it. Whenever I looked at the painting, a feeling of pathos overtook my pleasure of its beauty. I had wondered how desperate his situation must have been for him to sell something he had specially created for, dedicated to and made a legacy to his lost daughter. He told me that every day while on the bridge, trying to sell his paintings, he was also looking out in case his little girl should show up and call out, "Papa". He kept on living with the hope that one day he will find her and hug her and hear her voice.

'I left the canvas in its original frame and repacked it. I didn't have Josef's address, so I couldn't post it. I felt a deep sense of guilt for depriving a little girl of her legacy. I resolved to hand it over to him one day. That day came sooner than I thought.

I decided to attend a seminar at the University of Prague on, "The impact of art in Psychotherapy". It was a good enough excuse for me to visit Prague again. Josef, as usual, was there on the bridge concentrating on his artwork and hoping to attract customers. He was very surprised to see me again so soon. After an exchange of the usual niceties, I expressed my intention to meet him somewhere in the evening.

'He was apprehensive and enquired if I was, in any way, unhappy about the purchase of his painting. I told him that we would talk about that when we would meet. He suggested we meet at the Café Franz Kafka, at Siro ken, the coffee house Kafka used to frequent and not far from his flat at the Jewish colony. Accordingly, I went to the café, with the wrapped canvas in my cloth shoulder bag, and met him there.

'I told him how I felt about taking the painting from him. He was then on his third pint of beer and I was on my second cup of coffee. I told him that I did not want my money back but wished to give the painting back to him to keep for his daughter. He told me he didn't need that painting any more. He would never be able to give it to his Natasha. She was no more, had gone to heaven. The painting was causing him untold agony. He was at peace with himself that he had found a good home for it. He was now able to carry on living without the pangs of loss by shutting his mind from the memories of his daughter. That painting had reminded him of his daughter, creating a relentless agony in his heart.

'He told me that one day accidentally he had bumped into his estranged wife, Sofia, at a boulevard in a small town not far from Prague almost a year after she had left him. She was trying to avoid him. But he caught up with her, held her hand tight and demanded to see Natasha. She asked him to let her go to avoid creating a scene. He begged her to take him to see Natasha as he was dying to meet her. She announced, without any emotion, that she had died of leukaemia some months before. He let go her hand, almost fainted and sat down on a bench. Sofia looked at him and disappeared into the crowd without saying a word.

'Josef wanted to know how and when Natasha had died. Did she remember him and miss him at the end? He wanted to know where she was buried. It would have given him some solace if he could have heard from her mother about all the things that had happened to her and what she had said during her brief life. He told me that he was hard up, but not that badly to have to sell his masterpiece. He couldn't bear the constant reminder of Natasha, his lost treasure. He had donated the money from the sale of his painting to a children's hospice charity.

'I saw tears on his cheeks. He told me that he often wondered what it would have been like if the *IL Divino* master had also painted the Creation of Eve!'

That was the end of the story. Touching indeed, but not relevant to Rolf's predicament. He was silent, as if in meditation, his gaze still focussed on the painting. He didn't get up to say goodnight or open the door. I let myself out and slipped away into the quiet of night…

5

Those Lovely Dark Eyes

It was the beginning of the long summer holidays and all the undergrads had left town. Most of the British students had gone home to their parents, and the overseas students had the hassle of finding temporary accommodation out of Hall, but Postgrads who normally lived in rented accommodation, did not face the same difficulty. Laboratories and libraries were always open for normal academic activities, so closure of colleges made very little difference to me personally. The vacation did however allow us more time and opportunity for *adda* sessions.

The weekly activities at the British Council continued as normal during the University recess. Most of my fellow *deshi* students, however, didn't find the activities there exciting enough and found gathering at a hangout for a heated *adda* session more interesting. Their absence offered me the advantage of being able to improve my spoken English without the temptation of lapsing into my own language. Soon, though, I realized that talking to other foreign students, albeit in English, was not helping me much towards this goal. I wanted to meet English students thinking that I could learn more quickly from them. In particular, I wanted to learn how and when to use English idioms, and speak the Queen's English.

I was often reminded of my landlady, Mrs Capper's words of advice on getting to grips with the English language, thrown at me in anger. I was therefore quite excited when I met and become friendly with a pretty young girl from the Midlands.

Paula was an undergrad fresher at Somerville College studying mathematics. I met her at one of the British Council's functions. She was introduced to me by Lindsey, one of my acquaintances from the Voluntary Overseas Services Association (VOSA). Both were residents of the same college. Those days only about ten percent of the students were female and all of them lived in two of the all-female colleges.

I found Paula very charming and friendly. It didn't take me long to pick up courage to ask her for a date. On that occasion I took her for a drink to the senior common room of Oriel College. Being a postgrad I was privileged to have a personal key to the senior common room, where there was a bar and facilities for making coffee and getting snacks, but no bartender. The system was based on trust. I offered her a glass of red wine she declined and we ended up drinking coffee. She was easily persuaded to have a packet of crisps and I munched some biscuits. I was trying to impress her.

After that first meeting we often met for tea at a café or our respective places and often went out for walks together. Once I invited her to the Pakistan society's annual get-together party. We also went to *Moti Mahal* few times for slapdash spicy Indian lunches served mainly for hard up students, comprising of one type of curry of one's choice served on top of a pile of rice, with a dash of lime or mango pickle on the side. Anything else was extra and would be charged. The meal cost only four shillings and we usually went Dutch. It was quite fashionable in those days to be escorted by an Indian or Pakistani to an Indian restaurant. Some of my less scrupulous countrymen even masqueraded as princes and relatives of maharajas.

Paula and I got on so well that we talked non-stop whenever we met. She was a very good listener and liked to hear about my childhood, student life, my culture and about the people in the villages and towns where I grew up. Her curiosity knew no bounds and this led me to talk incessantly with great enthusiasm and pleasure. We even invited each other to dinner at our respective colleges. Before the summer break, one evening I got a chit from Paula, dropped in through the letter box at my flat. The message read, "Sorry, couldn't meet before I left for home for the recess. My parents and I would be delighted if you could come and visit us for a day. Please confirm a suitable date ASAP by posting a note to me." Below the name and address she wrote, 'Lots of love', and made a few crosses.

I was pretty sure that she had fallen in love with me and, naturally I fell for her too. I was, however, not sure of the significance of the invitation to meet her parents. In my tradition back home this would precede a courtship and entail approval by the girl's parents before engagement. I was also not sure of the meaning of the crosses at the bottom of the brief epistle. So, with some hesitation, a lot of trepidation and without much delay I made my way to my mentor, Masud's flat in Walton Street.

I had hardly seen him since his beloved wife had joined him two months ago. He and his wife, Banie *Bhabi*, were delighted to see me. It's customary to address an elder friend's or brother's spouse with a suffix, *'Bhabi'* following her name as an expression of fondness and respect. From their body language and the elation they showed for receiving a visitor I realised, merely two months' togetherness had lessened their hankering for each other's company. They were in the middle of their dinner and I profusely apologized for dropping in unexpectedly and interrupting their intimate dinner. Masud pretended to be angry at my formality and ordered me to get a plate from the cupboard, sit down with it at the table, and to "dig in". After the meal I took Masud quietly aside and showed him the note. He was by then holding his third can of beer in one hand and a Benson and Hedges cigarette in the other.

I was apprehensive about being ridiculed by this "wise man of the East" for being so serious about a simple hand-written invitation to a girlfriend's home. I was worried that his counsel would end up in characteristic scoffing and one of his interminable monologues. Surprisingly, he did nothing of the sort. He handed the note back to me after a quick glance, put his can down and then, took the note back again to concentrate on it with more attention.

'Do you know what the crosses at the bottom mean?' he asked.

I shrugged, 'I'm afraid not'.

He looked at me with a cryptic expression and said,

'These signs here are expression of kisses. 'He smiled, tapped my shoulder and continued, 'You are a lucky lad.'

We went back to the lounge and without even asking me he showed the note to Banie *Bhabi*. They exchanged glances and smiled at each other. Banie congratulated me and enquired when I was going to introduce my girlfriend to them. Masud cautioned me to go slowly and quoted, "Haste makes waste and spoils the broth."

I was over the moon and beginning to feel love sick. My answer to Paula would have to be by mail since she had only given me her parents address. The post typically would take two days to reach its destination. I was excited and immediately wrote to her confirming the earliest possible date. I didn't forget to put a few crosses after my name. My patience was wearing thin; I couldn't concentrate on work and was desperately waiting for a reply. It arrived without delay; the date was confirmed. On that day I boarded a train at Oxford railway station for Leamington Spa in Warwickshire, Paula's home town.

I was expecting Paula to receive me at the station with her characteristic childlike sweet smile, but when I arrived at the station there was no sign of her. So, I sat down on a bench by the side of the road outside the station. I got a bit worried, thinking – "Have I come on a wrong date or got off at the wrong station!" As I stood up to stretch my legs, suddenly a black car stopped in front of me and Paula got out of the driving seat and apologized profusely for being late. I assured her that I was waiting there only for a few minutes and the train was a bit late anyway.

Paula had got her driving licence very recently and she had to cajole her father to let her drive his new Volvo for this occasion. I was really impressed. She drove me to visit the famous Warwick Castle and also took me out for a long drive in the countryside. We stopped by a river and had a walk along the bank. I saw some young couples there, walking holding hands. I was tempted to do the same, but shied away remembering Masud's advice – "Haste makes waste", and I thought – "It will happen in good time."

I joined her family for both lunch and dinner. Unlike Paula, her father, the head master of a local private school, was not at all interested in my life history, my culture or my country. He seemed to be more concerned about the state of my spoken English than my physical wellbeing. Probably due to my mixed Indo-English accent he often misunderstood me and had to beg my pardon and ask me to repeat what I said. He most enthusiastically tried to correct my pronunciation and to educate me in the proper spelling of things and the names of trees in the immediate environment of his mansion. He pointed his finger at one of the big trees and said with the spelling, 'this is a, s-i-c-a-m-o-r-e tree, and then another one, p-i-n-e, and another, o-a-k, and went on with great enthusiasm. He also tried to teach me the names and spellings of English seasons, but surprisingly, never mentioned the weather, unlike Paula.

I managed to gather enough courage to give her a goodbye kiss on her cheek at the railway station. It was a most memorable day out for me. But it would be a very long two weeks before Paula would be returning to Oxford.

🍂

I had not seen Rolf for more than three weeks, as I had been away seeing relatives and friends living in other cities in England and some friends who were studying at other Universities. As a result I hadn't been able to attended Tuesday's gatherings at the British Council where we usually met.

Late one Monday morning I strolled passed the Ashmoleum museum to go to a café on Cornmarket Street before going to my department. Occasionally I made a detour instead of taking the direct route along Pusey Street for a change, and to have a proper cup of fresh coffee at a nearby shop. Often I would be so much preoccupied with a plethora of thoughts that the existence of the big museum building or the grand Randolph Hotel in front of it wouldn't even come to my notice. But this time a crowd of visitors going into the museum building drew my attention. This was quite unusual for this time on a Monday. Out of curiosity I dropped in to find out what was going on.

I thought of Rolf. Could it be something in connection with objects of art or antiquity? Rolf would not miss such a thing. I wondered if my unscheduled visit really was just an act of idle curiosity! Perhaps Rolf was amongst the visitors? Subconsciously I was probably missing his company and seeking him out.

I was, pleasantly surprised to bump into him inside the museum and exclaimed – "Think of the devil and he shall appear."

With pretend anger, he said,

'Feeling is mutual, my friend. But tell me, what the hell are you doing here of all the places, and at this early hour of the day?'

'Looking for the devil I suppose.' I replied.

'But this is heaven. You won't find any devils here,' he shot back.

'That is a matter of opinion. Your heaven could be someone else's hell, I submitted.

Rolf said, 'Never mind; now tell me why on earth have you been deliberately avoiding me for all this time? I popped into your laboratory this morning on my way to the museum and you were not at your desk and I couldn't find any trace of you anywhere in the building. When I asked one of your fellow research students about you, he sniggered and suggested that it was rather too early in the morning on a Monday for you to grace the laboratory with your presence.'

I was not amused by this baseless insinuation that I was deliberately avoiding him.

I said flippantly, 'The reason you couldn't find me at my desk is quite simple, because I was not there. I was here looking for you, wasn't I? I'm a bit upset by the cynical remarks of my fellow research student. It is true I do love my morning nap and hate rushing to my workplace early in the morning, particularly on Mondays. I bet you, he didn't mention that, unlike him, I work late into the night.'

Before I could give an explanation for my long disappearance and temporary severance of our companionship he unilaterally forgave me.

He was quite excited and said, 'Good job you are here. Today is the last day. Tomorrow priceless paintings by Raphael will go back to their permanent home in Italy. These have been on public display here for the last three weeks. You must have read about this event in the local newspaper or heard about it on the local radio.'

'Sorry, I don't read the local newspaper or listen to the radio.' I said.

Rolf continued, 'This is the third time I have come to enjoy these great masterpieces since these were on display here. The four selected works have been borrowed by the Ashmoleum museum through the auspices of the Italian branch of the International Committee of Fine Art Museums. It is the policy of the committee to lend such paintings to other museums in the Western world.'

He remarked with a touch of irony,

'It's funny isn't it that the publican opens his pub and people flocks to him rain or shine, whereas the milkman has to deliver his merchandise door to door at the cock's crow?'

A small room was dedicated to the display of the four paintings and nothing else. He pointed to the one depicting a bearded man with a pretty woman beside him holding a baby, and asked me to take a closer look. I read the title: 'God the Father and the Virgin Mary'.

Rather irreverently, I thought – "Here we go again!", and said, 'The picture of God in this one doesn't look anything like the one that you showed me in your flat the other day. It is not as compelling and mesmerizing as yours. So, whose God is the true representation of the godhead?'

'Take your pick,' Rolf said. 'The earthen statues of Hindu gods and goddesses are not the same or even similar throughout the Indian subcontinent. You have seen God creating Adam. Now you see him crowning his son baby Jesus.'

I read the titles of the other three of the masterpieces. These were 'Sistine Madonna' holding the baby Jesus and flanked by two saints and two winged cherubs. The other two were of a young woman entitled, 'La Donna Valetta' and 'Baldisseri Castiglione'. Rolf didn't utter a single word; instead he sat down on a nearby seat and fixed his gaze on the face of the woman in one of the paintings. Although there was no trace of smile in her face, unlike that of Mona Lisa, a magical and seductive aura emanated from it. I was sure that, had I been in a different mood, it could have taken my breath away.

I was not in the least interested in the paintings just then, but I did not make any comment about them and pretended to be keenly interested and enjoying them. I sat down by Rolf on a seat in the middle of the room and joined him in meditation, focussing my gaze on the paintings, hoping to get overwhelmed with feelings of heavenly beauty. I knew for this to happen I had to let myself undergo some sort of self-hypnosis. But I couldn't achieve this. Perhaps it was too early in the day or too crowded an environment. Anyway, I refrained from making any comment that might upset Rolf, thus avoiding another sermon on the beauty and deep meaning to be found in the paintings of the classical masters. Besides nothing mattered to me then since I was in love.

But Rolf did not know about my newly acquired status, and I was rather reluctant to interrupt his silent meditation, enjoying my own mental turmoil.

After a while I noticed he was back with me. The prevailing noisy environment and my presence by his side were preventing him from getting his artistic fix.

Bringing his mouth near to my ear he said, 'They were contemporaries and bitter rivals, you know. Both of them were products of the high Renaissance. Rather I should say they were the high priests who, along with some lesser fries were, so to say, 'midwives' of the European cultural Renaissance, the golden age of painting and sculpture.'

'Who on earth are you talking about?' I asked.

'I am talking about Michelangelo and Raphael, stupid. You ought to know that they were the people who have, through their work, helped us open the door to our inner world and to search for our souls and look for our origin.

He stood up and asked the time. Neither of us wore a watch. There was a clock on the wall so I drew his attention to it. After a bit of a pause I said,

'My built in alarm clock rings when it receives biological 'hunger signals' and it's ringing now, reminding me most earnestly that it's time for lunch.'

We left the museum together and went to a nearby café for a spot of lunch and a hot cup of coffee. Noticing my unusual quietness, concerned Rolf said,

'You look ill, Rafi. You seem to have lost your youthful liveliness and sense of humour. I also noticed that you were not at all interested in the paintings. Something must be bothering you. Tell me, my friend, what's the matter?'

I looked down at the floor and then made my confession, 'I'm in love.'

He did not double up with laughter as I feared he would. He was composed, and said,

'You know that I am an amateur practitioner of homeopathic medicine. I've probably told you that at one time I also studied medicine for my sins. What I didn't tell you is that, I am also a qualified psychoanalyst. I was observing your every movement and guessed your sickness from your body language as soon as I saw you this morning. But there is nothing to be alarmed about. I have, in the past, cured many patients with a similar illness. What you need is a therapy session with me, fairly urgently.'

"Do I really want to be cured?" I questioned myself.

In a funny sort of way I was actually enjoying my so called, 'sicknesses'. We made an agreement to meet that evening at his flat after dinner, at 8 pm. I made sure that I rang the bell of his flat exactly at 8 pm as agreed, although it was not a dinner invitation.

I was, however, surprised to see him dressed in a dark suit. It was not his birthday which had just gone. He immediately realized the cause of my concern and said,

'Don't worry my friend. The guest I am entertaining is aware of your participation in tonight's musical soiree. Your presence will make it a nice 'threesome' rendezvous, it is always better to have a well-trained audience, albeit a lone one.'

Rolf introduced me to his guest. But there was no need for that, as I already knew Susan Hill, tonight's special guest. I had been introduced to her before at a music concert held in one of the colleges, a couple of months ago. I remembered her telling me, she was doing research on the 'Application of Tantric Yoga in Applied Psychology' for her master's dissertation at the School of

Oriental and African Studies, a part of London University.

I gathered that they had already finished their quiet 'candlelit' supper sometime before I arrived. She was a fine looking woman and very elegantly dressed. I was aware that from time to time Susan visited Rolf to practice playing the piano and he always took the opportunity to make these occasions a kind of 'romantic' date. He would join in, forming a duet by playing on his violin in concert with her. He told me that he had never played violin in any public function, but took pleasure in playing in the company of a few close friends who really appreciate classical music and were moved by it. He considered me to be a member of his inner circle of such listeners and a close friend. By then, somehow, I was considered to be a connoisseur of classical music and paintings. I felt both of them enjoyed my presence as solo audience at their private music concert. I also enjoyed the private soirée in that lovely ambience.

Being one of a dying breed, Rolf, as per his family tradition, normally dressed up formally for musical soirées even though it was an informal gathering of merely three people. He told me once that to cultivate a heavenly art one needed to create an appropriate atmosphere, both in one's inner world and in one's immediate surrounding. A formal dress created the mood to cultivate such activities. Priests of all religions do the same.

For an hour they played scores from great maestros including Bach, Mozart and Tchaikovsky. Before starting each piece of movement he will announce the name of the piece and its composer for my ear. At the end of their performance Susan politely refused the invitation to stay on for a drink. She took leave of us explaining she had a long walk back to her digs and had an academic assignment to finish that night.

There I was again sitting down with Rolf on a sofa with a hot cup of coffee in my hand. He looked at me with a smile on his face but remained silent. He did not ask me about my so called "sickness".

I could sense from the gloat on his face and the anticipation in his eyes that he would have the upper hand in the session to follow. It would be like a 'doctor-patient' relationship.

At last he opened his mouth, 'Well my friend; so you are in love.' He then made a dramatic pause and continued,

'It is nice to be in love I suppose. I wouldn't know much about it as I have never experienced such a sickness. In my household, in my formative years, we talked incessantly about money, marriage, food and other family matters. Love and lust were taboo topics. Even within my circle of friends we kept our emotions hidden from others. But, it is good to be able to share the feeling with someone close to you. Please, tell me, how do you know you are in love? Could you also tell me of your assessment of what love actually is?'

I was quite annoyed by his school teacher-like manner; I was not a love-sick teenager asking for a tutorial on love.

I said, 'I don't know what love is and I do not want to know. Whatever it may be, it certainly isn't a sickness, I am sure of that. I do know I am 'in love' because I feel it in my heart. I can't explain it; it is most probably like being high on drugs. Despite all the trepidation and associated uncertainty it is providing me a 'feel-good' factor.'

Rolf let his characteristic sideways gaze fall on to my face and after a short spell of silence he apologised and said,

'I suppose that is an acceptable answer to my first question, but, forgive me for my audacity in asking a very personal but nevertheless prudent question, which would be relevant to my analyses and that is, do you also feel it in the groin?'

He produced a mischievous smile and waited for my response still looking at me. I shook my head with irritation at his implied innuendo. His smile disappeared and he continued,

'Platonic love then, I suppose! To be honest with you I don't know what that means. Even Plato didn't really give a plausible explanation. He merely gave some account of the genesis, purpose and nature of 'love' in one of his symposia.

'Come to think of it, I forgot; I *was* in love once, no doubt as passionately as you are now. We were at the upper school together and we were inseparable. He died of Pneumonia within a year and my world fell apart. I thought about him all the time; for a while I could hardly do normal things like eating, going out to play, and school homework. I often fantasised about being with him, caressing him and kissing him. Time is a great healer and slowly but surely his memory faded and my love sickness blew away with the wind. Anyway, I don't like to think back to sad episodes from my past. Now please tell me all about your platonic, or should I say romantic love episode.'

I narrated the events leading to my meeting with Paula's parents and of how much I was looking forward to seeing her on her return to college for the next term. I confessed that it was the first time I had fallen in love, and that it was affecting my health, studies and my social interaction with friends.

He asked me bluntly, 'Do you want me to cure your affliction? As I have told you before, I have a great deal of experience in treating love sick people.'

I was not sure of what to say and how to answer his question. I paused for a bit and said nonchalantly,

'Yes', and then I said, 'No, no' and, then I said, 'I do not know.'

Rolf stood up and said, 'Why don't you wait till she comes back to college? You need to let her know how you feel. You might even like to offer her a present as a token of your love for her. Only then you will find out where you stand with her.'

When I left him, I was very disappointed by his lack of empathy. He was supposed to be my mate and a mentor. 'Love' is not something one expresses with the offer of a gift, he should have known that. It has to grow naturally and one must not be hasty in this business. I appreciated Masud's counsel on this sensitive matter, 'haste makes waste'. But then again, Rolf was a thinker, an intellectual with knowledge and understanding of human psychology; therefore, he couldn't be wrong either.

All the analysis and dissecting of my emotionally unsettled state of mind didn't help alleviate my agony. The fact was, it was nearly two weeks before the new term, and that appeared to be a millennium to me. However, time passed and at last the day came; it was the Monday when she would be back.

When we met at the residence of Paula's parents we had talked about meeting up on the Tuesday evening at the British Council. That would, I thought, 'give her ample time to settle down after returning to her college. There was nothing concrete about the date. Nevertheless, I was eagerly awaiting our encounter on that day. Most of the regulars, including Rolf, were there, but there was no sign of Paula. I was chatting with people and participating in Scottish dancing with little or no enthusiasm. I kept looking at the outside door. Everybody was busy enjoying the evening and nobody had noticed my unusually meek behaviour and melancholy mood, that is, except Rolf.

Before the end of the event he came to me, put his hand on my shoulder and said, 'Don't look so dejected my friend. You know where to find her. Perhaps she is expecting you to go and meet her there.'

I took heart from these words of wisdom from the wise old man. I gathered as much confidence as I could muster and went to Somerville College the following evening. Paula appeared delighted to see me and allowed me to kiss her on the cheek. She asked me to take a seat and made some comments about the weather. I was not interested in the weather, not what it was like on the previous day or what it was predicted to be like the following day. I had no control over it; therefore I had no interest in it. I would do what I wanted to do, rain or shine.

I continued with the conversation, following my own traditional way, 'How are your parents? I really enjoyed meeting them.'

'They are well and asked me to convey their greetings to you.' Paula said.

'That's very nice of them.' I said enthusiastically, 'I liked your parents, particularly your father. He was very keen to improve my English. I would have learnt a lot about botany and spelling if I could have spent more time with him.'

Paula smiled, 'I am sorry I can't offer you any tea or coffee. I am trying to finish an assignment by tonight for my tutorial tomorrow morning, that's why I did not go to the BC yesterday.'

I was disappointed but I was able to make a dinner date with her on the following Friday night. I then made my own excuse for a quick exit, saying,

'I must go now; I also have some work to do on a paper based on my preliminary experimental results.'

The next day I bought the newly released Beatle's LP, 'Yellow Submarine' to present it to Paula as a token of my love, as Rolf had advised. I remembered her once mentioning that she liked that album, but couldn't afford to buy it. On the Friday I collected her from her college, but instead of going to my regular Mati Mahal I took her to the other Indian restaurant, The Taj Mahal, which was more upmarket and consequently more expensive. I thought it would be a suitable place for a tryst. I wanted this to be a romantic rendezvous for a memorable occasion, a secret one for the time being.

We had a wonderful time with a lovely dinner of rice and different mild curries. Although we had had slap-dash curry meals at Moti Mahal before, that was Paula's first experience of a proper full-course Indian cuisine. She found it very enjoyable and exotic. We talked and joked and laughed and, of course, ate to our heart's content.

After the dinner, while drinking coffee, I gave her the record saying, 'It is a present for you, a token of my fondness for you.'

The word 'love' did not come out my lips. Paula thanked me profusely, she was visibly embarrassed and with a trace of anguish in her tone she said,

'It is very kind of you, you are very generous but you really shouldn't have done it. Thank you very much indeed. I shall never forget this special Indian dinner experience in your company.'

She unwrapped the covering and looked at the record for a moment. Then she stood up, landed a brief kiss on my cheek and said,

'As a matter of fact I also have got quite fond of you, you know. I shall always remember you whenever I listen to these songs. These are really my favourite ones. I shall treasure it.'

She paused briefly and said while looking down at the table, 'Actually I have something important to say to you.'

I was stunned but relieved that the first talk of 'love' was to come from her mouth. But I was also apprehensive as to how I was going to respond to her unexpected offering of love towards me.

Her voice was hesitant and words were sticking when she dropped the bombshell, while still looking down at the table she said in a doleful tone,

'I am sure you will be happy to know that I have a boyfriend now and we are in love with each other. His name is Charles. He is in his second year studying mathematics at Brasenose College.'

She couldn't look at me, but went on, 'You will like him. I have already told him about you and our friendship and how fond I am of you. I would dearly like to have you as my soul mate. But you do understand that now we can't see each other as often as I would like to.'

I couldn't find anything to say to her. The sudden change in my mood and a lack of enthusiasm for conversation was very embarrassing and awkward for both of us. We both tried to continue our normal friendly conversation for a while without much success.

While walking her back to her college, I had to, for the first time, resort to talk about the weather. I pecked her on the cheek and bade goodnight in an impassive tone and came straight to Rolf's flat. It was nearly 11 pm when I rang the bell. I apologised for intruding at such an ungodly hour.

Rolf usually went to bed late and I was sure he would be still awake and wouldn't mind my intrusion at this ungodly hours. Before I could open my mouth to apologise he bantered,

'You need not apologise, my good friend, I was expecting you. You did tell me a couple of days ago about your impending tryst this evening. I knew you would come to thank me for curing your love sickness. Sometimes it is better to sacrifice the ecstasy than to suffer the agony. Matters of the heart are better resolved sooner rather than later lest these clog the brain, don't you think?'

He made me a mug of tea using a tea bag. He did not believe that tea should be served in a mug or made using a teabag; it should be brewed from loose tea leaves in a pot at a right temperature and over a precise period of time. He kept mugs, and teabags in a jar for emergencies such as this. He realized I was in desperate need of a hot drink and comfort. He put away the books and the papers on which he was making some notes in German. He leaned forward and prepared himself to listen to me without even asking me to recall the events of the evening.

I was not in the mood to take issue with his condescending display of prowess in forecasting the outcome of tonight's event. He knew I would follow his advice against my better judgement and present Paula with a token of my love. But what I didn't realise until now was that he'd also foreseen that this was going to cure my ailment.

Anyway, I was not going to talk to him about my relationship with Paula, my foolish infatuation and my display of emotion and the subsequent embarrassment I suffered. I knew this would give him enormous pleasure and he would simply gloat. My love sickness was gone and I didn't wish to dwell on it. So I remained silent.

Rolf kept a straight face, pretending that he had absolutely no interest in how my date had gone and, as a way of making a conversation he asked,

'What did you think of Susan Hill? I saw you trying to flirt with her after the recital the other night.'

I didn't know why exactly I was at Rolf's. Perhaps my unrelenting pull towards him was due to a need for sharing something important with someone close to me and, perhaps a sixth sense had told me that he was waiting for me. Once in his company, my enthusiasm for striking up a conversation disappeared completely. I tried hard to present a brave face as if all was well. I knew he was trying to make it easier for me by engaging in small talk.

I remembered that I had been warned by the warden of the BC not to trust English women since they were as unpredictable as the English weather. I should have been warned also not to attempt to read their minds. I recalled a Hindu religious scripture, 'even gods fail to understand a woman's mind.'

In answer to Rolf's question about Susan Hill I answered, 'I found her very pleasant to talk to and no one can deny that she is a fine looking woman.' I sipped some tea and continued,

'You must know it by now that I enjoy talking to beautiful women, even if they are with their boyfriends. The thing that interested me most was the subject of her research. Although I am from the Indian sub-continent, I know next to nothing about the cult of ancient *Tantric Yoga*. If I understood her correctly, she is researching the idea of the 'use of *Tantric Yoga* in modern psychotherapy. I would like to know about that. I would like to meet her again and build a good repertoire with her.'

Rolf shot back, 'So would I, my friend, so would I. She is not an easy catch, mind you. I have been playing music with her for some time and she has always been very friendly and respectful but always avoids intimacy artfully. You are most welcome to try your luck, you never know.'

He continued, 'By the way, 'Tantric Yoga' is not a cult; it is an ancient Hindu philosophy and a procedure for achieving a state of non-sexual orgasmic union between the Guru and his disciple. Great minds in the middle ages, Muslim scholars like Al Beyruni, Firdausi, Sheikh Sadie etc. and even the Persian prophet, Zarathustra, all scoured the ancient Vedic scriptures for wisdom and ideas. Even the later-day philosophers and poets like Rumi, Omar Khoums, Nietzsche, Jung and a host of others, in one way or another, had recourse to *Sanatan Tantra Yoga*, practiced by Hindu *Yogis* to seek an acceptable answers to the queries – the 'meaning of life' and the 'origin of consciousness.''

Rolf's definition of *Tantric Yoga* was fascinating, but for me it didn't hold water. I failed to fathom out how a non-sexual relationship could be orgasmic. I thought , perhaps the post-Freudian youths, like me, were so pre-occupied with the reality of sex and orgasm that, the age-old Hindu dictum of achieving orgasmic pleasure without sex was antithetical. I thought I may appear stupid to him for the time being if I expressed my ignorance of such an esoteric Indian philosophy, but if I didn't, I would remain a fool for ever.

When he paused briefly, as he always did while giving long sermons, I asked,

'Could you please explain the meaning and essence of the *Tantric Yoga* in layman's language?'

He answered my question with another one, 'Do you know anything about Dr Timothy Leary's counter culture, i.e., the cult he has created in recent time?'

'No, not much I am afraid.' I answered nonchalantly, 'But like most young men of my generation, I was also desperately seeking for the meaning and purpose of life. Being in the midst of this counter culture I had to read his latest book on the psychedelic experience and his philosophy of 'turn on, tune in and drop out', elaborated in that book with the same title. I borrowed it from a friend. It was a good read but the idea of achieving conciseness using psychedelic drug for 'turning on' was not my cup of tea. I found lots of 'mumbo jumbo' in his writings.'

'I am impressed that you've read the book. But I am afraid you read it quite superficially', Rolf said,

'Did you know that he took the idea from the Tibetan Book of the Dead? That book advocated a way of achieving new realms of consciousness, first of all, by completely emptying the mind, then by conditioning it i.e., 'tuning in', through mental and physical *yoga* and finally, by maintaining the statuesque, i.e. by dropping out'. Dr Leary advocated that, the 'turning on' phase was best achieved by using psychedelic drugs such as LSD. The *Tantric* philosophy, on the other hand, promoted the idea of achieving a clear state of mind through meditation and not medication. Such meditation needs to be structured and disciplined, as practised by the ancient Indian saints and more recently by present day *gurus*, following the guidelines in their scriptures.'

We decided to have a discussion with Susan Hill on this topic at a convenient time in the future. It was an unspoken ploy between two of us to get her engaged with us somehow. It was very late when we parted company. Rolf bid me goodnight and said with a mischievous smile,

'Now that you have achieved a clean slate, and your mind is clear of the illness, perhaps we might go to London one of these days. A few of Rembrandt's masterpieces are on temporary display at the National Gallery. The people of Louvre museum do not want their treasures out of their home for too long, so we have to make it pretty soon.'

I couldn't afford the time and luxury of accompanying Rolf for his pilgrimage to the National Gallery. I apologised to him, 'Perhaps another time. I have too much on my plate these days.'

Working on my thesis became my top priority. I remembered the 'words of wisdom' bestowed upon me by the Ceylonese chap I met and despised for his dictum, 'study's' for degree's sake'. I wondered if my starry notion of 'science for sciences' sake' had changed and acquiring a degree had become a priority for me.

Having got rid of my so-called 'fever' I felt quite relieved and relaxed. When I took leave of him well after midnight, the word, 'thanks' slipped out of my mouth and I could see the gloat in his face when he said,

'Why thank me, I didn't do anything.'

⁌

I focussed my attention to my academic commitments with renewed enthusiasm now that I had overcome my so called "sickness". I remembered Assad's advice, 'play hard and work hard'. However, intensive academic work, to which I was ill-accustomed, eventually told upon my mental health. I needed a break, perhaps an exciting adventurous holiday abroad. I thought it would be a shame to have come all the way to England from a remote corner of the Indian subcontinent and to miss out the opportunity of visiting mainland Europe, just twenty five miles away across the English Channel.

I suggested a grand European tour to two of my buddies - Akram Bhatti, a chartered accountant and the proud owner of a Ford Escort and, my flatmate Aziz Qureshi who had the enthusiasm and organisational ability for such activities. We needed a fourth companion to share the cost, making the trip in Akram's car economically viable. Of course, we had to share the cost of petrol and food. We enlisted Mahboob Khan, a fellow Bengali speaking East Pakistani post-grad. He joined the tour party on the condition that he would only share the cost and do nothing else.

I was in charge of navigation, for which I had no experience whatsoever. However, for this duty I had to occupy the front passenger seat, which allowed me the advantage of a better view of the scenery. I followed the wisdom of great thinkers of the ancient world, "the success of a journey is not in its end, but in the journey itself". I conducted my navigation with the help of a medium size map of Western Europe and a small compass. My philosophy was that the road will show the way. When we got hopelessly lost we stopped and asked people for directions, mostly using our made-up sign language, to a campsite for which we knew the name and the address.

We had an enjoyable fortnight, visiting a host of Western European Capital cities. We slept in a tent in various campsites and cooked our communal evening meals and breakfast on a portable gas cooker. I managed to have a brief visit to The Louvre in Paris and the *Rijks museum* of fine art in Amsterdam. My fellow travellers were not interested in such futile activities; instead they went out on city tours. In the evenings we had the opportunity to savour a bit of infamous Parisian night life at Pigalle and the red-light district in Amsterdam.

I felt the urge to visit art galleries in preference to places of both general and historical importance whenever I could. I believed this unusual interest had taken root in my psyche as a result of my close association with Rolf. I knew that descriptions of the Eiffel Tower in Paris or the canals of Amsterdam or the amazing cathedral in Cologne would be the last thing he wanted to hear.

More than three weeks had gone since we'd set out on our travels. I was enjoying the excitement of visiting new places, living in a tent with three others, cooking food, and often after losing our ways, eventually finding our destination. However, time to time I did spare a thought for poor Rolf, imagining him to be miserable and at a loss for things to do without me. Since I had visited two of Rolf's temples of culture in mainland Europe, there would be something interesting for us to talk about, I thought.

Two days after our return I was still recovering from the ordeal of an unplanned camping holiday abroad. I was leisurely helping Aziz prepare our evening meal of mincemeat curry and rice, and thinking of dropping in at Rolf's after dinner As we were about to serve ourselves dinner, there was a familiar knock at the door. I immediately knew who it was. Muttering – "think of the devil", I ushered Rolf in without showing any surprise, as if I'd been expecting him. I said with an expression of delight,

'You couldn't have come at a better time, my friend. We are about to have our evening meal.' Rolf was apologetic and said,

'Sorry to barge in at this inconvenient time. I never know if you have anything called dinnertime! Anyway, I shall be off now, and call in another time. Enjoy your meal, boys.'

He was about to leave when I said, 'On the contrary, you have come at exactly the right time. You are either fortunate or clever to catch us having our meal. According to our custom, if a guest unexpectedly drops in at meal time it is incumbent upon the host to share his food with him.'

'It's a very interesting custom. And now that I know about it, I will probably visit you regularly around this time.' Rolf said with a cheeky smile.

'But remember, if you start coming too often at meal times you will be considered a family member and not a guest. You will then be expected to share the cost and the labour.' I quipped.

It was Rolf's first experience of a real home-cooked curry meal, and a very hot one at that. He consumed a huge quantity of rice with the mincemeat curry. Occasionally he paused from eating to wipe his nose and eyes. Perspiration stood out on his forehead.

We ate our meal in the kitchen as we didn't have the luxury of a dining room or even a dining area. After the meal I asked if the curry experience had been painful.

'On the contrary my friend, it was a high adventure in the culinary field for me. Now I know why you are addicted to rice and curry. It is very satisfying. Rather too satisfying not to feel relaxed and lethargic.' Rolf answered.

I took the opportunity to give him a lecture on the effect of rice on human mind,

'Did you know that Friedrich Nietzsche understood the psyche of the Indian people without even undertaking a tour of that country or even embarking on a gastronomic adventure with curry and rice? He attributed 'the spread of Buddhism', not the origin, mind, to the excessive and almost exclusive reliance of Indians, *en masse,* on rice. This, according to him, led to a general loss of vigour and discontent with existence. He then went on to stipulate that, it also triggered weird imaginations culminating into the emergence of great, and at times bizarre philosophical ideas and weird religious rituals and antics.'

I knew Nietzsche had left hardly any culture or civilization untouched in his many books. His comments and analyses are literary masterpieces, but not gospels. I knew Rolf was a great admirer of Nietzsche and knew a lot more about him and his books than I did. So I didn't wish to continue a discussion on his philosophy on the spread of Buddhism.

Changing the topic, I said,

'Next time we go to London together I shall take you to a really authentic Indian restaurant in Brick Lane for an unforgettable culinary experience. In any case, now that you have had a first-hand experience of the effect of rice, you should eat it ritualistically every day to enhance your imagination and creativity.'

Rolf and I retired to my room from the kitchen with coffee and Aziz excused himself under the pretence of writing an assignment for his coursework. I asked Rolf if he would be interested in listening to a record of a *Sitar* recital by the famous Indian maestro, Ravi Shankar.

With a gesture of disgust he said, 'Please forgive me, but I must decline your offer. Not because it is Indian Classical music. I have been to a recital by him in London not so long ago, and I loved the experience. But my appreciation of music is different from that of most others. I never listen to music from a machine; either I make my own or I attend public performances by famous maestros. By the way, I nearly forgot why I came to see you this evening; it must be the intoxicating effect of your rice. Now I remember. I came to ask you a favour.' In an ironic tone he went on,

'Don't worry my friend; it is nothing to do with the secret agents or borrowing money. I know you hardly have two spare pennies to rub together.' With some apprehension I said,

'Now you have got me worried. You want my help in something which has nothing to do with the law or money: I can't think what on earth I can do for you, mister!'

'It's to do with the security of my possessions in my flat when I'm away.' He said.

I thought – "It's funny, he knows me well enough to understand that I am the wrong person for that." He continued,

'I didn't tell you before because it was rather a last minute decision to go away on this holiday. I was also not sure if I would get the flight booking at such short notice. I was hoping you might help guard my flat when I'm gone. It's not a big deal.'

I said, 'I don't understand what you are talking about. I don't possess a gun; neither do I know how to use one even if you provided me with one. How can I then guard your flat?'

'You don't need any weapons,' he said, 'You can help me simply by moving out of your flat and moving into mine. You would be staying there temporarily as a rent-free tenant. In fact, if you give your landlady advance notice you might be able to save four week's rent and the cost of electricity and gas.'

I was surprised and felt rather awkward that Rolf was asking my help for something which was alien to me and for which I had absolutely no experience. It would be impossible for me to take a responsibility like that, even for a close friend like him. I was a permanently broke student with meagre belongings. To my way of thinking, the ultimate security for material goods is to have none. I often left my room unlocked and joked with friends that if a burglar were to enter my room accidentally he would feel so sorry for me that he might even leave some money on the table when he left.

Of course, saving some money was a matter for serious consideration and a real temptation for someone in my position. But spending four weeks in such a big flat all on my own, bearing the burden of guarding his treasures, was simply out of the question. Besides, I couldn't get it out of my mind that his house might be haunted. I believed ghosts must exist in one form or other; otherwise people wouldn't have kept on saying they'd seen them.

I was taken aback by what felt more like a demand than a request. I couldn't use the excuse that I was going away for a holiday myself as he knew I had just returned from my own tour. When one does not have a genuine excuse to get out of a sticky situation like this, the devil usually provides one. Rolf was waiting for an answer and, the silence, while I tried to come up with some excuse, was unpleasant for both of us, to say the least.

Then I was inspired and came up with an effective excuse,

'I'm not sure you have thought this through before approaching me, Rolf,' I said in a patronizing tone.

He raised his head and looked at me and said in a sombre tone, 'I do not believe there is anything wrong in asking a close friend for a small favour. I do not think this will cause you any inconvenience. Besides, I can't think of anyone else whom I trust and who would be willing to do this for me.'

With my gaze still focused on his face, I said,

'You might be able to fumigate the flat afterwards, but layers of nicotine might cause permanent damage to your paintings. I believe any damage caused by cigarette smoke will not be covered under your insurance policy. Besides, have you considered the fire-hazard? With my addiction to this weed I can't guarantee that I will go to your bathroom every time I have the urge for a smoke.'

I paused to see his reaction and then continued,

'I am happy to stay in your flat, but I must have told you the episode of my ignominious eviction from my previous lodging by an incensed landlady, Mrs Capper. I am convinced, that was because of the fire hazard posed by my smoking in bed. I believe you will not have any piece of mind during your holiday if I looked after your precious belongings, as I cannot possibly put my addiction on hold during your absence.'

Rolf was a bit disheartened but convinced of the unacceptable risk and asked if I had any suggestions. I asked him what he'd done in the past when he went away on holiday.

'I used to give my flat keys to one of the neighbours and asked him to switch on the light in my bedroom at night and switch it off in the morning.'

When I asked him why he couldn't do the same this time round, he replied,

'Times have changed now. The burglars have become a lot cleverer. They know, from the pattern and regularity of house lighting and also from their own intelligence network, if an occupant is away and probably for how long. The 'light trick', according to recent police reports, doesn't work these days. You must have read or heard about the recent surge in artwork theft. My collections are insured against fire and theft. I may get some money back if they're stolen, but how would I ever live without my babies?'

I did not know what to advice. We put on our thinking caps on and sat silently, trying to come up with a way of solving the problem.

Rolf was thinking aloud, 'I know Mack's are living on a shoestring budget. I believe he will seriously consider the possibility of saving a few weeks' rent favourably.'

'Well then, why not ask them to stay in your flat!' I snapped. Rolf paused for a while and said,

'I thought about this possibility earlier, but discarded the idea. I was afraid they might reject the proposition forthwith. I thought – the bitter taste of the past incident, which I narrated to you earlier, could still be lingering on with them. But now that you have concurred with me on this possibility and I cannot see any other alternative, I feel tempted to give it a try. Let's both go to their place and put the proposal to them.'

I didn't have an axe to grind, so I went along to witness the encounter. I had met Mackentyre earlier, after Rolf had accused him of collaborating with an agent to defame him. Then I'd assured him that I was also a victim of the same accusation and had taken it as a misguided outburst from an otherwise quite normal and wise man. I also told him that Rolf did not bear any grudge against him or me.

It was well after dinnertime when we rang the bell of their flat. Mack opened the door and welcomed us in. I had not met his wife before. Rolf apologised for our unscheduled incursion into their privacy so late in the evening and refused to accept the offer of a hot or cold drink. He put forward his proposal directly. Mack and Hana did not reject the idea outright as we had feared they would, but it also came as a complete surprise to them, consequently they couldn't make a snap decision. Mack apologised and went to their bedroom with Hana to discuss the matter. A few minutes later, they agreed to the deal, although they did appear to be a bit apprehensive.

Rolf had mentioned once before that the couple were living on a shoestring budget with a small grant from the Dutch Government. The prospect of saving a few pounds and at the same time helping a friend in need had meant that they reluctantly agreed to move into Rolf's flat for a month. The arrangement suited them as they were already preparing to return to the Netherlands in a couple of months and only had to give one month's notice to their landlady before vacating the flat. They realised that they would be able to save a whole month's rent. The big thing for Rolf was that they were non-smokers. This caused for a small celebration so we all had tea together.

⁂

Symbols in ancient Indian religions were a subject of great interest to Rolf as he believed the clue to the origins of humanity lies hidden in such symbols of ancient cults and religions. He also believed that if deciphered with insight and intelligence, they might lead to an understanding of the origin of consciousness in early mankind. Rolf and Mack began a serious discussion on this topic using terminologies, most probably gleaned from psychology textbooks that I did not understand. Rather than listening to their conversation and feeling stupid, I chatted with Hana. Her personality was quite the opposite of Mack's. She was talkative, inquisitive and a good listener. But I noticed she was hiding a yawn – it was time for her to go to bed; she had to get up early the next morning to work in a shop. I looked at the clock and realized it was late. I stood up and said good night. Despite Rolf's request to hang on for a while and his warning that ghosts might be lurking at the shaded corners of the road leading to my flat at Bradmore Road at this time of the night, I took the risk of facing evil spirits, apologised for leaving unceremoniously and hit the road.

꘏

Rolf went away for his long foreign holiday. My life went on, as always, quite busy and eventful. I bumped into Mack one afternoon and he told me that he had received a card from Rolf and he was well and enjoying himself. I also received one with a picture of Titian's painting, "The Assumption". On the back he simply wrote, "Wish you were here". I often wondered why he visited Venice so regularly, and what did he do there? I wondered if he had a lover or even a wife there. But if he did have somebody like that he would certainly have told me about it. Perhaps he spent the days gazing at paintings of various masters in the museums, art galleries and churches scattered around Venice to get his regular fix. Perhaps he searched for the origin of man in those paintings.

I felt his absence and missed his company, but it was not a big issue. New excitement came in the form of a storybook episode of love, betrayal and reunion between Masud and his beloved wife, Banie. Being the wife of a senior civil servant and the daughter of a retired General she had connections in high places in Pakistan and also within the Pakistani High Commission in London. It was unthinkable that someone of her social standing would visit my flat unaccompanied and uninvited instead of summoning me to her own place. But one afternoon she surprised me beyond measure by doing just that.

She was in a terrible state, incoherent and at times incomprehensible, repeating Masud's name over and over. In floods of tears, she said she desperately needed my help. I offered her my shoulder to cry for a little while. When her weeping was over, she composed herself with some tissue papers. She sat down and appeared a little calmer. Then she narrated the unbelievable story of her predicament.

She wanted me to go to Masud forthwith and persuade him to come to his senses and leave that "bitch", Maggi, and come back to her. She assured me that if he did so, she would forgive his misdemeanours as a bad dream or a bout of sudden madness. She asked me to do that without any delay.

Accordingly, I went to see him at Margaret's flat in Summertown. He was delighted to see me. While talking about his decision to leave his wife he also shed tears, but did not need my shoulder. He opened a can of beer and after a long sip said,

'I have at last found the thing that has eluded me throughout my life. I deluded myself by pretending to be happy and assuming that I was happy with Banie. But now I know what love is; and it has overwhelmed me – body and soul.'

He paused and then recited Robert Burn's famous love poem, "My love is like a red, red rose," changing the words "My bonnie lass" with "my English lass", and ending with the mantra, 'Maggie is my life, Maggie is my death, Maggie is my world.'

I felt a bit embarrassed to hear such romantic claptrap from a mature and serious man with two little boys at home in Pakistan and a lovely wife here pining for him.

Gravely I said, 'I understand your feelings, Masud Bhai, I was the victim of just such an attack of madness not so long ago.'

'Did you say, 'attack of madness?' He retorted in an angry voice, 'You are talking nonsense. Your use of English phrases leaves a lot to be desired, young man. It might have been an attack of craziness in your case with Paula, because it was simply a youthful infatuation. You are not mature enough to know what real love is. But in my case it is neither an attack nor madness. It is a cool-headed decision to erase my past and set sail on a boat with Maggie for an eternal journey and to face the challenges of a new life together and to find our destiny.'

Masud was not drunk, except perhaps on love. Sensing the purpose of my visit, he said,

'Please go and tell Banie, that the old Masud is dead and buried. She must go back to Pakistan and seek her own destiny in a new life with a new man and with her two little boys.'

I couldn't believe what I was hearing. I felt as if I were in a theatre taking part in a Shakespearian tragedy. Maggie stopped by briefly to say hello and to give us some tea and biscuits. I was sure she was, by then, aware that I was working as Baine's agent.

Masud's personality was such that I couldn't continue with what I wanted to say. I knew that the last thing he would accept was advice or persuasion from someone his junior and, as he saw it, a learner in the course of life and a mere apprentice in the business of love.

Holding me by the shoulders with both hands, he looked at me in the eye and said, 'You are just like my younger brother, and also a good friend. I need your help at this moment. I want you to do everything you can to pursued Banie to go back home. Promise you will do this for me?'

I found myself between the devil and the deep blue sea. He knew the game he was playing. He changed the subject before I felt obliged to make a false promise, and said,

'By the way, if you are free, why not join me at the Town hall tomorrow? The Afro-Caribbean society is holding a cheese and wine party there. Maggie does not like reggae or funky music, and neither do I. But I had to promise a friend that I shall join him there for a drink.'

That was a good moment for me to escape the awkward situation and I took my leave, saying,

'I have an appointment and must leave you now. I will see you tomorrow.'

As I was leaving I looked into his eyes and realised that he was not planning to go to the Afro-Caribbean society's event the next day and that he did not expect me to be there either.

The next day was a Friday. I casually flicked through the pages of the Vide Mecum at the departmental common room. I noticed that there was indeed an Afro-Caribbean function that evening at the town hall. So Masud was not bluffing after all. But, it was out of question that he would let Maggie out of his sight for the whole or part of that evening. It was also most unlikely that an aspiring connoisseur of classical music like me would be interested in loud Afro-Caribbean beat music.

In the evening I went to have my dinner at the *adda khana* at the back of the Moti Mahal, hoping to have a good time with my mates. For some queer reason that evening, members who were usually very vocal and experts in stoking and maintaining heated arguments until they reached boiling point, were absent. I wondered if they knew something I didn't! I escaped from the company of two dull acquaintances, discussing the cost of living in England and how to economise.

I found myself at the entrance of the Town Hall, forking out five shillings for the Afro-Caribbean party with the faint hope that Masud might not be telling porky pies after all. Cheese chunks and pickled onions inside wooden sticks, sticks of crunchy celery pieces, crisps and dry biscuits were laid out on tables around the hall. A huge Hi-Fi audio system was blasting out beat music, a fusion of pop and rock, from the centre of the stage. Boys and girls were dancing in the centre of the floor.

In my subconscious I was expecting to see Masud there. My thought of him evaporated instantly when instead, I noticed Rolf. I could hardly believe my eyes when I saw him at the centre of the hall, dancing like a crazy young man.

Now that I'd located Rolf I need look no further for company and amusement in that crowded place. With a few pieces of cheese in the stick and some crisps and biscuits on a paper plate in one hand and a glass of drink in the other, I took up a seat in a position where I could watch people dancing and, at the same time, partially hid myself from Rolf, in case he got embarrassed.

I was amazed and greatly amused to see Rolf dancing with a slim and beautiful African girl with braided hair, doing his utmost to copy the funky dancing of the young Afro-Caribbean people. Rolf danced like a madman, or someone who has completely lost his inhibitions owing to drugs or alcohol. He was twisting and gyrating, moving his hips, and at times, holding the girl by her waist and turning and twisting her around him. The pair of them monopolised the dance floor to such an extent that one by one the other couples moved back to watch the hilarious and engaging performance of this middle-aged man and his young partner. Both of them appeared oblivious to the presence of the watching crowd and lost in their frenzy.

I found it very hard to believe that my wise and mature mentor, Rolf, would make such a public display of silliness here. Taking part in a silly walk along St. Giles Avenue was a different thing altogether and was quite acceptable. But this is sheer madness. However, when the music stopped there was applause from the spectators. Rolf and the girl, holding each other's hand, took a bow and he suddenly turned to the girl and landed a kiss on her cheek. She was visibly embarrassed but did not lose her cool and pecked his cheek in return. A new piece of music started and Rolf asked her to carry on dancing with him. She declined and headed for the washroom to powder her nose.

Once she'd gone, I was drawn towards Rolf like a piece of iron to a magnet. I congratulated him on his masterful dancing, asked him about the girl and commented as a way of flattery that she was lucky to have a partner like him. He beckoned me out of the crowded room towards the entrance to the hall. I lit a cigarette and waited while he went away to fetch his dance partner. He came back with her after a while and introduced me to Afariva Mathe, a Nigerian undergrad and a fresher at Somerville College, studying social sciences.

In an unusually and unnecessarily loud voice Rolf asked Afariva if she would like to go back to the dance floor for some more fun. In the meantime, her friend, who was also an African student, came up and informed her that it was time to head back to their hall of residence and that she would prefer to walk together with her friend back to their college. Rolf led Afariva away to a corner to have a private conversation.

His voice was so loud that, despite a considerable distance between us, I could hear what he was saying,

'There is an African art exhibition at the fine art museum in London next weekend. I would be delighted if you were to accompany me to the event. It will be an opportunity to share your thoughts and interpretation on the background and the subject of the paintings.'

I did not hear what she said in reply, but noticed that she was in a hurry to leave him to join her waiting friend.

Rolf handed her a note saying, 'This is my telephone number. Please let me know as soon as you can.'

He kissed her on the cheek and said good night and returned to me.

Still shouting, he yelled, 'How the hell did you know I would be here?'

'We are looking for the same thing and this must be a common hunting ground.' I said in a sarcastic tone.

'Can you speak a bit louder?' he shouted.

I got a bit concerned, he might have become a bit deaf during his holiday in Venice or perhaps the loud music inside the hall had damaged his hearing.

I said in a loud voice, 'You thought you will get away with it. But I caught you, didn't I?'

'Are you surprised to find me here with my girlfriend? 'He asked.

'Not a bit my friend, not a bit, I am not even surprised to see you dancing like Gene Kelly on drugs. But I cannot understand how a man with such a sensitive ear and taste for fine classical music could stand such loud music for so long!'

Suddenly he remembered and took the rubber plugs from his ears, muttering, 'You do not have to tell me about the perils of loud music. I thought about this and remembered to bring my ear plugs with me. Otherwise, the music at the hall would have made me go bananas. The funny thing is that I forgot until now that I was wearing them.'

Crossing the High Street, we walked passed Carfax Tower, along Cornmarket Street and ended up at the fork leading to the Woodstock and Banbury Roads at the end of St. Giles. We were about to decouple to go to our respective abodes along different routes when Rolf pleaded with me to let him come to my flat for a cup of coffee. I knew it was not coffee he was after, he simply wanted to talk. I was in no mood to talk about his childish exploits at this time of night. Besides, I had already done my bit for humanity the day before and endured a humiliating monologue from Masud. But Rolf was my best buddy, perhaps the one and only when it comes to common interests and respect for each other. I couldn't bid him good night unceremoniously when he needed to share his joy of new-found love with me. Inside, we made ourselves comfortable on my lumpy sofa and I put a shilling in the meter to get the gas fire going. We looked at each other and I broke the silence,

'I know you really don't want coffee, now let us talk.'

'What about?' He asked.

'Well to start with, you can tell me when and how you met Afariva? I said.

'I met her at the Bodleian library.' Rolf started, 'We were looking for similar books and articles, we got acquainted and started to talk. One thing led to another, and we became friends. You saw this for yourself tonight. She is also my dancing partner and most probably going to be my soul mate and girlfriend. You never know!'

With a mischievous smile, I said, 'You are a lucky man, she must be talented and, surely charming and beautiful, perhaps as beautiful as the queen of Sheba, and surely she dances like a butterfly. Sheba was exquisitely beautiful according to the scriptures or legend – you probably know that.' Rolf smiled and said,

'Your skill in flattery has often pleased me and I like what I am hearing now. My gut feeling is that she will not betray me, unless of course, the agents intervene. Now tell me, frankly what do you think of her?'

'I shall tell you what you really want to hear. Like it or not, for most people from the Indian subcontinent, female beauty is primarily associated with skin colour, the fairer the skin, the prettier the woman. But, there again, a lover looks for other attributes and sometimes even invents some, believing them to be true. Such is the name of the game, my friend. Let me translate one famous Bengali poem by Tagore, exalting his new found black beauty – "Dark? No matter how dark her skin is, I have seen her most beautiful dark eyes, like those of a deer." How does it sound?'

Rolf was charmed by my adulations of his girlfriend and visibly relishing the moment of glory when he said,

'I must commend you for noticing the most wonderful attribute of this girl which has both fascinated and captivated me – those lovely dark eyes!'

It was late when Rolf finally left, without having had any coffee, but with a smile on his face and a sound of confidence and satisfaction in his voice when he bade me goodnight.

6

Magic of the Shaman

A Real-life drama in the life of my mentor, Masud was unfolding, but I could ill afford the time to act as the "piggy in the middle" in the estrangement and enmity between my friend and his once beloved darling wife Banie. Unfortunately, I didn't seem to have much choice but to get embroiled in it. I had a premonition that a new demand on my precious time was imminent and in case it turned out to be true, I did a lot of serious academic work over the weekend.

Come Sunday I was pleased to have made good progress with my studies and sure enough, as I had feared, on the Monday morning, Banie came straight to my corner of the laboratory in the Engineering Department. She couldn't find me at my desk as I was in the library on the 6th floor, but she hunted me down there and demanded that I went with her to the 'Dear Friend' Chinese restaurant right in front of the department building, behind the church. After ordering a small meal for two, she expressed her disappointment in a peevish tone,

'I've been waiting for news from you all over the weekend. What had happened to you?' I apologized profusely,

'I meant to come and tell you about my meeting with Masud Bhai, but I had a deadline to meet for the submission of a paper on my research for a conference presentation ...'

Before I could continue, she shot back, in a dramatic tone and with an angry face,

'I'm nearly dying and all you are concerned with is your bloody paper and deadlines! What has happened to your commitment to our friendship? Can't you understand that I sought your help as a desperate friend in need?'

She paused for a moment, not particularly waiting for a response but to allow the gravity of her predicament to sink in me, and then said in a commanding tone,

'Now tell me what happened.' I replied without any prelude or hesitation,

'In my opinion Masud Bhai is afflicted with a bad bout of mental illness. He is in need of some very strong medicine. However, you need to be patient.' After a brief pause I added with conviction,

'Some form of exorcism will surely help to wean him off the influence of that witch.'

'Don't you worry about that my dear friend,' she said, 'I shall administer stronger and stronger medicine until I succeed in exorcising the devil out of the stupid man. I will surely get him out of the claws of that bitch. But I will need your help to do it.'

I couldn't, for the life of me, guess what was in her mind. Apprehensively, I said,

'But Banie Bhabhi, Masud Bhai is like my elder brother. He always looks down on me as an inexperienced immature young man in matters concerning the heart. He wouldn't even talk to me about this affair. How will I be able to help you administer your medicine?'

Gazing at my worried face she smiled widely, leaned forward, touched my hand and whispered in Urdu which means, 'Don't worry, my dear young friend; I won't ask you to do anything which is too difficult for you or will be detrimental to your relationship with him.'

Carefully taking a small envelope out from her handbag, she leaned across the table and handed it over to me saying,

'This is my suicide note to Masud. You must describe, in the most earnest fashion and passionate tone, about my mental state; how I am constantly talking of ending my miserable and meaningless life, suggesting that it is even possible I may not be alive tomorrow. You must try to convince him that he should come back to me immediately, before it is too late, at least for the sake of his two darling little boys, if not for me.'

I knew in my heart of hearts that this subterfuge wouldn't hold water. Masud would simply disregard it and see through the charade. He would recognise it as emotional blackmail. It was a very difficult task she had given me to do but I had to do it, just in case she wasn't bluffing. So reluctantly I made my way to Maggi's flat that evening and knocked on her door. She informed me that Masud wasn't in, and was most probably still at the library.

I didn't stop and hurried to the Bodleian and caught him coming out of the door. He greeted me with a wide smile and a friendly voice,

'Good to see you Mr 'go-between' friend; what news have you brought me this time?'

I didn't like the way he belittled me with his sarcastic comment, although what he was implying was close to the truth. I responded to his question in a concerned tone and with a grave expression,

'Can we go to the coffee house on Cornmarket Street to talk?'

'I have a better idea', he said enthusiastically. Let's go to the Lamb and Flag at the corner of St. Giles. I can quench my thirst there with some holy water. The pub also serves freshly made Brazilian coffee.'

At the pub, after a big gulp from the glass of beer and without the usual niceties he looked at me and said,

'Now talk, that's what you came here to do, isn't it?'

I gave him the envelope and said,

'Banie Bhabi asked me to give this to you in person. I don't know what she has written but I could see from her mental state that the situation is dire. Please take this seriously; otherwise something terrible might happen. I am just doing my duty as your younger brother and well-wisher. Please do not forget you have left two lovely children with their grandparents in Pakistan.'

I could see that he felt insulted, after all who was I, being an immature youth, to give him such a condescending counsel. It was patently obvious to him that I was lying about not knowing the content of the note. He took out another cigarette, lit it very carefully and gave a long puff after downing another gulp of beer. He leaned back on his chair and casually opened the envelope. He read it with a deadpan face and put it back in his pocket.

After straightening his back and looking at me for a moment, he said flatly,

'I know you mean well and that you have reluctantly become embroiled in our affairs. But you must understand that I know my wife better than anybody else. So, don't worry about this matter. If you must, just tell her that I said, "I am doing what my conscience dictated and she should do the same with her life. If she wants to end it without any thought about her boys then I wish her success".' There was nothing more to be said and as we parted company he shouted after me,

'Best of luck for Banie; I am afraid I can't wish you success.'

Next day, during my morning coffee break at the departmental common room I saw someone reading the local newspaper. I borrowed it to briefly skim the headlines for any news about the suicide or attempted suicide of the spouse of a foreign student on any of the pages. There was no such news. Of course, I hadn't expected to find anything, but I looked for this anyway, just in case.

Initially, in a weird sense, it had been quite exciting for me to be a 'go-between' and try to help my estranged friends to get back together. After my initial experience as a 'middle man' I realised how difficult the task was and that it would be wiser in the future to avoid such a futile and thankless role like a plague. I was getting tired of being an unwitting party to the games estranged married couples sometimes play.

I was expecting Banie Bhabi to arrive at my door the next morning with a plan B. But before she could get hold of me, a severe bout of flu did. I managed to walk down to her flat late morning and dropped a note through her letter box noting –

"I have contracted flu, which I believe is highly contagious, so I will be in quarantine for a few days."

I was bed-ridden with fever for three days, sneezing, coughing and spluttering and desperately pining for visitors and sympathy. Dilder came to find out if I was still alive since he had not seen me at the *Moti Mahal* for the last few evenings. Observing my condition, he took his leave as quickly as possible under the pretext of an appointment. I was pretty sure he was afraid of infection and didn't want to take any unnecessary risk. He did, however, offer to inform the University welfare office.

The rumour started like this – 'Rafi had contracted an infectious flu'. Friends thinking of visiting me were cautioned by one another to consider taking all necessary precautions to avoid contracting and spreading the disease. Therefore, none of my mates from the *adda khana* showed up. Even Banie Bhabi stayed away, despite her announced suicide attempt! That was probably a blessing, and for the moment I had relief from her schemes.

The news spread like the Chinese whisper: Rafi has a cold; he is suffering from flu; a highly contagious one at that; he is on his deathbed. I don't think it went as far as "he is dead". The world appeared to have turned its back on me. I was feeling very ill but also sad, thinking of the mental torture my friends were enduring for not being able to visit me in my time of need. I imagined people were waiting for the funeral date, hoping to rid themselves of the guilt of not having had the courage to risk becoming infected with the virus by visiting me.

My good friend Rolf, however, was not deterred by these

rumours and came knocking at my door as soon as he heard the news. He said with the familiar smirk,

'I heard from one of your admirers, Reza Huque that you are dying, so I hurried here to take the last confession of your sins before it is too late and the undertakers beat me to it.'

In a feeble and croaking voice with my eyes watering and nose running, I said. 'Very good of you my friend, I am hanging on to life by the skin of my teeth, waiting for the last rites from you, a non-believer and a Jew. That's just what I need before I say goodbye to this world and embark on the journey to meet my maker. I wonder, how Reza knew about my condition, he didn't come to visit me.'

Rolf took out a box of tissues from his plastic bag and said,

'Please, get rid of that toilet roll and use these. You should understand that there are a few things in life on which you cannot economise and tissue paper is one of them. I grant you, toilet paper might serve the purpose, but it is made for the exclusive use of another part of the body. Decorum forbids its use to wipe a running nose.'

After thanking him kindly for his advice, I said,

'Now, tell me, as a doctor, are you going to help me recover from this debilitating flu? Or, as a good friend will you hasten my demise to end the suffering?'

Rolf snapped, 'You have made two mistakes in one sentence. First of all, although I completed and passed my medical exams, I am not a fully qualified doctor and I've never practiced medicine. It's a long story for another time.

'The second mistake is your wrong self-diagnosis. You haven't got flu. What you have got is a bad bout of a condition known as 'hay fever' caused by high levels of pollen in the air. Some people are more susceptible than others. In extreme cases it appears to be flu. The fever is partly a psychosomatic effect.'

'Whatever it is, either cure me or kill me.' I shot back.

'Under the present circumstances, the first option will be easier than the second. There is no allopathic medicine to cure hay fever. Nevertheless, I have used homeopathic medicine quite effectively for such ailments.' I expressed my surprise,

'You practice homeopathy in this modern scientific age!'

'I have always been an admirer of the 18th century visionary healer, Samuel Hahnemann,' he said, 'and like him, I also believe modern allopathic medicine does more harm than good. I have been practicing homeopathy for almost 10 years now. It is more or less a hobby and is certainly not for earning a living. You may regard it as one of my research projects.'

'Where and when did you qualify in this field,' I wondered.

'Great artisans of the world don't need a paper certificate to practice their trades. Homeopathy, for your information, is more of an art form than a scientific procedure. Anyway, now I have to say "Auf wiedersehen". I will be back tomorrow morning with some pills. I guarantee that you will be fighting fit in a day or two.'

Rolf left and I felt relieved that I no longer had to suffer his overbearing presence. Being of a scientific mind and the son of a medical practitioner, I could never trust in homeopathic treatment. I found it difficult to tolerate Rolf bragging about his prowess in that regard. Miserable and depressed, I took to my bed late in the afternoon with a hot cup of soup and a couple of aspirin.

My flatmate, Aziz, like my other friends, also believed that I had contracted a deadly influenza infection and was very cautious about direct contact with me. He made a large pot of soup and announced that it was ready and I had to help myself from the kitchen in his absence. As soon as I finished my evening meal of more soup and a chunk of bread, I heard a familiar knock at the door. I wasn't expecting him until the next day, but Rolf couldn't wait that long. He wanted me to get better as soon as possible. When I opened the door he barged in, forsaking any formality or protocol and parked his bottom on the old sofa.

I was in a reclining position on my bed. When we were face to face he produced a small bottle containing white pills from his jacket pocket and said,

'You are very lucky. I had the right medicine in my box. This is left over from some I bought for another of my patients. I buy these from a specialist homeopathic shop in London during my occasional visits to the art galleries and concert halls there.'

He picked up the bottle from the table and handed it over to me saying,

'Start by taking two tablets now and continue by taking two at four-hourly intervals. I can guarantee that you will be amazed by the result.'

I didn't know what to say. No way was I going to take his pills, but I couldn't say so to his face. Instead, I thanked him politely for his concern about my wellbeing and for bringing me the medicine. Jokingly I asked if I had to pay him a consultancy fee.

Rolf said, 'I told you before I do not practice homeopathy professionally. But if you like you may pay for the cost of the pills, after your full recovery. It isn't much.'

He took the pill bottle from me and poured two white pills on to my right palm and asked me to swallow them then and there.

On the pretence of needing some water to swallow them, I went to the kitchen drank a bit of water and threw the pills down the drain. He took leave early because of a prior appointment, but promised to come back the next day in the afternoon to celebrate my recovery from the illness once and for all and to take me out for a walk.

I was boiling with rage at the audacity of this crazy friend of mine. How could he ever think that I would trust him and swallow such unknown pills? For all that I knew these could be poison. Taking such medicine from a man who was not a qualified homeopathic doctor is tantamount to believing in witchcraft by shamans or taking a talisman from holy men. From what little I knew, homeopathic medicines are composed of poisonous substances in small doses.

I was cursing myself for being associated with this time-wasting, over-bearing crazy man. I pondered if the famous old French quotation, "A fool always finds a greater fool to admire him", could also be applicable with the word 'fool' replaced by the word 'crackpot', otherwise why would I be attracted to him? I decided to do all I could to avoid regular contact with him in the future.

The thought that played in my head – "He was already trying to embroil me into his phantom world inhabited by secret agents in a grand international conspiracy, and now he wants to harm me with these pills which he claims are homeopathic medicine. Perhaps he thought I would be cured with faith healing. He must be out of his mind, otherwise why would a properly educated medical doctor, albeit a non-practicing one, resort to psychoanalysis and then leave everything and start practising homeopathy?

I thought perhaps he has a propensity for showing off his diverse talents to impress people, particularly young girls. I even started to doubt his claims of being medically qualified or of having a certificate to practice psychoanalysis. Maybe these were simply lies or perhaps figments of his imagination which he had started to believe to be true. Possibly he supported such false claims by reading around the subjects. Perhaps he was a conman! My imagination got the better of me. I took the pills out of the bottle and flushed them all down the toilet and threw the bottle in the bin. I was angry, agitated and sweating. I made myself yet another cup of soup and after drinking some felt a bit calmer.

I lay down on my bed and thought about Rolf, and his face appeared before me – beaming. There was no trace of insincerity in it. His smile and enthusiasm now appeared to be quite genuine. He had taken so much trouble to deliver the pills to me! There was absolutely no reason why he should wish to impress me with his healing prowess. He must therefore be a true friend and a sincere well-wisher. He rushed here to see me while others stayed away. I felt ashamed at what I had thought of him in a fit of unprovoked anger.

My anger and anguish disappeared and I visualized his smiling face beaming through the gloom, reassuring me that I would be well soon. I felt closer to him than ever before. I was sure that from his past experience with homeopathic medicine he genuinely believed and wished that I would be on my feet within days if not hours. I felt I had not thanked him properly for his kindness. I needed to try his medicine even if it was only to prove to him that the practice of homeopathy was like witchcraft or faith healing, which had been replaced by advanced scientifically tried and tested allopathic drugs.

But, alas, it was too late, I had flushed the pills down the toilet, and he was coming to see me the following afternoon to find out if his medicine had worked as he expected it would. I was feeling very uncomfortable about the whole situation – "what would I tell him when he comes to see me tomorrow?"

I would not be able to tell him that I had flushed the pills down the toilet. That would hurt him beyond measure and end our friendship. On the other hand, how could I tell him that I had taken his pills when he was going to ask me about it looking at me and waiting for an answer? I was not used to telling white lies and he was a psychologist to catch me out easily. But it seemed I had no alternative but to take a chance of pretention.

Still coughing and sneezing, using the tissues from the box he left for me, I hit the bed and pulled the quilt over my head, hoping I might feel more at ease about concocting a lie in the morning after a good night's sleep.

I had a bad night, often waking up and worried about the

impending encounter with Rolf and at times, having nightmares of being caught red handed telling a lie. I got up fairly early and decided to go ahead and tell him that I had taken the pills as prescribed. I had to have some tangible proof that I have taken the pills which could only be a visible display of my quick recovery and cheerfulness. Normally I have a bowl of cereal with milk for breakfast. That morning I made an exception and cooked myself a hot breakfast with a fried egg and a grilled tomato and couple of pieces of toasted bread. I ate my breakfast without difficulty, unlike the previous few mornings when my appetite had all but disappeared. I lay in bed the whole morning, preparing in my mind how best to act like a cured patient when I would meet Rolf that afternoon. I was preparing the smile and the posture that I would have to use to convey the effectiveness of the pills. By keeping a straight face and not being nervous I might be able to avoid lying. I hadn't had a bath for about 4 days. I thought a good bath would make me feel and look better. With special permission from my landlady, I took a long bath without having to pay an extra charge. I also treated myself to a shave to get rid of my stubble. I put on a clean shirt and trousers. I finished off the remainder of Aziz's soup for lunch while waiting for Rolf.

At about ten minutes past four in the afternoon I heard the familiar knocks at the door. It is uncanny how the strength and timing of the knocks becomes a signature tune for the person behind the door. I opened the door forcing a broad smile, pretending to be happy to be cured of the hay fever. I greeted him,

'Welcome my good old medicine man. It goes to show that some homeopathic medicine does work miracles after all. Now you deserve a hot cup of tea.'

Rolf looked at me with a gleeful expression on his face, sat down and said,

'I would prefer a cup of coffee, if you have some. It is incredible to see such a drastic change in you during a span of merely 24 hours. How many of the pills have you taken so far?'

To avoid answering I pretended not to have heard the question and went to the kitchen, and came back to tell him I had run out of milk and asked if black coffee would do? He nodded with an affirmative nod. I brought him a cup of coffee and told him that I was very keen to know the origin of homeopathic medicine and its history. I was not really at all interested, but I knew he wouldn't miss the opportunity of giving me a lecture, and in so doing forget everything else, thereby saving me telling any direct lies.

'I have an appointment to see somebody at the library so I have to take leave of you now,' Rolf said, 'But if you are really interested in this fascinating history and the origin of homeopathy I will have to have a long session with you another time. I just dropped in to see if my medicine has worked, and you have, as I see, all but recovered. I am very pleased.'

He left after advising me to continue taking the pills and to take a walk in the fresh air. After he'd gone I felt elated, believing that I had been able to pull the wool over his eyes, despite him being a so-called qualified psychoanalyst. At the same time, I felt remorse because as a good friend I should have told him the truth – I had recovered without his pills. I was not pretending any more, I really did feel almost completely well. I wondered if he had performed some sort of exorcism on me! Perhaps this was the so called "faith healing"! I was itching to tell him that, I had hoodwinked him into thinking that homeopathy worked as well as modern medicine.

Next day, in the late afternoon, I rang Rolf from my lab and said in an elated tone, 'Good morning my good friend. It was indeed a magic of the *Shaman,* the medicine men in remote areas back home. Your pills have not only cured my illness, but also have given me a big appetite. I am thinking of going out, hunting for some good nosh somewhere. Your company in this gastronomic adventure is very desirable.' Rolf quipped,

'I knew for sure you would soon be cured. I am pleased, but what I didn't know is the side-effect of my medicine – creating an appetite. I shall make a note of that.

'Anyway, I have no hesitation to join you in your hunt. Have you any thoughts on the location?'

I didn't answer his question and said, 'Please hurry, I am waiting for you in my flat,' and rang off. After getting ready I occasionally peeped through the window for any sign of the "great medicine man". I joined him on the pavement as soon as I spotted him, sparing him the trouble of coming down the steps and thereby saving a bit of time.

His first question was, 'Which way are we heading for this culinary adventure?'

'You are a wise man of the West. You choose the destination and let me have the pleasure of a surprise.' I answered.

Rolf started walking and I kept up with him as best I could, he hardly ever walked at a leisurely pace. After crossing the Banbury road and the Woodstock road we hit Walton Street. I thought he was taking me to the *Dil Dunia*; the newly-opened 3rd Indian restaurant in the city, which we'd, visited a couple of times as a change from the *Moti Mahal*. Since I was not expecting to go out for an Indian curry that afternoon, he might have thought that it would be a big surprise for me.

When he walked passed the *'Dil Dunia'* I was a few steps behind him and ran to catch up with him and said,

'Now that you have brought me to the edge of the city and appear to be heading towards the countryside, I'm not sure I am going to like the surprise, I should point out that a hungry Bengali is a dangerous man. Cannibalism isn't unheard of back home'

At that Rolf came clean, 'Truth be told, we are heading towards the Trout Inn. I was going to surprise you but your threat is a bit scary so I assure you this will be a surprise for you, not only because of the destination, but also because of the journey. I believe you had been to this public house once before, but I am sure you have never walked there and never dined there.'

Flabbergasted, I said, 'Do you know how far that place is?'

Rolf quipped, 'It's about three miles from here, so we will be there in about forty minutes. It is only half-past-six, and the sun does not set till about half past nine. So what's the hurry? As you know, the bigger the appetite the better is the taste of food.'

There was no point in arguing with him. Besides, I had asked him to make the choice. I might as well enjoy the walk in the midst of pleasant scenery and the company of my healer friend. I lit a cigarette in the hope it would suppress my hunger, and we walked on until we hit a narrow little-used footpath along the river Thames.

I started to enjoy the walk, stopping briefly from time to time; chatting with anglers sitting comfortably on folding chairs along the bank, enquiring if they had caught any fish, or simply exchanging a word or two about the weather. I was surprised to learn that the anglers here caught the fish for sport and not for consumption. I thought - spending hours and hours and a fair bit of money to catch the fish, only to throw them back into the water; what a peculiar sport!

Having caught up with Rolf I complained,

'Would you please slow down a bit? We are supposed to be enjoying a leisurely walk. Have you thought that we could have a heart-felt conversation if you did that? Perhaps you could take the opportunity to give me a lecture on any one of your favourite topics.'

He liked the idea. Reducing his pace, he started a monologue:

'I find the countryside in England, particularly on a sunny summer day, quite enchanting. Its beauty and tranquillity had been immortalized by some great poets and captured in many exquisite paintings by world class masters. I am not a literary man, you will probably know more about romantic poems than me. I know one or two things about paintings. I enjoy reflecting on such English paintings by artists like John Constable, Thomas Gainsborough. Joseph Turner etc. They appreciated and enjoyed the charm and beauty of the English countryside and captured these scenes on canvases for the posterity and for all to enjoy. But unfortunately, these paintings are scattered across different art galleries both in this country and abroad. Sadly some of them are inaccessible, being in the ownership of private collectors.'

'Isn't it more fulfilling to experience the beauty of the nature by your physical presence and through your own eyes as we are doing now, rather than seeing it through the eyes of a painter while standing in the confines of a gallery?' I said. At this, Rolf became more enthusiastic and continued with his lecture:

'To appreciate a diamond you don't go to a diamond mine. The precious stone has to be quarried by labourers cut and shaped by craftsmen in factory and set it in a gold or silver frame by expert jewellers. Only then it becomes a thing of beauty and a part of the tiara of a queen or a loved one's ring. A gifted master painter is a miner, a craftsman and a jeweller all in one. As a miner, he captures the beauty of nature in his mind in its raw form. As a craftsman and a jeweller he then puts down the image on canvas after weeding out the unsightly or irrelevant bits, until it emerges as a perfect jewel for us to behold and enjoy. I hope I have answered your query?' He concluded by saying,

'The truth is, modern man hasn't changed much from his primitive form. Using their masterpieces as a universal language, modern man is telling posterity that "a god is born", just as primitive man, through his hand prints or cave drawings communicated the message to his descendants, "a man is born".

I was a bit confused by his philosophical commentary on the creation of "god". I was already struggling with his hypothesis on the creation of "man". I thought perhaps he was trying to introduce the Hindu philosophy of the transmigration of man and god.

Having walked for over 50 minutes on an empty stomach I was in no mood to embark on a futile discussion on a topic about which I knew next to nothing and least interested. By then we had arrived at a village called Wolvercote, not very far from the river bank. In the centre of the village was an old public house. It appeared to me that the place was an old English village with an interesting history.

Despite being tempted to hang around the village centre for a while we continued our journey towards the Trout Inn. After ten more minutes of brisk walk, passing the old village church, we arrived at the Inn on the bank of the river Thames.

Rolf wanted to drop in to the church for a quick look – I supposed, in case any valuable old classical paintings were lurking in there. I discouraged him and hinted that one couldn't evaluate a work of art just by a quick look in dim light; besides, there was the real possibility that the restaurant might stop serving food if we were late.

The Trout Inn is not an 'inn' at all. It is primarily a drinking house, where food is also served; generally known as a public house or a "pub", for short. It is well known for its fish meals. The fish served there, we were told, were fresh ones caught from the river right in front of the Inn. The river is fast flowing, hence quite suitable for Trout firming. A bridge over it led to the enchanting woodland on the other side. There were trees and fields on all sides. In fact, the Inn stood in an isolated location.

The broad paved forecourt provided seating places for a large number of customers. This was crowded with people enjoying a glass of beer, soaking up the atmosphere, feeling the cool breeze, listening to the almost musical sound of flowing water and the occasional bird song. There was a resident pair of peacocks, one showing off its beautiful feathers and startling the visitors with their piercing screams.

'Without the screams of the peacocks and the crowd of people, this place would be an ideal rendezvous for one of your evening trysts with Afariva,' I said playfully.

'If you were anywhere near as interested in poetry as in painting, and could have recited romantic verses from Omar Khayyam to her in this place on a quiet afternoon, she would have melted and have been yours for ever,' I added.

He completely ignored my banter and was looking out for a free quieter place to sit down. The Trout inn was extremely crowded that night. When I told Rolf that we wouldn't be able to enjoy our meal in the cacophony of that open-air space, he sounded pleased,

'Good, I don't like eating my evening meal outside in a half-lit environment. That's mainly for fear of eating live insects but also for fear of inadvertently eating fish bones. Besides, although the sight of the colourful feathers of the peacocks pleases me, I hate their screams. Let's go inside,' Rolf commented.

We ordered, and the meals came to our tables soon enough – grilled trout with steamed vegetables and some pieces of bread. The atmosphere inside was relatively quiet, although hot and stuffy. I knew Rolf took his dinner very seriously and generally wouldn't indulge in any serious discussion over the meal. I enjoyed my fish, thanks to a dash of hot Tabasco sauce and a shake of salt. Rolf carefully unfolded his napkin and tucked it under his chin before starting on his meal. He didn't use any condiments as these, in his opinion – destroy the delicate flavours of the fish and steamed vegetables.

I told him the joke about the notice someone had put up below the advertisement on a billboard, "For 'safe sex use a condom; for safe food use condiment".

The joke cut no ice with him. His sense of humour, related to frivolity, was surely different from that of mine. He didn't react. We indulged in some small talks and finished our dinner at around 9 pm. After the satisfied meal we decided, this time without any argument that we would return by bus from the Wolvercote village square. The last bus to the town centre was scheduled to leave at 10 pm.

Having jointly settled the bill we came out to the open courtyard with our cups of coffee, crossed the bridge and sat down on a wooden bench to enjoy the sound of flowing water. Sunlight, though rather subdued at this time of the day, was seeping through the openings in the branches and leaves of big trees and we could still see the distant corn fields glittering in shades of gold from the reflection of the soft sunlight.

Rolf took the last gulp, put the cup on the floor, stretched his legs and with an egotistical expression and a gloating tone said,

'I am very happy to see you recover so swiftly from your ailment. Thanks to my homeopathic pills; don't you think?'

He paused and continued, 'Let me tell you something which will amaze you. It is mandatory for me to keep the *modus operandi* of my treatment protocol – a trade secret from my patients. But I just cannot do that in your case, you are my only close friend. I know this technique will not work with you a second time, there again you will never be my patient again.' I was a bit perplexed and asked,

'Could you please explain what on earth you are mumbling about?'

Rolf replied, 'If I tell you the truth you might think that I am a pompous git. But I can't help feeling proud of my skill despite the fact that I stopped professionally practising psychiatry, many moons ago. However, my technique of curing many ailments for friends and some odd patients still works effectively. My ability as a medicine man is still intact. As you said, and rightly so, it was the "magic of the Shaman".'

I was agitated by his shameless conceit, and displayed my displeasure in an excited voice,

'Listen to me, my friend. I have been feeling bad by leading you up the garden path. I have given you a false sense of achievement. It will upset you, but truth be told, although I did not tell a lie as such, I did give you the wrong impression about taking the pills. I did open the lid of the small bottle of your supposedly, homeopathic pills, but, read my lips, not a single one went down my throat. All were flushed down the toilet. I got better by myself, by my own will power.'

I was so agitated having to tell him the truth at the risk of breaking the trust and undermining the integrity of a wise friend and a good companion that I broke out in a sweat. I lit a cigarette and tried to calm my nerves by taking a long draw and slowly releasing the smoke. I looked at him and waited anxiously for his response. I was surprised to see a look of utter satisfaction on his face. He looked at me in his usual sideways manner for a while to make the situation a bit more dramatic.

After an uncomfortable pause he said in a composed voice,

'You don't need to tell me that, I knew you would discard the medicine as soon as I left your place. You mentioned once that you did not believe in the scientific validity of homeopathic treatment. I was sure that being a man of science and with the logical mind of a modern man you wouldn't take homeopathic pills from me, not even from a qualified practitioner. I didn't think you will get better so quickly even if you took the pills, as I made them at home with arrowroot flour and a bit of sweetener. Faith-healing applies only to someone with "faith", you don't have that.'

I realised that I had got into trouble trying to hoodwink him and now I was tangled in the web of his psychological role play.

'In that case, what was your game?' I asked.

'The outcome was exactly as I expected my dear friend. I knew you to be a conscientious man who would be greatly disturbed at deceiving a well-wishing friend. To eradicate the discomfort caused by your prick of conscience we both had to play a part and in the end, the pretence became the reality. Don't be troubled, the treatment worked and you got better. Next time you will have to go to another *shaman* for your ailment.'

I was moved and a bit embarrassed to realise what had happened. I had nothing to add or to ask in response to this revelation. Rolf took advantage of this lull and continued his discourse on the introduction of homeopathic medicine in psychiatric treatment:

'When I started practicing psychoanalysis and psychiatric treatment, I followed the codes and procedures prescribed by Jung's school. I found out that in some cases, depending upon the nature and character of the patient, a placebo worked more effectively than real medicine. I started to introduced homeopathic pills as these were home-made, non-descript and absolutely harmless. For some, I use them as a placebo pill and for others, such as you, I used it to create a shock effect as a way of treatment. Because we cannot have a doctor-patient relationship, I have, as they say, let the cat out of the bag. This was my first and last treatment for you because, although you might have developed a trust on my healing power, you will have, at the same time, lost faith in my words. I am afraid I did hoodwink you rather than the other way round.' While he paused for breath I said,

'I suppose this is, in a way, simply a matter of faith healing. This is still widely practiced by the religious preachers, *Shadhus*' i.e. holy men, snake charmers, and sometime, by the village elders back home. They use talisman, blessed water etc. to exorcise and cure physical and mental ailments.'

Rolf retorted, 'As a matter of fact, my practice of psychiatry is quite similar to those practices which also took place here in this country and throughout Europe in the past. The problem is that 'modern man' has lost faith in a divine or supernatural power able to cure his ailments. That's why we need to recreate faith in him by introducing a medicine which 'modern man' can believe in., "will is the source of power", according to Nietzsche and that helps to cure.'

'For the primitive man "will" was a part of his instinct. I believe this instinct will come back to the modern man in the near future.'

I realized Rolf was now digressing and was on the topic of his thesis. I found out the time from a passer-by and asked him to get ready for a run to catch the bus. As we came out of the Inn's grounds, most unexpectedly we encountered Masud and his mistress, Maggie. He was equally surprised to see me there, particularly with an elderly man and not with a young girl. I introduced Rolf to both of them. Maggie offered us a lift back to town in her Vauxhall Viva, I was tempted, but Rolf rejected the offer politely. We ran towards the bus stop despite our heavily overloaded stomachs and ultimately, puffing and panting, just managed to catch the bus for our journey back to the city centre.

7

Frailty – Thy Name is Woman

Hayfever had provided me with an excuse for a temporary respite from the dry and strenuous academic world and relief from vexing social duties in favour of the comfort of my bed. Eventually I have had enough seclusion and become utterly bored and was pining for a heart-felt *adda* session with my friends and foes at the *adda khana (rendezvous-venue)*. I pondered – "Lots of catching-up to do." The long confinement followed by commitments to overdue academic chores didn't allow me much opportunity to see my buddy, Rolf since our meal together at the Trout Inn; although I had often thought of him.

It was a fine Saturday afternoon and I had nothing planned for the week-end. I thought it was high time I looked up my friend. I could hardly wait to find out about his antics in his very recent love life. I was pretty sure he also would be desperately waiting to open his heart to me, recounting the trials and tribulations with his new-found sweetheart. I went to my laboratory to phone him to enquire about his well-being.

On receiving my call and recognizing my voice he humoured me in his own characteristic style,

'I am afraid Rolf is not in at the moment; I am his ghost, you may talk to me instead if you like.'

He then continued normally,

'How are you, my friend? What have you been up to since our little adventure to the Trout Inn? I wondered if you have left the country! Some people even leave the world unceremoniously due to the stress and trauma of preparing their thesis and the fear of failing to defend it! Tell me your news, tell me all?'

'Sorry, I couldn't contact you earlier.' I said, 'I've been busy with a backlog of work and had some deadlines to meet. I was thinking neither of leaving the country nor this world, just because of this trivial business of writing and defending a doctoral thesis. I needed to devote myself to work simply to escape the stress and trauma of life outside of academia and to maintain my sanity.

'Anyway, I am now fed up with my obsessive pursuit of academic goals and have allocated myself a little time for more trivial distractions. Therefore, I am enquiring whether you have spare time to accompany me this evening on any activity of our mutual interest.'

He paused then said in an impassioned voice,

'I am extremely sorry to have to tell you, my dear friend, on this occasion I have to deprive myself of your company. It is unfortunate. You know that I always enjoy your company more than anything else.'

He paused again and added in a hushed tone, 'I have a date this evening.'

I expressed my surprise and pleasure and hid the disappoint--ment in my voice,

'Its great news and I didn't know you were secretly dating someone. Anyway, I am delighted to hear this and wish you a very enjoyable evening and a good future together. Now then, my friend, would you like to tell me about the lucky girl?'

'Don't pretend that you haven't guessed who it is! He replied, 'You have already met her. Remember the party at the Town Hall.?'

'I guess she must be the Nigerian beauty, Afariva, who you introduced to me at the cheese and wine party,' I said.

'You are right', Rolf said in an animated voice, 'She is coming to dinner with me tonight. I have kept our trysts a secret for some time; even from you. Now that it's no longer a secret between us

I shall tell you the whole story of my romantic escapade in due course. I have a lot to do right now.'

'That's absolutely fine with me but remember, don't keep me waiting too long to tell me about your story-book romance. I am happy for you; as a matter of fact I am thrilled. I do understand that you only have a couple of hours left to prepare the meal, laying the table with right crockery, choosing and preparing yourself with suitable attire and then creating the right ambience by romantic light and so on. I'd better let you get on with the preparation.'

I rang-off wishing him good luck and hoping to see him soon.

Having failed to secure a desired companion for the evening I walked back to the flat, a bit down hearted, and rested on my bed for a while. I decided that the next best thing I could do would be to go to the Moti Mahal.

That was the place to go, to overcome homesickness, love sickness and loneliness. There we could get solace in the company of a few other Bengali students, eating a plate of rice with a dollop of hot spicy curry and, a bit of mango pickle and couple of fried red chillies on the side as free extras for an affordable fixed price. If lucky, the proprietor would add some 'staff-curry' to our plate without charge. Staff-curry was an authentic Bengali-style hot fish curry with thin gravy, specially prepared only for members of the staff.

A small corridor at the back of the main dining hall was reserved for our use as *adda khana,* and a private dining area. This was also the passageway to take dishes to and from the kitchen for serving customers in the main dining hall. There we were free to eat our meals using our fingers, which were a real luxury, rather than struggling with knives and forks. This part of the restaurant was strictly out of bound for the other customers.

The décor of our 'reserved' part of the restaurant was more like that of cheap and cheerful restaurants in the back streets of

Dhaka, the provincial capital city where I studied back home. It had peeling wall paper, a precariously dangling light bulb without a shade, uncomfortable wooden chairs, and a wobbly oblong wooden table. Sometimes old newspapers were used as disposable tablecloths. The strong smell of curries wafted through the open kitchen door, not far from us. The sound of music from the speakers at the front of the restaurant was modulated by the chattering of the customers, high on alcohol and low in inhibition, and also by clanking-clunking noises from the kitchen.

The décor of the main dining area, on the other hand, attempted to emulate the atmosphere in the banqueting hall of an Indian Maharaja's palace. The walls were adorned with flowery flock maroon and gold coloured wallpaper, glass chandeliers hung from the ceiling for a regal lighting effect, and strategically placed incense burners spewed out intoxicating aroma. Non-stop Indian music was being piped out from a hi-fi system placed at one side of the reception desk at one corner. The later was, of course, a must for authenticating the ambience of regal India. Often, LPs of classical sitar recitals by the music maestro, Ravi Shankar would be played. He was, of course, well-known in the Western world because of his association with the Beatles. Sometimes, for the benefit of the staff and Indo-Pak customers like us, popular Bollywood film scores were played.

On the signboard outside the restaurant, below the name, 'Moti Mahal' in big letters was written the words, 'Authentic Indian Cuisine'. India, to the British was known as the 'Jewel in the Crown' of the British Empire. It was a colony with great treasures, exotic spices, incomprehensible social customs and whose people practiced erotic bedroom antics prescribed in their ancient book, the *Kama Sutra*. The Bengali proprietor had the sense that it wouldn't be good for business to call it a 'Bengali or Pakistani Restaurant', serving authentic Bengali cuisine such as, fish curry and lentil curry, to English customers. For them the name 'Bengal' was associated with a place where one goes hunting for a big cat', The Royal Bengal Tiger' and the place of origin of the infamous 'Cepoy Mutiny' or worse still the Black hole of Calcutta.

To inspire my depressed mood, having failed to have the company of my buddy, I went to the restaurant fairly early in the evening and found my friend, Dilder, engaged in a heated argument over the ideals put forward by Karl Marx in *'Das Kapital'* for the emancipation of the under dogs of the world. He was struggling to defend communism against an excited verbal onslaught by Reza and a Panjabi ally, Khalid, both die-hard supporters of capitalism. I wasn't really interested in politics. Nevertheless, I felt it to be incumbent upon me to take sides and join the fray, raising my voice to display my debating skills. Normally I would have supported the capitalist viewpoint, but when I noticed my friend's argument was weak and he was losing ground trying desperately to defend his views on communist ideology I instinctively came to his rescue.

That evening, while tucking into my rice and curry I became his comrade in arms and sided with him, shouting in support of communism as the only way of ending the suffering of the hapless mass of Asia, Africa and the Latin America, as well as the oppressed poor working class of the Western world. The attacks soon became personal, attacking individual's backgrounds and life-styles. There was also some table banging and shouting. Normally when the argument reached fever point, as was customary, we broke the debate, stood up and shook hands just before it could deteriorate into a fist fight. We took leave of each other after exchanging mutual apologies and 'good nights', wishing to continue with the debate next time we met.

I felt it was futile having an acrimonious argument with friends, knowing very well that our shouts and hollers from the back room of the Moti Mahal would hardly be heard outside the confine of that small corridor to make any difference what so ever to the trials and tribulations of the 'have-nots' of the world. I was particularly sad having to participate in personal attacks in a political discourse.

🖎

It was about 10:30 pm when I got back to my flat. I promised myself that in future I wouldn't be provoked into futile arguments and would refrain from personal attacks. At first, I tried to read a book but couldn't continue. I then flicked through some old magazines, but couldn't concentrate. I thought, "why not listen to some classical music, not the over-played and, perhaps over-rated Ravi Shankar's sitar recital, but some Western classical music perhaps."

I never had any interest in, or experience of, listening to such music. I had the impression that people with such taste and interest belong to a class known as 'cultured', an esoteric class with the taste for the finer things in life. I convinced myself into thinking that Western classical music sounds unpleasant to my ear only because of my pre-conceived idea that whatever was not 'Indian' must be rubbish.

I thought "Perhaps my mind needed to be trained to develop an appreciation of Western classical music. Liking or disliking something must be a matter of familiarity, and it is surely the purpose of intelligence to guide and train the mind to develop one's tastes. Only fools remain a slave to their prejudices."

I felt guilty for my unreasonable bias for Indian classical music.

I pondered over my recent experience at Rolf's flat. I remembered how a reproduction painting of the birth of Diana by Botticelli had moved me and had given me a feeling of pleasure and elation that I had never experienced before. I trained myself to share the ecstasy of *Il Divino* through his painting of the Creation of Adam. This suggested to me that the mind could be trained, perhaps with some guidance, to accept and enjoy something inherently but not obviously beautiful. For some time, I'd been wondering whether this could be true.

I had borrowed some records from a friend a few days ago. I thought "perhaps now is the moment to find out whether I could train myself to appreciate Western classical music." I took the records from the shelf and browsed through them, looking at the writing and the pictures on their sleeves. I saw names like Beethoven, Mozart, Tchaikovsky, Vivaldi, etc. These meant nothing to me; neither did words such as, sonata, symphony, overture, appassionato etc.

My attention was drawn to a picture of a young, Middle Eastern looking sailor on board a sailing ship, with a turban wrapped around his head. The sleeve cover described the content of the record as a 'symphony movement'. The scene depicted the journey of Sinbad, the sailor from the tales of the 'Arabian Nights'. The name of the music was 'Scheherazade' and the composer, 'Rimsky Korsakov' as was written below the picture.

I decided that this record might be a good introduction for me to Western classical music. I tried to prepare myself mentally before putting the record onto my record player (which I had bought from a hard-up fellow student a couple of months earlier). I sat down on my old sofa with a cup of tea in one hand and a cigarette in the other. I then closed my eyes for better attention to the sound. I tried to visualize a picture in my mind – "The slow and gentle motion of a ship sailing on calm waters, propelled by the wind filling its billowing white sails. The sailors are busy doing their work, quietly humming ballads in memory of their loved ones left behind. Albatrosses are gliding overhead. The sun is at its zenith like a disk of gold, creating a line of purple hue along the horizon by its subdued light, thus creating a mesmerising scene on the calm sea."

I took the cue from the picture on the sleeve of the record.

I had read the fairy tale stories of Sindbad's adventures at an impressionable young age. The picture engraved in my memory of Sinbad, the sailor, was like that on the LP cover – "An alluring young man, looking at the horizon from a vantage point high on the main mast, holding on to that with one hand and protecting his eyes from the direct light from the setting sun with the other. He is scanning the horizon for something or someone."

Despite considerable mental effort I failed to associate the music I was listening with the scene that was engraved in my mind. By the end of the first movement I couldn't help wondering, "I have spent most of the time trying to convince myself that the music should move me and be pleasurable. The style, composition and rhythm were excellent but, did I really enjoy the music?"

I came to the conclusion – "No one can enjoy art or music by analysing it." I realized that a resonance of my feeling with the music was lacking; my mind was not in tune with its wavelength. I had to accept, albeit reluctantly, that Western classical music might be something I would never learn to enjoy. I remembered an oft-quoted line from Rudyard Kipling – "East is east and West is west and never the twain shall meet."

Perhaps I should give up trying to achieve the impossible, and try for that which could now be easily attainable – get some sleep. It was well past midnight.

I was about to hit the bed when I heard a familiar knock at the door. My flatmate was already fast asleep. I was surprised, but I knew instinctively and almost certainly who was on the other side of the door. No one would knock at my door, not even in an emergency, at this late hour, except one particular friend.

But still just to be on the safe side, I shouted, 'Who's there?'

The sound came out, 'It's me, quick, open the door. I know you are awake.'

Pulling back the bolt, I said in a sarcastic tone, 'I know you are a ghost. I swear I am asleep, go away, leave me in peace.'

I opened the door and, as soon as I saw his face in the dim light of the hall I guessed what had happened. I had feared that it could happen but sincerely wished that it hadn't. I felt very sad seeing my friend standing in front of me with such a long pathetic face. He looked pale. I ushered him in. He sat down. Putting his head in his hands, and leaning on the side of the sofa, he kept his gaze fixed on the floor and remained motionless without uttering a word. I went to the kitchen and made him a cup of coffee without asking if he wanted one. He looked at me, took the cup and started to drink. Breaking the silence, I said,

'I am very surprised to see you here at this time of night. Did something go wrong with your date? I only hope whatever it is it's not too serious, perhaps just some misunderstanding! Well, never mind. You are now with a friend and a well-wisher. Tell me all about it. The night is yours.' Raising his gaze up Rolf said,

'Yes, you guessed it alright. She has betrayed me, or should I say those secret agents have once again successfully intervened in my private life. What happened tonight was most unpleasant and shocking. I have come here to share the tragic episode with you; as you are the only friend to whom I can unashamedly and unreservedly open my heart. I believe you will understand my predicament and sympathise with me which will give me comfort and some consolations, which I desperately need right now.'

He paused and continued, 'Besides, nobody else would open their doors for me at this ungodly hour for a surprise visit. For the life of me, I wouldn't think of knocking at anyone else's door either.'

I said politely, 'Please dispense with the superfluous prelude and get on with the facts – what exactly has gone wrong?'

Rolf paused, and within that he finished the coffee, put down the cup on to the table, reclined on the sofa, took a deep breath to sigh and began his story:

'Agents of the organization are still following me like shadows. What happened tonight was not unusual or even unexpected. The fear of their intervention in my private life was never far from my mind. However, I had convinced myself that by now they would have washed their hands of me, considering me to be an insignificant nobody.

'I haven't published a paper detrimental to the organization's reputation for the last two years and I am not officially involved in any psychiatric practices. I mistakenly thought I am no longer a threat to them. The agents must have orders to complete the task assigned to them, not stopping until the job is finished. The organization is determined to eliminate any threat to its survival. Its plan is to drive me crazy, literally mad, by making me out to be a fraudulent professor and by depriving me of any female company.' Sitting up, he looked at me at a tangent and said,

'By now you have surely guessed what has happened?'

In a sympathetic tone I said,

'Yes, of course I guessed it. Please tell me the whole story in detail without any deviation, and let me analyse the situation and counsel you on this matter.' Rolf continued,

'After our first date, when you met Afariva at the party my relationship with her became progressively closer and closer. One evening she came to my flat and cooked a Nigerian meal for the two of us and we had a lovely evening together discussing the life of the ordinary people in her exotic country. In particular, I learnt quite a lot about the practices of 'black magic' amongst some tribes and cults. We drank wine and she wanted to dance, but I didn't have a machine to make music, never the less we moved together in close embrace.'

The calmness and clarity of his voice assured me that Rolf was then fully composed and accepted the event as a *fait accompli*. He continued,

'As a matter of fact, only two weeks ago we went to London together. She wanted to see a solo exhibition of modern paintings by a well-known Nigerian painter at the Tate gallery. Although, as you know, I am not at all interested in modern art still I was happy to go with her. Her company, her childlike inquisitiveness and her keen interest in my opinion and explanations did make my day at the art gallery a very memorable one.

'We walked along the path by the Serpentine in the Hyde Park, holding hands. We also had an evening dinner at an Indian restaurant; we couldn't find a Nigerian one. We talked and laughed all the time. I found her youthful liveliness and innocence quite alluring. She surely stole my heart. I began to feel love sick.'

'I know the feeling,' I commiserated,

'I had no doubt that she was growing fond of me and I thought perhaps that was a prelude to her falling in love.'

'What made you think that?' I interrupted again.

'Give me a moment, for god's sake! I was about to tell you that. Last week she came to dinner for the second time. She accepted a very expensive present from me. In exchange she gave me a kiss on the lips. She also gave me a beautiful gift, a wooden figurine of a very tall African man and a woman in a close embrace. It was a fine example of a modern wooden figurine by a famous Nigerian sculptor, that's what she told me.

'I couldn't tell any of this to anyone, not even you. It is not that I have lost trust in you but there had to be a right moment for me to announce an event which was going to be a watershed in my life. But alas that dream had been shattered. Tonight's debacle has put the final nail in the coffin of my dreams. I am mourning the loss of my hope and the death of my dream. I am here to share the pathos with a friend.'

Staring at the carpet with a melancholy expression, he continued in a normal tone, 'My excitement was overwhelming. I invited Afariva for dinner tonight for a very special purpose. It was so much so that I did not feel the slightest remorse for rejecting your offer of companionship. I took heart thinking that you will not be sulking on your own this evening as I was sure that you would find something exciting to do with your compatriots.'

I remained silent and was eagerly waiting to hear about his account of the tragic end of an exciting love story. He continued,

'I prepared a dinner of cold salmon and salad and put a bottle of expensive white wine in the refrigerator to chill. I put on my best suit and expensive cologne, waiting for her in anticipation. I asked her to be at my place at 7:30 pm sharp. As the time approached, I looked impatiently through the window.

'The agreed time came and passed away. I was impatiently kept on looking through the window. When it was about 8 pm I thought about you "The Indian custom of adding half an hour to the scheduled appointment time may be a part of African culture too."

'When it was nearly 8:30, I got worried. It was unthinkable that she had forgotten about the date. There must be something wrong, perhaps she has suddenly fallen ill.

'I came out of my flat at about 9 pm and walked up to St. Hilda's college. Her room was locked and there was no light. I wrote a note on the back of an old envelope that was in my pocket and pushed it through the small opening between the floor and the edge of the door. In the note I reminded her of our dinner date tonight. I noted that I had come to see if she had fallen ill and was unable to call. I also added that I was on my way back to my flat in case she had arrived late and was waiting for me there.

As I was leaving, I saw that her next door neighbour's door was slightly ajar. I took the liberty of knocking and asked about Afariva. I couldn't believe my ears what I heard her say, "She has gone out with her boyfriend."

'I felt as though the sky had fallen on top of me. I came out of the hall after thanking the girl. I thought Afariva must have forgotten about the date and had gone out with her brother or a close relative for a dinner – wishful thinking!

'But, even that was unforgivable, considering our hitherto unexpressed commitments to each other. I was at a loss as to what to do next. I couldn't rest until I had confronted her and demanded an explanation and an apology. I was walking along the footpath by the side of the Magdalene Bridge, not very far from St. Hilda's. I knew she had to return by 10:30 pm along this path. I noticed many undergrads coming and going, chattering amongst themselves, some quite boisterous, but no sign of Afariva.

'The road was getting quieter as the deadline for returning to the college approached. Suddenly I heard the familiar sound of her laughter from the other side of the bridge. I hid in the shadow of a tree by the end of the bridge. She came nearer, having crossed the bridge. Rafi, I couldn't believe my eyes what I saw. She was drunk; that was obvious from her body language. My sweet-natured, soft-spoken sweetheart was walking partially supported by a tallish African lad. Both of them were laughing, horse playing and passionately kissing each other time to time.

'I was stunned. She was passing by me, but didn't notice me. I wanted to call out her name, but was so choked-up that I couldn't make out a sound. I thought I was having a hellish nightmare. My desire to stop and confront her vanished. At first I was disgusted and enraged and began to walk briskly back towards my flat. Then I started to feel sad, beaten, betrayed, demeaned, belittled and helpless. I reached the door of my flat but did not go in. I turned round and here I am. He paused briefly and continued,

'As you probably know by now, love and hatred are two faces of the same coin, both borne of the same passion.' He turned his face away from the wall towards me and I let him open his heart to me as much as he wanted,

'My anger and disgust towards her has all but gone. I no longer feel bitter or betrayed. To be honest with you, I don't feel anything at all about the episode. But I couldn't go back to my lonely flat without sharing the intoxicating pangs of my heart with you. Now that I have done it, I feel no remorse or sadness. I can now go back to my flat and have a good night's sleep. Perhaps, you should think of this as being the confession of sins to a priest. As far as I am concerned, you are as good a confessor as any other.'

'Isn't it in Shakespeare's Hamlet that we get the famous saying – "*Frailty, thy Name is Woman*?" I said, 'Fiction and drama are not subjects of my forte, as you know. We don't need Shakespeare's dictum to prove the point. We both have personal experiences for that now. It is just that women are born with this attribute; otherwise, lives of people like you and me would have been quite dull. Don't you agree?'

He wasn't waiting for a reply. This, however, provided him the opportunity to continue with his monologue:

'I am sure you know me well enough to agree that I am quite rich both materially and spiritually. I can also tell you without reservation that I am also sexually as potent as any other young men. I know, and you must have noticed that girls are attracted to me, but none can get too close to me. These agents will not allow anyone to develop a permanent relationship with me. It's not the fault of the people who betray me, deliberately or unwittingly. After all, they are normal human beings with their share of weakness and temptation for material and personal wellbeing. Now you tell me, how can these impressionable young girls avoid their influence, temptation or persuasion?'

I didn't attempt to answer his query. Instead I went to the kitchen to make more coffee to give myself a break from his phobia about the organization. Lately, having listened to his comments of the activities of the so called 'secret agents of the organization' many a times I was beginning to feel irritated whenever he brought up the topic. I couldn't be sure whether the organisation and their activities were real or merely a figment of his imagination.

It would have been easier to empathise if he had told me who they were, what their background was, and why they were out to destroy him. It wasn't that he did not want to tell me; in fact he was desperately keen to do so. But, it was not a simple story. It was something that had controlled his life for more than a decade. It's a very serious matter. He didn't feel ready to tell me the tale, or perhaps, not quite sure that I was the sympathetic listener he was looking for. I knew I must wait for the right moment for him to tell me the story. I generally tried to avoid the subject if at all possible.

For now, though, to make things easy for him, I asked,

'Are you insinuating that Afariva has been tempted by material gain or by blackmail to betray you? Perhaps the agents have, somehow, spread false rumours about your character to frighten her off.'

He said, 'You mean that I am a dirty old man! Your guess is as good as mine. The agents must have found out that our relationship was on a very strong footing and that temptation and threats would not work. It is clear to me that they have engaged the African boy to take her away from me, using him as bait to seduce her. He must have been guided by an agent as to how to poison her mind against me with rumours, such as that I am a fraudster. However, I am confident that she will soon understand her mistake and realize the value of true love. She will come back to me in good time, that's for sure.'

It was quite late at night, or should I say, very early in the morning. I wanted to change the topic of conversation to something light to ease the situation and to cheer him up. I took the opportunity of the pause to give him my counsel on the matter, which I'd been preparing while partly listening to his account and partly analysing the events of the evening:

'Listen to me my dear friend, listen attentively. Most people are not blessed with the gift of true love, a treasured attribute of the human heart. Sadly, most people don't even know that they are deprived of this most wonderful gift of God, or 'nature', if you like. The fact that you have loved her and given her your heart is the gift of your very resourceful mind. You can't find such a quality in many human beings. The flowers bloom and fade away after giving pleasure to their beholders, and nectar to the bees. Great poets and philosophers have created memorable verses and wonderful words of wisdom for posterity to ponder. Tagore wrote, *Spark got a moment of rhythm, it flew away and was lost, and that was its pleasure'*. He also used the description of a bird's feelings to capture passing pleasure, *'I haven't kept any trace in the sky, but I did fly, that was my pleasure.*

'You may not have left a deep mark in Afariva's heart, but the very fact that you had a spark in you and have loved her passionately should be your pleasure. Forgive me, I must quote again. This time from a poem by the great English poet, Lord Tennyson – 'Tis better to have loved and lost than never to have loved at all'. After you have taken these words of wisdom into consideration you should feel contented. Besides, a wise man of your status and taste for the fine arts and music should not get dejected at being jilted by an ordinary woman.' After a brief pause Rolf countered accusingly,

'You haven't understood me at all. You're just showing off your prowess in literature. Fine art, music, culture, these are not the things of my love, and these are the things of my passion and my intoxication. I get uplifted through these, others get addicted to religious devotion, hemp, cigarette or LSD. In that sense you may consider me as religious as others. I am emotionally very impoverished, that's why I am religious. Can't you understand that these agents have kept me poor by depriving me of emotional and physical contact with females?'

I had no doubt that his attraction towards young women was

essentially of a physical nature and not something platonic. It had nothing to do with 'love for love's sake'. It was more like the attraction insinuated in Omar Khayyam's poem describing an old man with a long white beard, caressing a beautiful young maiden carrying a jar of wine. I was used to his rather unhealthy attention to young girls and his sometimes "falling in love" episodes with them. I had accepted this aspect of his idiosyncratic behaviour as a tolerable weakness on his part which I could put up with as long as it did not become too toxic.

For anyone who did not know Rolf as much as I did his behaviour with and attitude towards young girls would certainly have seemed inappropriate. Although nobody knew his actual age, nature is cruel and it was all too evident that Rolf was much older than the rest of us. The difference in his age made his attempted relationships seem odd. However, in those crazy days of swinging sixties it was fashionable to oppose discriminating against age, race or sexual orientation in relationships. Partly as a joke and partly to give some advice I said,

'According to ancient Vedic scripture, "love for women" had always been driven by carnal desire and was branded as a form of mental illness, albeit quite harmless. However, religion, based on faith, can lead towards self-awakening and the ultimate truth, where beauty and true love lies. In the dedicated journey in search of true love there is no place for materialism or carnal desire between you and your beloved. The sages of by-gone days, as you know, always denied themselves any form of physical pleasure.'

'Not always, my friend, not always,' Rolf re-joined, 'When one is deprived of material pleasures or is sick of them then one is attracted towards spiritual goals which can turn someone into a saintly person. That, I believe is the truth. But I have not the slightest desire to be a saint or a holy man. As a matter of fact, I have a strong aversion to the status of sainthood. I am an ordinary man like the rest of you. I want to enjoy life to the fullest, with emotional attachment and physical pleasures, particularly with young women. I have been deprived of this phase of life. I cannot accept becoming old without experiencing physical passion with women.'

'My dear Rolf,' I said to ease the tension, 'Nobody has to pretend to be old. Time, as a dragon in its eternal one-way journey devours childhood, youth, and ultimately, old age, until we are no more, and yes sir, for each of us time begins when we are born and ends when we die.'

Rolf retorted, 'Age is all in the mind, you are as old as you feel. Some of my compatriots have aged prematurely and the only thing they are doing now is counting their days until they meet their maker. You jolly well know that I am not like one of them. I haven't lost the spring of my life. My physical and sexual prowess is intact and I shall not allow my enemies to break me and take my spirit away.'

I did not wish to hurt his feelings, but at the same time, as a good friend and well-wisher, I needed to point out the reality of the situation,

'I understand what you are saying, but I feel strongly that if you really want to fulfil your emotional and physical needs with the opposite sex you should look for mature women who will understand you better.'

Rolf barked, 'Are you insinuating that I look old? Perhaps I do, but my appearance is deceptive. I am not as old as you think my friend. If I do what you suggest I will become really old, the 'dirty old man' as I am known in some circles. Examples of physical and emotional liaisons between mature men like me and young girls abound in all ages and all around the world. So, what is the big deal that I look old? I have charisma, education, wealth, although not a millionaire, mind, and most importantly, I have physical vitality. So why do you suggest that?'

Embarrassed at having raised the matter of his age, I remained silent.

'The organization cannot tolerate my involvement with young women. They want to see me dead, or drive me mad. That's why I am in this situation today'. Rolf muttered.

'You must have been a very handsome man in your younger days, Rolf, please tell me why you deprived yourself of female contact then? By your age now, most people have had their flings, romances, sexual encounters, probably got married, had kids and then continued with the struggle for survival with all the trials and tribulations that life had thrown at them. I wonder why these eluded you!'

'I assure you that this gap in my life is not because I wanted to avoid the trials and tribulations of life, as some do. It is because of some tragic events in my life during that formative period. My story is a sad one and a long one for that. If you are really interested I will be pleased to share memories of those unbelievable events in my life. One day, at an opportune moment, I would like to do that. Yes, I really would, and perhaps, then you will understand me better.'

It was getting very late. I was not sleepy but I needed to go to sleep. At the same time, I was reluctant to give him any hint that I wanted to be left alone to catch up with my sleep, as I knew he desperately needed my company at that time, I didn't, however, want to dwell on the current topic and diverted it to something different.

The record albums which I had been looking through earlier were right in front of me on the floor and provided the perfect topic. I picked them up and said,

'I have recently borrowed these vinyl records of classical music from a friend. I wonder if you would like to explain these to me. You told me last time that you never listen to music from a machine. Otherwise I would have liked to share the music with you in my machine.' He took them from my hand and browsed through the labels on the sleeves and commented,

'There is not much to comment about classical music, either you like it or hate it. The choice of the album depends on your mood, familiarity and the environment. You have to train your mind to like it, my dear friend. I am delighted that you are experimenting with Western classical music. Such music, in the right environment and with the right orchestra, will provide ambrosia to nourish the body and the soul. I must take you to one of the concerts by the Royal Philharmonic orchestra at the Royal Albert hall one day. It wouldn't cost you much – the tickets are heavily discounted for students.'

I expressed my eagerness to do that. He was quite chuffed at this and appeared to have forgotten about the sad episode which broke his heart. But, there was no sign of him making a move to take his leave, neither did I give any indication that I was getting sleepy.

Rolf continued, 'Do you know, Afariva once expressed her wish to visit Shakespeare's birthplace and enjoy a play at the theatre there. I bought two tickets for a coach trip to Stratford upon Avon tomorrow which also included the tickets for the play – "The Merry Wives of Windsor". I do not like plays at all, but I was ready to do anything to have the pleasure of her company. I was going to surprise her tonight by inviting her to accompany me. I knew this Sunday she did not have any commitments. After what has happened this evening, that isn't going to happen anytime soon.' Hesitantly, he went on,

'I was just wondering if you would be interested in accompanying me to Stratford. That is, if you don't have any prior commitment. I am not going there on my own. If you are interested then perhaps we both can make the trip an experience to remember. I hate to see the tickets go to waste, it is like burning money. By the way, you do not have to pay for it, it's free. The only problem is that you have to be at the coach station very early in the morning, to be precise, at 8 am sharp.'

'Did I hear you say it's free? I exclaimed, 'In that case I must hit the bed forthwith and so must you. We have to get up early.'

Rolf left without further delay and with a cheerful disposition, bidding, 'good night' and reminding me,

'See you tomorrow morning at the Gloucester Green Coach Station before 8 am – Read my lips – 8 am.'

8

Long Reach of the Agent

The coach station was a fifteen minutes' brisk walk from my flat. Thanks to my old alarm clock, surprisingly still in working-order after a fair amount of mishandling, I was able to arrive well ahead of the scheduled departure time. There were a good number of passengers, mostly foreign students, gathered by the side of the coach, and a few others were trickling in to join the crowd. I saw a sprinkling of middle aged couples also loitering nearby, all eager to board the coach bound for Stratford-Upon-Avon. Only fifteen minutes remained before the coach was scheduled to leave and still there was no sign of Rolf.

I was tense and pacing to-and-fro inside the coach station. After a while I sat down on a bench and lit a cigarette to calm my nerves. The passengers were taking their seats one by one and they were making themselves comfortable for the long pilgrimage to the Shakespeare's birthplace. I got up and resumed my pacing, agitated and resenting having missed out on the pleasure of my routine morning lie-in, just because it was a free event. From time to time I stopped and looked towards the short passageway through which I expected Rolf to enter the station, standing tiptoe to see further.

The coach driver noticed my predicament. With a touch of humour, even at this early hour on a Sunday morning he shouted,

'There is a small step here mate. You can use it to get a better vantage point to look out from, if you like.'

I was in no mood to respond to his friendly banter. I thought it was likely that my good friend had taken an overdose of a nightcap when he had returned home to drown his sorrows, and over-slept. All the passengers were on board and the coach looked full. It was exactly 8 am shown on the big clock on the wall inside the building. The coach driver shouted,

'If you are coming with us, young man, I'll give you another two minutes, if you are not on board by then I am afraid I shall have to leave you here.'

By this time, I had given up all hope of seeing Rolf and was about to start walking away when, lo and behold, there he was; seeing the coach beginning to move off, running frantically towards it. Without a word of greeting he signalled me to follow him to the coach, which was just turning for the exit. Fortunately, the coach driver spotted our Laurel and Hardy double act with amusement, and stopped to let us on board. He got all the other passengers to applaud. Without any hesitation or embarrassment, Rolf nodded, took a bow and sat down, breathless. When he had his breath back, he muttered,

'Sorry I am late; I couldn't find the tickets when I was ready to leave the flat. I searched everywhere, including my wallet several times, as I usually keep such things there. I panicked and gave up all hope of finding them in time to catch the coach. Self-pity overwhelmed me and I sat down. I was thinking of you – "How was I going to face you?" At that moment I remembered that after showing the tickets to you last night I put them back into my back trouser pocket, as I was going to wear them for the journey.'

I looked out of the window to avoid face to face encounter. I was fuming inside and thought of giving him a piece of my mind. Not particularly for this event, but to take revenge for his lecture on me for being late for dinner. I turned around to say something rude but when I saw his expression I felt sorry for him and couldn't say anything.

After leaving the city centre the coach entered the countryside along a relatively narrow scenic road. The early summer sun was up; light was shining through the foliage of trees lining the undulating bendy road. Small clusters of houses came into view from time to time. These were beautifully adorned with unique flower gardens. I saw some isolated ones which were equally as exquisitely beautiful and bewildering. It was like a painting on an endless canvas with no mismatches or anomalies anywhere. I was enjoying the scenery and pondered – "How different this is from the rice fields and palm trees back home." Breaking the silence Rolf mumbled,

'I had a terrible night, couldn't get a wink of sleep.' I responded in a harsh tone, 'Spoiling sleep and suffering mental agony for the so-called 'love' of an ordinary, childish young girl is absolutely unbecoming of a mature intelligent man like you, Rolf. She is not worth your losing even a wink of sleep. It is time to get such feelings out of your mind.'

'No, no, no, you silly man,' he shot back, 'You don't understand. My failed love or, as you sometimes call it, my infatuation for Afariva is not the cause of my mental agony and sleeplessness. I know that love comes and love goes. It's not a novelty. I have dated many girls before. But it is the interference of those heinous agents in my private affairs that is the cause of my worry. Last night's episode is typical of how they play their hands. They follow me all the time, everywhere. They believe they will be able to make me mad so that I wouldn't be able to publish anything against them anymore. But they are mistaken. They make me sad, but they will never make me mad. Every event, like the one that has happened with Afariva, had upset me immensely but had not caused any mental breakdown. Neither have these events diminished my resolve to fight them and win. I haven't had the opportunity to tell you about what happened to me in Innsbruck last autumn! If you hear the story you will understand the gravity of my situation. You will then understand why I am concerned about the motive of the organization. Its agents follow me everywhere, even when

I am on holiday abroad. The most disturbing thing is that no one seems to believe this, not even the police.'

I thought it would be better to listen to his 'Innsbruck saga' as it would drown the monotonous annoying background noise from the diesel engine of the coach. I asked him to go ahead with his story as we had a couple of hours to kill before arriving at our destination.

Rolf began his story with relish:

'It happened when I went to Venice for the third time last year. That's when I asked you to stay in my flat, remember? Well, when in Venice I always stay in a particular cheap and cheerful Bed & Breakfast place in a rather rundown part of the Jewish quarter. I prefer that not only because it is light on my wallet, but because the landlady, a 40 something Italian widow, is also a connoisseur of fine art and we really get on very well with each other.'

'Now I know why you frequent Venice so often!' I sniped.

He shot back, 'I knew, with your single-track mind you would jump to such a conclusion. But no, she's not really my cup of tea in that sense. As you know, I don't go for older women.' He smiled mischievously and paused. Taking advantage of the silence I said,

'Love shouldn't be based on age or physical beauty. A woman with artistic aptitude and an intelligent brain is what you should go for. Mature women are like vintage wine. You are a connoisseur of fine art and you love everything antique. So what is wrong with an antique woman – mature, cultured probably intelligent and most importantly, has a similar Jewish background' He ignored my banter and continued in a serious tone,

'It's all very well for you. You have the youth and can look forward to a future in which you will find a nice young woman with whom to share your life. But such a dream eluded me because of the intervention of external forces; anyway, let me continue with my story.

'Three weeks in Venice passed by very quickly. My daily routine was visiting fine art museums and cathedrals in the daytime and going to concerts or theatres in the evening and frequent some of the selected restaurants. You will probably have guessed that my visits to the cathedrals were not for religious purposes. Some of these churches hoard collections of paintings by great masters. A few of the paintings are by unknown painters, but I felt as if they were masterpieces. I sometimes wonder if the Church authorities know the real value of these collections. I worry that the soot from all the burning candles and incenses inside the churches will soon degrade the paintings beyond restoration. I have tried to buy paintings from churches in the past. None of the custodians wanted to part with their treasures, at least not until the time when a tipping point is reached because of a desperate need for cash.

'Of course I was not absorbed by art work all the time. I walked around the streets, browsed items in antique shops, got into conversation with shopkeepers and other customers. You will be pleased to know that I thought of you from time to time and you must know it because I sent you a card soon after I arrived there. I also sent one to Mack at the same time. Your card had a painting of virgin and child by Titian. The original is at the Galleries de Academia there. This has a large collection of Titian, Giovanni Bellini, Tintoretto and other masters. I often spent a long time gazing at these and got, as you say, my fix of intoxication.

'At the end of my holiday in Venice I got the irresistible urge to drop into Innsbruck for a few days on my way back to England. So I re-organized my flight back to England from Munich which is only an hour's train journey from Innsbruck. I took an intercontinental train ride from Venice for Innsbruck with a change of train near the Austrian border.'

At that moment the coach stopped at a service station for a

break. I informed him that I was desperate for a puff, so, we both got down and had coffee and as usual, I enjoyed a cigarette. We also exchanged pleasantries with a few young fellow passengers during our brief stop.

As soon as we were back on board and settled in our seats for the resumption of our journey, Rolf asked me,

'Now, can you remind me how far I got with my story?'

I was sure the reason for the question was not that he had forgotten how far he got, but to find out if I was seriously listening to him. Without hesitation I replied,

'You were on your way to Innsbruck by train.'

He appeared happy with my interest in his story and continued,

'As the train crossed the border onto Austrian soil, nostalgic memories of my childhood holidays there went through my mind like a motion picture of a series of unconnected events. I was day-dreaming while the train was approaching Innsbruck station. The apprehension overtook me. Would I be able to recognize the beautiful riverside hotel where we used to stay during our family holidays? Would the anglers still be lining the bank of the river Inn? Would the opera houses, concert halls and churches scattered around this beautiful small riverside city be there to welcome me? It had been a long, long time since the last time I had visited this place with my parents.

'When I arrived at the station it was well past midnight. The terminus was nothing like I remembered. There were no gas lights or horse driven carriages waiting outside. Even the trains did not puff smoke or make a whistling sound. Anyway, I didn't expect to see those scenes in today's automobile, dominated world, but I was saddened to find the station appeared more or less similar to those in other West European cities. The information centre at the station was closed and I did not want to go through the hassle of looking for a hotel room or a bed & breakfast place in the middle of the night. It was not that cold, so I decided to spend whatever was left of the night on a bench outside. The decision seemed economically sensible, since there were just a few more hours before sunrise.'

He looked at me and said in a sarcastic tone,

'I shall punch your face if you make any pun relating my Jewish genes in this decision.'

I retaliated 'I was not thinking that at all; but now that you reminded me, what you are implying is probably correct, but I am not going to say it, because I don't want to be on the wrong side of your fist.'

He snapped, 'You are being flippant, but please note that the characteristics of the particular Jew you are referring to do not represent those of the whole Jewish race, only those portrayed in popular fictions and dramas.'

'Like the Jewish moneylender, Shylock, in the, 'The Merchant of Venice'; by the very dramatist whose shrine we are going to visit now', I added.

After he had put me right following my comment he continued with his tale,

'I tried to make myself as comfortable as I could with a small shoulder bag as my pillow, the overcoat as a blanket and the holdall as a foot rest. I closed my eyes. Travelling all day had made me tired and I nodded off quite quickly despite a rather less than comfortable bed and the exposed surroundings. A sweet female voice, speaking in pure German, woke me up. She excused herself and said in a polite tone and mild voice that she hadn't seen anyone spending nights sleeping on a bench here before. She enquired if I was broke! If that was the case she offered to arrange a hostel for homeless people, for me to spend the night.'

'I got up and rubbed my eyes to make sure that I was not dreaming. I looked at her – a beautiful young girl, probably in her mid-twenties. I was surprised and deeply moved by her kind words and concern for me. I thanked her profusely and expressed my gratitude for her offer of shelter. I explained to her that my decision to spend the night on the bench was indeed related to financial considerations, but that I was not a pauper. My pecuniary situation was not as bad as she had thought. I told her that I did not believe in wasting money and liked to save and spend as and when deemed necessary. I asked her politely not to misunderstand me and with the intention of knowing her name, I extended my hand, saying: 'Miss -.'

'Petra, Petra Hutner', she replied while gently shaking my hand.

'I expressed my delight to having made her acquaintance, and introduced myself in my mother tongue. I told her that I was of German origin but had been living in England for a long time. I also told her the reason for my sojourn there. I asked her what she was doing outside of the station so late at night. She said she was a student and worked at the cafe there at night to earn some extra money. She wanted to run along and ask her father if he would be willing to put me up for a night at their house. He was waiting for her nearby in his car. She added that her parents were very hospitable to foreigners.

'I stopped her and said that if I was not a slave to my prejudices and my pride I would have immediately accepted the offer and gone with her, subject, of course, to her father's approval. I thanked her for her kind offer. I told her that I was wired-up not to accept a favour when it is offered, but not to hesitate asking for it when needed. So I would have no hesitation in asking her for a favour. She was waiting to hear what that might be. I asked her if she could give me company whenever she would be free during my stay in her city.

'Petra jotted down her contact details on a chit, and said while handing it over to me, that she would be delighted to keep me company when possible and asked me to contact her the next day. She had to rush since she didn't want to keep her father waiting. She wished me goodnight and disappeared. I remained in a trance for a while.' After a brief pause Rolf asked, 'You can't believe it, can you?'

I answered in an irritated tone, 'There is absolutely no reason to doubt it. It is quite natural for an innocent young girl to feel sorry for a pauper spending the night on a bench in the open. What I am wondering though, if you are getting carried away telling me yet another tale of romance and chivalry on the pretext of telling me about the so called, "long reach of the agent".'

He snapped, 'You should know that all good stories must have a prelude. Without the background, you will not be able to appreciate the seriousness of what took place involving Petra. You need to know how and, to what extent I became involved with her, only then you will be able to see the parallel between the events that took place in Innsbruck and those which took place here at Oxford involving Afariva. It has been quite unsettling for me to find out that the agents were following me, even when I was abroad on a holiday.'

By this time the coach had arrived at Stratford-upon-Avon. While we were getting ready to disembark, Rolf promised to continue with the story on the return journey. I realized there wouldn't be any respite for me then, either.

The play was supposed to start at 5pm. That was quite a while away and we had several hours to kill. I suggested that we moved around the town before the ultimate pilgrimage, i.e. visiting the house, now a museum, where the literary giant was born and spent his childhood.

Rolf said, 'Let's do first things first. This morning I had no time for breakfast. I don't know about you; you must be hungry too.'

It was nearly lunch time and we had indeed both missed our breakfast, so we decided to have brunch. We found a suitable restaurant and after waiting in a queue for some time we were eventually seated and we managed to appease our hunger pain at a reasonable cost.

Stomachs full, we moved around the town from one end to the other, visited many Elizabethan houses some of which had once belonged to Shakespeare's family members and were open to the public. Memorabilia connected to them were on display for tourists to see and plentiful souvenirs were scattered around tables for purchase. No wonder we came to know the pun about the British – "Race of the shop keepers". We were not really interested in Shakespeare's birthplace, where he spent his childhood, or in his relatives' houses and the various artefacts on display, but it was a way of passing time. After two exhausting hours following the recommendations of the tourist office's guide book, we made our way back to the park by the riverside, close to the theatre. It was a very hot and sultry day. I was so shattered that I collapsed onto the grass ready for a slumber.

Rolf showed no sympathy. Instead of giving me some words of comfort he asked me in a sarcastic tone,

'Do you want me to call an ambulance, mate? They have stretchers which may be used to transport you to the theatre.'

'That won't be necessary.' I replied, 'I shall be alright after a bit of rest. It is just that, unlike your forefathers, my ancestors utilised a contraption which took advantage of wheels for transportation to escape the drudgery of walking. Therefore, we were not quite used to over-use our god-gifted pair of legs.

I got up and we headed off for the theatre. There was already a long queue, but we weren't bothered as the seats were numbered. I enjoyed the play and I knew Rolf didn't. He considered dance, plays, cinemas, even contemporary paintings as lower class of arts, suitable for the taste of common people and remedy for some occupational and mental ailments.

By 8 pm we were back in our seats on the coach. We noted the expressions of amused surprise on the faces of our fellow passengers, because this time, we were among the first few to board the coach.

❧

Rolf waited until the coach started its journey back to Oxford before resuming his Innsbruck saga. He began with the remark,

'I am sure you are as much eager to hear the finale of my story as I am to tell you that.'

I nodded reluctantly and he continued with his story; this time without checking if I remembered where he had to stop the story:

'I kept looking at Petra disappearing from my view and remained in a state of daydream until I opened the chit she handed over to me and read her contact details. I then realized that I was not dreaming. I went back to my horizontal position to try to catch up with a bit of sleep. I thought god must have taken pity on me and sent this wingless angel to cheer me up. Then I said to myself "It can't be true, I don't believe in god. How can there be a miracle then?" Well, it must have been a coincidence that I was at the right place at the right time. It must have been the realization of an event, based on statistical probability. I did fall asleep eventually. It must have been a deep one, as I woke up quite late and felt good despite the noise of the locomotives and people wandering about. I enjoyed a big German breakfast at a nearby café and booked myself into a cheap and cheerful hotel not far from the station. After a quick shower and shave and putting on a fresh flowery shirt I went out in search of Petra's address.

'The city had grown in size over the years, expanding quite a bit vertically, but not much horizontally. Her address was in the central part of the city and it didn't take me long to find it.'

Rolf checked to see if my eyes were still open and that I was not nodding off. After all it had been a very long and tiring day for both of us. I assured him that I was awake and listening and pleaded for him to go on with it avoiding unnecessary innuendos. He continued: 'I checked the road name and house number and then rang the bell. A buxom middle aged lady with blond bob haircut, wearing a white blouse and a long tartan skirt opened the door. She replied to my greetings in a soft and kind voice and asked me if I was the gentleman whom Petra had mentioned that morning at the breakfast table. I answered in the affirmative and asked if I could speak to her. She told me that Petra had gone to the public library to study and I could meet her at the cafeteria of the University near to the library right on the river bank at around 5 pm. She invited me to have a cup of coffee and expressed a few words of sympathy at my predicament in having to spend the night outside the station on a bench. I refused her offer of coffee politely, thanked her profusely and took leave of her saying that I would be delighted to accept her offer for another time.

'I returned to my hotel and tried to rest for a while. I took a map of the city from the lobby and found out the location of Innsbruck University. It was close enough for me to take a stroll to the library, perhaps less than a mile away. After a brief nap and a leisurely lunch at the hotel I was on the street walking towards the University following the concierge's directions on the map. I arrived there nearly an hour before I was due to meet Petra. I decided to savour the collections at one of the fine art museums in the neighbourhood before our meeting. I chose the one which was supposed to have a good collection of fine art objects including some classical paintings. There was a good collection of baroque and contemporary arts but I was rather disappointed by the lack of Renaissance paintings there. Anyway, the spare time passed pleasantly and I was back at the University cafeteria a few minutes after 5 pm. I recognized Petra through the glass window of the cafeteria. She was sipping a drink with a friend. When I approached the door she came out smiling and greeted me with a brief hug. I reciprocated with a light kiss on her cheek.

She introduced me to her companion, Alexander. He was a friend from her school days, from the same town. He was studying classics at that University. After exchanging niceties Alexander said goodbye, leaving us alone.'

It was a welcome relief for both of us when the coach stopped at the service station. I took advantage of the break to have my fix and use the facilities. I must admit I was by then enjoying the story. I wished he would cut out the description of his chivalrous adventures and come straight to the point where the so called 'secret agents' came in. But he just could not do that. Probably that's why he hadn't found a sympathetic listener to his stories, let alone anyone to believe in them. I happened to have been gifted with patience and had the ability to give the impression of believing in his tales. I had grown fond of this man and was keen to know his past to understand his present state of mind, so that maybe I could be of some help in alleviating his torment.

Back on the coach I said mockingly,

'Glances exchanged, heart pounding in anticipation, lips meeting in passion, romantic embraces; I assume it was love at first sight, or rather 'at first encounter in daylight'. Carry on my friend. I can't wait to listen to the finale of the ballad of your romantic antics with the young lady. Don't worry. I understand how delightful it must have been for you to discuss philosophy and recite poems in your mother tongue, bewitching an impressionable young woman.'

Rolf was not at all amused by my sarcastic remarks, not because I was mocking him, but because he felt it undermined the seriousness of what he was about to unfold. Nevertheless, without a trace of annoyance in his face he continued,

'As I was saying, we sat down face to face, and she bought me a cup of coffee. After enquiring about my wellbeing she asked me if I had been living in England for a long time. She then asked me a succession of questions, about my home in England, my family, my profession and my pastimes. She also appeared to be genuinely interested in hearing about my sweet memories of childhood in Innsbruck.

'In response to her barrage of queries I talked about my background and current circumstances in details. She looked blank when I told her I was a freelance researcher in social anthropology. I knew it would have been completely futile to give her even a brief synopsis of my research. Besides, it was neither the time nor the place for such a discourse. The only thing that I told her about my research was that it was to do with human instinct and the transformation of Homo sapiens to modern "man". I doubt if that meant anything to her. I thought it must impress her a lot. As for my childhood memories I simply pontificated that these could only be enjoyed in day dreams but words fail to communicate to others.

'As for my hobbies, I mentioned that there were only a few and, these were all connected to fine art and artefacts, music and psychology.' I interrupted with a sniping remark,

'You seem to have omitted the main one.'

'What do you mean by that?' He shot back.

'I mean the hobby of, "skirt-chasing!"'

'Don't be flippant, this is not the time for a joke,' he snapped with disgust and continued regardless:

'I asked her to tell me about her life her interests and hobbies. In particular, I asked her opinion about modern youth culture in Austria. I also sought her observations on the soul of her beloved city which was a 'fairyland' to me in my childhood days. Petra looked bemused and said that as for the soul of the city, if I meant its treasure of fine arts and artistic cultures, like classical music, then she would be the wrong person to ask. She did however tell me a little bit about herself. She was studying for masters in social sciences at the University of Salzburg and was in her final year of a two years course. She came back home during the vacations to spend time with her parents. She had planned to travel to India with a few friends during the approaching Christmas vacation that's why she was working part time to earn some money.

'She also told me that she desperately wanted to move away from the rather claustrophobic environment of her parent's home, and a change both from the stressful student life and the boring old city where she had spent the last 25 years of her life. The offer of a small stipend from Salzburg University had enabled her to move out of Innsbruck. Her periodic visits here meant she could meet up with old friends.

'I asked her what she wanted to do with her life in the long term. She didn't have a clue, but she knew what she wanted to do immediately after University. I asked her to tell me if it was not a secret. Petra laughed and said that it was a top secret but she was happy to share it with a new-found friend and mentor like me. She said that she wanted to spend some time abroad, either in France or in England. Her preference was England, mainly because she thought her English was much better than her French. She also believed that England had kept its history and traditions alive, and was a fairy tale kingdom run by a queen. According to her, young people in England were less restricted by social constraints and taboos than their French counterparts. She was not religious but followed the tradition of accompanying her parents to Church every Sunday and joins in prayers before family meals. Even when back at the University, although not under their direct influence, she said that she felt guilty doing anything that would not meet with her parents' approval. Like most youngsters she dreamt of being a part of the western youth revolution, the flower power movement of free love and peace.

'When I told her that I was also in the thick of this revolution she was surprised and probably thought I was joking. I suggested that she should come and live in England for a while to be a part of this emerging new horizon in Western civilization. Petra asked me how long I would be staying in Innsbruck. I said to myself, "It all depends upon you my beautiful darling." I told her that I was in no hurry to leave Innsbruck, and that I usually decided things like that on a whim. My flight from Munich to England was open, the date to be confirmed.

'We talked about her studies, her friends and her hobbies. I bought her a drink. After a while she looked at her watch and announced that she had to call it a day and get back home. I asked her when we could meet again, reminding her that she had kindly agreed to keep me company when she had some spare time. I emphasised that it would make my visit worthwhile and memorable. Petra thought for a moment and said that she worked only four nights a week, keeping two nights, Friday and Saturday, for domestic chores and socializing, while on Sunday she went to church with her parents and stayed at home, occasionally either visited or entertained relatives. She said she'd be happy to spend some time with me the next day, which was a Friday.

'It was a chance for a romantic date, so I invited her to a concert. I assured her that the antipathy of the young generation to classical music was due to both their unfamiliarity with the music and to their addiction to modern popular music. I implored her to give herself the chance to enjoy such heavenly music in my company, assuring her that she would enjoy it and also mentioning that I would certainly enjoy it more in her company. Petra readily agreed. I told her that the concert started at 8 pm and that we should meet for dinner at 6 o'clock at a restaurant of her choice near to the concert hall. Petra agreed and hurried away. I waited for a while, watching her disappearing from view, and then came out of the library and took a leisurely stroll back to my hotel.

'I felt elated. That evening I had a light dinner at the hotel. I was dreaming of a future liaison with Petra when she came to England. Perhaps she could be my guest for a while and I would chaperone her on various tours and tell her all about my research.

I thought she had an inquisitive mind and a sweet disposition. I was sure I could get through to her, explaining the theory of the evolution of consciousness and get some useful response. "What a lovely girl" I thought.

'I took the concert brochure from my pocket and looked through it again. It was to be a performance by the touring Viennese Philharmonic Orchestra, including a Rhapsody with violin accompaniment. I thought it would be ideal for an evening out with Petra and give her a new appreciation of classical music. At that moment, the last thing I was thinking about was the secret agents, but the thing that did worry me was if there would be tickets left for good but not too expensive seats.'

Rolf checked to see if I was still listening before launching into the finale of his saga. By this time I was resigned to the fact that I had no other option but to listen to the next twist in his ballad of romance. The alternative would have been to put him off by suggesting a break from the story until a later occasion, citing the excuse of lack of concentration due to tiredness. That would have been an act of cruelty on my part. From the fluency of his narration and the details he provided of specific events, places and times I was convinced that the story he was narrating was a true one and not something he was making up. He continued:

'After an early breakfast at the hotel, I was able to buy two suitable tickets for the concert from the hotel reception. I spent most of the day wondering around the city and the riverside. I found precious little there to bring back my childhood memories for a dose of nostalgia. There were no anglers on the riverside, patiently gazing at their floats, waiting for a fish to bite. The natural distribution of trees and foliage I remembered were gone, replaced by manicured shrubs and plants adorning new concrete statues and high rise flats. I realized that either the child in me had died leaving only an empty shell, or time had taken its toll on this once naturally beautiful city. Perhaps both contributed to my disappointment. Anyway, I took solace – "The past is history, never to return and the future is a mystery, yet to unfold. What mattered was the present. I had to capture the present with a developing friendship with Petra, giving promise for the future."

I felt Rolf was getting a bit carried away. I accept that emotion is a prerequisite for writing good fiction. It is also an essential ingredient for captivating an audience in a market place or in a caravanserai. It is however simply embarrassing to display it to a friend on a coach in the midst of a chattering crowd. After a dose of "The Merry Wives of Windsor", the last thing I wanted was another drama, albeit a real-life one, presented as a one-man show. What I wanted to hear was the bare facts, without any emotional clap-trap. But with Rolf, one either took the whole story or got nothing.

'We had a wonderful time together,' he continued, 'The dinner was excellent. I couldn't have chosen such a good but not overly expensive restaurant on my own. We never had a dull moment, finding out about and amusing each other, except of course, during the concert. Coming out of the concert hall she told me that she really had enjoyed it. I wasn't sure if she just being polite. I wanted to take her home by taxi, but she preferred to go on the bus. I would have walked her home if I'd had the choice. While we were waiting for the bus, I asked her about her plans for the next day, which was Saturday, as she had told me before that she did not work on the weekend. She said that she was meeting some friends during the day and was going to a University disco in the evening. I asked her if I could accompany her to the disco. She looked at me and appeared surprised, and I could see that she thought I was joking.

'I told her that I would go anywhere for her company. I also talked to her about the new-age revolution of the youths of

Europe; the erosion of barrier between sexes, faith groups and between people of different ages. It was about challenging traditional values. Petra had no hesitation about taking me to the dance, but still mumbled her concern that I might feel like a fish out of water, as it was really meant for young people. I indicated that I was young in my heart and keen to participate in youth culture anywhere. After hesitating briefly she asked me to be ready at the hotel at about 8:30 pm the next day. Her bus was approaching. We exchanged hugs and kissed one another on the cheek. It was thrilling.

'I slept soundly that night with pleasant dreams. I spent the next day roaming around the city, walking along the narrow cobbled streets exploring a few antique shops. Additional expense for restaurant meals and concert tickets had taken a toll on my budget. I had just about enough money to buy the coach ticket to Munich and pay for the cost of rescheduling my flight to England from there. From past experience I felt that I was growing attached to Petra rather too quickly to be healthy and sustainable. I decided that I should cool things down for now, inviting her to be my guest in England in a few months' time after she had finished her studies. We would then be able to get to know each other better and I might be able to improve my chances of having a successful relationship.' At that point I couldn't help interrupting,

'Excuse me, but I find it strange that you were planning on only stopping overnight at the city where you were born, before returning to England. You spent nearly four days in Innsbruck reminiscing about your childhood holidays, but have not mentioned anything about your memories of Munich, where you were born and grew up as a child. I find it very odd.'

Rolf looked out at the passing scenery in the twilight of the summer evening. He breathed a sigh. I thought he did not like the interruption near the finale of his story. He did not turn around towards me and, as if talking to the passing trees, he deviated from the main story and carried on with his monologue:

'Knowing you as much as I do, I was afraid you were going to ask that question. I only wished, somehow, you hadn't. It is quite a natural question, particularly for a friend and well-wisher like you. I can tell you that there was a reason why I deliberately avoided visiting my 'ancestral home'. It is in no way relevant to the present story or to the 'secret agents'. However, since you asked, let me oblige you by responding.

'About a decade ago, I visited my childhood home for the first time since leaving my homeland with my family. What I saw and found there really upset me beyond measure. The house and the surrounding area had disappeared, everything had gone. I realized that a combination of the allied bombing and post-war urbanization had wiped out all of Munich's past without a trace, and replaced it with a concrete jungle. I still had the memories of this beautiful city and my childhood there, although a bit faded. I could have lived with those sweet memories of my fatherland. My visit erased that, replacing it with a keen sense of loss that was better to forget. The very thought of going back to Munich was painful.'

I apologised profusely and expressed my sympathy for the great loss he felt, quoting the fact that such was the inevitable casualties of all major armed conflicts, and similar fates had befallen many millions of peoples in the last two world wars. Of course, this was hardly any consolation for Rolf, but it didn't deter him from finishing his story, and I anticipated that the appearance of the agents in his story was imminent. He continued:

'As I was saying before you interrupted, I went back to my hotel room for a spot of lunch and a bit of a rest after finishing my travel arrangements for the following day. There was not much to see in Innsbruck. The memories of younger days had faded and as in Munich, there was precious little left of the olden days. But I was happy that when I returned to England, I would take with me the pleasant memory of my new friend, Petra and the lovely time we'd had together. I dressed up in my colourful shirt and a rather tight-fitting, pair of trousers. I was, after all, going to a dance with a beautiful young escort.

'Petra, as expected, appeared in the hotel lobby just after 8 pm. She was wearing a floral dress and a matching ribbon on her hair. She looked like a doll. We walked to the University along the familiar route and went straight to the hall. It was dimly lit and a projector was displaying coloured patterns on the screen behind the stage. The DJ was piping out loud western pop music through two large speakers at the two corners of the stage. He was controlling the level of the sound and choosing the type of music from long playing vinyl records.

'We chose two empty chairs on the edge of the dance floor. Some people were already bopping. Within a few minutes Petra excused herself and went to see a young chap, standing behind the bar on the other side of the room. I must admit I was a bit jealous to see them kiss each other and start chatting and laughing. Petra's friend introduced her to a roughly-dressed, butch looking companion of his. Suddenly I felt as if an electric shock had run through my spine. I had met that guy this afternoon while returning from the travel agency. I was sure it was the same person. I remembered him approaching me and taking out a map and asking me for directions in German. When I apologised and said that I was myself a stranger there, he said that he was aware of that. I was rather perturbed and asked him how he knew that and why then had he ask me for directions. He replied that it was his job to know the whereabouts of strangers in this city and warned me to be careful as the city was crawling with criminals and undesirables. Being uncomfortable in his company, I had excused myself and moved away from him as soon as I could. I decided that he was probably deranged, a type often encountered when travelling. I didn't think much of it.'

Rolf looked at me with a searching expression. When I did not react, he continued unabated,

'I wondered what he was doing here. Petra came back and sat beside me, saying that the man she had spoken to was her ex-boyfriend, Frank. He was studying engineering at that University and it was an unexpected encounter. When I asked about the other chap she shrugged and said that he was Frank's mate, but she did not know him.

'I couldn't help telling Petra that I'd met the same stranger earlier that same day, and suggested that he might be a secret agent. Petra laughed and said that I was mistaken. According to her, the person who had accosted me must have been a vagrant or a conman. Frank's friend couldn't possibly be the same person. I reluctantly agreed, but remained troubled. Still, I wasn't going to let anything spoil my last evening with Petra. After a short while I noticed with some annoyance that Frank and his friend were standing directly behind us. Frank asked Petra for a dance and she obliged. His friend took her empty seat. I felt a bit uncomfortable in his company. Suddenly he leaned forward and asked me in a mocking tone if I was Petra's dad. I was extremely agitated and angry and told him that I didn't talk with strangers, but for his information, Petra was my friend and dancing companion. He laughed and said that he knew what I was up to.

'By then I was sure that he was the same guy who tried to intimidate me in the morning. My heart was pounding. I got up and moved to another seat away from him. When the music stopped, Petra came off the dance floor, found me and asked me to dance with her. I was waiting for this moment and sprang into action. It was a modern Jazz number, dominated by electric guitars and drums. I got into the tempo and tried to show off my skills. Petra was a good dancer too and we soon dominated the floor. Most of the other dancers moved away and joined other spectators watching us intently. When the music stopped, there was an ovation and I took a bow. I then turned to Petra and did the same. She returned my bow with a curtsey, bending her knee and bowing her head. She whispered in my ear that I was a great dancer and gave me a short and unexpected kiss on my cheek. I was chuffed by all this and forgot about the intimidation by Frank's friend.

'The next piece of music was a slow one. I held her ballroom style and she clung on to me, holding my shoulder. We were moving slowly in step and on tune to the music. Overwhelmed, I got carried away. I told her that although I was a quite a lot older than her, I was young at heart and that I was falling in love with her. I wanted to kiss her on the cheek, but right at that moment she turned her face towards me to say something and, my kiss landed on her lips. I must have lost my bearing and I felt the urge to linger on that passionate kiss a wee bit more than was acceptable for the occasion. But alas, at that moment Petra did something quite drastic and completely unexpected. She pushed away from my embrace and ran towards Frank. She said something in a panicked and agitated voice. He and his butch friend approached me and tried to drag me outside. During the commotion, I fell to the floor and started to bleed from my forehead. The events took place so suddenly that I felt helpless and did not know what to do next. I started to think that surely this thug had something to do with the secret agents, the same story was unfolding. I was, by then, sure that the stranger who had tried to intimidate me was the one who had pushed me. I thought I would get a sympathetic hearing and justice from the Austrian police, more so than I had experienced with their British counterparts. I was hopeful that at least they would be able to find out who the assailant was and which organization he was working for.

'I took a taxi and went straight to the local police station. They treated my wound with first aid and were very sympathetic. A policeman drove me back to the dance hall. We found that the dance was still going on, but Petra and her friend Frank were not there. I saw the thug lurking about and identified him as the man who had assaulted me. The policeman asked him to come with him to the police station for questioning, along with a witness. At the station two police officers took the accused and the witness to another room. I was asked to wait outside in a chair. I was very surprised, thought "I should be present while the police questioned them." After a little while, both of them came out, shook hands with the officers and left.

'I was amazed and began to fear the worst. The officers called me inside and after we sat down one of them began to barrage me with questions while the other one took notes. I demanded an explanation as to why they were interrogating me when I was the victim and the accused had been allowed to leave without being charged. The officer told me in a stern tone that since I was a foreigner and was filing a criminal charge against an Austrian citizen it was mandatory for them to record details of my status and circumstances. After they had finished their questioning I enquired what they were going to do about the perpetrators of this crime against me. This time the second officer, who had mostly remained silent during the interrogation, spoke.

'I couldn't believe my ears what I was hearing. He said that, from the description of events provided by an independent witness they were convinced that I was a predatory man attempting to groom young impressionable women. He said that the witness had confirmed this and that the other young man had simply come to the rescue of a petrified girl who was being sexually assaulted. He warned me I should leave the country as soon as possible and said that this was a civilized country and had no place for people like me.

'I was stunned by this and left the police station for my hotel room after giving the police a piece of my mind, accusing them of accepting a bribe to act against me and saying that they were most likely a part of the conspiracy. I threatened to complain to the British embassy and issue a press release back home.

'Next morning after breakfast I packed my bag ready to leave. I am so used to such incidents that I am able to recover quickly. My train was scheduled to depart at 1:30 pm. so I had some time in my hand. I thought of Petra, I was sanguine that she had nothing to do with the conspiracy, but she might be able to give me or send me some information about her friend and his mate. I felt an urge to ask her to accept my apology for any unintentional wrongdoing, if that's what she felt it was. Besides, I wanted to give her my contact details for when she visited England in the spring, should she wish to contact me. I assumed that she would be coming back home from the church long before lunch time. I left my luggage at the reception of the hotel and set out.

'I was very apprehensive about facing Petra, knowing that she must be quite upset at her over-reaction which had caused me to be hurt and distressed. When I arrived at the house, I glimpsed her through the front window, seated in the lounge. I was a bit nervous and rang the bell. Her mother opened the door, sour-faced, and without saying hello asked what she could do for me. I didn't like her tone a bit, but asked to see Petra. She told me rudely that Petra was not at home and shut the door in my face. I went back to the hotel and caught the train to Munich. That's the end of my story my friend. This is certain prove of the long reach of the agents. They are responsible for the miseries of my life. It is up to you whether or not you believe me.'

We were approaching Oxford; the dreaming spires were visible in the neon light. We both kept silent for the rest of the journey.

9

A Brief History of Man

'Gone away', the last three years of my life at Oxford, 'just like that', as Tommy Cooper would say, snapping his fingers. My eventful student life would soon be a thing of the past. Reality was dawning on me – submitting and defending my thesis, preparing to leave Oxford and facing the real world where I would have to do some real work for a living. But I wasn't going to let these morbid thoughts get in the way of my enjoying life, not just yet. I still wanted to make more memories of unforgettable experiences of student days in Oxford, for reminiscing in later life.

The twilight period within the end of swinging sixties and the beginning of seventies brought in the pinnacle of events which took roots in mid-sixties. The pop culture with its Rock music came to a biblical status in Woodstock. Ordinary people of the industrial world took to streets for anti-Vietnam war demonstration and civil-right movement in the USA. First man landed on the moon and started a giant leap for mankind. The cold war reached its pinnacle, making an uncompromising North-South divide. While the north was enjoying unprecedented prosperity, the south was suffering famine of Biblical proportion. The world was changing in an accelerating speed; and all that was led by the youths of that generation. Old values were undergoing re-evaluation.

While all these were happening in the wide world, I was cocooned in my small world of the *adda* circle with Rolf at the centre. I kept myself away from getting seriously involved in any international events, except for attending a meeting here and a demonstration there. I thought of the common saying back home – "What is the point enquiring after the departure time of the cargo ship by a mere ginger merchant?" I had long since abandoned the dream of changing the world. Instead, I decided to change myself to get on board in the changing world. My world at Oxford had never been dull.

Activities at our *Adda Khana* waned. Regular members joined sessions in dribs and drabs, some had abandoned it altogether. For some of us, it was the most pressing time being the final year at the University. I went there only when my flat mate was away or didn't feel like cooking his tasty minced meat curry and rice. For speed and convenience I stopped going to the Moti Mahal and started to go to the Lamb & Flag pub, just round the corner from my lab, for my regular 'chicken and mushroom pie' lunch. That's where one lunch time I had an unexpected encounter with Margaret. I couldn't recognize her at first. She was having a drink at the bar with a male companion. She came to my table and asked,

'You are Rafi, aren't you? Remember me?' I sprang up and extended my hand shouting,

'Maggi! It's great to have met you again. Of course I remember you.'

'I can't talk to you now, I am with somebody. I would like to have a chat with you some other time.' She said in a low voice.

'I am here most lunch time, if you want to catch up with me.' I said.

'We'll meet tomorrow then!' She confirmed, and took leave to re-join her friend at the bar.

Next day she was at the pub, waiting for me while sipping from a glass of something. I bought a drink and joined her across a table. When the waiter came around she asked me what I wanted for lunch.

'Please allow me the privilege to treat you with lunch.' I quipped.

She snapped, 'Don't forget you are still a broke student and I am an executive at the Oxfam head office here, besides, it was I who invited you to meet me.'

I didn't quibble and we started to talk over lunch. She wasted no time and asked me point blank,

'Have you heard from Masud at all?'

'Not a dicky bird!' I said, 'He didn't even say goodbye before he left. I received a brief letter from Banie about six or so months ago. She didn't mention Masud by name, but only that, she accomplished her mission and was happy with her family. She repeatedly thanked me for my friendship and help. I didn't reply, she didn't ask for it either.'

She said, 'Good for you; not wasting a postage stamp. She was nobody's friend anyway. When she realized that you are too small a fry to be of any real help, she dropped you like a used tissue. She needed to use big guns. To start with, she contacted his academic supervisor, then the provost of his college. They were sympathetic to her predicament, but could do very little; it was his private domestic matter. Then she contacted her father, a retired general who belonged to a powerful old boy's network. Soon he was summoned by the Pakistani high commissioner in London. He was asked to pack-up and leave the UK within a fortnight. "Some sort of state security risk in his social activities", was stipulated in a letter to him through the office of the commission. We were both extremely distressed and took legal advice for political asylum. The only option available for him was to go back, divorce his wife, leave his job and then marry me. Only then he would be eligible to come here to live permanently. We were madly in love and couldn't imagine a separation. But there was no alternative.

'I took him to the airport – there were a lot of hugs, kisses and tears. Banie had left a week earlier. He assured me that six month would pass away soon. By that time I would be in Pakistan, marry him and we would make our way back to Oxford together, "to live happily ever after"; like the finale of a fairy tale.'

Magi paused, I looked at her face, eyes were wet, and she excused herself to go to the ladies. I realized she wanted to hide her emotion. I was impatient to know the end. Fully composed, she resumed her story:

'My world fell apart. Regular telephone conversations and doses of hope kept me going with life. He was living with the family of his friend and occasionally went to visit his children at the mansion of Baine's parents, where she was living then. Masud, as far as I gathered was in a trap. He didn't have any legal ground asking for a divorce and she was willing to forgive him rather than agree to a divorce.

He was neither able to leave his job, nor able to travel. I offered to go and help him out of the situation. But there was nothing I could do in that hostile environment back in Pakistan. The situation became so hopeless that I couldn't bear him to suffer anymore agony and I made the decision to break up. That was more than a year ago.'

Sadness gripped me; I asked her, 'What happened next?'

'Nothing', she snapped, 'That's the sad thing. I didn't expect him to take my word as gospel. I was hoping he will find a way to make my dream come true. His love for me was so inexorable that I thought he would be able to move mountain for me, but it turned out to be skin-deep. I waited for several weeks and then I abandoned my pride and rang his number. The lady who answered the call at the other end didn't know who I was talking about; she rang-off, saying 'wrong number'.

Maggie couldn't control her emotion at this time. She took out a tissue paper from her handbag to wipe her tears. She continued:

'I have now picked up the threads and got on with my life. My heart was broken into pieces once before. After two years, he was bored with me and found my close friend more exciting and fun. I got over that acrimonious messy break. It was, however, my decision to have a clean break with Masud, even so, you know, it's always painful and leaves a permanent mark. Hopefully it will get fainter as time goes by. When I saw you yesterday my curiosity to know about him got the better of me. It was the first time I'd heard that Masud was re-united with his family, "Living happily ever after"; our short affair brushed off as an anecdote in his life.'

She thanked me profusely for being a good listener and said,

'I feel relieved now that I have been able to open my heart to someone who I could relate to somehow. Please let me know if you hear any news about him in the future. Here is my contact number.' She handed me a card. We both stood up to leave, she said,

'Please don't feel sorry for me. I am now happy, engaged to be married and looking forward to have an exciting life and an exciting future. I can't deny though that I do still nurture a soft spot for Masud.'

After giving me small goodbye hug she looked at my eyes and with a smile made her parting remark,

'Frailty thy name is man'; don't you agree Rafi?'

I walked to the bar, after she left. The pub was then getting empty. I bought a cup of coffee and sat down, reminiscing the time when I had a coffee here with Masud before delivering Banie's suicide note. I pondered about Maggie's last remark. My thought took me back in time, recollecting Rolf's anguish after being betrayed by a woman. 'At first it was Mosses gave Eve this attribute, and then Shakespeare made it proverbial by assigning this to Hamlet's mother. Why women? I wondered! Men could be and had been equally frail in the matter of heart! Maggie's comment has justification. I asked myself, 'shouldn't it be, 'frailty thy name is human'.

The waiter nudged me, they were closing the pub. I stopped day-dreaming, swallowed the remaining dregs of the coffee, putout the cigarette butt on the ashtray and hit the road for my lab.

🌀

Of late, Rolf and I had cultivated a common interest, not in competition but in collaboration, and that was flirting with Sabiha, a smart and cute undergrad at Somerville studying PPE. She had dated a few Pakistani boys but soon found out that they were mostly after gaining scores and not the marrying type. They were mostly interested in chasing, 'emancipated' Western girls. Besides, her close liaison with any young man might become the 'talk of the town' as a rapidly-spread gossip. For a young ambitious girl from an upper crust background in Pakistan such gossips and rumours wouldn't be good for her marriage prospect. So she adopted a different style of social life.

Her growing friendship with Rolf, an elderly and academic looking gentleman was not likely to cause for any raise eyebrow or spread any gossip. We often went to functions, meetings and parties as 'three-some' and it was, just about acceptable as '*kosher*' to our community. She found him amusing, interesting and a harmless jolly old fellow, and got very fond of him. They both flirted with each other without getting physical and often in my presence. Sabiha's father, a Sandhurst trained graduate gave her the taste of Western classical music. Rolf took her to a concert in London and it was, according to him, a date. I was not able to join them for some previous commitments; it was just as well, a scope to be two-some for a change. Such innocent relationship between intellectual-type elderly teachers and impressionable young women are not uncommon in our urban societies back home.

I was, however, worried, "He might take it the wrong way,

fall in love again, and end up with a broken heart and blame the phantom organization for it." I hoped that he had learned a lesson from his previous failed romantic escapades, and would be cautious in the mater of heart – 'Haste makes waste'; I remember Masud gave me the advice once.

The scorching summer was nearing its end, making way for my favourite season, the autumn. It arrived gradually, painting the trees in different colours as the days progressed. While I was enjoying the season's bounty, the fear of the approaching winter, after a short-lived autumn, was not far from my thoughts. At the fag-end of my student days, I couldn't help being in a melancholy mood, dwelling on Shelley's words, replacing the seasons to suit my feeling of concern – "If autumn hath come can winter be far behind!" Winter arrived too soon for my liking. However, I consoled myself with the English proverb – "every cloud has a silver lining", and wishing – "the cold and miserable weather would allow me to work on my thesis for long uninterrupted hours."

Although I dreaded the coming of winter, I did look forward to the possibility of seeing and enjoying winter snow during the Christmas period, just as much as children do. Snow, for me, was still a novel experience, refreshing and enchanting, following my mesmerizing experiencing the first snow of first winter in England three years ago.

"Christmas" replaced "weather" as the topic of conversation amongst my English colleagues and friends, since weather was no longer a topic with any real prospect of any drastic change over that season. In most encounters they would greet me saying, 'cheer up Christmas is nearly here'.

We were all looking forward to a welcome break from the drudgery of everyday routine. Travel and parties during the holiday period were other common topics. The hype around the impending Christmas holidays and listening to other people's plans was beginning to bore and annoy me, particularly when I had nothing much to talk about for myself.

Most of my English friends even knew what presents they would be receiving from friends and relatives and, were compiling lists of presents for reciprocation. We, the people of the so called 'developing countries' do not plan anything much in advance. Being fatalistic by nature, we are never sure whether we will be here tomorrow, next week or next month. Besides, our cultural background is such that we believe advance planning takes away the charm and pleasure of surprise.

However, remembering the saying – "When in Rome, do as the Romans do", I had resolved to act like an Englishman while in England. Consequently, I was starting to think like one. But where could I go and what could I do to mimic my English colleagues! I had no parental home, and therefore, couldn't observe the annual ritual of Christmas with the family.

One afternoon in early December, I bumped into my supervisor, Professor Walsh, while I was coming out of the departmental library. I hadn't met him for a while and it occurred to me that he might be deliberately trying to avoid me. After all, Christmas was not far away and he wouldn't be happy to be lumbered with reviewing my boring thesis during the break.

He asked me the same question I had been asked throughout the last week or so,

'What are you doing over Christmas?

I toyed with the idea of wearing a placard announcing, "NO PLANS YET FOR CHRISTMAS", to avoid the hassle of explaining things. Although I didn't have any plans, I made up a fictitious plan there and then, informing him that I was going to Paris to see a buddy for a few days.

'What are you planning to do during the Christmas holidays?'

I asked in return.

'Christmas is not for doing anything,' he replied, 'On the contrary; it is meant for doing practically nothing, except eating, drinking and cracking nuts and watching special television programmes in front of a log fire if you have one.'

He made no mention of church services or praying and continued,

'Christmas day is not the true birthday of Jesus Christ; nobody knows exactly when he was born. It's simply the adoption of a mid-winter pagan festival by Christians.'

He wished me a good time and fun with my friend in Paris before taking his leave.

Behind the impulsive idea of meeting my buddy, Mushfiq, was a long-standing wish to visit Paris on the cheap. He was a one-time partner in many of my misdemeanours during our wilder days at the University back home. He started at the Sorbonne the year before I went to Oxford. I wrote to him about a possible rendezvous in Paris during Christmas recess. His reply was sharp, but made me totally flabbergasted – "I am now convinced that it is silly and futile to waste any more time doing research on a meaningless topic, in pursuit of a useless qualification. I have, therefore, abandoned my studies in pursuit of peace and happiness here in this world, and hereafter. Consequently, the University had withdrawn its grant and I have lost my seat at the hall of residence."

I read on, "I am now at peace with myself and found some like-minded people to help me establish the first mosque in Paris and to launch a *'Tabligh'* organization, with the goal of promoting and spreading the message of Islam amongst the non-practicing believers and also of converting people of other faiths to Islam.'

He was ecstatic to hear of my plan to visit him, as he hoped for another lost sheep returning to the fold, perhaps a potential *Emir* who would sacrifice worldly ambition in favour of carrying out God's work. Moreover, he emphasized that my participation in the journey on this glorious path would allow me to collect "*Swabs*", sort of 'tokens', which would help me find a place in heaven after death.

The idea was to travel from city to city, taking advantage of the hospitality of local Muslims living in close-knit communities. It would usually involve sleeping on the floors of other people's houses at night, while the day would be spent going door to door preaching the good words of El-Lah. He assured me that I would have the experience of a lifetime and that it would be a watershed in my life.

I got worried. I remembered how I had escaped the clutches of the sole vendor of the so called, 'Fourth Internationalist', avoiding the life changing experience of becoming a member of the Naxalite guerrilla movement in India. That had been easy; he was no friend of mine. But this member of the Parisian *Tablighi Jamaat* was my onetime blood-brother. I feared that if we were to meet face to face, his persuasive prowess might be irresistible. However, the promise of a place in heaven surrounded by 70 beautiful and firm-breasted maidens as a reward for following the path he had set out was tempting. After much soul-searching I decided, with some regret, to forgo the opportunity of seeing Paris in the company of my dear friend in this world and a secured place in heaven, in the next.

I realised that such an experience could jeopardise my immediate ambition of securing my qualification, a vital commodity for my survival in this world. The risk was too great. I decided to stay put in Oxford despite the miserable weather and depressive mood.

At last Christmas arrived, with its three episodes – Christmas Eve, Christmas day and Boxing Day. I spent Christmas Eve watching television in our college common room. There were only a few foreign students and no '*deshi*' boys for an *adda*. I made my way into the department building after brunch. There was not a soul in the whole building and it was a bit eerie. I feared that ghosts normally haunt empty buildings. I crept back out without much delay.

It was the first time during the last three and a half years that I was spending the Christmas recess on my own. It was a big challenge to have this experience of living like an Indian *Yogi* or a Buddhist monk, spending time in isolation and in meditation to achieve '*gnosis*. I decided to spend the whole holiday of nearly 9 days all told, in pursuit of excellence in the art of fighting and defending my thesis against the enemy within (the internal examiner) and the enemy outside (the external examiner). I withstood the loneliness of a five full days, including the three days of Christmas, but alas, I made very little progress in my planned pursuit.

The deadline for completing my thesis was approaching fast. I could ill afford the time for socializing, let alone meeting up with my mate, Rolf. Despite the pressure and urgency of my academic work I had been nursing an insatiable desire to know more about his 'organization' and its 'secret agents'. I had put this on the back burner, prioritizing on more urgent matters, and by the end of 5th day I found myself mentally exhausted, having been confined in the library and totally preoccupied with piles of papers and experimental data, trying to get some sense and meaning out of them all.

It was Friday evening and the end of the fifth day of my self-imposed solitary confinement. I knew most of my friends and acquaintances were out somewhere relaxing after the gruelling week. I felt left out and was craving for company and a fix of *adda* session. I could not withstand the loneliness any longer and went out to the *Moti Mahal* for my evening meal. I was surprised and disappointed to find none of my *deshi* friend there. I wondered if they knew something that I didn't.

In hindsight I felt lucky that none of my *adda baz* friends were there and I didn't have to get bogged down in futile, time-wasting argument. I returned to the library with the intention of continuing with my thesis write-up. It was early evening and I could hear the chattering and laughter of youngsters passing along the Banbury road, from my office cum laboratory on the first floor. I couldn't settle down to work and was wondering what to do next. Suddenly I remembered that there was an event in one of the colleges which could be of interest to me, but I couldn't remember what it was about. I dug out the *Vade Mecum*, the weekly news leaflet which lists university events. I found out that there was indeed a lecture on the art and craft of Japanese flower arranging with a practical demonstration at Balliol College, starting at 7 pm that evening.

My resolve to concentrate only on academic work vanished and I found myself queuing at the door of a small auditorium inside the College campus, just in time for the start of the hour-long event. I managed to squeeze into a seat and looked around the hall. It was almost full with an audience of roughly fifty odd people. Rolf was not amongst them, I would have spotted him instantly. "The ancient Japanese art of flower arranging would be just his sort of thing" – I thought.

I was sanguine that he wouldn't miss such an event. Apart from the aesthetic aspect of this art form, he would be tempted to have the pleasure of watching and speaking to a cute and nimble-fingered young Japanese lady in a Kimono. Then I wondered "Why on earth I had come here?" I had no interest, whatsoever, in the art of flower arranging. I didn't really believe it's an art form in the traditional sense. I felt embarrassed to realise that I went there for no other reason except for a subconscious desire to meet Rolf.

I tried to convince myself that his absence was a blessing in disguise. I justified my attendance as a well-deserved break that would help rejuvenate my brain for serious academic work. Although I was, to some extent, disappointed by Rolf's absence, I was quite unhappy not to see a pretty, delicate young Japanese lady hosting the event in sweet broken English. Instead, a smartly dressed ethereal young man, sporting a manicured French-cut beard, was introduced to the audience as an expert on "oriental flower arranging" and the high priest of that occasion. Although I had very little interest in the topic, and other things were cluttering my mind, I tried to listen to him attentively.

As far as I could gather, "Ikebana" had a spiritual aspect that supposedly helped uplift the mood of both the creator and the appreciator of this art form. The buzz word was, "Living in the Moment". I felt, I did not have much time for this stuff, and left as soon as the lecture finished and before the discussion session started. As I was hurrying through the small corridor of the auditorium leading to the gate, I almost crashed into Rolf. I was stunned,

'Where was he rushing to?'

'Let's get inside quickly,' he said, gently touching my shoulder, 'The presentation is about to start. We have to get seats to enjoy it in comfort.'

I realised what had happened, "Too many engagements and no diary." Stifling my laughter, I said sardonically,

'Calm down my friend, there is no rush. You are only an hour late and have missed the show and I am afraid there wouldn't be a second one for a while.'

He looked at me, sussed out the situation and broke down in laughter with his typical display of double-upping, while trying to control his outburst.

After recovering from his amusement he stood up and said,

'I am sorry to have missed the encounter with the kimono-attired Japanese beauty. I was hoping to approach her for some private lesson in flower arrangement.'

I didn't let on as to the true identity of the demonstrator. After we went out of the college gate, Rolf stopped and asked,

'Now what?'

'Don't be stupid,' I interjected, 'the question is, "Now where?"'

'You must bless your stars. If I was not stupid, you wouldn't have the good fortune of bumping into me. Keep up, my friend, I have to learn everything you know about Japanese flower arrangement.' He shot back.

At the end of Cornmarket Street we passed St Giles and then headed up the Banbury road. I knew the location of tonight's rendezvous was going to be his flat. I tried to talk to him about the event I had just attended, but in response he muttered briefs like, 'yes', 'no', 'later' etc. I could sense that, like most other times, he was going to be a silent walking companion, so I put up with it and kept quiet for the remainder of our walk together.

Once at Rolf's flat I settled down on the sofa while he went to the kitchen and came back with two cups of instant coffee. He sat down on the sofa opposite, as usual and demanded to know all about the art and philosophy of Japanese flower arrangement. I corrected him,

'The word is not, "arrangement", but "arranging". I continued with an impromptu introduction, showing off my newly acquired knowledge on the subject:

'People in the West take flowers and a vase with water and put these together so that eventually their full blooms, with their varied colours, are vividly displayed. There is no subtlety in this. In the Orient, particularly in Japan, "flower-arranging" has been transformed into a fine art form. A few flowers, a non-descript vase, a few freshly cut twigs with leaves and most importantly, the space in the surrounding environment; all together have to make a symphony to serenade the earth, the space in the vicinity of the viewer, and the sky above.'

Rolf interrupted, 'So you think these interpretations of the spiritual aspect of *Ikebana* are all clap trap!'

'Of course they are. But if you have faith in the artist and his or her interpretation in its art form then, like religious dogmas and addiction to fine arts it is not considered to be nonsense. If you do not see the beauty and the deep meaning of the art form produced by a so called 'recognized' artist you are branded as a philistine. But then doesn't beauty lie in the eye of the beholder?'

Rolf's unusual silence and interest in my interpretation and analysis of the art of flower arranging encouraged me to continue:

'My first impression of the *Ikebana* is that, to brand it as a fine art form is a misnomer. It should be classified as a craft or a commercial art form. The commercial entrepreneurship of the Japanese is recognized worldwide and had always amazed me. After the destruction of its economy and the degradation of its cultural heritage at the end of WWII, the nation sprang back with economic regeneration through industrial revolution. First exporting its food, such as *sushi*, sports such as Kung Fu, mirror paintings etc., as art forms; they are now exporting *Ikebana* as a fine art form to the West.

'The Japanese understood the mind-set of Westerners, who aspire to be recognised as cultured and intellectual. They are drawn to anything which is exotic, oriental and amenable to philosophical interpretation. After a dose of Indian *Kama sutra* and *Maharishi Mohesh Yugi*, *Ikebana* had to be the next best thing here. This thirst of the modern man to create something out of nothing and see something where there is nothing must be the sign of his instinctive effort to regain his lost soul.'

I stopped after my long monologue. My scathing remark on

the lack of Japanese spiritualism probably had evoked a deep feeling in Rolf's mind. Usually he wouldn't allow me so much time to shed light on a topic of great interest to him and on which he thinks he was gifted with much more knowledge than I would ever have. He would usually assume the authority to talk about this and correct me as and when necessary. He had been mentally preparing his response while half-listening to my speech, interpreting the Japanese art of *Ikebana*. Now it was my turn to listen:

'You are mistaken my friend', Rolf began, 'It is not a matter of losing soul. Modern man is totally consumed by materialism. His apparent thirst for novo-art is his effort to mask the ugly reality of materialism. But, the modern 'Man' is wired up ultimately to dig out and re-connect with his primitive instinct. I believe the primitive instinct of 'Man' is returning to modern Man at a new psycho-physiological level. This is basically the title of my book, the "*Magnum Opus*", for which I have been working for the last three years.

'I believe that modern man will, one day, inculcate "flower arranging" as a part of his worship, as primitive Man did. These ancestors of ours had both faith and the instinct of the art of flower arranging, so they could worship their god with flowers. Modern man has buried his god in ugly materialism. In the upcoming future he will be looking desperately for his god with a meticulously composed garland of flowers in his hand with which to worship. He will soon realize that the god he is looking for is not out there. He will then compose his own god to worship. Flower arranging, body painting such as tattoos, body piercing for adorning with jewellery, music, dance all these things will be a part of his arsenal of god worshiping. Primitive Man did the same.'

Rolf paused with a glare of satisfaction in his face, probably with the feeling that he had delivered a convincing prelude to his book to a phantom audience on the event of launching it. He had done extensive and intensive studies of old and new literatures on the origin and evolution of cults, occults, religion etc. He had found good justification for his conviction and accretion that the instincts of primitive 'man' will come back to modern Man. But most importantly, he had the courage of his convictions to actively promote his ideas against many odds. For a man like me, who only understands something which can be proved scientifically, Rolf's deductive logic made me wonder, but did not influence me enough to change my outlook on the field of art and culture.

I enquired, 'I am sorry Rolf, you did not explain what you meant by the instinct of primitive Man. Or if you did, I did not understand it. If you could explain this in the language of common men, not using jargon of psychology or philosophy, perhaps I would then be able to understand the subject of your research.'

'The attribute that we call, 'understanding', my friend, is something you have to cultivate within yourself. Perhaps, one day when you find your god, he or she may bless you with that gift. I can only try to communicate the idea as best I can, with my limited linguistic ability. But I can't give you 'understanding'. You have to listen, not only with your ears, but also with your mind.'

Rolf continued with his sermon, 'To understand the instinct of primitive man, yes my friend, you need to understand what I mean by "instinct". Even before that you must know what I mean when I speak of "man", and the history or so to speak, "the origin' of man". Just wait, before you mentally relapse into a state of despair, thinking that I am just tagging on to Darwin's theory on 'the origin of species'. No my friend. I am not talking about Homo erectus or Homo sapiens. These upright apes developed intelligence and dexterity. They invented fire and then the wheel. Through the rotation of that wheel they have arrived at the 21st century with the title, Homo sapiens.

'I am not talking about them when I talk about "man", for which my definition lies in the true meaning of the Latin word, 'sapiens' which is 'wise'. Darwin's theory of evolution describes the process of natural selection, establishing intelligent modern man through the instinct of 'survival of the fittest', but it does not give a clue about when and how Homo sapiens became 'the wise man'. My book will start with a new theory of the origin of that human attribute, 'Self gnosis', commonly known as 'consciousness.'

I asked him to give me a break for a brief stroll outside. He knew it was not for fresh air, but for a puff of the 'holy smoke'. He was happy to comply with my request' as he knew, under its influence I become a better listener. When I returned refreshed, he resumed his theory of the origin of man:

'In my theory of the "origin of consciousness" there is no evolutionary process involved. The attribute had always been wired into the genetic code of the apes, in the single-cell life form, and even in the atoms and molecules which make up the Universe. This attribute had been waiting for millennium for the arrival of Homo sapiens through an evolutionary process which occurred over a brief period of time of just a few million years. It needed a starter, an unprecedented lighting or thunder, or an impact of meteorite or, if you like, the command of God, to instil the 'the consciousness' in Darwin's Homo sapiens.

'For some Homo sapiens, the burden of sudden 'gnosis' was unbearable. They screamed out to declare this watershed event in their lives. Newly acquired consciousness drove them to venture into remote caves to put imprints of their palms on the walls using coloured mud. They even engraved profiles of animals such as the bison, to communicate to posterity, to declare the arrival of a new species of Homo sapiens with consciousness, 'the origin of man'.

'That was the beginning of a new world with a new chain of species which was not a part of Darwin's evolutionary process but will continue in a loop, stretched and expanded by a parameter called 'time'. The ends of this expanding circular chain are destined to meet to continue reforming the loop with modified parameters. This is the primitive "man" in my definition, who is omnipotent with a sudden miraculous beginning and whose end is ingrained in this beginning.

'Those creative activities of the primitive man were not based on logic or faith. They were not for promoting or expressing skill. They were the outcome of his instinct, like the cry of a new born baby, instinctively declaring his arrival in this world.'

I was at a loss to understand the relevance of this hypothesis to the subject of his book. Noticing this, he said,

'I was not very optimistic that you would be able to quite apprehend my hypothesis on the miraculous appearance of consciousness in Homo sapiens. To understand this you need a great deal of faith and meditation and the ability to come to logical conclusions without getting confused by half-baked, poorly understood psycho-science or religious dogmas.'

To show my keen interest in his hypothesis I commented,

'You said it quite succinctly my friend. But isn't it the same proposition that the religious apologists have been making to reconcile the heavenly message on the creation of 'man' in the scriptures with the theory of evolution, propounded by Darwin and widely accepted as a fact? You must be talking about 'conscious man', as mentioned in the scriptures; modern man, transformed from Homo sapiens by the command of God.'

Rolf interjected, 'The difference is that the chain primitive man started has a beginning but no end, whereas the chain created by man through heavenly intervention, as mentioned in the scriptures, has a beginning, when God said, 'let there be man' and an end which is the 'Doomsday'. Abrahamic religions provide some solace and comfort to modern man desperate to find a meaning and purpose of life, an identity and a personal 'god'.

But these do not mention or allow any question on the evolution of 'consciousness. You see how this cave-dwelling primitive man, through the evolution of 'intelligence', has conquered and exploited nature and became its master. He has become a 'super man' which Nietzsche called 'over man' in his book, 'Thus Spoke Zarathustra'. But unfortunately, amongst all the material gains, scientific and technological advancements and within the mountains of religious books, the idea of the manifestation of consciousness is lacking.'

Pointing his finger at a small but original painting of a sailing ship on a stormy sea by a less well known Italian classical master, Rolf said in an emotional tone,

'Look at this painting. Look not only with your eyes, but also with your mind's eyes. Can you read the message encrypted within the brush strokes in the paint of the picture?

'No, my friend, you cannot. You, like millions of other modern men, are in a chain defined by Darwin. But I believe I can read the message. It says, "I am a notch ahead of the primitive man and still bear his instinct despite being almost drowned in modern materialism." Perhaps, beyond my own knowledge, I do, at times, undergo a kind of metamorphosis and temporarily turn into an *Ubermensch*.' To add some fuel to fire, I said,

'But instinct never goes away. Instincts of the primitive man are hidden in the genetic code of the modern man. Such codes exist in the genes of other species such as birds and fishes. These codes are almost certainly the guiding force which makes them travel thousands of miles to arrive at specific destinations to lay their eggs, making the link with the next generation, just as their parents did previously. So why do you assert that the instinct of man will come back to modern man?'

The fact that somebody was listening with interest and questioning his arguments made him pick up with renewed enthusiasm,

'Yes, for instincts of survival and the propagation of the species your comment is absolutely correct. Modern man is no different from his ancestors. The only difference is, he has lost his finer instincts, the instincts of spontaneously playing music, drawing, painting, singing, laughing and crying. Perhaps this is the destiny of the modern man. It is also written in his genetic code that, in the fullness of time, he will return to the state of primitive man.'

'If you think about it you will realise that the need and the greed of modern man has given rise to this ugly materialism, of which one of the consequences is the international arms race. The evolution of intelligence has transformed him into a monster with unprecedented power for self-destruction. I believe that primitive man will reappear from the mass grave of modern man. He will again sing, dance and paint pictures on canvas to re-start the spiral of the chain, of course in a new psycho-physiological manifestation.'

I knew Rolf was a devotee of Nietzsche, and one of the founder members of the Nietzsche Appreciation Society (NAS) at Oxford long before I arrived there. They met every month to discuss some chosen aspect of his philosophies. Once, Rolf cajoled me into attending a session of their gathering. There was a dozen or so members and most of them were listeners. I have read Nietzsche quite extensively and enjoyed reading his books, but analyses of his philosophy were, mostly, beyond me and not of much interest to me. Once I asked Rolf if he was aware that Nietzsche's writing had anti-Semitic elements which influenced Hitler and the elite members of the third Reich into believing that Jews were sub-human and the Aryan Germans, superhuman. He answered, "Yes, of course". I then asked him how he could be at peace with himself appreciating and adoring an anti-Semitic philosopher like him. His answer to my query was an emotional out-burst,

'The peacock has gorgeously beautiful feathers, but ugly feet. Flowers have poison and nectar. Good and evil, both are divine attributes of human kind. Man must train himself to appreciate and get benefit from the good and beautiful attributes for the preparation for his journey to achieve the status of being an 'over man'. I must confess that I have taken the cue for my book from Nietzsche's philosophy.'

To make him feel that I was at one with him, I tried very hard to look at the picture with my mind's eye while listening to his words of wisdom. But I have to confess that I was not able to decipher the code in the brush strokes. I knew why "I was not a believer like Rolf and I did not have a clean slate. Lots of agenda items were jotted down on my slate. It was getting quite late and I feared soon Rolf might extend his lecture on Nietzsche's concept of the transmigration of 'over man' to 'ultimate man'. Before he could start, I stood up and said,

'I think I have had my fair share of your hypothesis, whatever you may call it. You must give me time to digest it, before providing me with another dose of your or Nietzsche's philosophy, to avoid me having a mental diarrhoea due to an overdose.'

Rolf wished me good night adding, 'I enjoyed the discussion on my hypothesis. Perhaps we will have another session on this topic very soon, now that I know you are so keenly interested in this topic.'

As I was getting ready to leave, Rolf said,

By the way, I forgot to mention that I have received a letter from Sabiha from Pakistan last week.' He continued in a sarcastic tone, 'Hope you are not feeling jealous. She did, however, send her greetings to you. As a matter of fact she is planning to come here couple of months' time to attend her graduation ceremony. I am going to invite her to be my guest during her stay at Oxford. We will have a wonderful reunion party, just three of us, what do you think?'

I also received a card, thanking me for arranging a farewell party at his flat on the eve of her departure. I deliberately didn't mention this to him, in case he didn't' get one and felt jealous.

On the way back to my flat I was wondering about Rolf's fascination for Sabiha. I was not unusually worried about that; "Out of sight - out of mind"; he will soon forget about her and get involved in another project.

10

The Death Camp

The similarity between Rolf's love escapades with Afariva in Oxford and Petra in Innsbruck, both ending in fiascos, was rather uncanny. I started to question the basis of his conviction that the "secret agents of an organization" were behind these debacles. I began to think that there had to be some mental block which prevented him from realizing the truth.

The truth was that he had passed his youth many moons ago. Natural aging is a relentless process and all of us have to succumb to it, there is no reprieve. One can be youthful in one's mind and spirit, but, at the end of the day, the face gives it away. Rolf's eyes saw his balding head, lined forehead and sunken eyes in the mirror, but his mind failed to register them as signs of approaching old age. If anyone bothered to point out to him that this was the cause of his failure in romantic liaisons with young girls, he would reject the suggestion as utter nonsense and strike his or her name from his list of friends.

He needed an explanation for the fiascos of the romantic adventures he had undertaken so far. I was beginning to believe that he had to invent the so called 'secret agents' as a plausible explanation for those debacles to keep his sanity and console his tormented mind. Rolf had not yet found anyone to testify against them. Besides, the agents, allegedly hell-bent on unbalancing his mind, were supposedly acting within the law.

I didn't know much about his past, but from occasional references and titbits during conversations on several occasions I picked up his basic portfolio – "He is a German Jew, who had studied medicine in Berlin. He had to leave Germany for England sometime during or after the Second World War. He never told me what he did for living, but I guessed he was probably a part-time art dealer, not that I was particularly interested in his source of income. He dabbled in homeopathic practice, but as far as I knew, it was not to earn a living.

I didn't wish to pry into his private life, particularly the time that he had spent in Germany during the Nazi era, in case I touched a sensitive nerve. I even thought, – "Being a Jew and living in Germany, he could be a survivor of the Holocaust, Hitler's final solution for the elimination of the Jewish people. That could provide an explanation for his state of mind.

I discussed the symptoms of his paranoia, under the promise of secrecy and without mentioning any names, with a fellow student doing research in neuroscience. He told me it was possible that my friend was suffering from schizophrenia, which is often triggered by trauma or shock. He also mentioned that although there was no known permanent cure for that condition it could be controlled through a combination of drugs and psychotherapy.

I researched the symptoms of schizophrenia, but they did not fit with Rolf's normal day to day behaviour. I read that psychotic paranoia might possibly be overcome by exercising the practice of imposing mind over matter. For that, Rolf needed a trigger or a catalyst in his conscious state of mind and he would have to want to be cured. Someone whom he trusted and felt quite close might be able be an effective catalyst. I would have dearly liked to be that catalyst. I was also warned that, in the case of mental illness resulting from a life-changing event in the past, wrong diagnosis and treatment could cause untold damage to an otherwise generally normal person. To be able to help him, I felt I had to know the past life history of this enigmatic and visionary friend of mine.

My thesis was with the typist. I felt I had done enough preparation to defend it during the viva voce, the date of which had not yet been scheduled. I felt relaxed and stopped further preparation, finding that, the more I went through my thesis, the more I got frightened by finding that there was much more I needed to know and write. I had accepted the fact that, as far as the thesis was concerned, enough was enough. I felt it was time before it was too late to confront Rolf. I became desperately interested to know his life-shattering story. I gathered that he knew it would soon be time to say good-bye to me; therefore, he was also desperate to tell me the intimate story of past events that, according to him, had been defining moments in his life.

One afternoon instead of going to Moti Mahal for a supper-cum-*adda* I decided to take Rolf out for dinner. I walked down to my lab and rang him from there. As soon as he heard my voice he, as usual, answered in a deep, serious voice – "Rolf is not at home at this moment."

'Could I talk to his spirit, then?' I asked with equal seriousness.

He started to giggle loudly and I imagined him doubling up in conjunction to his own humour. '

You are talking to his spirit; talk then, whoever you are,' he said.

'What the hell are you doing there in the company of "Undeads" within the confines of the four walls of your claustrophobic room?' I asked; and then told him, 'You are missing out on the fun the "Livings" are having in the world outside.'

He shot back, 'But you don't understand, if I were outside, who the hell would have answered your call?'

I asked him if he was ready to face the cold weather for another culinary adventure with me, this time as my guest. He couldn't believe what he'd heard and asked,

'Did I hear you say, – 'as my guest'? If that's correct, then I must say I am surprised, pleasantly of course. It is quite unusual for you to use that word. There must be an occasion for such generosity on your part. Tell me then, what's the big deal?'

'It is very simple. The sun is shining this afternoon after a few days of rain and gloom. It cheered me up and I thought I shall share my joy with a good friend over dinner. What's unusual about that?'

He was not convinced that I was giving him the real reason. He insisted on knowing the real purpose of the celebration, remaining adamant that he would not otherwise accept my invitation.

'It's a secret matter and can't be divulged until after the dinner, I said, 'Therefore, my good friend, I am sorry not to have the pleasure of your company on this occasion. Thanks anyway. I am sure it won't be difficult for me to find another taker of my offer of a free dinner, even at this last minute.'

I knew Rolf well enough to guess what would be his response and as expected he shot back,

'Well, 'a friend in need is a friend indeed'; therefore, under the circumstances I have to make an exception. Tell me the time and the venue. By the way, is there any dress code?'

Rolf arrived at my flat at about 7:30 pm and from there we went to the *Dil Dunia* restaurant in Walton Street. Rolf enjoyed a chicken *korma;* a lightly spiced chicken curry cooked in yoghurt and ground coconut, with plain rice. Although at home, he would never cook anything with even a trace of spices other than a pinch of salt and a shake of pepper, he had no hesitation in trying spicy food, particularly when it was free.

At the end of our enjoyable meal I told him what I was celebrating, 'On this very day, many moons ago, I was born, that's what I am celebrating.'

When he'd finished congratulating me, I responded,

'I can't claim any credit for it, that's why I normally never celebrate my birthday. Tonight I decided to make an exception and make it an excuse for us to have dinner together, as there may not be another opportunity. My time here in this country and in Oxford is coming to an end very soon.'

I continued, 'Back home we have many annual festivities, including thirteen Hindu festivals, several Muslim religious festivals and many other cultural and social festivities celebrating the arrivals of the seasons, birthdays of great poets and others, etc. Therefore, we do not need to mark birthdays of mortals like us as another excuse for a celebration.

'I knew if I did not tempt you with a free meal, you would automatically take it that we would be going Dutch and having Jewish blood in you vein, you might not want to join me for such an extravagant event on a cold winter afternoon when you could have a better meal at home for a fraction of cost that a restaurant would charge.' Rolf retorted,

'You silly fool, you could have used this occasion to squeeze out a present from me if you had told me about it before.'

He suggested that we go to his flat for coffee after the dinner. He also said he wanted to show me something very interesting.

At his flat I settled down comfortably on the sofa. He switched on the heater and prepared coffee. Then he brought in a couple of lamps and set them strategically in front of me while switching off the ceiling light. Next he brought an easel and set it in front of me and asked me to close my eyes.

I heard him approaching from one corner of the room and resting something, most probably a painting, on to the easel near me. He then sat down on the sofa by my side and asked me to open my eyes while studying the effect of the painting on me from my facial expression. After a while he left me alone with the iconic painting.

I kept my eyes focussed on it. It was a black and white painting of the face of a beautiful young oriental woman in a mirror. The absolutely flawless facial profile was set against the background of black hair, tightly braided in two parts and running along her smooth slender shoulders, each tied with a single white ribbon. She was endowed with well-proportioned nose, eyes and ears. I thought she was looking exclusively at me with a pair of dreamy mysterious eyes, which evoked a deep emotion within my heart. The feeling couldn't be described in prosaic fashion. Her beauty was so alluring and her gaze so inviting that I felt she was alive and coming out of the confinement of the mirror towards me. I was truly mesmerized.

Although the maiden in the mirror was looking at me at an angle, an aura of seductiveness emanated from an unfathomable and indiscernible smile on her face. Perhaps such was the nature of the smile on the face of Leonardo Da Vinci's Mona Lisa at the Louvre. My gaze was deeply focused on the painting when Rolf entered the room quietly and observed my fascination.

It was a triumph for Rolf and a shame on me for my involuntary weakness induced by a mirror painting. As soon as I realized that, I composed myself, straightened my legs, and sat upright. Rolf was staring at me with a smirk on his face. The situation was a bit tense, as in, "who blinks first". I couldn't stand the gloating expression on his face as if to say – "I can read your mind; I know what you are thinking." I said,

'Not a bad painting. I don't know much about Japanese art and it would be audacious of me to make a judgement on its inherent quality and beauty. Please tell me more about it.' Rolf needed no encouragement he continued,

'You see, "painting" is unique amongst all art forms arising from natural human instinct. From the dawn of civilization, humans have sung and danced as expressions of their inner mood or feeling. Paintings do the same, but with one big exception. They can convey a message to posterity, like the ones in caves or those of the masters in modern times. Classical paintings bring out the hidden messages and can only be deciphered if viewed with heart and soul and accepted as an article of faith. When you become a connoisseur of such paintings, they become pieces of heavenly beauty and carriers of messages for you and those who will inherit the earth after you.

'Da Vinci's 'Mona Lisa' became a masterpiece when 16th century poets in Europe wrote ballads on this. Later this happened when the elite and powerful, the kings and popes of that era started to recognize and patronized the artistic talents and the visionary minds of the masters, likes of Michelangelo, Raphael and Leonardo Da Vinci. So, my friend, to really appreciate and enjoy such a creation and get the nectar out of it, you need to have a very sensitive mind and have faith in the existence of its inherent beauty, and also the message a masterpiece carries. By the way, this mirror painting is not Japanese; it is Chinese, a late 18th century Cantonese masterpiece; such paintings were once very popular in Europe.'

I took offence at his comments and was hurt at being accused of being a philistine and for not being sufficiently sensitive, and also for exposing my total ignorance of oriental art. It also made me angry because I realised that he was able to read my mind and tell me unpleasant and unacceptable truths about myself. I snapped,

'I am sorry to have to tell you that, with a sensitive mind and a vision for – god knows what, you have been taking and enjoying the heavenly nectars created by others, but you haven't given anything to anybody in return. The manifestation of humanity, to which you claim to belong, arises from sacrifice and giving and not taking. Besides, how do I know that you are not living in a fool's paradise with your heavenly paintings? Could the beauty emanating from the mirror painting in front of me, or even that from that of the Mona Lisa be a mere 'exposure effect'?'

Despite being a self-declared psychoanalyst, Rolf did not guess that his general comments would upset me and spoil a lovely evening. After a rather long pause, he said,

'You have a very valid point there, my friend. I am aware of the fact that while the 'Mona Lisa' was hanging safely on the wall of the Louvre museum not many spectators stopped by to look at it. However, when it was stolen and disappeared for nearly two years, and made national and international news, there was a long queue of people who wanted to see the empty space where the picture used to be hung.

'You should know me well enough by now to realize that I am not an ordinary man of the street. I go for the intrinsic quality of a painting with a clean slate of mind, without any preconception from external stimulus. Exposure does not affect me. Anyway, let us not fall out by being personal about the attributes of art and culture and leave discussion on the subject, by accepting that – "Beauty in an art form, lies in the eyes of the beholder or ears of the listener, in the case of music; ok, my friend?'

He paused and commanded, 'Now, get up and follow me, I have decided to give you a surprise present for your birthday. Now just follow me.'

I followed him to the music room, which he also used to store more paintings and other memorabilia, in addition to his grand piano.

He continued, 'As you know I never play my violin for the pleasure of others and certainly not in public concerts. I play for my own pleasure, particularly to express and enjoy sad thoughts and memories, sometime happiness as well. I feel happy tonight and want to play for your ears only as a present for your birthday.'

I was chuffed and took a comfortable seat in the music room. Rolf took the violin out of its case and unwrapped it from its muslin cloth gently and very carefully, muttering,

'You wouldn't believe it but this is a priceless instrument, a masterpiece you might say, with superb quality and exquisite beauty. It is one of roughly 500 odd surviving 17th century Stradivarius violins in the world. I am the lucky and proud possessor of one of these. There is a very interesting story about how this elegant instrument came into my possession. Perhaps there will be another occasion when I can tell you that.'

He set the script on the music stand in front of him and played a very melodious piece for nearly half an hour. I closed my eyes as if in a deep meditation and remained as such for a while even after the playing stopped. Rolf asked if I was asleep.

'No,' I said, 'that was splendid, superb, bewildering. I now understand what you were saying earlier about the birth of masterpieces. Indeed, it requires a combination of the gifted talent of a master craftsman and the sensitive receptive mind with a deep feeling. This is the best present that you could have given me. You couldn't have pleased me more if you were to give me your mirror painting. Please tell me about the music.'

Rolf was pleased, feeling that he had at last converted a philistine to a lover of classical music and said,

'This piece is from Wagner's, 'Siegfried', especially adapted for violin. He composed this for his wife, as a birthday present, and it is also my favourite. Don't you think, it is very appropriate that I present this to you on your birthday?'

I said, 'As far as I know, Wagner was a well-known anti-Semitic who inspired Hitler and the Nazis to conceive the policy of creating a pure Aryan race. Don't you have any hatred or revulsion towards him or against his music?'

Rolf was impressed by my comments and knowledge on the famous composers and reply passionately,

'You asked me a similar question in connection with my great admiration for Nietzsche, allegedly an anti-Semitic philosopher, who also supposedly influenced Hitler. I wonder if you remember the answer I gave you. I judge people by their creativity and contributions towards making Homo sapiens into 'the man' in my definition. My answer to this question will be the same – "I hate the sin, not the sinner". How can I deprive myself from the nectar that Wagner has left, or the treasure in the works of Nietzsche?'

He continued, 'True artists do not belong to a class, race or religion. They are humans with bursting creativity who leave something for others. You mentioned about sacrifice a few minutes ago. I sacrificed hate, revulsion, even love and concern for humanity quite some time ago. I like to share the pangs of such sacrifices and for this I need a medium. The fine art created out of the combination of the sacrifices and the agonies of old masters and maestros provide that media for me.'

His emotional outburst resonated with my own feelings. I was, however, concerned that I might have evoked a burning and painful episode from his past, perhaps the pain of losing something or somebody during the war. I was sure he wanted to share this memory, a poignant melody for me to listen and which would make it easier for him to bear the burden of the past.

'Do you mean the pangs of losing your fatherland?' I asked with an intense eagerness. Rolf replied with equally intense emotional outburst,

'No, the thing that I have lost has caused immensely deeper agony than losing either my birthplace or parents. What I have lost is faith in humanity and in myself. I had been in this country, a living dead for a long time, trying to overcome the guilt of my survival and to forget the ordeal that I suffered in my fatherland. Behind my apparent youthful exuberance I bear a broken heart and a lost soul.' Worried now, I asked him directly,

'I believe you were in Germany when the Nazis were in power. Tell me Rolf, is it true? I wonder, as a Jew in Hitler's Germany, if you suffered persecution at the hands of the Gestapo? Please do tell me all about it, if it helps you to get some relief from the agony of the past. I will listen with sympathy. You have my undivided attention and the whole night at your disposal.'

It was the best opportunity and the right moment for him to get on with his story, and, without any hesitation and with a short prelude he began:

'You will be astonished to know that I owe my life to an army major in the Nazi SS, who happened to be at the concentration camp in Poland, where I was an inmate. Although I am a Jew by birth and in name, I had no faith in the Tora or any other religious books. I never believed in miracles in my youth, but I have to admit that miracles happened and saved my life.

'The events leading to my escape from the camp and certain death are a story of utter brutality, extreme sadness and debilitating agony. It is an almost unbelievable story which changed me beyond measure, both physically and mentally, making me who I am now, one of the living dead. It is indeed a tale, "stranger than fiction."

Engrossed, I pleaded with him to continue with his story. So he did:

'My family moved from Munich to Berlin mainly to facilitate our higher education. My elder brother was already an adult while I was in my teens. He had completed his university studies and was looking for academic assignments when we first became aware of anti-Jewish discrimination. In our close-knit Jewish community, with families living around a synagogue, in a relatively wealthy suburb of the city fear of alienation and discrimination by Hitler's Nazi regime was spreading. From time to time we heard of people immigrating to other countries. We too, within our family, discussed the political climate and the threatening mood within the society and also the possibility of us emigrating.

'After a lot of discussion and soul searching, it was decided that I would stay on to finish my medical qualification and the rest of my family would immigrate to the UK. The choice of this destination was influenced by the fact that, except for our mother, we all spoke English well enough to get by and settle down there with little difficulty. The move was suggested and encouraged by my father's cousin who lived in Scotland. Knowing someone in the UK made it a more attractive choice than the USA.

'My mother begged me to abandon my studies and go with them, as she foresaw a gloomy future for the Jews in Hitler's Germany. I comforted her by saying something like, "take heart mother, every black cloud has a silver lining." I assured her that it was only a year before I qualified as a medical doctor. I would then leave the country to join them in Scotland if the discrimination against us continued. Besides, I reassured her that Germany would desperately need doctors for the war effort and could ill-afford to discriminate against me on the basis of race.

'After the family left Berlin I moved to the college dormitory. I received news of the family from my father who wrote regularly. He was a qualified medical doctor himself and had practiced medicine for a long time in Berlin. His qualification, from a little known college in Munich, was not recognized in Scotland. In addition, his ability to communicate in English was not good enough for him to practice medicine there. As a result, he could only find a job as a laboratory assistant in the pathology department in a local hospital. With some contribution from my brother, who received a regular income from Edinburgh University as a post-graduate research student, the family managed to survive with a shoe-string budget, with no scope for spending on luxuries.

'When I qualified as a doctor, the whole country was on a war footing. There were marches and jubilant celebrations all over the country, particularly in Berlin, the capital city. German aggression began with the annexation of Austria and then the invasions of Czechoslovakia and Poland. We were troubled by the gradual imposition of restrictions on job opportunities, property purchases and business opportunities for members of the Jewish community. I felt a shiver down my spine when it became blatantly apparent that the Nazi regime did not want Jews. I was not allowed to join the mandatory placement to a teaching hospital for a year-long training needed to obtain my certificate of qualification. I joined a small practice as an assistant to a medical practitioner in the city centre. It gave me an opportunity to learn and, at the same time to earn a little bit of money. My boss was a very polite and efficient middle-aged German doctor who tried his best to teach me and to encourage me whenever possible. I confided in him about my concerns and of my plans to leave the country. He told me that there was an acute shortage of medics, mainly because of the draft of a large number of doctors needed at the war front – Germany desperately needed more qualified doctors, he assured me, there was no reason for me to be worried.

'I knew that my medical qualification would be internationally recognised and I would be able to earn a good living in the UK. But how could I get a certificate without the hospital training? Perhaps I could persuade the authorities in the UK to allow me to complete my hospital internship. Although the thought of leaving my homeland was painful, I comforted myself with the thought that after the inevitable fall of the Third Reich and the demise of Hitler, I could return home with my family.

'News of Jews being sent to resettlement centres and labour camps abounded. Fear within our community was heightened by rumours of the unthinkable – the mass murder of Jews in these places. I decided not to waste time and went to the foreign office to submit an application for permission to leave the country for a holiday in the UK. The officer who interviewed me was unbelievably rude. He humiliated me by asking in a mocking tone if I was aware that our fatherland was at war and how could I be thinking about going away for a holiday? He told me that he knew my real intention and accused me of being a fifth columnist.

He crumpled my application form into a ball and threw it at me shouting,

'The Führer was right to adopt a policy of getting rid of you lot.'

'I was shocked and frightened, and left the office forthwith. I was trapped in Germany with no escape route. I had no alternative but to continue with my work as best as I could and wait for an opportunity to leave the country. I, and most others I knew, had the same dream – finding a way of getting to Switzerland. This was the only country bordering Germany which was neutral and not under the influence of the Nazis.' I took the opportunity of his brief pause and said,

'This is the most engrossing first-hand account of the persecution of the Jews I have ever heard. You must finish it even if it takes the whole night. Just let me go outside and get a bit of fresh air, before you continue.'

'Don't lie to me, Rolf snapped, 'you don't need fresh air, it is bad for you. You need a nicotine fix. You are welcome to use the bathroom, as you did before, while I make another cup of coffee.'

When we'd settled down again, he continued:

'A newly qualified doctor joined our practice under the same boss and started to work as my colleague. I felt, he disliked me from the very outset and, from occasional brief conversations during the lunch break I realised, he bore an anti-Semitic sentiment.

'One day he deliberately picked up an argument with me on a minor matter of protocol on the treatment of a patient. He complained against me to our senior. When he heard my side of the story he reprimanded my colleague in front of me. Outside the door of our meeting room he looked at me and said in a vindictive voice, "I will see to it that you never, ever get a chance to practice medicine in this country." A chill passed through my spine.

'I continued with my work as best as I could. One evening, when

I was playing my violin after dinner, my boss unexpectedly called on me at my flat. I was surprised and perplexed as he had never dropped in to my flat before. I ushered him in, sat him down and offered him a drink. He refused and apologised for his sudden intrusion and said that he had to deliver his message personally. I sensed it was bad news. He informed me that he had received a secret circular from the Ministry of the Interior, instructing him not to employ anyone of Jewish origin and to get rid of any such employees forthwith. He was visibly upset and found it difficult to say this. He also mentioned that the authorities did not invite questions and did not give explanations. In an apologetic tone he told me that his hands were tied and he would miss me and wished me luck. He shook my hand, looked at me and said goodbye. On the way out, he turned back – I saw him take out a handkerchief and dab his eyes.

'Now that I was unemployed I needed to find some means of earning a living. I started to practice medicine privately from my flat, mostly amongst my own community members, even though it was illegal to do so without a licence. I sold whatever valuables I had at giveaway prices and withdrew whatever cash I had so that I could make a dash by land to Switzerland with a few fellow Jews at an opportune moment.

'But alas, that opportunity didn't come, and within no time I received a visit at my flat from a couple of plain clothed SS men.'

I interrupted, 'I have never understood what these two letters stood for. Could you please tell me?'

'They stand for *Schutz Staffel*,' he said, 'literally meaning, Protection Squad – the special force created by Hitler and Himmler to police and deal with the race issue. The SS were responsible for the 'protection' of German racial purity and the implementation of what later became known as the "final solution of the Jewish problem." I am sure you understand what this means.'

Rolf continued, 'These men were very polite and after confirming my identity and profession, one of them explained to me that it was the policy of the third Reich to resettle all German and Polish Jews in new camps in Poland. He said, these camps were newly constructed with all mod cons. There was a shortage of doctors there and professional people like me were needed. Therefore, I had to go with them right away. We all knew that those people did not like any questions. It was a matter of, do or die. I asked if I was allowed to take some of my belongings. They let me gather up what cash I had in the house, some personal clothing and some medical equipment.

'Suffering from the shock of these events I became numb. I couldn't think beyond the immediate present. In a daze, I followed their instructions with little or no concern for the future just like a ship in a flock. They took me to a railway station, where I was man-handled by the military police and packed into the compartment of a goods train with dozens of fellow Jews.'

Rolf paused and I looked at his antique grandfather clock. It was long past midnight, but that did not matter. I was used to all-night *adda* sessions and he was also a late-night party animal. In the meantime I took a break for another smoke. On my return he continued with his saga:

'I was placed in one of the smaller camps, where I was allocated a bunk bed in a dormitory, along with many other male Jewish inmates. The SS men who ran the camp were not as merciless as we feared and even allowed us a biggish hut for use as a synagogue. The job of the day-to-day management of the inmates was left to a council of members handpicked from the inmates by the camp commandant. In practice, this council was obliged to do their dirty work for them under the constant threat of death. Council members considered themselves to be privileged, albeit temporarily, and occasionally were given improved rations. They allocated jobs to the inmates and had the most unpleasant task of deciding who lived and who died, by reporting on our ability to work. The fate of an inmate was sealed once he was deemed to be nonproductive and therefore surplus to requirements and a liability. Of course, in the end the threat hung over everyone, since eventually even council members could be deemed 'surplus to requirement.

'Josephs Stein, the nominated camp Rabbi, took to me and, took me to the synagogue for the first time. He gave me the task of medically examining the suitability of persons selected for hard labour outside the camp. Thanks to him, I also sometimes got a special diet such as a bigger piece of bread, a piece of cheese or if I was very lucky, a Frankfurter sausage. The selected inmates, despite being allocated for hard labour, considered themselves lucky for; they knew they would then get a better diet so that they could work harder.

'The business of making these life and death selections, as Josephs asked me to do for him, was repugnant to me. Apart from my stethoscope and a thermometer I had precious little to diagnose illness. Besides, there was no real provision for any treatment or medicine. I knew that the only cure for the illness there was a proper diet, which most of us were denied. It would have been a sin to give my fellow inmates false hope. Even if there were medicine and a healthy diet I couldn't have stopped or delayed their death.

'The drudgery, degradation and depravation were so severe that humanity, as such, all but vanished from us. Rabbis, murderers, doctors, lawyers were all thrown together with no distinction between them. I managed to keep my body and soul, whatever was left of these, together for the long seven months from May to December. I was able to do that because of Josephs' words of wisdom and his kindness and his invaluable lessons of the art of survival.

'He was more than 12 years older than me and, I suppose a

human being with normal carnal desires. At times I felt that his unusual physical and spiritual attraction for me was getting too much for comfort. Sometime I found his touch to be different from that of just a friend's. I took tacit precautions to avoid any further physical contact, hinting that I abhorred the practice of homosexuality. I couldn't let anything happen between us to spoil our friendship.

'We talked and dreamt about freedom. Rumours abounded about a Polish-led secret army insurgency going to take place to rescue us and also the imminent fall of the Third Reich and our rescue by the advancing US led allied forces. We had to have hope. That was what kept us living and breathing. If we lost hope we were as good as dead.' Rolf looked at me sideways and asked,

'Are you getting a bit bored listening to the monotonous monologue of my personal tragedy? Please don't hesitate to tell me if you are. I can stop it now if you like. I could tell you the rest another time.'

I quipped, 'It's quite funny. You sound like Scheherazade, the story teller in the book, "1001 Arabian Nights", who captivated the disgruntled king Shahryar, nights after nights to stop him killing her in the morning. But you do not have one thousand and one stories to tell, my friend, but only one. I am probably the only listener you have found who believes every word you say to be true. You are a living legend for me; your story is more real for me than similar stories I have read about survival and escape from concentration camps in Nazi Germany. I have to know the end of this amazing episode now. If you do not finish your story tonight, there will be a big manhunt tomorrow for a fugitive murderer on the run from this flat.'

He continued with more enthusiasm:

'As I was saying, the dream of freedom, to be reunited with my family and to live like a normal human being brought out my deep seated survival instincts. Besides, from the many tales of horror we heard from inmates transferred from other camps, we considered ourselves privileged as far as ration and work quotas were concerned. But we were still very much a part of Hitler's horrific "Final Solution." Those who were infirm and useless were sent to their deaths in another camp. In our camp there were three main categories of work – "Manual, technical and administrative." In some ways my task was probably the most soul destroying and unbearable. If I certified someone fit for work, he would be condemned to a slow and painful death in labour camps. If I decide someone was unfit to work, he would be taken to the 'alternative re-settlement camp' where the gas chambers were always operational. Inmates learnt of my medical background and started to approach me with their problems. Without medicine I could do nothing for them. I begged Josephs for help.

'Being a prominent member of the council of management he had some influence with the SS. One day he called on me and informed that the SS no longer needed medical certificates for inmates. Everybody had to work to live. I turned pale and asked him about my own fate. He told me not to worry; he had managed to persuade the authorities to assign me to assist him in preaching Jehovah's word to the inmates and also to assist him in the synagogue on the Sabbath day. This charade of religious activity was devised by the SS to keep the inmates orderly, like lambs for the slaughter, enabling a smoother execution process. We were being used like sheep dogs. I was extremely grateful to Josephs, realising that my good friend had saved me from a debilitating outside work assignment, which would have caused my slow and painful death.

'On Sabbath days, the synagogue was always full. I was amazed to see that even under such degradation, squalor and the constant threat of death, inmates maintained their faith in Jehovah. The temperature in the synagogue was almost comfortable compared to the freezing dormitories. Besides, the weekly Sabbath congregation was the only occasion for us to find out who was still with us and who had gone to meet his maker. Besides, this gave us the opportunity of catching up with rumours, allowing us sustain our hopes for survival and liberation.

'Josephs told me not to delude myself into becoming a godly man, but to keep up the pretence of being one. He sensed that I had faith neither in the Torah nor in a God of any sort. He confided that he also did not have faith in religion. He qualified as a Rabbi to earn an easy living with very little physical work. He was, however, a good soul and helped inmates whenever he could, often risking his own privileged position and at times even his life. I developed a fondness for him as we were both pretending to be Jehovah's preachers. I wondered if the famous quotation of the French poet, "a devil always finds a bigger devil to admire him", could be applied to us, replacing the word "fool" with "devil".

'Sometimes, there were only standing places left in the synagogue. As I had mentioned earlier, this was not because these passengers on a journey to their final destination had all suddenly became very religious. Almost all believed that Jehovah had forsaken them. But they still assembled there because, Josephs' highly emotional sermon convinced them that their present situation was a test of their faith and urged them to keep their hope alive – "There was always a trace of light at the end of the tunnel." I learnt the tricks of the trade as a lay preacher and was allowed to conduct services sometimes in his absence.

'Josephs came from a wealthy family of jewellers. Their shop was raided by the Gestapo and his father and younger sister were taken away, never to be seen again. He rushed back home from Bonn, where he was studying to be a rabbi and found his mother on her death bed in a relative's house. She passed away a few days later. She gave him the account details of a Swiss bank where his father had stashed away a fortune for his family. He had memorized the account details.

'He had a dream which he shared with me – One day, he would be free and redeem his fortune from the bank and rebuild his life with a family and a small house on the bank of a lake at the foothill of Swish Alps. He did not have anyone else left in the world and he wanted me to be a part of his new life and share his fortune if we both came out alive from this earthly hell. He even gave me a small note with the account details and signed authority for me to withdraw the funds in case he died and I survived. I kept the note hidden inside the fold of my collar. Overwhelmed by the kindness of another human being in the face of utmost adversity, the only thing I could do was embrace him tightly for a long time. We never shed tears in the camp, only a human being with feelings could do that.'

There was nothing I could say to make it easy for him to tell his compelling story of hardship and the ever-present threat of death. Never the less, he continued unabated:

'There was never any reliable news from outside. There were only rumours and speculation. There was a strong rumour that a group of prisoners was collaborating clandestinely with a group of underground Polish freedom fighters, who were training some of them to use fire arms and helping them smuggle weapons into the camp. There was also the rumour of an escape tunnel being dug by this same group. I personally took such rumours with a pinch of salt, but it did not stop me and the others dreaming about an uprising, escape and freedom.

'One night, after light was out, I was visited by a young man named Mark. His bed was not far from mine. Almost all the inmates were asleep, but such a visit was still very dangerous for both of us. I knew Mark well as he was a regular attendee at our weekly services and stayed over after the service to talk with me about God and the promise of an afterlife. He handed me a smallish cardboard box and begged me to keep it safe for the night. He assured me that he would collect it early the next morning. He then slipped away.

'It all happened so suddenly that I didn't have time to ask him any questions. I hid the box under my bed hoping that it wouldn't get me into any trouble. I was both excited and frightened and couldn't sleep. Curiosity got the better of me and in the dead of night I fished out the box from under the bed, untied the string around it and opened it very carefully under my blanket so that no one awake could see it. It was pitch-dark and I felt the contents with my fingers. To my utmost horror I discovered that the box held two revolvers wrapped in cloths. I was petrified and my heart was pounding.

'I could hardly sleep a wink whole night. Very early the next morning, I managed to go to the hut where Josephs slept. He was not there. I knew where to find him. When he had work to do for the SS masters he would go to the shed used as the synagogue cum his office. I was shivering with fear. Somehow, I managed to tell him what had happened the previous night and gave him the box for safe keeping. He was as much startled and most probably as frightened as I was, but unlike me, he put on a brave face, kept the box and waved me away.

'After our meagre breakfast of a chunk of bread and a cup of watery tea, I went out to carry on with my mentoring rounds. I was extremely nervous – If the SS found out I had helped smuggle firearms, I would be a dead man. After lunch, which consisted of some thin soup with a few bits of vegetables in it and another chunk of bread, I helped clean our accommodation as a part of my rota. While I was doing this, two SS officers came up and ordered me to follow them. I knew this was the end, but resolved – Under no circumstances would I incriminate Josephs. I was so frightened that I could hardly say my name and number. One of the SS officers told me to sit on a stool and wait.

'After several minutes, the second man came to the room and led me to another room in the administration building. Laid out on a table inside, I saw a body covered in a white cloth. A chill went through my spine and I stopped dead. The SS man pulled back the cloth – it was Mark; his face was so badly battered and bloodied that it was hardly recognizable.

'In a conversational tone, the officer said, "He isn't dead yet; but he soon will be. Confess and make my job easier, and I promise you I will make your end painless"

'He nodded at the broken figure between us and added, "Unlike this bastard gun runner."

'I realized Mark had told them I had the guns. Everyone has a limited threshold for pain and fear; I did not blame him at all. I told them that I was a peace-loving priest and knew nothing about Mark's gun-running. I suggested that as I was his religious mentor, he must have mentioned my name in a state of delirium, perhaps given it out of fear of death or further torture. I implored them to believe me that Mark had wrongly incriminated me.'

'The officers had already searched my bed space and clothes and found no clue as to the whereabouts of the firearms. The SS officer opened a connecting door and shouted a name. A Gestapo thug came into the room, looked me up and down, and smiled.

'The SS man said, "Give me a shout when he talks. The torturer came up, grabbed me by the arm, pulled me into another room and forced me down on a chair. My legs were trembling so much I could hardly walk. Except for the bentwood chair, a small table and a wood-burning stove, the room was bare. He tied me up tightly. Then he picked a poker, opened the stove door and shoved it into the embers. When it was glowing red he pulled on a thick glove, took out the poker and shoved it into my left eye. The pain was so excruciating that I collapsed with a scream which must have frightened even the perpetrator of this barbaric action, and then I fainted.

'Later, when I came to my senses, I found myself lying on a hard bed with a bandage over the injured eye. Blood was still oozing out of it. Someone brought me a glass of water. I realised they wanted to keep me alive, at least until they got the information out of me. The pain was still terrible, but I was able to speak. The first SS officer came to the room. Mark's body had been removed. He asked me if I was going to talk before they burned out my other eye. I knew they would kill me even if I told them the truth. I thought it was better to die than suffer any further torture.

'My only hope to be alive, albeit a faint one was to tell them that Rabbi Josephs had the weapons. But I couldn't do this to my trusted friend. But I knew if I didn't, I would die slowly in great pain. I managed to create a self-induce state of unconsciousness, a defence mechanism from the intolerable pain in my eye. The SS officer who had come to interrogate me told the Gestapo thug – give him another day to think it over".'

I glanced at the clock and looked at him; it was nearly half past two in the morning; he smirked.

'Never mind the time,' I said, 'please get on with the rest of the story.'

He continued, 'I was delirious with pain all night. For the first time in my life I believed in God, and begged him earnestly to take my life without delay. In the morning one of the camp trusties brought me a bowl of soup and a piece of bread. It was amazing that while I was praying to die, I ate the piece of bread with the soup – A primeval survival instinct, I suppose. The Kapo marched me back to the first room. "Sit there," he said, "and don't move."

'Not knowing what was coming next, the waiting seemed interminable. In the end, I must have dozed off.

'I woke up in a daze; someone was calling me. I opened my unharmed eye and saw a face I thought to be familiar. I heard the voice again, coming from a smartly dressed SS officer sitting behind the desk opposite:

"What is your name?"

I thought I was hallucinating again. I rubbed my good eye, looked around, pinched myself and realized that it was a reality. The officer was Karl Hoffman – "How could I have forgotten Karl?" Not so long ago, he had been my buddy. I couldn't believe that he hadn't recognized me, or that he had forgotten my name. I thought he was pretending to be a stranger. In a faint voice, I told him my name. He stood up, came close to me and asked me to speak louder. I couldn't speak for fear and the pain and exhaustion. He must have heard me, as he didn't ask me again, but went back to his chair and started to look through some notes in a file.

'Suddenly a floodgate opened up and a stream of memories rushed into my mind. The images unwound – Karl had been a very good friend. We were studying medicine together in Berlin. Not only were we in the same class, we also shared the same college dormitory. Music was our common interest and we played violin together at college concerts. He invited me to his house and introduced me to his parents. We spent lots of time together and had lots of happy memories. He didn't enjoy studying medicine, and left after the first year and joined the army. That must have been nearly five years ago. We had exchanged letters for the first couple of years, at longer and longer intervals. Eventually, we lost contact with one another."

'After he finished looking through some notes in the file on his table, he looked up and ordered the sole Gestapo guard to leave the room.

'The guard said, "Ja, Herr Major," and gave a Nazi salute and bellowed – "Hail Hitler". Once we were alone, Karl turned to me and said in a matter-of-fact tone, "My dear Rolf! I would recognise you anywhere; even in here. I haven't forgotten your name, or our friendship."

'He told me that he had been called from Berlin by an urgent telegram message to investigate some lack of security at this camp. There was intelligence that some of the inmates were collaborating with Polish insurgents on the outside. He had read the full report provided by the commandant on his arrival. He couldn't believe that one of the collaborators named in it was his one-time old chum until he saw me in flesh and blood.

'Karl warned me not to let anyone see or know that we knew each other socially. He said he was prepared to risk his career and even to face a court marshal and imprisonment to help me. He was quite passionate when he told me that we both loved our fatherland, and were prepared to give our lives to defend it. But he hadn't sold his soul to the devil. He was doing what he had to do for the sake of humanity and friendship.

'Karl said that such incidents were usually dealt with by the junior Gestapo officers in the usual brutal way. They would usually take the shortcut, as with that lad, Mark, to eliminate such a problem. But he had not been alone in this conspiracy to smuggle firearms into the camp. The report said some of the Gestapos, although carried out their assigned duties, were not entirely loyal to Hitler's cause and were prepared to collaborate with the insurgents for the right amount of money. This was the reason for sending a high-ranking official from the central SS office in Berlin.'

'I thought – This is a sheer miracle; perhaps God does exist after all. I felt a flicker of hope to keep alive despite the unbearable pain in my eye. I told Karl what had actually happened, and that I was innocent. He told me that his conversation was against all SS orders and could result in the gravest consequences for him. He gave me an ultimatum – "You have very little time, and if you want me to try to save your skin you have to talk right away and come clean." He said quite categorically that even if I were truly innocent, my name had been mentioned and there was no allowance for the benefit of the doubt.

'On the face of it, Karl was sympathetic but the only person I knew who had been involved was now dead. I was sure everyone here would die sooner or later. The conditions were so dire that death was much more desirable than living. Ironically though, everyone was still desperately trying to cling on to life. Like all of us here, Josephs would certainly be going to the gas chamber, sooner or later. They had now closed down the religious service facility and he was not suitable for manual labour.

'The trace of a soul that was still in my fragile body, tiptoed away from it. Humanity bade me farewell. I had the opportunity, although a very small one, to survive by offering Josephs as a scapegoat. To my lasting shame, the primeval instinct of self-preservation got the better of me. I had to take the chance. I told Karl what had taken place in detail, stressing the fact that neither Josephs nor I had taken any part in the arms smuggling episode. He thanked me and summoned a Gestapo officer to take me away. I looked up and saw no outright emotion on his face, but he nodded at me and I saw the hint of something in his eyes that was unusual and somewhat reassuring. I was taken back to the same room where they had tortured me. The pain returned with a vengeance and I sank back into a state of delirium. When I returned to my senses, I heard the voice of somebody lying on the adjacent bed – "Take heart my friend, we will probably arrive at the gates of hell at the same time, such is our destiny." He sounded near death.

'It was, as I feared, the voice of Josephs. I was mortified and desperately prayed that I might die rather than face him. He told me that I should not feel guilty, as he would have certainly done the same under the circumstances. I felt that the survival of my good eye had been bought by my betrayal, and was costing the life of an innocent and good man, a trusted friend and a mentor. Two guards came in at that time and dragged Josephs away. I never saw him again.

'A Gestapo officer came in after couple of hours and marched me back to the same room where I had been interrogated by Karl and then left. Karl was sitting behind the desk. I stood by the side of it. He handed me a card and said, "This is your new identity badge, a talisman. Wear it at all times and memorise the name and the number on it, it may very well save your life."

'From that moment on I became Igor Kowalski, a German speaking Polish labourer. Karl called for the guard and nodded to him. The private took me to the camp gate, where a bus was waiting to collect Polish labourers for work elsewhere. I showed a corporal my pass and they let me get on the bus.'

Rolf got up and went into his bedroom. After quite a while he came back, turned the wall lights on, and handed over to me an old faded card inside a plastic folder. I could only recognize the name and the number written in German. I couldn't decipher the rest of it. He took the identity card away from me and stared at it for a while. Then, for the first time in the telling of his marathon story, he gave a deep sigh and translated card details for me – "Name: Igor Kowalski; Place of birth: Warsaw, Poland; Age: 26; Religious Affiliation: Christian." It was dated and, signed by someone he did not know.

I was overwhelmed by seeing this lifesaving memento, one that represented such a watershed in his life. With great care, he slid the card back into its plastic folder and took it back to his bedroom. When he returned, he was fully composed and resumed his story:

'I was transported from one labour camp to another, along with the other members of the Polish work gang, which consisted mostly of convicted criminals or suspected freedom fighters who were serving life sentences or under execution orders. None were of Jewish origin and hence not subject to Hitler's plan for the final solution of the Jewish problem. My injury got better over time and I learned to get by with only one eye. Life was hard and absolute drudgery, but we got plenty to eat and were fit and able to work hard.

'For us, the regime in most of the work camps was just about tolerable. Most importantly, we could expect to live and dream of being free and human again one day in the not too distant future. For many others, that day never came. The physical and mental horror of the camps, the lack of medical care, the poor living conditions and the harsh winters all took their tolls. The contractors who managed us had treated us badly, but compared to the Jews in the concentration camp, we were lucky.

'When I'd been working with the Poles for a couple of months, another miracle happened. I was assigned to a gang of labourers constructing a wire fence along a short length of the Swiss border with Germany. One morning, early, a few of them risked their lives and made a dash for freedom. The German border guards chased after them, shooting indiscriminately. Most of the men were either shot dead or caught alive with gunshot injuries. Only two made it across the border into Switzerland alive. I had not tried to escape, but I thought – "I will be shot anyway, so why not take a chance with the others?'

'So while the guards were busy with the dead and injured, I edged closer to the gap in the fence and then started running. I heard gunshots behind me, I survived and surrendered to a couple of Swiss border guards and asked for asylum. Within three months, my papers were processed, contact was established with my family in Scotland and I was able to travel to England and then on to Scotland to be with them.

'The agony of sadness was so severe that I had lost the will to communicate with other family members. I became a stranger and spent most of the time thinking about Josephs and felt how strong our bond had been, I wished I had died rather than betray him. I started to hate myself. I realized that I had betrayed my friend and mentor only because of my selfish desire to keep the body and the soul, whatever was left of these, together. I felt, my soul was not mine anymore but belonged to the devil. I often thought of committing suicide. But I was too cowardly and loved life too much to be able to do that. I had survived, but the cost had been very high – Loss of faith in myself and the sense of humanity.'

That was the end of his amazing story. But it was not the one about the 'secret agents' that I had expected to hear. It was very late. Rolf's story reverberated in my mind, driving out all other thoughts. I got up and wished him good night. Opening the door, he pointed at the grandfather clock and smiled; the sky was getting clearer.'

11

The Organization

The amazing and almost unbelievable story of Rolf's time in a Nazi concentration camp and his miraculous escape from certain death overwhelmed me beyond measure. I was totally captivated and emotionally disturbed and remained in a daze for several days. It was almost as if I had been through the whole thing myself. During lonely moments in between my busy schedule, trying to tie-up loose-ends of my thesis and preparing, both mentally and materially, for a new life back home. Rolf's gruesome story lived in my mind.

My imagination took me to that concentration camp in Poland and I visualized the events of his time in there, followed by the miraculous escape. These appeared very real and vivid to me. Obsession with his story overwhelmed me so much that I started to fantasise, re-living his life and most surprisingly, beginning to think that it had not been so nightmarish at all. I had undergone a transformation, becoming Rolf, the chivalrous hero, who overcame all odds, suffered near-death experiences and came out alive to tell his story with cool and dispassionate manner. I felt like a hero myself, so complete was my transformation into Rolf.

"Dead men tell no tales", but he had survived to tell me his. I had read articles and books about the Nazi concentration camps; the gas chambers and the torture and dehumanization of the Jews, and seen films and documentaries on television. Was Rolf's suffering any different from that of thousands of others who had survived the Holocaust to tell their horror stories? Most of them had long since gone to their graves unknown, along with their accounts of personal tragedy. Their melancholy melodies had been lost in the wilderness of the Universe.

Rolf did not want to leave the world without telling his story. He tried to write it down, but gave up for two reasons – firstly, not knowing where to start or how to end it, and secondly, for fear that the book would end up being a fiction, or at best the memoir of an "ordinary" Jew; a "nobody". Already desensitised by overexposure to the events of the holocaust, readers had become apathetic. In any case, a good storyteller is not necessarily a good story writer. I was lucky that I'd been in the right place at the right time to satisfy his insatiable urge to tell his story to someone who he felt would be able to write it down for the world to hear.

At last, after all those years, he had found that person in me – a sympathetic and understanding listener and a potential writer of his amazing tale. To me, Rolf was like the vagabond sailor, roaming around the shores, trying to find someone to tell his tale, the tale of guilt and suffering, in Coleridge's famous poem, 'Rhymes of the Ancient Mariner'.

The only difference was that, unlike Coleridge's mariner, Rolf wouldn't tell his story to just anybody. I wondered if he had had the premonition that one day he would find someone who would be his perfect listener and who would eventually immortalize him by writing his ballad for posterity for others to experience the ecstasy and the agony of a tormented soul. A quote from Shelley came to mind, "Our sweetest songs are those that tell of saddest thoughts".

Much had changed in my life at that time. I felt a lot more relaxed as my *viva voce* had gone well. The examiners decided to recommend the conferral of the degree of Doctor of Philosophy, subject to some minor changes and corrections. I was given a 3 months' extension of my grant and time to complete these for the degree. In addition to work on tidying up my thesis I also applied for a one-year post-doctoral fellowship in the UK before returning home. I still made time to go to concerts and parties, often in the company of Rolf. We laughed and joked as before. The only thing that had changed drastically was my feeling towards him. I felt I was his one and only 'soul mate' and not merely a friend for intellectual exchanges, having good times and chasing skirts. I'd been sceptical about his tales of secret agents trying to destroy him. But since he'd told me about the concentration camp, his suffering and his miraculous survival, I was beginning to believe that there might be an element of truth in that story, too. I wondered if his phobia about secret agents had something to do with his gruesome past experience in the death camp.

My insatiable desire to know more about the so called, 'secret agents', particularly the reason why they wanted to harm him, and the organization that they belonged to, grew stronger than ever before. To him, the story of his life at the concentration camp was simply a fatalistic event over which he had had no control. It was much less significant for him than the 'secret agent' conspiracy.

Rolf had tried and, for all intent and purposes, had succeeded in accepting his act of betrayal and the consequent death of a friend in the concentration camp. He had stopped having nightmares, hearing gunshots and the haunting voice of Josephs, calling his name, repeating what he had struggled to say on his death bed. It had been a question of self-preservation. That episode of his life was in the past, time had blunted those feelings and its memory was fading.

※

But he had been finding it increasingly difficult to live with the consequences of another episode that had taken place only a decade ago. This was the disturbing and haunting story of the organization and its secret agents and his unfortunate involvement with it. This was the other story he desperately wanted to tell me, the one I had been waiting to hear for the last three and half years, since my acrimonious encounter with him at that time.

From the outset of our friendship Rolf had suspected I might have some connection with the agents, inadvertently or otherwise. But he had given me the benefit of the doubt. We were both waiting for the right moment, when we would both have the right time together. Once I had left Oxford to return to my own country, the chance of finding such an opportunity to listen to his story would be practically – nil.

My student life here would soon come to an end and it would be time to say goodbye to everybody before I return to my country, my family, sunshine and most importantly, to real life and living. I would probably miss the place and some of the people for a while. I would certainly miss Rolf's company for a long time. I reassured myself thinking – "Surely time will look after that, old memories will gradually fade away to be replaced by new ones, born out of new events and adventures." But what I didn't want was to leave before hearing him out.

One afternoon I ventured into the department after a quick brunch at the Lamb and Flag pub. I wanted to make use the facilities at the departmental library to make the suggested amendments to my thesis. I was not expecting any distraction during the Easter recess. But I couldn't settle down to any serious work and tried in vain to contact some of my *deshi* chums who had access to a telephone. I knew Rolf would be in Edinburgh with his brother's family over Easter. He told me that he wanted to get to know his brother's family, particularly his nephews, whom he hadn't seen for 15 years.

I don't know why, but I dialled his number without thinking, out of habit perhaps, since I knew that he wouldn't be there. I couldn't believe my ears when I heard the familiar voice – "Rolf speaking, hello."

With utter surprise and great delight I said, 'Goodness gracious me! Is that really you, Rolf Kosterlitz? For a moment I thought it was your ghost. Anyway, what on earth are you doing here? You are supposed to be spending the Easter holidays in Edinburgh with your brother's family!' At the end of his familiar laughter he replied,

'To be honest with you, Rolf is not at home. Indeed, it is, as always, his ghost speaking. But don't worry; it will not make much difference, you may speak to me. I can answer for him just the same; we live in the same body.'

He continued, 'The answer to your question is that Rolf changed his plans, considering the possibility that you might call. If he went away who would have then answered it? Now you know why he changed his mind and stayed waiting by the telephone. Anyway, the real Rolf will be home and free after 7:30 pm. Why don't you drop in for a bite to eat and a cup of coffee any time after that and before midnight? Rolf will be informed immediately, have no fear.'

I realized he was as desperate for company as I was, and I accepted his invitation forthwith. The telephone rang after about a minute or so – "It's Rolf himself speaking this time and not his ghost. I cannot ask you to read my lips over the phone, therefore I repeat and you listen carefully, "Dinner will be served on the table at 6:30 pm precisely." He rang off. I knew from my past experience that he would be very upset and annoyed if I were to be again late for dinner. I didn't stay long in the laboratory. I went back to my flat and did some tidying up; a duty no one could have accused me of ever discharging until recently when the landlady, Mrs Malik threatened to evict me if I didn't make an effort in that direction.

Mrs Malik, despite her affection for me, wouldn't allow me a bath for free unless it was deemed an emergency or as an act of charity. I couldn't afford the two shillings for a paid one. So, instead of a bath, I washed thoroughly and shaved and put on my one and only maroon suede tie, tucked away under the button down collar of my striped shirt, which had never suffered the torture of a hot iron. I was determined to impress Rolf by being well-dressed and, most importantly, by presenting myself at his place just before the specified time for the dinner.

I left home at about 6 pm. Rolf's flat was a brisk ten-minutes' walk away from my flat at Bradmore Road next to the University Park. I took a leisurely walk along Banbury road, since I knew Rolf wouldn't like his dinner guest to be at his door any time much earlier than the scheduled time. From a passer-by I found out it was 6:25 pm. I decided that it was the right time to ring his door bell. This was based on my estimation that by the time he opened the doors of his fortress and climb down the stairs it would most probably be exactly 6:30 pm on the dot.

Rolf was ready and expecting me at that moment and rushed down the stairs and said, 'Good evening and welcome. I am very pleased to see that at last you have learnt the importance of time keeping, especially for a dinner appointment with me. I can gladly forgive you for being two minutes early. I realise it is not easy to keep track of time when you do not have a time piece or a wrist watch.'

Showing a hint of frustration, I said, 'You people have become slaves of time. Time controls all aspects of your lives. I never thought that I would have to conform to such a ridiculous stricture. But, there again, I realized that to maintain friendship with people like you I have to make some sacrifices. It is your loss my friend. You have made yourself a slave of time, whereas we are its master and enjoy riding it.'

When I saw only two plates on the table I realized that I was the only guest for tonight's dinner party. Rolf's formal dinner parties with more than one guest were usually associated with musical soirees or serious discussion session on a specific topic. For him, this was like the Hindu ritual of offering '*Prasad*', a small amount of food offered to the gods. It goes without saying that well-presented food on his dinner table filled the eyes with delight, but did little to satisfy the appetite of a rice-addicted Bengali guest.

After dinner we made ourselves comfortable on the sofa in his library room, as we always did whenever I visited him. He sensed that I was in no hurry to leave early and felt comfortable and relaxed. I was in a receptive mood and he seemed prepared to talk intimately. It occurred to me that it was probably the right moment for him to tell me his story about the 'organization and the secret agents'. I prepared myself mentally to ask him to tell it. Before I could do that, he started to talk,

'All these time during the last three and a half years since I have known you I have told you many stories of my life and my work and my failed love affairs. Some were quite intimate and very personal, but I had the urge to share these with you without reservation, sometimes without any shame, often with some guilt. I felt a lot better for that. But during all this time I haven't had the opportunity to share the story of the most important episode of my life which is haunting me all the time. I tried to tell this to one or two friends of mine in the past. But it turned out that they were not genuine friends and laughed off my story as simply a figment of my imagination, a cock and bull tale of my making.'

'Now that you are here with a clear mind, and since tonight we have no fixed agenda for discussion, I feel this is the opportune time to reveal the mystery to you, if you are happy to listen.'

I snapped, 'Of course I shall be most delighted to listen; it doesn't matter how long it takes. 'Please go ahead and do share the story with me. By doing this I hope you will be able to lessen your burden and reduce the mental anguish. As for me, I can't be at peace with myself until I know the whole episode in detail. It bothers me to hear time and again that you are being constantly persecuted by some agents of an organization. I am sure I will be able to understand you better and empathise with you if I know the full story. Please, go ahead, open your heart.'

Rolf stipulated, 'Before I begin my story you have to tell me how much you know already. It will help me avoid duplication and allow highlighting the relevant aspects of the story.'

I thought if I showed my anger or annoyance at this unexpected and vexed request I would miss the chance of listening to his story for good. I said with a cool but firm voice,

'For heaven's sake Rolf, you should know by now that I do not lack integrity and honesty. Please take it from me that I know nothing more about your past life than the things you have told me so far.'

Rolf started his saga thus:

'I arrived at the English port of Dover, thanks to the good offices of the British Red Cross. I was kept in a camp in Geneva for about a month, waiting to be sent to the UK as an emigrant. I have probably mentioned this before that because of my family connections I was offered asylum in the UK as a refugee. All official formalities were processed at the transit camp before I was put on a ship bound for the English sea port of Dover. From their immigration records the British authorities were able to trace and contact my family in Edinburgh. My elder brother, Euhan was at the port to receive me.

'I found it sickeningly sad to find that the elapsed time, the news of the plight of the Jews in Europe and our past and present circumstances had blunted our feelings so much that when we met for the first time after nearly 5 years, we did not hug or embrace each other or display any emotion. Euhan simply shook my hand saying, "Welcome to Britain Rolf. Good to see you. Hope you are well and had a good journey".

'These were not questions for answering or making a conversation. So I responded by enquiring after the wellbeing of our parents and talking about the weather here in England. He reminded me with a dry smile that I would be living in Scotland and not in England. For me it made no difference where I would be living then. Anywhere would be better than the concentration camp in Poland, the labour camps in Germany or even the transit camp in Switzerland. On our long bus journey to Edinburgh, I did try to make conversation with Euhan. I asked him lots of questions about the family and his situation. He gave only short answers. Only once did he mention that they had all feared that I was dead, except for my mother who never gave up hope of seeing me alive again. They finally received news of me a month ago through the Red Cross in Geneva. He also told me that since then our mother spent most of her spare time at home praying and visiting the local synagogue whenever possible.

'The events of the last two and a half years had mentally scarred me so much that I felt emotionally numb. I had no enthusiasm for life or living as a free man. I did not have any interest in anything or anybody or even in myself. It was neither a feeling of depression nor of frustration, but of emptiness, simply nothingness. Whenever I tried to shake off the feeling, the question of my right to exist by betraying the trust of my friend and mentor came up, and the life appeared meaningless. I often suffered from deep depression. The 'will to live' is such a potent instinct that these questions did not arise during my short confinement at the transit camp and the comparatively long stay in labour camps.

'My parents lived in one of the terraced houses in a rundown area near the city centre. These were council houses allocated to homeless families and immigrants. I lived there with my parents for about four months. My father's fluency in reading English was quite good, but he had difficulties in making a proper communication with members of the host community. He lost the will to improve his English to enable him work as a doctor.

Therefore, we had to live on a shoestring budget from his meagre income as a laboratory technician at the local hospital

'Perhaps the sadness of having to leave his homeland, friends and a comfortable lifestyle in an affluent suburb in Potsdam city near Berlin bothered him. He became a loner, and progressively more and more of an introvert. He devoted his spare time to reading books on history and religion. There was no life or laughter in our home. Always there existed an uncomfortable quietness which was often unbearable to me. My brother Euhan now worked as a post-doctoral fellow at the University and lived in a one-bedroom flat outside the city centre. He joined us for the family dinner most Sundays, as was the custom and, perhaps out of an obligation to our parents. During such family gatherings, we all sat down for dinner around the table in our kitchen-diner, the only sound being that of the cutlery and occasionally the discussion on the cost of living.

'Amazingly, no one dared ask me what had happened to me for the last two and a half years in Germany. Of course, they were aware of my confinement in the concentration camp and my escape from a Nazi labour camp. I assumed they wanted to avoid tormenting me by opening a raw wound. They were expecting me to tell the story of my own volition. In desperation, my mother once asked me the question. I said that I was saved by an SS officer, an old German friend. He provided me with a false identity as a Polish convict. That had saved me from certain death and allowed me to get out of the concentration camp for work at various labour camps. My watered down and censured description of life in the camps gave her a great deal of solace.

🕭

'During my short stay with my family I rarely ventured out of our house. My spoken English was poor and I did not have any money to go to the cinema or to a restaurant. My father didn't have "two pennies to rub together", so to say and I loathed asking for pocket money. He did suggest that I seek temporary work in a shop or a factory. He had very limited contacts to help me find a job. He had never tried to assimilate or integrate into the local community. Besides, in those days, jobs were scarce and there was overt discrimination against immigrants, particularly of those with a German accent. In any case, I didn't want a job there. I wanted to escape from my claustrophobic home environment at any cost. Sometimes I used to go for a walk along the high street and spend time inside the Art Gallery in the city centre. These occasional walks outside the home helped my circulation and gave me a bit of fresh air. But I spent most of my time lying down on the bed and aimlessly looking at the white featureless ceiling and thinking about the past, trying to erase the memories and aimlessly wondering between heaven and the earth in my imagination.

'My brother felt sorry for my pathetic condition and helped me fill in an application form for admission to New College at Oxford University to study theology. Another miracle – I got an offer with a small stipend. It was probably at the end of 1944, if my memory serves me right, when I matriculated to study there.

'My luck ran out. Something was not right in my head. I had to quit the course a few months later, unable to cope with academic life at the college, the pressure of meeting deadlines and the stress of meeting new people when my spoken English was not that good. Besides, I felt uncomfortable being the only mature student amongst the new matriculants in my college. My family were deeply disappointed in me for losing such a golden opportunity to make something of myself. I had to return to Edinburgh to live with my parents again.

'Life couldn't go on like that. So, one day, following my father's advice, I took the plunge and made my way to the city of London. My uncle in Edinburgh had a Jewish acquaintance there. Through his good offices, I landed a job in a jewellers shop in Golders Green. The area had a sizable established Jewish community. The Jewish owner of the shop was very generous to me with his praise and advice but not so when it came to payment for my work. I was considered as a trainee shop-assistant. He deducted a fixed sum of money from my pay packet for lodging and meals at his house. My duties were to run various errands as and when deemed necessary, and at times, to mind the shop. Working from 9 am to 6 pm, with a break for only an hour for lunch, time crawled. It was so boring that I sometimes thought life, in a way, had been more exciting and bearable in those labour camps.

'The landlady was generous with breakfast and dinner but very careful about heating the house. I had to go to bed early every night with a hot-water bottle. I thought I must get another job and move from here or I shall go mad. We all knew in our heart of hearts that anti-Semitism was not only confined to members of the Third Reich or to the German race, but also existed amongst the British people, and was probably more prevalent amongst Londoners. To find employment we needed qualifications and skills, for which there was a desperate shortage. Even with the appropriate qualifications the Jewish immigrants had no option but to take up jobs which the indigenous Britons did not want to do. At that time, there was an acute shortage of medical doctors. I had studied medicine for four years at the Berlin Medical School, of which, in this country only my family knew. Being out of practice for nearly 4 years and with no certificate to prove my qualification, I did not have a 'cat in a hell's' chance of getting a job even as an auxiliary trainee doctor.

'I felt certain that all documents of the Berlin medical school would have been destroyed during the British bombing blitz at the tail end of the war. Besides, I wanted to do something different, something which had no connection whatsoever with my past. I wanted to make a new beginning in my career and in my life. After a long and hard look at the prevailing socio-economic circumstances in this country, I decided to qualify and earn a living as a psychiatrist. The main reason for this decision was my keen interest in the topic from my early student days back in Berlin. Reading was a passionate hobby in my formative years and I had even read books by famous psychologists and psychiatrists like Jung, Freud, and Alder etc. I must confess that some sections of those books, although written in German, puzzled me.'

Rolf paused to let me have a fix of nicotine in his bathroom and to have a stretch and then resumed his story:

'I thought it was time to do some serious reading on the topic and to find out how I could get into the profession. I found the field to be most absorbing and interesting and open to subjective interpretations with scope for the introduction and incorporation of innovative ideas.

'You are probably aware that the field of psychiatry does not strictly belong to science or logic. It is a black art. A revolution in the treatment of mental disorder started in earnest in Europe when the famous psychologist, Sigmund Freud propounded his controversial but ground breaking theory in the early 19th century in Vienna. According to this theory, the seed of an adult's personality is sown in his childhood experiences with adults and particularly with the child's relationship with his or her parents. These experiences, according to his theory, which was later supported by Carl Gustav Jung, stem from a sexual desire which lies hidden deep in the child's subconscious. Taboos and guilt introduced into the child's subconscious may, on occasions and under some circumstances, transmigrate into the conscious state of the adult mind. These then manifest themselves as mental conditions which include, amongst other things, nightmares, rage, depression, paranoia, schizophrenia etc. The way to treat any such mental illness is to bring these suppressed fears and guilt feelings from the subconscious to the patient's conscious state. This, according to these famous psychoanalysts, would allow the patients to make a conscious decision to revert back to normality. For this to happen, a rapport needs to be established between the patient and the analyst. Hence there is the need for a comfortable couch for the patient to lie on during long sessions of one-to-one counselling, to allow the analyst to extract the patient's inner thoughts, fears and dreams and to bring these to his or her conscious mind. As you can see, this procedure has both subjective and objective elements and the outcome is most likely to be influenced by the personality and skill of the analyst.'

I was infuriated by Rolf's assumption that I would be interested in his lecture on the subject of 20th century psychiatry. I couldn't tolerate it any longer and burst out in anger,

'I am sorry to have to interrupt your lecture exhibiting your knowledge in the field of psychoanalysis. You may gloat in self-glorification, but, to be honest with you, I am not and never have been interested in psychiatry. I was mentally prepared to listen to your story about the mysterious organization and its heinous agents, but not to listen to your illuminating lecture on 'the ground breaking' Freudian or Jungian theories on psychoanalysis.'

It wasn't like me to be rude to my beloved learned friend, although I had hardly ever let an opportunity go by without taking the mickey out of him. My voice choked and I felt a trace of sweat on my forehead. I was expecting him to be enraged for this wanton rudeness. I looked at him with apprehension. There was no expression of disappointment or anger in his face. He said apologetically,

'My dear friend, I will never, I repeat, never again try to promote my prowess in this field. In the past I did take a gamble, trying to achieve fame and recognition by showing off my prowess in the field of psychoanalysis. I didn't achieve my ambition; instead what I got was the secret agents chasing me everywhere to make my life a hell. I am paying a heavy price for my misadventure.

'Please do accept that the background to the story I am about to narrate has everything to do with what I have been talking about. That's why I feel it necessary to brief you on the basics of the theory of Jungian psychoanalysis. Otherwise, you wouldn't be able to understand why and how I got into trouble with the multinational Jung organization. So please bear with me for just a little while. I shall minimize your suffering by being as brief as possible on the prelude to my story.'

I felt ashamed for my uncharacteristic outburst and my incorrect assumption as to Rolf's motive for his lecture. I apologised profusely and asked him to continue with his story. So he did:

'Following a period of high-level collaboration with Freud, promoting a unique method of psychiatric treatment, Carl Gustav Jung parted company with him and started his own, extremely elaborate research and practice on analytical psychology. He became a prolific writer of books on complex and often controversial topics such as, dreams, memory, symbolism, religion, personality, collective sub-consciousness etc. His international fame overshadowed that of other giants in the field, including that of Freud, who was eventually debunked. He also incessantly published articles on these topics in relevant German and Swiss journals. Some were translated and published in relevant British and American journals. At the end of Second World War, his fame was at its zenith. He founded The CG Jung Institute of "Analytical Psychology for Training and Research" in Zurich. In those days, he became a cult figure for intellectuals, particularly amongst the youth.

'I was then an angry young man, hungry for adventure and a career in an intellectually challenging field. I became a devoted follower of Jung and read most of his books and also tried to get my teeth into some of his papers in the Journal of Analytical

Psychology, published in the USA and available at the British Library in London. In my spare time at the weekend I went to the library and read articles on such topics as, symbolism in the religions of modern 'man' and, comparison and contrast with that in the cults and occults of primitive man. Understanding human psychology became my obsession and I started to enquire about the nature of 'instinct' in the psyche of primitive man. I read widely about the ancient Indian Vedic philosophy of consciousness and studied the nature of symbolism in their rituals both during the Vedic time, and now. I read about Jung's visit to India and his close, but brief encounter with intellectuals in the field of consciousness studies there. I decided it was time to stop reading and start writing.

'Reading helped me to appreciate the wisdom of great thinkers such as Jung and the way they interpret and analyse psychic phenomena. I was, however, quite careful not to let knowledge of, and devotion to these giants in the field of psychiatry blinker my own thoughts and interpretations. I was concerned that if I was not on my guard, my originality of thought would vanish along with my ambition to make an impact in this field, and to become rich and famous.

'I thought – "Having my ideas and thoughts in print would boost my ego and raise my profile among the people who might be able to help me obtain a qualification in this field. Therefore, I had to write about something close to Jung's heart.

'So, after a lot of research and thinking I wrote an essay entitled – "Symbols in primitive cults and their influence in modern man."

'I wrote a letter addressed to Professor Jung and posted it to his Institute's address. I was not very optimistic that the letter would find its way into the hands of such an internationally famous and busy man, through the Institute's administrative chain. I thought – "Nothing ventured, nothing gained."

'Once again, it was nothing but a miracle and, to my utter surprise and joy it did reach him. In my letter, in German, I briefly wrote about my academic and personal background and included the essay. I requested him to consider its publication in the journal of his institute. I had read about his background and knew that he was qualified as a medical doctor and had written against the Nazi doctrine, albeit after the end of the war.

'I had hoped he would feel guilty for tolerating and perhaps tacitly supporting the atrocities committed by Germany against the Jews. I mentioned my desire to get training in the field of analytical psychiatry and to get accreditation to practice as an analyst from his institute. I also enquired about the possibility of a bursary citing the family's refugee status and pecuniary disadvantage. As a way of attempting to do a bit of buttering up I also mentioned that I had read all his books and he was my hero.

'It worked. I got a reply from an official, designated as the executive director of the Institute. He was instructed to write to me on behalf of Professor Jung. I was invited to attend an interview with him. I was ecstatic. I couldn't believe what I was reading. I read the letter out loud several times. For the first time in a very long time I felt a level of confidence in myself. I was determined to take up the opportunity and face the challenge.

'I didn't waste time. I left the job at the shop and moved back to my parent's home in Edinburgh and started to prepare for the impending interview in Zurich. My parents were happy to help me out with travel and subsistence costs as I was assured that these would be reimbursed by the Institute.

'I was very nervous when I sat face to face for the interview with such a famous psychiatrist in his office. But his manner of welcome and body language immediately made me feel at home. He asked questions in such a way that I felt I was talking to a mentor or an uncle. After the preliminary niceties, he started to ask more probing questions, such as my reason for wishing to become an analyst and the differences between his and Freud's methods of Psychoanalysis. I was sure of one thing; he would easily recognise any falsehoods; so I decided "honesty" in my responses, would be the best policy. I answered the first question by saying that since body and mind are practically two sides of the same coin, my medical qualification would help me treat the ailments of the mind, something he would identify with as a qualified doctor himself. Responding to the second question I explained that I wasn't as familiar with Freud's work as with his, so was unable to comment on the difference in the two approaches. I mentioned that the subject would probably be a part of my study and training, if I got the chance to undertake the course in his Institute.

'He seemed happy enough with my answers. He made some notes on a piece of paper and put them back in a file. He then took out the manuscript of the paper that I had sent, stared at me and said in a matter of fact tone that, one of his editors had reviewed the paper and made some comments on it. While handing it over to me he advised that I needed to read more on the topic and make some major revisions before it would be considered for publication. He told me that I would be informed about my application for a bursary in due course. He shook hands and said goodbye and wished me good luck and I left feeling relieved that the ordeal was over.

'I returned to Edinburgh filled with great apprehension and a little hope. While waiting to hear from the Institute I started an hourly paid job at the city's main library, rearranging books on shelves and carrying out errands.

Rolf paused and asked me if I still wanted him to continue as the night was coming to an end. I nodded, and so he did:

'The hope of a positive response from Zurich gradually faded as time passed. I gave up all hope, although my mother kept reassuring me – "No news is good news." I couldn't fathom out how my mother's dictum could possibly be true. Then all of a sudden, after about three months, I got a letter from the Institute. Now it was in my hand, I wished I hadn't received it. Before its arrival I had suffered trepidation, at the same time, enjoyed a spark of hope. I thought: 'as soon as I open the letter all this will be gone. I will be confronted with the stark reality of disappointment – the death of my hope.

'Then again, I took courage thinking – This might bring a positive message which would be a watershed in my life. Perhaps, my mother could be right.'

He paused for a dramatic effect and then announced,

'Yes, my friend, the letter bore a positive message. I was offered a bursary for a full-board studentship at the institute. It was for a six months' intensive course, leading to accreditation to practice as a psychoanalyst, initially working for a year under a fully qualified psychiatrist approved by the Institute. The offer was conditional – within the year of internship I would have to write a dissertation on a topic chosen by me and approved by my senior. The dissertation has to be successfully defended in an oral examination before I would be entitled to a certificate of accreditation to practice independently. The other condition was that I had to give a written undertaking that I would be loyal to the Institute and practice according to the exact protocol inscribed in its published manual of the Institute. The Institute had the right to revoke my certificate of accreditation in case of noncompliance to those conditions.

'Nothing, but nothing would deter me from fulfilling the requirements for getting the accreditation. I did not give a second thought to accepting the offer with all the conditions attached to it. After attending the residential training course for two semesters in Zurich and submitting a dissertation I got a certificate of qualification and started to practice as an analyst under a renowned psychiatrist in Cheltenham, England, arranged by the Institute.'

'What was the topic of your dissertation?' I enquired.

'It was my favourite subject, of course, "Primitive instinct in modern man".'

He continued, 'As I was saying, at first I was simply a trainee, learning through observation of my senior's practices, procedures and dealings with patients, and making notes dictated by him. After a few of these sessions, as well as undergoing a required psychoanalysis on me by my senior, I was allowed to run one-to-one sessions with the easier cases under the hawkish eyes of the senior. I took notes incessantly of the patient's fears, concerns, obsessions, worries, dreams and anything else that they threw at me. I tried to analyse their dreams and relate these with real circumstances to pin down the cause of their problems. I then discussed the conclusions of my analyses and judgements with my senior for his advice on whether there was a need for further counselling and if so, how it should be directed. I did this with each patient for many months.

'Our patients kept returning to the clinic. Sometimes I felt that they didn't want to be cured and looked forward to coming back to the clinic and enjoyed lying down on the comfortable couch, talking to a keen and dedicated listener. For the rest six months of my time at the clinic I was involved with only a handful of patients. I tried to correlate their dreams with their mental states and hidden inner feelings, based on Jung's protocols. But I couldn't find any standard or correlation between any two arbitrarily chosen patient's symptoms.

'I could have fabricated one if I hadn't remained true to myself. The whole business appeared to me to be very subjective. I found my senior's explanations and analyses so woolly and often so illogical that they couldn't be applied to correlate one patient's problem with another's. I started to lose faith in Jung's principles of psychoanalysis as a treatment for mental illness. But I didn't give up. I thought perhaps my senior was a cowboy and was not good enough to apply the Jungian protocol of applied psychoanalysis properly. I devoted most of my spare time preparing my dissertation and within a year I submitted and successfully defended it in a viva voce in front of two experts in London. After receiving the accreditation from the Jung Institute, I applied for a post in a clinic in London. I told my senior that I had to move to London for family reasons and I needed a reference for a job there. He seemed to be quite happy about my explanation and with my request. Patient numbers was dwindling and, he was probably finding it hard to pay my salary.

'Thanks to a glowing reference from him, I got the job and moved to London. It was a much bigger clinic. I got to know my colleagues and carried on conducting sessions with patients as a senior in waiting. Everything went well at the beginning, but soon I realized that this clinic operated in the same way as the Cheltenham clinic, except on a bigger scale of course.

'It was customary to have occasional informal social get-togethers with my colleagues and a few other professionals from other clinics, usually at restaurants or public houses. On one such occasion I commented to one of my colleagues that during my two and a half years of practice I hardly saw any of the patients make a permanent recovery. I couldn't believe my ears when he said, "That is the good thing about the profession, you see. We have captive clients all year round, guaranteeing us a steady income and lucrative career. I would accept the 'status quo', if I were you, without questioning our results and practices. Why rock the boat?"

'I was astounded by such a flippant reply from a professional colleague. My doubt about the validity of Jungian principle of psychoanalysis for the treatment of mental illness got stronger. I also doubted the integrity of my fellow practitioners. I felt that the secret door to the patient's inner world, the subconscious mind, is permanently locked from the outside. The key or the code to this lock is hidden in his subconscious. Analyses of dreams and his outward expressions cannot unlock the door to this hidden world of the patient's consciousness and allow the clinician to affect a cure.

'I began to read and think more about Jung's "modus operandi" and the concept of consciousness in general. I focussed my studies on this topic in literatures on ancient Eastern and Middle-Eastern cults and religions such as Hinduism, Buddhism, and Zarathustrianism. The more I thought the more I came to the conclusion that modern day psychoanalysis, using Jung's methods, was flawed and based on a very subjective and half-baked understanding of the concept of consciousness.'

Rolf continued with his saga without any concern about the time or the state of mind of his sole listener. For both of us it was a chance of a lifetime to satisfy our long desired wishes and sacrificing a night's sleep was well worth it. He continued to speak thus:

'It was quite obvious that Jung took the concept of consciousness from ancient Hindu scriptures, coloured it with Nietzsche's concept of the ultimate man and, propounded a theory and procedure for psychiatry using verbosity and invented terminologies. I didn't quite understand his theory of so called, 'collective unconsciousness', which was not even based on statistical data from a large number of samples, but I managed to follow his procedure enough to keep most of my patients happy. I started to believe that Freud, Alder and Jung were all high-profile and highly intelligent conmen who have achieved fame and wealth by being merchants of mystification and by taking advantage of human frailty and haplessness. Some sceptics, like me, were branding them as, I quote, "excavators and exploiters of the catacombs of unconsciousness."

'I felt a strong urge, a compulsion perhaps, to do something about it. Freud had been debunked. It was time to do the same to Jung. An effective and sustained attack had to be made on his theories and practices. I felt that money-making institutions like Jung's Institute in Zurich needed to be targeted. The onus was on me to take the initiative. I believed many more would follow my example and join me in re-evaluating the use of psychoanalysis in the treatment of mental disorder. I did not feel any guilt for "biting the hand which fed me", or failing to abide by my oath to the Institution. I felt like a knight – perhaps a "Knight Templar" on a crusade, ready to fight against the lies and deception, to establish a true and effective treatment for mental illness.

'In my search I came across the use of rhythmic and synchronous body movement to exorcise mentally ill people. The idea is innate to the human psyche, and the practice had been prevalent amongst our primitive ancestors. It is still employed in some cultures. I was fascinated by the ancient ritual of naked dancing by young females as an important aspect of making an offering to the gods in Hindu temples. I thought perhaps dance, like painting and music, may be used for the treatment of mental illness.'

I butted in, 'Are you claiming to be the originator of this idea?'

'Not at all, my friend, not at all,' he shot back, 'The idea of the interdependence of the body and mind in the analysis of psychic phenomena had been known for a long time. The use of movement, both by the patient and the healer, for the alleviation of psychic illness was then known as, "applied behavioural therapy". It came to my notice that a Hungarian born choreographer, Rudolf Von Laban, had already formalized the idea through dance sequences in a guild he established in London.

'I became an associate of the 'Art of Laban Movement Guild (LMG)' and studied his philosophy of inter-dependence of mind and body movement. I became obsessed with the prospect of using body movement for psychiatric treatment. In collaboration with another member of the Laban Guild, I started to promote the idea of his innovative dance sequences as an element of treating mental patients. I participated in many programmes at the Guild, gave lectures on this topic, not only at the Guild, but also at some Universities as an invited speaker. I was so taken by the idea that I even undertook a visit to Bali, where dancing by young maidens had been elevated to the status of fine art and is viewed as an act of spirituality, providing fulfilment for both performers and observers. You will be surprised to know that I even published a few papers on this topic.'

At this point he stood up and went to his bedroom without excusing himself. After about 10 minutes or so I took the opportunity to go to the bathroom to get my fix. When I retuned I saw Rolf sitting down with some papers in his hand. He was very apologetic for leaving me suddenly and unceremoniously and said,

'I am sorry, I got carried away. In a rush I could only find one of the papers.' He handed me the paper and continued, 'I am sure the others are somewhere in the flat, certainly I would not have thrown them away.'

I looked at the paper. It was entitled, "The Application of Movement to the Treatment of Psychological Disorder", published in the LMG Newsletter, in 1950. It was quite brief and I read a bit of it while he watched me from the sofa opposite.

'Excellent, your command in written English is very good.' I commented.

'It is not the language on which I wanted your opinion, stupid. I wanted to know your thought on my hypothesis?' he snapped.

I retorted, 'As you know my good friend, my knowledge of psychiatry, for all intent and purposes, is next to nothing. But I always encourage innovation. Your idea may not be a success

story, but you may take heart from the words of wisdom from philosophers who believe that the success of a journey is not in its end, but in the journey itself. I am impressed, please continue.'
So he did:

'I found moral support for my crusade against the Jungian school amongst some prominent members of Laban's Guild. I published a few articles on applied behavioural therapy, using Laban's protocol of dancing and also, among other things, making use of homeopathy for a placebo effect. It worked on you didn't it?'

'It worked on my physical ailment,' I snapped, 'It had nothing to do with my mental condition.'

He smiled, and then went on,

'I wrote a rather toxic article, entitled, 'The Relevance of Jung's Modality in Modern Psychiatry and Alternative Approaches'. After a lot of thought and some hesitation, I sent it to the editor of the Swiss Journal of Analytical Psychology. I thought that the article was topical, original and controversial enough to be considered for publication. After about two months, the article was sent back to me with the referee's comments. I was advised to make a few changes where facts were uncorroborated, the arguments were unclear and to correct grammatical and typographic errors, before resubmitting. Without wasting any time I did just that. Over the next few weeks my initial excitement subsided. I almost forgot about the paper. My excitement, however, came back with a vengeance when I received a letter from the publisher informing me that it had been accepted for publication and giving the number and the month of issue in which it would appear.

'The excitement was, alas, short-lived. I got another letter. This was not from the publisher, but from the Jung Institute, addressed to my present work place. I was informed that my accreditation to practice as a psychiatrist had been revoked and a notice had been sent to my present employer in this regard. One of the reasons cited in the letter was my alleged self-promotion as a professor at Oxford University, which was, of course fraudulent. It also accused me of breaking my signed oath of loyalty to the principles and protocol of the Institute in my practice as a psychoanalyst.

'I was also warned to refrain from seeking any employment or starting my own practice under the auspices of the Institute or its accreditation forthwith. If I ignored this demand there would be drastic consequences, including legal action.

'Later I found out through the grapevine what had happened. The paper was sent to one of the directors of the Jung Institute for further review, and considering its damaging content, it was withdrawn from the list of articles selected for publication on that issue of the journal. It was obvious that the organization didn't take my 'betrayal' kindly. I was informed of their decision to reject the paper in a letter from one of the sub-editors of the journal, citing – "Lack of substance and evidence" on further review.'

'That was understandable,' I thought, 'I was however, totally flabbergasted to receive such a drastic threat from the Institute. My anxiety levels soared. Immediately I wrote a letter to the president of the British Psychological Society, of which I was a fellow. In my communication I included my manuscript and a copy of the letter from the Jung Institute. I urged him to use his good offices and high standing in the mental health carer's community to expose the Institute's intransigence and malpractices. I received a quick response, to the effect that his organization had no jurisdiction, moral or legal, to interfere with, or intervene in the businesses of the Jung Institute. I realized then that they were all in it together. I was disappointed but undeterred. Before the clinic could sack me, I resigned to continue unabated with my battle against the Institute.'

I interrupted, 'I appreciate your spirit and courage in fighting for what you believe to be right. But to take on such a big and internationally recognized organization you need to have financial backing and high-level support. As far as I know you have none of these, and now you are telling me that you resigned from your lucrative job. I wonder, you being a little 'David' how you thought you were going to finance your battle against 'Goliath', let alone being able to keep your body and soul together?'

'That is indeed a very pertinent question,' he said, 'It shows that you are finding my story quite absorbing, I am glad. That is a different, but equally amazing story, albeit a short one. I probably would have told you even if you hadn't asked. But before I conclude the story of my fateful episode with the organization we must have a break for some refreshment.'

We both took the opportunity to stretch. Rolf went to the kitchen and came back with a tray laden with his favourite cheese and biscuits, couple of pieces of toasts and two glasses of drinking water. He seemed to prefer talking rather than wasting time in eating. In between small bites of biscuits and finishing his drink of water he continued with the saga:

'It's too early in the morning for breakfast but have something to keep you going. It's that special Swish cheese with holes again' and he continued while I was munching the bread and cheese:

'It is a little deviation from the main story, but you have to know the answer to your query to complete the jigsaw. This is the story of how I became rich overnight, allowing me to take on the "Goliath"; that's what I felt like doing'

Hastily, he added, 'No, it was not a bank robbery or a lottery win. I had a windfall, idiomatically speaking – "Pennies from heaven."

'It was shortly before the debacle surrounding the publication of my toxic article. One day, completely out of the blue, I got a registered letter at my London clinic's address from the American consulate in London. I was advised to make an appointment to see a certain councillor there in connection with an inheritance from a relative in the USA who had recently expired. I was not unduly sad by the news of the demise of my estranged uncle, but rather pleasantly surprised to be informed that he had left an inheritance for me in his will. It was, once again – a miracle indeed.

'My father was the youngest of three siblings. His sister died of some illness at a very young age while his brother, Rudolph, immigrated to the USA. My father stayed with his parents in Germany, studied Medicine in Munich and took up a job at the local hospital. After the death of his parents he moved to Berlin with his family, my uncle never returned to Germany and was completely estranged from us all. I heard from various sources that he studied accountancy, married a colleague and started a consultancy firm in New Jersey. He was a very wealthy member of the local elite society and became a venture capitalist.

'Everything was perfect and full of promise for them. Unfortunately, their only son was kidnapped by a Mafia gang while he was studying medicine at the Albert Einstein College of Medicine in New York as a campus boarder. The kidnappers demanded a large ransom for his release. Rudolph agreed to pay the ransom and not to contact the police. He hadn't intended to honour the agreement and informed the police of the kidnapping and ransom demand with a strict verbal confidentiality agreement and an assurance that his son would be rescued unharmed without any exchange of money.

'Following his clandestine contact with the police, the hijackers broke off all further communication with him. After a couple of days, the police recovered his son's dead body from the Hudson River. My uncle was convinced that there must have been an informer inside the police force who had passed on the information to the kidnappers in return for payment.

'According to my information, my uncle was helpless to take any action, since the identity of the kidnappers was unknown and they were, in any case, protected by a key member of the law enforcement agency. He and his wife were devastated by their son's murder, and moved to the countryside to live a secluded life. His wife never recovered from the shock of losing her one and only beloved son and died within a year. Through an Interpol search, my uncle found and bequeathed all his wealth and properties to me and my brother equally. He had no one else remotely related to him, not even a close friend. He didn't leave a penny to charity. Now you know how I became rich. The legacy allowed me a comfortable life-style, and to pursue my passion for fine art and my new-found passion of trying to debunk Jung.'

'You lucky devil,' I said, 'Enjoying a handsome pay-out without even doing a single day's work. No wonder you are, "undoing your belt and looking for trouble." I am sure you didn't take on the Jung Institute without an ulterior motive.'

'What do you think that is?' He asked.

'Fame, perhaps!' I replied.

He nodded his approval and resumed his marathon tale:

'I decided I must continue my fight against the Mafioso type practices of the organization. You see, money is not only an aphrodisiac but also an elixir of life. I became obsessed with the idea of becoming immortal by acquiring fame. I didn't need to work for anybody or any organization for my living. I was able to devote most of my time in pursuit of fame and recognition, knowing that this is neither easy nor safe. The path to success has many obstacles, paved with failures and is often quite hazardous.

'I needed a focus to find a well-thought out strategy to attack and cause mortal damage to the organization. I decided that the focus had to be my knowledge and, the effective weapon had to be my pen. I also needed contacts and supporters in high places. My unusual and uncharacteristic determination in this matter stemmed from my unshaken conviction of the futility of Jungian psychotherapy. However, I would be cheating to you and myself if I do not admit that my desire for taking on the mighty organization was fuelled by an insatiable hunger for fame.

'This must be an indication of the primitive instinct in a modern man. Primitive man, once he was assured of his survival, with adequate shelter and ample supply of food, sought fame and recognition by putting his fingerprint or drawing a picture of an animal on a cave wall. Ordinary modern man, on the other hand, seeks such recognition by showing and sharing his wealth. But for me it had to be about the prowess of my knowledge and wisdom. That's why I moved to Oxford. There, I hoped, I would be able to cultivate my passion for collecting paintings and also be in direct contact with scholars and luminaries in the field of psychiatry.'

My interest in his story remained as strong as ever despite the imminent approach of sunrise. Rolf continued with unabated enthusiasm:

'I made contact with Dr Watson, a professor of psychology at New College. In a private audience with him I explained my situation and requested him to take me on as a part-time mature research student to read for the degree of doctor of Philosophy under his supervision. I expressed my willingness to pay the fees for the studentship and assured him that I have the means to pay. He asked many questions and listen to me very attentively. He was not a man of many words. I was assured that he would discuss the matter with his colleges at the senate. Before that I had to send him an application along with my curriculum vitae and a brief description of the topic I wanted to cover in my thesis.

'In my résumé I did not mention my last published paper and the letter from the Institute. I chose a tentative title for my thesis – "Body language and its contribution to the origin of consciousness in primitive man." I was interviewed by a panel of three faculty members, including Professor Watson. On the basis of the certificate of accreditation from the Jung Institute and the strength of my responses during the interview,

I was offered a part-time research studentship for the degree of Master of Philosophy in the Psychology department. I was very disappointed, but the prospect of transferring to a doctoral level at a later stage, depending upon my progress, was good enough a justification for me to accept the offer.

'I got myself enrolled and started my research in earnest. I had occasional discussion sessions with my supervisor and he encouraged me to attend the relevant lectures and seminars. I was very enthusiastic and became very committed to my work. Within a year I completed my dissertation for the degree of Master of Philosophy with very little help from my supervisor. I decided to present the conclusions of my research in the annual symposium of the International Society of Applied Psychology held at University College London.

'I started my topic by citing examples of the failure of modern Psychiatry based on psychoanalysis for treating mental illness without directly referring to Jungian theory and protocol. I suggested an alternative approach based on the Vedic philosophy of consciousness, use of specially choreographed body movement and the use of homeopathy as a placebo. The door of the subconscious world of modern man could never be opened by external stimuli. This has to come from within. There is a real need for role reversal in the treatment procedure. The patient should be in a position to be the analyst and, the analyst needs to play the role of the patient.

'Ultimately the role of the analyst must be to help the patient find a 'god', to relate and to receive a stimulus from within, just as his ancestors did. This would allow the patient to bring his hidden instincts from the sub-consciousness into the real world, governed by the "will to live instinct", and fashioned by his conscious mind.'

I interjected, 'I am awake and listening, but I am not yet sure how these are relevant to your phobia about the heinous agents?'

'Everything will fall into place soon, my friend, please have a little bit more patience and listen,' Rolf said in a pleading tone, and continued:

'My presentation didn't go very well. I couldn't answer many of the questions they put to me, and in some instances, I exposed my ignorance by misunderstanding the questions and replying foolishly. After the session, I saw Professor Watson in the distance. He was talking to two gentlemen in the corridor. As I approached him the men rushed off in different directions. I clearly heard them saying to each other, "Auf Wiedersehen". Professor Watson told me that these two gentlemen were delegates to the conference from the Jung Institute. I was concerned but didn't think much of it, considering that it couldn't have been anything to do with me or my paper or presentation. I was unknown and unlikely to be of any real concern to them.

'I submitted my M. Phil thesis hoping to be recommended for the continuation of my research leading to a doctoral thesis. I did it against the advice of my supervisor. He commented that some of my arguments were half-baked and advised me to do some more work and to make revisions before making my submission. I was fed-up and adamant and I couldn't wait any longer and submitted it anyway.

'After my viva voce, I was informed that I had failed to defend my dissertation and the examiners were not satisfied and could not recommend it for an M Phil qualification let alone for transfer for further work for a Doctorate degree.

'I was not disappointed, but angry, angry beyond measure. I made an appointment to see Professor Watson urgently. I accused him of being anti-Semitic, a Jew-hater, and an agent of the Jung organization. I had found out that he had received a grant from the Jung Institute for a 'D Phil studentship on a topic of interest to the organization to promote its profile. I accused him of being on the Institute's payroll.

'He listened to my wild and furious outburst and said in a very calm and composed voice, that I should have taken his advice. I shouldn't have taken on such a mighty and well-established organization with inadequate, ill-defined and unverifiable data. He asserted that he was an atheist and did not judge people on their colour, religious or ethnic background. He insisted that he was a man of unquestionable integrity who would not have accepted payment from the Jung Institute to collaborate as its agent as accused.

'I was ashamed of my sudden outburst and misbehaviour, angry with myself and disgusted with the organization's heinous actions aimed at thwarting my academic career.' Catching my eye, he continued,

'What has been happening since then is known to you. I don't believe these agents want to kill me, at least not yet; but I do believe they would like to see me kill myself. At times, I despair and feel life to be unbearable, being unable to confide in anyone who will be sympathetic to my suffering. But I am sure that you now understand my predicament. I would have liked to tell the whole world about it. When I try to write about this my pen stops moving, my mind goes blank, and I get writer's block. All this is due to my deep-rooted conviction that, sadly for me, the world is not only blind, but also deaf. I feel quite light-hearted now that I have been able to tell you my story, and hope that one day in the not too distant future, you will tell it to others who, like you, will believe it.'

Rolf offered me a bed in his spare room to sleep off what remained of the night. I refused his offer politely, left the flat and hit the road. In the distance, I saw a milk van distributing milk from door to door.

12

Oxford Revisited

For three and a half years I'd been Rolf's closest friend and confidant. I had known him well enough to vouch for his complete integrity. It was unthinkable that he would fabricate such a serious accusation, that the Jung Institute and its agents were hell-bent on destroying him. In any case, many of the events he had described were verifiable. I couldn't find any reason why he would seek to dramatize the situation. The story made my heart bleed for him, but didn't fill me with quite the same compassion as the story of his experiences in the concentration camp, as when it came to taking on the Institute; he had been the master of his own destiny. He'd taken a calculated risk and it had backfired. But while I had no doubt as to the authenticity of the events in his story, I still nursed some doubt as to the veracity of his interpretation of these events.

Most of his acquaintances found him to be an elusive character, who gave the impression of being a happy-go-lucky middle aged man vainly trying to hold on to his lost youth. To those who knew him well socially, he appeared to be a connoisseur of fine art; a lover of classical music; a dance enthusiast; someone with a keen interest in psychology and sometimes, a dirty old man with an unhealthy interest in young women. Nobody gave any credence to his stories involving secret agents, and some even laughed at him, believing the whole thing was merely a figment of his imagination. But I had always maintained and open mind.

A person is not important until he has acquired important enemies or critics. I wondered if Rolf had invented the 'secret agents' of an esteemed and powerful organization! A clenched fist in front of the eyes will hide the mighty Himalayas. Was something as simple as a clenched fist preventing him from seeing the truth? But, what was that clenched fist?

I was getting rather too engrossed in Rolf's story. Nobody else could read his mind like I can, and no one was as sincere a friend as I was. It was no surprise that while others laughed and joked about his phobia behind his back, I had kept an open mind and remained sincerely sympathetic. I could neither accept his assessment, nor dismiss his fears as delusory.

～

Rolf and a few other adversaries of Jungian principles and practices of psychotherapy had gained some exposure through publications in journals and presentations in conferences. Rolf told me that in the beginning such propaganda by a handful of mostly unknown individuals had been largely ignored. But the organization couldn't afford to be complaisant. Its bosses and shareholders had a vested interest. They knew that the debunking of their high priest – the *guru,* might start with a small trickle of challengers, but it might eventually become a mighty flood, engulfing their empire and causing its collapse. They couldn't take any chances and had to nip any challenges to Jung's theory and protocol in the bud. They were afraid of Rolf's group, albeit insignificant to start with, might gradually gained prominence and one day take on and debunk him. The consequences would be devastating for its worldwide practitioners and a disaster to the expanding and lucrative business.

It is possible that, with these considerations, the organization might have taken measures to root out opponents. Perhaps, the best way for them would be just what they were trying to do to Rolf, the alleged leader of the group. They were depriving him of status, female contact and making him appear to be a fraudster professor.

These were just my conjectures of course. It all appeared to be stranger than fiction, except that I was playing an important factual role in it.

My obsession with the trials and tribulations of Rolf's life did not subside for a long time. I thought of visiting the Jung Institute of Psychiatry in Zurich and try to dig out more about his paper, his time there and the record of his meeting with Jung. But this was simply wishful thinking. Reality did not permit any such undertaking. As far as the mighty Institute was concerned he was, in any case, too insignificant an individual to warrant records of his involvements with them or the record of his interview with Jung being kept after such a long time. My imagination wandered, I even wondered if the idea of the secret agents of the organization had taken root in his subconscious during his time at the Nazi concentration camp.

Even so, the need to establish the authenticity of his tales got the better of me. I started to think and behave like a detective. I went to great lengths to befriend a young lady working as an office secretary at the New College archive, and persuaded her to look through the administrative documents to find out about Professor Watson and Rolf Kosterlitz. She obliged. Professor Watson had retired nearly two decades ago and had passed away almost a decade ago. But she found Rolf's name in the registry book as a part-time post-graduate student, so that much was true. She couldn't, though, confirm if he'd ever completed his dissertation or obtained his qualification. I was at a loss as to what else I could do to establish the truth.

꧁꧂

It so happened that I was unable to return home from Oxford straight after receiving my qualification, owing to the outbreak of civil war there. My grant stopped and I was literally stranded with no financial support. My supervisor was quite sympathetic and managed to offer me a short-term post-doctoral fellowship at the department and this enabled me to carry on working there and to publish a couple of papers.

These events brought about a drastic change in my lifestyle. I had a reasonable income now and was no longer a perpetually broke student. I was aspiring to become a responsible professional man and trying to behave like one. I was becoming involved with a new circle of friends and most of us were pairing up with girlfriends. Rolf probably felt alienated in our presence, having no lady friend to accompany him to parties and functions.

I maintained a good friendship with him and we continued to meet on and off, but our youthful exuberance and silliness were things of the past. I had become a senior in the eyes of the new students from the Indian sub-continent and had to set a good example.

Once I went with Rolf to a monthly discussion session of the "Nietzsche Appreciation Society." He told me in an impish tone that he would introduce me to his new friend, who was apparently sexually attracted to him. He explained that his friend was an archetype, being sexually aroused by a person's intelligence and wisdom rather than by physical attributes. I joked – "If that was the case, a humble good looking chap like me, with little or no intellectual prowess would have nothing to fear, I suppose." I knew Rolf abhorred homosexuality, but got on quite well intellectually and socially with gay people, as long as there was no question of intimacy.

The gathering was in a small room at the Queen Elizabeth Hall and attended by about a dozen or so people. I cannot remember what the topic of discussion was, but most of it went over my head. I kept quiet and listened most of the time, except when Rolf asked me to comment on certain issues. I only obliged if these were related to Indian culture and Vedic philosophy, otherwise I admitted my ignorance and apologised.

After the session he introduced me to his so called, *sapiosexual* friend, Leonel Pane, his deputy in the society, a man from Midlands in his forties, with a goatee beard. He had known Rolf for about a year. There was nothing much in common between them except their interest in philosophy. He worked for the local authority, was settled in Oxford and was a bachelor. I never went to any other session of the society after that. During that time I also went to a performance by a touring Indian dance-drama company at the town hall with Rolf. He was fascinated by the dance sequences of the *Bharat Nattyam* dance style. It was choreographed in the style of a Vedic ritualistic temple dance and performed by beautifully-dressed women. Rolf commented that such a dance style could be used to induce a trance-like state in a mentally-ill patient, and that similarly choreographed dance had been used by primitive people in the past, and, was still being practiced in the treatment of mental illness by some tribes, not yet engulfed by the influence of modern civilization.

However, our intimate intellectual sessions, which had also provided him with the opportunity to tell me about some important and private events in his life had all but ceased. He most probably felt that he had achieved his goal. He had been able to off-load the worst of his experiences on me. I felt that he probably did not need me anymore, as he had nothing else to tell me. Similarly I also felt I have grown out of him and needed to venture in a wider world

🌒

The life style and composition of the student community from the Indo-Pak subcontinent had also changed since my arrival in Oxford some four years earlier. Some of my intake had finished their studies and left, some were making preparations to go back home. New faces were arriving and forming their own circles for *adda*. The Pakistani association had ceased to exist. A very uncomfortable co-existence replaced the chummy relationship between the Pakistani students and us, Bengalis from the former East Pakistan at the end of the bloody civil war between these two wings of Pakistan. Now we had separate identities. The dinner time gathering for *adda* at the back of the Moti Mahal restaurant also ceased. Freshmen were not as enthusiastic to join groups or societies which dreamt of changing the world. I could sense there was much more interest amongst the new-comers in more worldly things such as joining the computer user group, the popular science society, the literary society or the book club. It dawned on me that the ebullience and ideology of the swinging sixties was slowly fading. A new generation of worldly wise students was in the making.

A couple of months after my final viva, I was summoned to the graduation ceremony at the Caledonian Theatre, where certificates were handed out in an elaborate traditional ritual spoken in Latin. I was allowed only two guests inside the theatre. I invited my girlfriend, Estelle, and Rolf. After the ceremony, he said that he was once aspiring to attend as a recipient of a certificate here, not merely as a spectator. But the agents had other plans. He said he didn't want to dwell on it. He invited Estelle and a young friend of mine, Fakhruddin, who was a Rhode's scholar studying chemistry at Christchurch, back for a tea party at his flat. I asked Rolf to entertain us with a violin recital on this auspicious occasion, and he obliged. We were about to call it a day, when he asked us to wait and went to his study.

After a few minutes, he came out and handed me a rather big box and said,

'This is my advance wedding present for you and Estelle. I know you are planning to wed but I don't know when the event will take place and where I will be at that time, or even, if I will be invited. This is very fragile, but authentic, not a reproduction. It will bring you luck one day – if you believe in such things. As you know I don't have any faith in God; but I do believe in miracles.'

One afternoon, I was at my desk at the laboratory, trying frantically to finish a paper which was to be submitted for presentation at a conference. I had to submit the manuscript by the close of day. Lo and behold, Rolf suddenly appeared in my office. Those days it was quite unexpected and unusual for him to drop in at my workplace. Without any preamble he pulled up an empty chair and sat down next to me. I was not only surprised, but also quite annoyed to see him.

Not attempting to hide my annoyance, but remaining polite I said,

'You don't look very happy. I hope no bad news?'

Moving a bit further away from the desk, he leaned back on the chair and burst out, 'Where is Sabiha? I want her address. I am told by one of your fellow countryman that you have met her recently and you know where she is staying now! She was supposed to be here around this time to attend her graduation ceremony.'

Calmly, I asked: 'Who told you such a fib?'

'Jamshed Khan', Rolf answered angrily. He then repeated, 'Where is she?'

Jamshed, a Pakistani undergraduate, studying law at Oriel College was Sabiha's contemporary although not in the same year. I was annoyed by Rolf's insistence and shot back,

'You should understand that Jamshed is still jealous of your intimacy with her and still trying to make a fool of you. Anyway, even if Sabiha was in this country how the hell would I know her present address? I am not her keeper. She is supposed to be your close friend.'

'Jamshed told me that she had either met you or contacted

you,' Rolf asserted, 'And I believe him. You are supposed to be my trusted friend and confidant; you cannot hide this from me. I had told you before that I was going to host her at my house at the time of her graduation ceremony.'

Normally Rolf would ignore Jamshed's sniping, and avoid meeting him. But this time, for some unknown reason, he believed him. He glared at me, waiting for an answer.

In a calm and composed voice I said,

'I'm surprised that you have spoken to that idiot at all. And I am really perturbed that you believe anything he said.' Rolf was adamant,

'I am a psychologist and I know if someone is telling the truth or not. I know that Jamshed was not lying, but you are. I want her contact detail and I want it now. I shall not leave you until you tell me the address where she is staying. You have been secretly writing to Sabiha knowing jolly well that she and I were very close. If you are, as you claim, a true friend and wish to continue to be so then please come out clean with it.'

I was at the end of my tether and wanted to scream. Somehow, with great difficulty I maintained my cool. I got up, approached him slowly and said sternly,

'Listen to me my friend. I did not meet Sabiha. I do not know if she is here. If I had her address I would gladly give it to you, just to get rid of you and save my sanity. I have a very urgent assignment to finish by the end of the day. I desperately need to get on with my work. Believe me for heaven's sake, I do not have any information whatsoever about Sabiha's whereabouts. I beg you, leave me in peace'

Rolf kept quiet for a little while, looked at me, moved his head left and right and said in a stony tone,

'You are mad.'

That was it. My blood had suddenly reached boiling point. I lost any sense of composure. I shouted,

'It is you who is mad and always have been! You are deranged, and that's why you think agents are after you. Please leave now, otherwise I will become really crazy and may harm you.'

Rolf stood up, walked towards the door of my laboratory room, paused and turned around towards my direction and said calmly,

'I shall find her alright, but you have lost a true friend for ever.'

I watched through the window as he walked away down the Banbury Road. That was the last time I ever saw him.

I tried to erase the memories of my days as Rolf's closest friend and confidant, but they never go away. The memories keep coming back to haunt me and to play melancholy tunes in my heart. Nothing haunted me more than the memory of our last encounter. I often felt the bite of guilt for my outburst of madness and anger. I had tolerated his idiosyncrasies for the last long four years and built up a deep friendship and trust, often under adverse circumstances. But alas, all that had blown away with the wind, as if all that happened during that time was a drama or a dream. My sudden loss of temper had destroyed our friendship. It was completely out of character for me, but it was beyond my control.

I knew I had to live with regret and guilt for the rest of my life. I wished I could go back in time and undo that happened at my last encounter with him to wash out the bitter taste of that memory. I often fantasized about bumping into Rolf in the street or at a gathering, and asking him to forgive me and to forget that unfortunate episode. He would then touch my shoulder and say – "Don't be silly, it was just a momentary madness for both of us. I was away to Bali for a long holiday." I often wondered if he was ill or still alive and what he was up to! Knowing him as much as I did, I feared, unless there was a miraculous change in his psyche he would never ever make amends with me after what had happened. But then miracles do happen.

The bursts of hurt and agony in my heart became progressively less frequent. I convinced myself that it was human nature to have a limited level of tolerance and that the occasional outburst of anger was an inevitable aspect of our humanity. I expected Rolf to take the initiative and seek to make amends. Although my obsession was gradually fading, my resolve to write down his story became stronger than ever. It is the life story of a man who befriended me and captured my imagination. Someone who introduced me to a 'brave new world' filled with fine art, classical music and a deep quest for the origins of human consciousness and culture. Rolf had held my imagination captive for nearly four years.

I was preparing to get married, and settled down to work in a new job as a MoD scientist at a defence institute in Oxfordshire. I couldn't stop myself from sending Rolf an invitation asking him to attend our wedding reception in the garden of the Queen Elizabeth Hall. He already gave us a Ming vase as a wedding present well in advance.

He never acknowledged the invitation. Many of my old friends scattered across the country attended the ceremony. I was, hoping against hope that Rolf would have forgotten that episode and, for old time's sake, surprise me by turning up at the reception. But alas, there was no surprise; I looked expectantly at the gate from time to time. It was painful for me to think that he had now put me on the list of people in his "enemy category", after all those years of intimacy.

One summer's day, many years later, my wife and I went to visit friends in Oxford. She, like many of my friends at that time, had also come to know Rolf well. We decided to look him up, hoping that by then he had forgiven and forgotten the bitter episode of the past. With some trepidation, I rang the bell of the top floor flat at 101 B, Banbury road and waited. There was no shout – "Wait a minute I am coming"; but I heard footsteps, louder and louder, while my heart was going faster. A middle-aged English gentleman came down the staircase and opened the door. We all looked at each other, nonplussed. I broke the silence,

'We are old friends of Rolf and dropped in to look him up. We hadn't seen each other for a long time. He lives here as far as I know.'

He was silent for a while, and then in a sombre tone said, 'I am sorry to have to tell you that Dr Kosterlitz doesn't live here anymore. He passed away nearly two year ago. I was told by one of my neighbours that he was knocked down by a drunken driver while returning home from the city centre late one night. I had never met the gentleman, but I am told that he was a highly educated man, a professor or something, a bit of a loner.'

The news struck me like a hammer blow to the head. I was speechless. I couldn't bear the thought that it was now too late, I would never be able to apologise for my outburst. Remorse descended on me like a black cloud; why had I waited so long to come and see him? I would never be able to forgive myself. The grief of losing a friend and the thought of a lifetime of guilt overwhelmed me. I had never experienced such sadness before. Noticing my condition, the gentleman kindly offered us a drink in his flat.

I couldn't bear the thought of going up to the flat and not seeing Rolf, surrounded by all the antique furniture and paintings. I refused his offer politely. Estelle and I spent some time at the University Park, reflecting on Rolf and my carefree days at Oxford in his company. We drove back home in silence.

This news strengthened my resolve to write down Rolf's story for others to read so that they would know about the man who wanted to 'live on' after his death.

This would have been the end of the story if I haven't had a chance encounter with a middle-aged man in a café on the High Street, the same one I had frequented in my Oxford days, and which I still visited from time to time out of nostalgia. I was there with Estelle when a gentleman came over to our table and asked if he could join us. I was a bit surprised as I saw there were some empty tables around.

I have always been at ease talking to strangers and said,

'By all means, go ahead, be my guest' then I asked, 'Are you a visitor here?'

'No. I am not a visitor and neither a stranger to you. You may have forgotten me but I recognized you the moment I saw you.'

I looked at him, puzzled, and then after a while I remembered the wiry man with a goatee beard I had met at the Nietzsche Appreciation Society meeting who, according to Rolf, was one of his admirers and was physically attracted to him.

I said, 'I think I can remember meeting you at the Nietzsche Appreciation Society's meeting some years ago. You were a good friend of Rolf; weren't you?'

'That's right', he said. 'I am afraid I don't remember your name. But I remember you very clearly, for two reasons. Firstly, you were the only non-white person in that meeting and for that matter in any meeting before or after, and secondly because you were the least vocal participant there. I'm Leonel, by the way.'

We shook hands and introduced ourselves properly.

When the waitress came to collect our empty cups and plates, I asked for another round of coffee and cake for the three of us. I asked,

'When did you see Rolf last, Leonel?'

'Over couple of years now. I think, nearly a week or so before he was murdered by a motorist,' he replied.

'Murdered?' I exclaimed, 'I was told by someone that he was accidentally killed by a drunken motorist.'

'The news appeared in the Oxfordshire Gazette', Leonel said 'There was no mention of the killer being a drunken motorist. It was a hit and run job. I have never heard or read since then whether the killer was ever apprehended and tried.' He went on,

'Over the couple of years before his death, Rolf and I became very close friends. We had a good rapport. This was mostly to do with the society and our private discussions on philosophy in general. Since his death, I've taken over the business of running the meetings of the group, but the meetings are now quarterly instead of monthly.'

He looked at me and asked, 'Why don't you come to the next one?'

'I no longer live in Oxford, but I shall certainly try to do that. Anyway, can you tell me any more about the accident?' I asked.

'About a month or so before it happened, Rolf gave me a paper he had written in English and asked me for some editorial help, Mike continued, 'His English was not as good as his German. He was planning to send it to the Journal of the British Psychiatric Society for publication, following its presentation as an invited paper at the annual conference of the society in London. The paper, if memory serves me right, was about something to do with an alternative to Jungian psychotherapy'. I congratulated him for such a bold and innovative perspective on the treatment of mental illness.

'Rolf told me that he had a growing following amongst British Psychiatric practitioners since the publication of a similar paper in the same journal. But he told me that after that publication he also had received threats from the Jung Institute of dire consequences if he did not keep quiet and stop creating trouble. He expressed concern about what would happen when this new paper in English would be published.'

He paused, swallowed the last gulp of cold coffee and said, 'I obliged him by editing his paper, although I didn't understand most of it.'

'What happened then, Leonel? Really?' I asked.

'The paper was published in the journal posthumously with a short obituary. He stood up, put on his jacket, shook hands with me and left, saying,

'Life is for living, my friends. See you at our next Society meeting. We advertise the event in the Oxford Gazette.'

That evening, at home, we sat down to relax and reminisce on Rolf's story of the organization and its agents. He had always pretended to me that he was not anymore involved in the crusade against the organization. I now realized that addiction to achieve fame and recognition was inexorable for him and he did continue with his struggle unabated.

I was wandering if his death was an accident or murder. My eyes fell on the Ming Vase on the mantelpiece. It was always there, a memento from Rolf, the wedding gift for the wedding he never attended. I rarely noticed it. I got up and approached it and was about to lift the beautiful lid when I stopped, fearing that all the memories that both Rolf and I had shared would suddenly emerge along with Rolf's ghost, and overwhelm me with a sadness beyond control.

Printed in Poland
by Amazon Fulfillment
Poland Sp. z o.o., Wrocław